George James Atkinson Coulson

The Lacy Diamonds

A novel

George James Atkinson Coulson

The Lacy Diamonds
A novel

ISBN/EAN: 9783337000646

Printed in Europe, USA, Canada, Australia, Japan

Cover: Foto ©Andreas Hilbeck / pixelio.de

More available books at **www.hansebooks.com**

THE LACY DIAMONDS.

A NOVEL.

BY THE AUTHOR OF "THE ODD TRUMP," "HARWOOD," ᴇᴛᴄ.

New York:
E. J. HALE & SON, PUBLISHERS,
Murray Street.
1875.

PREFACE.

The gracious reception of "THE ODD TRUMP" and "HARWOOD," by the Public, encourages the Author to offer the present volume.

He would fain believe that his effort to produce a series of Novels which, at least, should not be hurtful in tone or teaching, has been successful.

In the hope that this negative merit will atone for imperfection in diction, plot and construction, he presents the third volume of the "ODD TRUMP SERIES."

NEW YORK, *September*, 1875.

CONTENTS.

CONTENTS.

THE LACY DIAMONDS.

CHAPTER I.

DOCTOR CUNNINGHAM'S TESTIMONY.

IT was raining—I was going to say, cats and dogs, but it was a
great deal worse—it was raining pins and needles. I was riding
in a north-easterly direction, and the little, sharp particles of frost
scarified my nose and my right cheek in an extremely unpleasant
manner. My horse winced and snorted as each gust swept over
us ; and as my road lay along the west bank of the river, we were
ever and anon exposed to the full violence of the storm, as it came
roaring across the broad water. Sometimes a curve in the stream,
which the road did not follow, would give me the slender protection
of a clump of dwarf cedars, but I never had the friendly shelter
long at a time ; and it always seemed, as I emerged from the lee
of the bushes, that the fragments of sleet were considerably heav-
ier, sharper and more numerous than before.

I had left home early in the afternoon, before the rain, and as I
had a long ride before me, and some prospect of detention, I told my
wife that I should probably be away all night. I was called out
to visit a poor patient, John Hawder, who lived full eight miles
from my home. Had he been a richer man, I should have postponed
the visit until the next day ; but I promised myself, when I first
began the practice of medicine, that the poor should always have
my services upon demand. Hawder was very sick. He had no
near neighbours, and he lived alone with his little motherless boy
in a log house near the river bank. I don't know how the man
lived, but he never seemed to be in actual want. I left him with
a heavy heart, after I had prescribed for him, and was the more
saddened by the cheerfulness of little Elbert, his son, who listened
with great gravity to my instructions as to the administration of
the medicines. I had intended to go to a farm house two or three
miles back from the river, where I also had a patient, but as this

case was not at all urgent, I concluded to go back home from Hawder's. The storm caught me before I had ridden a mile on my homeward journey.

It grew worse and worse. I pulled up my horse under the lee of a "yaller pine," *Pinus mitis,* a stunted tree which afforded very insufficient shelter. There were three long miles of exposed road right up the river bank before I could turn my back upon the water and the sharp blast that whistled over it. The sleet rattled through the thick foliage of the little tree, sounding like a rain of shot upon plate glass. I rubbed my nose, wondering how long I could keep that useful and ornamental feature if I faced the storm again. There was a ferry just at this point, and while I was debating about the dreary prospect ahead, I heard the sound of oars, and presently saw the boat come up to the landing, and a passenger leap lightly to the bank. I saw him hand a piece of money to the boatman, and heard him say: "You will have a hard pull back, old fellow, and ought to have double fare. Good night!"

He came up the bank, crunching in the sleet that now whitened the ground. As he reached the level of the road he saw me.

"Hillo, stranger!" he said, in a cheery voice, "are you going to Baird's?" and he drew nearer. "I beg your pardon, sir, but I was thinking how jolly it would be if you could put me across the creek dry shod."

He was a handsome fellow, about twenty-five, frank and manly looking. While he waited for my answer, his blue eyes twinkling, and his white teeth glistening in the twilight, I made up my mind. Baird's tavern was a little country inn, rather more than a mile from the river. I had never been there, but I knew it was on this road, leading west from the ferry.

"I think I *will* go to Baird's," I answered; "my home is so distant, and the storm will then be behind me at least. Beppo will carry double, so I can put you across the creek, if there is one to be crossed. Will you mount at once?"

"Thank you, no," replied the stranger; "I have been cramped up in that boat, and want to stretch my legs a little. I can keep up with you for a mile, anyhow," and he started up the road at a brisk pace, ahead of me.

As I followed, I noticed that he had a knapsack strapped to his back. He was dressed in coarse, homespun garments, the legs of his trousers stuffed into his boots, and his coat collar turned up, covering his ears and most of his face. The brim of his slouched hat drooped around his head, and he looked as though he could endure the pelting of the storm far better than I could. As we advanced into the woods the pines grew larger, and we were a little more protected from the sharp wind and sleet.

"This is a dreary country," he said, as he strode along beside me; "it affords a striking contrast to—to—lands that I have seen elsewhere. The hand of man has not done much towards smoothing the rugged front of nature in this locality. The inn is a mile from the river, and two hundred yards beyond the creek." He said this with the air of one repeating a lesson.

"You mean the country is dreary in comparison with your own."

"In comparison with my own?" he repeated.

"Yes, with England. You are an Englishman?"

"I don't know why you should think so," he answered.

"Oh, you called Baird's an 'inn' just now. Besides, there is a certain accent which distinguishes your countrymen."

"Do I drop my H's, or make too liberal a use of them?" he replied, laughing. "I wonder if I may consider it complimentary to be taken for a Britisher. I cannot discover any remarkable difference between my speech and yours."

"You have decided then that I am an American?" replied I.

"Yes. I don't know, though. I can't say, I'm sure."

"There you go again! Americans don't say 'I can't say, I'm sure.' They are not sure, they guess."

"Well, I shall count you for a countryman till you deny it. I am Mr. John Smith, at your service."

"I think I have heard the name before. I am Dr. Cunningham, at *your* service, sir."

He pulled off his mitten and gave me his hand, which was white and soft. Altogether, he impressed me with the idea that his ordinary dress was not homespun, nor his proper name John Smith.

Baird's was a lonely country tavern, where all the inmates seemed to be just waking from a nap. I saw Beppo sheltered in a comfortable stable and supplied with a sufficient quantity of hay and oats. Mr. Smith stood by while I gave my directions to the hostler, and then we entered the public room together. The landlord went behind his bar, expecting us to imbibe some of his potations, but he was disappointed. We told him we wanted supper and beds, with the privilege of smoking by his cheerful wood fire after we had satisfied the cravings of hunger. We soon had some hot coffee, some broiled ham and good biscuits and butter. The evening meal appeared to be over, as my companion and I were the only persons at the table.

"I feel so much invigorated," observed Mr. Smith, as we drew our chairs up to the fire, "that I could face the storm again now if it were necessary. Yours must be a hard life, doctor, if you are often exposed to weather like this."

"I am accustomed to it," I replied, "and I do not find the duties of my profession irksome. In many cases I am able to relieve suffering, and then I am amply repaid for toil and exposure."

"I have often fancied," returned he, "that the most trying part of a physician's experience must be his constant contact with humanity in affliction. It is true you can sometimes ameliorate the condition of the sick and suffering, but there are also many cases beyond the reach of your art. And when you know, as you often *do* know, undoubtedly, that your patient will die, you must suffer somewhat in advance in your natural sympathy for those about to be bereaved."

"It is not the actual sickness of my patients that makes the largest drafts upon my sympathies. More frequently the attending circumstances affect me more. Now, to-day——." I paused.

"You were saying——"

"I hesitated," I answered, "because I don't know that I would be justified if I tell you a story that will sadden you, especially as there seems to be no remedy."

"You make me only more eager to hear it. Pray tell it, unless there is some other reason."

"No. It may be told in a few words. There is a poor fellow living on the river bank, a mile or two below the place where I met you, who is sick. His name is Hawder. I think he is going to have typhoid fever and will probably die. There is no one in the house with him excepting his son, a child probably not over ten years old. I do not know whether or not the man is in absolute poverty, but his dwelling is not comfortable, and he requires careful nursing. While I was there this afternoon I was struck with the little boy's intelligence and cheerfulness. He listened with attention to my directions, and I have no doubt he will obey them faithfully. But, somehow, I have not been able to shake off the melancholy feeling that comes over me whenever I think of that child."

Mr. John Smith sat there opposite to me with sympathy in his big blue eyes. As I proceeded with my story he threw the stump of his cigar into the fire, and when I finished, he rose and buttoned his coat.

"Please repeat your directions to me, doctor." he said simply; "I am going right down there."

"You?"

"Yes, I! God forgive me! here am I, brimfull, running over with health and strength, with nothing to do, and that infant is fighting a giant's battle alone. Yes, I am going down there immediately. Here, Mr. Baird! I am going out again. I shan't be back to-night. Take care of my knapsack till I return."

"Why, sir," answered the astonished landlord, "you can't go anywhere to-night. The storm is worse than ever. It is a regular nor'easter!"

"That's the kind of storm I'm partial to, Mr. Baird. What are the directions, doctor?"

"I shall order a strait waistcoat for you if you don't sit down here and be quiet," I answered. "What has put this insane project into your head?"

"Doctor," he said, gravely, "I am going down to that sick man's house. I am going if I have to encounter ten devils in my path. If you won't tell me what ought to be done, I'm going all the same. I can shield that boy at least; besides, I know something of enteric fever."

"My friend, you don't know all the case. This disease may be, and probably is, contagious; and you have no right to throw away the health of which you boast. Is there no one living who has an interest in your life?"

"Pooh!" he replied. "Perhaps there is; but I am not going to take any disease. I am going to start when I count twenty. If you'll tell me what ought to be done while I'm counting, I'll listen. Here goes. One, two, three, four, five, six, seven, eight—but I'll take my knapsack."

"Stop an instant and listen. Landlord, is there a near way to Hawder's?" Mr. Smith was strapping his knapsack to his back.

"Yes, there is a road right down the creek. There is a bridge at the mouth of the creek near his house."

"Nine, ten, eleven, twelve, thirteen, fourteen, fifteen——"

"Stop again, if you please. I left four or five powders with the child. The patient ought to have one every three or four hours.

If he sleeps, don't waken him. If he has fever and is thirsty, give him some sleet in a spoon. It will be better than water, and you can get it at the door."

"Sixteen, seventeen, eighteen—how much sleet may he have?"

"As much as he wants in moderation. You had better take a sober second thought——"

"Nineteen, TWENTY! Good night, doctor!" and he banged the door after him as he issued forth into the storm.

Mr. Baird stood looking stupidly at me, listening to the strong voice of his departed guest, as it came back to us outroaring the tempest. He was singing "A wet sheet and a flowing sea," and I heard his voice dying away in the announcement that "Old England was on his lee." He had reached the pines below the tavern by that time, and we heard him no longer.

"Well," said the landlord, drawing a long breath, "he sings nice, don't he? But it is a mighty quare start. I wonder what he is after at old Hawder's? He didn't pay for his supper, neither."

"He'll be back again, landlord, to-morrow or next day. I'll pay for his supper, though. Put it in my bill to-morrow."

"Oh, I'm not partick'ler, doctor. What do you want, Nelly?" The question was addressed to a beautiful child that came into the public room at the instant.

"I want the key," she answered.

"You mustn't come in here, Nelly, when anybody is here," said Baird as he walked behind the bar. The girl made no reply, but looked curiously at me.

"Come here, my dear," I said, and she came immediately. I took the little thing up on my knee and kissed her. "You are a fine little lady. What is your name?"

"Ellen."

"What else?"

"Nothing else; only Ellen."

"Here, Nelly, run out now. Here is the key," said Baird hurriedly. I kissed the child again and put her down. She took the key and vanished.

"What a beautiful little daughter you have, landlord," I said. "She is your daughter, I suppose?"

"No, sir," replied Baird; "she is some relation to my wife. I've got no children."

"What is her name? I mean her surname."

"Nelly Willis, I s'pose," answered he discontentedly. "You see, her mother wasn't married."

"Pardon me. I did not mean to ask an improper question. But the child is so beautiful that she interested me. Do you know how old she is?"

"About seven, I s'pose. It's storming again wonderful. He'll have a nice walk!"

"Who—Mr. Smith? Yes, he will have an unpleasant walk. How far is it to Hawder's by the creek road?"

"Two miles, good. Where is he going to sleep? Hawder ain't got no place to put him."

"I don't think he intends to *sleep* there to-night," I replied; "but I believe I'll try to get some sleep myself, if you will show me my room. I was called out very early this morning."

He lighted a candle and led the way through a passage behind the bar. I passed him at the first landing on the stairway, and when I reached the hall on the second floor I saw the child standing in a doorway. I held out my hand to her as I passed.

"Good night," she said.

"Good night, little darling," and I stooped down and kissed her again.

"There, there, Nelly!" said Baird, impatiently; "run in now and shut the door." She smiled and nodded her little head to me, and obeyed him.

I have so often been compelled to sleep away from home that I am somewhat hardened. It is always a luxury to stretch myself upon my own bed; but when I have to accept a sleeping place at the houses of my patients, I am mainly concerned about the quantity of the covering and the cleanness of the couch. But I have always hated to sleep at public houses. I don't know why, but the repugnance grows upon me instead of diminishing. Everything in my chamber was clean and comfortable; but I sat down, when the landlord left me, and concluded to wait until I was more drowsy. There was a fire in the room, and a log or two of wood on the hearth. A rocking-chair, made of split hickory, stood in one corner. It was rough in appearance, but decidedly comfortable. I drew it up to the fire-place, put out my candle, pulled off my boots, and resting my feet on another chair, I lighted a cigar and waited for the drowsy god. The sleet was rattling against the window panes, and I could hear the wail of the wind sweeping through the pines near the house. I thought of the generous young man who had voluntarily encountered the fierce blast and the pelting of the storm to minister to the wants of a poor creature, whose only claim upon his sympathy was the possession of a common nature. Then, when I remembered little Elbert, I wondered that I had tried to dissuade him when he announced his intention to go at once to the child's relief. I thought of the loneliness of Hawder's house, and wondered what possible concatenation of circumstances had brought the man there with that boy, and had kept him there for some years isolated from all his race. The man who brought me the message in the morning was a chance traveller, who met the child on the bridge near the house, and who found out, somehow, where Doctor Cunningham lived.

The logs fell apart on the hearth, and I put their points together again and thought I would go to bed. But the fire was still comfortable, and I stretched myself out on the chairs again and began to think of the little girl, and then I fell asleep.

I dreamed that I was half floating and half swimming in the river, and near the bank where the ferry boat had landed Mr. John Smith. It was a very pleasant sensation. The water seemed to be particularly dense or my body unusually buoyant, as I floated without any effort. Suddenly I saw Baird come down to the margin, leading the child by the hand. He waded out a little way and then threw the child far out into the stream. I tried to call out to him, but could not utter a sound. He waded back to the shore and walked up the bank and out of sight. I then struggled violently to reach the girl, whose intelligent face exhibited no sign of alarm. Her head was above the water, and her curls floated away from her neck as she moved with the current. I could not reach her. The dense element mocked my efforts, and my strongest exertions appeared to accomplish nothing. Then I saw Smith and Hawder come down to the water's edge. I tried to call out to them, but again I had no voice. They looked at the girl as she floated down the stream, and Smith appeared to talk very composedly about her situation. He made no effort to rescue her even when she floated near the bank. Then she began to sink, and she stretched her hands out to me, crying, " Doctor! doctor!" and I awoke.

I was in total darkness. The fire had gone dead out. I got up and began to remember where I was, when the voice came again:

" Doctor! doctor!" and the door-knob rattled.

" Who's there ?" I said.

" It's me—Baird," he answered. " I'm sorry to wake you, but my wife is sick. Won't you please come see her? I've got a light."

I stumbled to the door and admitted him. The dream was still upon me, and I felt inclined to take him by the throat for the murder of the child.

" Did you call me before ?" I asked, as I drew on my boots.

" Yes, sir; I called you once or twice. You haven't been abed?"

" No, I fell asleep in my chair. I am ready now."

He preceded me along the passage, and opened the door at which the girl was standing when I went to my chamber. There was a little crib in a corner, and she was in it asleep. Although I was now broad awake, yet somehow the memory of the dream clung to me, and the sight of the child relieved me. Baird's wife was lying in the bed—a gaunt, hollow-eyed woman, who looked anxiously into my face as I felt her pulse.

"Am I going to die, doctor ?" she asked in a husky voice.

" Not at present. You need not think about dying. I will tell you whenever I think you are in danger."

She sunk back on the bed with a sigh of relief.

" Where is your pain ?" I inquired.

" I am sick at the stomach all the time, and my feet are cold; and I feel so drowsy sometimes, that I fall asleep till the sickness wakes me again."

" What have you eaten to-day ?"

" Oh, nothing to hurt. I had some pork steaks for supper, and eat purty hearty of them—but I did'nt feel sick till I was in bed."

" I want some hot water, Mr. Baird."

" The fires are all out, and——"

" Well—kindle one somewhere and heat some water. I will prepare some medicine while you are gone."

When he left the room I sat down at a table and made up a prescription. The woman fell asleep while I was thus engaged. The table was near the crib and I looked at Nelly again. She was sitting up, bolt upright, watching me with her round bright eyes.

" Lie down, Ellen, my child," I said in a low tone, " and go to sleep."

" I want my mamma. Can't you take me to her ?"

" Not to-night. Don't you hear the rain? Where is your mamma ?"

"I don't know. Don't you?" and she looked eagerly at me.

"Is your mamma named Mrs. Willis?"

"No! she is not my dear mamma. Oh, I want her *so bad.*" I heard Baird coming up the steps.

"Go to sleep now, my darling," I said hurriedly; "Mr. Baird don't like you to talk to me. I will take you to your mamma if I can; but you must not say a word till I tell you. Do you understand?"

"Yes. You are a good man and I love you!" she answered as she laid her head down again. I believe she was asleep in a minute. When Baird came in I was at his wife's bedside again. She awoke as he closed the door. I administered the medicine. She was somewhat relieved when I left her, telling Baird I would see her again in the morning before I left the house.

When I got back to my chamber I threw myself upon the bed and tried to sleep. But it was in vain. The gray dawn came in at my windows before I closed my eyes. That child! Could it be possible that any villany, of which she was the victim, was perpetrated in the midst of a civilized community, where the laws were administered and their sanctions dreaded? Besides, what possible object could Baird have in view, if the girl was stolen away from her parents? He was a thick-skulled, inoffensive sort of man, and did not look like a rascal. Could I account for his evident uneasiness, when the girl was talking to me, by accepting his story of her relationship to his wife and her illegitimate birth? He did not seem unkind to her, and she did not manifest either fear or dislike when he talked to her. But the dream, and the child's eager demand to be taken to her mother, and her denial of Mrs. Willis's right to that title—all these things confused and troubled me. As the light increased I grew more composed, and when I went down to breakfast I had decided upon my course. I only needed my wife's approval of my plans, and I would do nothing and say nothing until I saw her and communicated the facts in the case.

Baird's wife was worse. Her symptoms, without being exactly alarming, were very annoying. The weather was less inclement, and I ordered my horse, intending to visit Hawder and Mr. Phillips, a farmer residing at no great distance from the Creek Bridge; and, if the weather improved, to return to Baird's in the evening. I did not see the child either in Mrs. Baird's room or down stairs. While I was waiting for my horse a stranger came into the bar room.

He was a tall, muscular man of about thirty. The first thing I noticed about him, when he removed his oilskin cap, was a long red scar across his forehead, about an inch above his eyes. I wondered if he had ever been in a battle and got a sabre-cut there. He wore a long bushy beard, and without looking exactly vulgar he had a flash appearance and manner. His dress was made of good material, though somewhat worn and shabby. He walked up to the bar without noticing me, and asked for brandy and water.

" How is the——filly ?" he said as he set his tumbler down.

"About the same, I reckon," replied Baird ; " but my wife is sick."

" Much sick ?" asked the other indifferently.

" Yes ; the doctor there says she is purty sick," and he pointed over to the fire-place where I was standing. The stranger turned and nodded civilly to me.

" It is a raw morning, doctor," he observed. " I think last night was the worst night I ever saw. I was out in the storm, down there by the river. I wanted to stop at Hawder's, Billy"—here he turned to Baird—" but he was sick abed."

" Did you go in ?" inquired the landlord.

" No ; the boy told me his father was sick. While I was talking to him at the door, a queer looking chap came out of the back room. He had his face tied up in a handkerchief and he stuttered dreadfully. But I managed to understand that he was nursing Hawder."

" What time o' night was it ?" said Baird.

" Nigh midnight, I s'pose. I went a mile up the road and got shelter at a farm house, after fighting a cross dog half an hour."

The hostler here put his head in at the door announcing that my horse was ready. I stepped up to the bar to settle for my entertainment, and interrupted a whispered conversation between the pair. I overheard the new comer say: "she will have to stay a little while longer. I'll take her when I can find a safe place." It suddenly occurred to me that they were talking of the child, and I waited for Baird's answer, but only caught fragments of sentences. "Nobody to watch her;" then another whisper, and then, " if you can get Kitty to come here "—" never mind your bill, doctor ; I'm afraid you will have one against me bigger than mine." I had no excuse for lingering, so Beppo and I were speedily on the road to my home.

When I related to my wife all the incidents concerning the little girl, I could perceive that her woman's heart was touched, and

2

that I might safely rely upon her coöperation. My plan was discussed and approved, with some slight modifications; the changes being suggested by her fears that I might get involved in some serious trouble, and suffer some bodily injury, if I came into collision with the men I had seen in the morning. But we agreed finally that I should endeavour to find out any secret that might be hidden under the story told by Baird, and as I would undoubtedly be at the tavern every day for a week or two to come, I should have an opportunity if I kept my eyes open. I had scarcely a doubt that Baird's wife had typhoid fever, and her symptoms were on the whole unfavourable. If I found in the afternoon that the disease had developed itself positively, I should give orders to remove the child's crib from the sick room. The question of contagion is an open one, but I have always thought it wiser to use all possible precautions to avoid the risk. I rode away after an early dinner, for Hawder's first, then for Mr. Phillips's, and finally for Baird's, where I would again remain all night if the case was urgent.

CHAPTER II.

Child Stealing.

I FOUND Mr. Smith walking up and down the road near Hawder's, smoking a cigar. He told me some of the sick man's most prominent symptoms before I entered the house. Little Elbert was with his father when I went in, looking fresh and cheerful. He told me Mr. Smith came there " before he was sleepy," and soon put him to bed in the front room, while he staid with his father. I thought Hawder would recover, with patience and careful nursing, the disease with him not having assumed any of its alarming aspects. I have never been able to get rid of anxiety, however, when I have had patients with " continued fever;" neither have I ever got my own consent to subject any healthy person, except a necessary nurse, to the risk of contagion.

" It is my duty to tell you, Mr. Smith," I said, when we had left the sick chamber, " that you are incurring more or less risk by attending upon this man. He has typhoid fever, and will require incessant attention for two or three weeks, if he is to get well."

" Pooh! doctor," he answered, " do you think I am afraid of such a bugbear as contagion? Never fear for me."

" I heard this morning that you were far from well. You had your head tied up last night, and had a serious impediment in your speech."

He laughed uproariously, and little Elbert joined in the laugh with great glee. I told him to come to me and tell me all about Mr. Smith since he first came.

" I gave father one of the powders last night, and came in this room for some water for him, and then Mr. Smith knocked at the door. He was all wet when he came in, but he took off his coat and then he hugged me, and told me you had sent him to help me nurse father. Then he opened that black bag yonder, and got out a pair of little shoes, and he took off his boots and put the little shoes on. Then he got some of the snow off the window sill in the tumbler and gave father some with a spoon. Father said it was so nice. Then he told me to go to sleep there on them chairs," and he pointed to an extempore sleeping place in the corner, " and he told me to say my prayers, and he tucked the blanket all round me. When Mr. Butler was a knocking he woke me up. He told me to get up and tell Mr. Butler—you know, he has got a red mark on his face—to tell him father was very sick, and he could not stay here. But Mr. Butler wanted to stay because it was a-raining so hard, and then Mr. Smith came out of father's room with his head all tied up with a handkerchief, and he told Mr. Butler that he might catch the sickness—but he talked so slow and funny! So Mr. Butler went away and I went to sleep again. This morning Mr. Smith went into the river and washed himself."

" Into the river ?"

" Yes, sir! he undressed himself and jumped right into the water, and then he dressed himself again out there in the cold."

" The lavatory arrangements are not extensive in Mr. Hawder's residence, doctor," remarked Mr. Smith; " but I prefer the river anyhow. One has more room out there."

" If you have no objection to tell me, I should like to know why you changed your appearance last night ?"

" None in the world. I thought I recognized the voice of the visitor, and I did not wish to be recognized in turn. So I wrapped my face up and put a couple of bullets in my mouth. It would have been quite annoying if he had insisted on remaining; but he went very quietly when he heard there was some danger of contagion. This boy is a bright little fellow."

" Yes, I must manage to get him away from here for a week or two. I think Hawder may escape a very severe illness, but the case may be protracted, and he must have a nurse. I am going now to Mr. Phillips's, and think I can get a woman there to come here for two weeks."

"I will pay the expense, doctor, and I will also stay here until the man is better. I have special reasons for remaining in this neighbourhood. Perhaps I may go back to Baird's to-night or to-morrow, if you get a nurse for Hawder. Where can you put Elbert?"

"I want to stay with father," said the boy earnestly.

"Your father will get well sooner if you are somewhere else, Elbert," I said. "You want him to get well soon, don't you?"

"Yes, sir! But I may come and see him?"

"Yes, you shall come whenever he is well enough. I know you will be a man, and wait until I tell you that you may come."

"I'll do whatever father says," replied the child; "but I think he likes me to nurse him. He took the powder last night without anything to take the taste out!"

"Well, he won't have to take any more medicine just now. I am not going to give him any more powders."

"Before father got sick," said Elbert, after meditating a few minutes, "he said I might go stay a day with Johnny Phillips. Mr. Phillips was here and asked father to let me go. I could walk over here from Mr. Phillips's house; I know the way—I've been there many a time."

"Very well. I'll see Mr. Phillips this morning—I am going there now: and if he says so, I'll take you over on my horse to-morrow."

It was so decided when I left Mr. Phillips. He very kindly offered to send for the boy, and to keep him until his father recovered. I also got a black woman, the wife of one of his farm hands, to stay at Hawder's and nurse the sick man. She went there the same afternoon. I had several other patients in the neighbourhood, and it was near nightfall when I reached Baird's.

As I expected, I found Mrs. Baird worse. Her symptoms were more strongly marked and decided. There was very little to be done except to give directions to the woman I found in her room, whom Baird introduced as "Mrs. Willis." I asked her if she was prepared to stay with the sick woman for two or three weeks. She replied in the affirmative, and I then endeavoured to explain to her the nature of her duties, and the precautions she should observe to avoid the constant danger of contracting the disease herself. She listened to me attentively and promised to follow my directions. I told Baird the child's crib must be removed from the chamber. He looked doubtfully at Mrs. Willis, who promptly proposed taking Nelly into her room.

"Where is your room?" I said; "let me see it."

"It is next to the one you slept in last night, doctor," replied Baird.

"Very well. I think there is danger of contagion, and it will do no harm to keep on the safe side. No one ought to *sleep* in this chamber. Mrs. Willis and you can relieve each other in watching the patient, who will probably be worse and worse for a week, or perhaps two, and who will require attention all the time."

"Do you think she will die, doctor?" said Baird tremulously.

"It is impossible to say. She has typhoid fever, and her symptoms are not very favourable. I hope, however, she will recover. There is nothing alarming in the case at present, and if she is well nursed, and her mind composed, she may be better next week."

"Her mind?" repeated her husband, inquiringly.

"Yes. It is very important that her mind should be perfectly composed. There are some slight appearances of cerebral derangement now, and there will be more to-morrow."

Baird and Mrs. Willis exchanged a rapid glance. I caught it as I stood near the door, for I was watching them.

"Does the child's presence in the chamber annoy or disturb your wife?" I asked. "I see she is not here."

"I believe it does. Nelly is in the kitchen. Mrs. Willis will put her to bed in her room, and she shall stay there till—— till——."

"Until your wife is better; very well. But Mrs. Willis will have to stay in this room most of the night."

"Oh, Nelly sleeps all night. She is a good little gal, and does whatever we tell her."

"Well, you had better remove the crib at once. Take one end; I will help you." So saying I took one end of the little bed and we carried it along the hall to the room he had designated. As we set the crib down in a corner I glanced around the room. It was similar in every respect to the one I had occupied on the previous night. Two windows looking out upon the pines and a door communicating with the hall.

"I shall remain here to-night. I suppose I occupy the same room again?" I said, as we walked down stairs.

"Yes, sir. There's a lot of drovers in the bar room who will stay here to-night, but I'll put 'em all in the back building. I s'pose I needn't tell 'em there's a catching sickness in the house?"

"It is not necessary. You may caution them to keep quiet, as your wife will be disturbed if they are noisy."

We went down stairs, and I returned to the sick room after supper. Mrs. Baird was sleeping fitfully and muttering incoherent sentences. I tried to listen, but it always happened that Mrs. Willis spoke to me before I could catch more than a word or two. Once I heard her say "that child!" I was careful to manifest no interest, as part of my plan was to appear indifferent to everything relating to the little girl. It was my duty to remove her from the sick chamber on the patient's account, and I excited no suspicions when I ordered this change. I could find no fault in the matter or manner of Mrs. Willis's frequent interruptions. She always managed to attract my attention, and always made some appropriate remark, or asked some appropriate question. I began to conclude that she was very nearly a match for me in the game we were playing. I could not decide whether she was merely watching against any possible revelations the sick woman should make, or whether she suspected me of an undue interest in the child.

For two or three nights I was at the inn until bed-time, watching the progress of the case, as the more unfavourable symptoms began to appear. I had but little hope of Mrs. Baird's recovery from the first; and during the second week, when she began to exhibit those manifestations which a medical practitioner so quickly recognizes as the precursors of death, I intimated to Baird that he would probably soon be a widower.

At last the climax arrived. It was on Saturday, and the night was clear and cold. I had ordered the man in charge of the stable to put my horse away for the night, and when I entered the bar room I saw Mr. Smith sitting by the open fire-place, astride of his chair, with his face resting on his arms, which in turn rested upon the back of the chair. I recognized him by the outlines of his handsome person and by his homespun dress, and by the slouched hat which concealed his features. The disagreeable looking man, Butler, was leaning idly against the counter, and looking with a puzzled expression at the stalwart form of the only other occupant of the apartment. Butler nodded to me as I entered, with a "Good evening, doctor." I walked up to the fire; Smith was breathing deeply and apparently in a sound sleep.

"That chap's doing a good deal of sleeping, doctor," said Butler. "I've hollered loud enough to wake a dead man, but he hasn't stirred for half an hour."

"Better let him have his nap out," I answered carelessly. "Have you heard how Mrs. Baird is?"

"No, sir. Baird is in the kitchen, I believe. I'll call him." So saying, he left the bar room.

"And I'll go to bed," said Smith, quietly raising his head. "Good evening, doctor. Mr. Butler is so noisy a companion that I will take advantage of the present opportunity and get rid of him for the night. I will see you in the morning, I suppose? I think I overheard you tell the hostler you would remain here to-night?"

"Yes," I answered, "I shall stay to-night. Are you off? Good night;" and he passed into the hall leading to the chambers as Butler re-entered the room, accompanied by the landlord.

If this was the proper place, I should like to record my opinion of the course, crises and termination of the disease known as continued fever. Mrs. Baird's case was an exceptional one. The symptoms and the course of the disease up to this Saturday night were identical with nearly all the cases I have attended. I had concluded, when I visited her on the previous evening, that she would die within the next twenty-four hours, but had decided to pass the next night in attendance upon the case if she were still alive. I also thought, if she should die in the course of the night, I might have the opportunity for which I had long waited—to converse a little with Nelly. I had had occasional brief glimpses of the bright-eyed little girl, who had always looked cheerful and particularly knowing as she nodded her pretty head to me in passing.

There was no perceptible change in the condition of the patient. I could detect no difference in her pulses or in the general symptoms. She was sleeping, looking gaunt and cadaverous, but she had presented the same appearance from the first. It was near midnight when I left the sick room, directing Mrs. Willis to call me if there should be any necessity for my presence, and also recommending her to remain by the bedside for the next hour or two. I then walked swiftly and quietly along the passage leading to my sleeping apartment and tried the door of the child's room. It was locked. Without pausing, I passed into my own chamber, and drawing a chair to the fire-place I sat down to think.

It was probable that I should have an hour or more at my disposal, and the first thing to be done was to gain an entrance into Nelly's room. There was no key on the outside of the door, and I inferred that it was reposing in Mrs. Willis's pocket. Perhaps the key of my door would unlock Nelly's. I decided to try it, and was about to re-enter the passage, when I thought I heard some one step across the floor of the little girl's room. I drew back, and leaning against the thin partition, I hastily concocted an answer, if it should happen that I found any one older than Nelly in the chamber, to inquire into my motives for paying her so unseasonable a visit. Then I very plainly heard Nelly's voice raised a little above a whisper. I listened intently, but could distinguish no words. After a moment's silence I heard a step again and the creak of a boot. It was undoubtedly a man's footfall, and he was walking with great care. Matters were getting complicated, and I sat down once more.

Who could be in the room? Butler, of course! How did he get there? What devil's work was he doing? And, hardest question of all, what was my duty? I don't know how long these perplexing questions chased each other through my troubled brain, or what rash conclusion I should have reached if I had not been suddenly aroused by Mrs. Willis's voice at my door:

"Doctor, come quickly, please!" she said; "I believe she is going!"

This abrupt summons effectually dispelled all my doubts for the present. I had just time to congratulate myself upon my good fortune. If Mrs. Willis had found me trying the lock of my little neighbour's door, I should have had all my well laid plans frustrated at once and forever. Mrs. Baird's case was urgent—Nelly's could wait.

There was nothing peculiarly alarming about Mrs. Baird. She was more restless and flighty, occasionally muttering some incoherent sentences, but I fancied that her pulse was better than when I saw her earlier in the night. Her attendant looked pale and careworn, and somewhat awe-stricken as she stood at the foot of the bed. Baird was sitting in the corner, looking glum and ugly.

"She's quieter now, sir," observed Mrs. Willis, "but she has been going on awful."

"What has she been doing ?"

"She has been talking kind of wild like."

"I want the gal!" said the sick woman distinctly; "I want to *see* the gal! I tell you she is——"

"There, there!" said Mrs. Willis; "don't go on so. I'll bring her to you if you want her."

"Give me some water," answered Mrs. Baird. I put a spoonful of wine in the tumbler before she took it. I walked over to the corner where Baird was seated, and the fellow looked as though he expected me to decapitate him on the spot.

"Your wife is not so ill, after all," I said; "she may even recover if her mind is undisturbed."

"She has been calling for Nelly, sir," replied he, starting up, "and if you say so, I'll bring her in here. I think she misses the child; she used to sleep in the little crib over yonder, and she misses her."

"Not at present," I said, as he moved towards the door; "if she asks for her when she wakens, you may bring her in."

She slept for more than half an hour, probably forty or fifty minutes, and when she awoke she looked steadily at me for a moment, as if trying to recognize me.

"How do you feel, Mrs. Baird ?"

"I think I'm better doctor; I've had a good long sleep. May they bring little Nelly in to see me ?"

"Yes, Mrs. Willis will bring her," and in obedience to my look she left the room. I heard her walk along the corridor; heard the rattle of the key as she put it into the lock; heard the snap of the bolt as it shot back, and then I heard her walking swiftly back; she pushed the door open and, standing on the threshold, beckoned me out.

"The child is gone!" I caught her arm as she tottered away from the sick chamber, and taking the candle from her shaking hand, I went to Nelly's room, Mrs. Willis following me mechanically. The chamber was empty. The little crib in the corner had been occupied, the bed clothing was turned down, and the impression of little Nelly's head was plain on the pillow.

"I locked the door after she was asleep, and have had the key in my pocket ever since," said Mrs. Willis. "Her clothes were on the chair there by the crib; they are gone. I remember putting her shoes on the chair——"

"Where is Butler?" said I, interrupting her.

She looked at me with a half scared expression, but made no reply.

"I do not doubt," I continued, "that Butler has carried the child away, and probably by your connivance. If my suspicions are not entirely unfounded, you two have committed an enormous crime, of which this child is the victim, and I swear to you that I am resolved to ferret this mystery out. If you will tell me all of the matter, truthfully and unreservedly, I will befriend you as far as I may be able to do so. I am willing to believe that you have been misled by a worse criminal, and it may be possible to save you from any worse punishment than the gnawings of your own conscience."

"You are partly right and partly wrong, doctor," replied the woman after a pause. "Before I called you to-night, I saw Butler go into his room down stairs too drunk to do more than fall upon his bed. If you don't believe me," she added, in answer to my incredulous look, "step down stairs now, you will find him in the little room behind the bar."

I took the candle, and leaving her in the chamber, I went down stairs, wondering if this could be true. I heard the man's stertorous breathing before I opened his door. There he was, doubled up upon the bed, with swollen features and such marks of helpless intoxication about him as could not be simulated. I was only a minute absent, and found Mrs. Willis where I left her.

"I think I know what has become of the child," she said, "and, God knows, I am only glad she is gone. If you want to hear a long story, I will tell you every word of it. If you can quiet Mrs. Baird and send her husband to bed, I will tell you to-night."

The crisis of Mrs. Baird's case was passed. She was sleeping quietly when we returned. I advised the landlord to leave the patient with us, telling him that all her symptoms were favourable. I may say here that she recovered her usual health, and seemed to mend more rapidly after she was made to understand that the little girl was in safe hands. I sat down near her bed, placing the light on the hearth, and Mrs. Willis commenced her story.

CHAPTER III.

MRS. WILLIS'S CONFESSION.

I AM an Englishwoman. I was born in Devonshire. I am not going to tire you with a long account of myself, but some things I am obliged to tell you, as you would not otherwise understand a great deal of the story I have to relate. I know that you will be most interested in that part of it which includes the child's history, but I must tell it in my own way.

Lady Lacy was very frequently in the village in which I was born. It is called Lavington, and belongs to a barony of the same name. The Lacys had once owned large estates adjoining the lands of Lavington, but the family had been unlucky for two or three generations, and Sir John Lacy inherited only the old house and park, and I think there were some mortgages on this small remnant of the old estate when he took possession. I don't know how he managed to get his wife, who was the only daughter of Lord Morton, of Lavington, and who brought him enough money to pay off all the debts on his estate, and more besides. He was a careless, good sort of a man, of whom I never heard much good or bad, and I suppose he attracted more attention because he was the representative of the old Lacys than from any other cause. All that I have to tell you about him is, that he was killed by a fall from his horse a year after his marriage, leaving his young wife with a little baby girl, just born. This happened just seven years ago.

Lady Lacy remained in the old house, though it might be called a new house then, as Sir John had repaired it very thoroughly before he took his bride into it. It was called the Red Hall, not on account of its color, for it was built of gray stone, but on account of some bloody legend that belonged to the family. I don't know rightly what the legend was, but I remember some poetry referring to it, which predicts the early death of the head of the house. No, sir, I don't remember the lines exactly. Maybe they will come back to me before I finish the story. I know that I heard people repeating the poetry when Sir John was killed, and the villagers seemed to consider his death as the only sort of death that a Lacy of the Red Hall could die. I wish I could remember the poetry.

Maybe I ought to mention here that Sir John was the second son of the former baronet. Before he died—that is, Sir Elbert, Sir John's father—he had quarrelled with his old er son, a boy less than ten years old, and at the end of the quarrel the boy left his father's house and never returned. It was said that he ran away and came to this country and died here. I was a little girl then, but I can recollect Sir Elbert and his remaining son going into deep mourning. I am telling you all this to give you some idea of this queer family. There has always been some kind of a curse following them, that is certain.

Very soon after Sir John's death I went to the Hall to nurse little Ellen. Yes, sir, the little girl who has been stolen away from this house to-night.

I don't understand the laws, and don't know anything about Sir John's estate. Lady Lacy had plenty of money in her own right; but I have heard the neighbours speak of the Red Hall going to some male heir of the Lacys, who, however, never came to claim it. There was one gentleman, Mr. Lacy Barston, who lived in the neighbourhood, and who was a relation of Sir John's, and it was said that the lawyers thought he was the rightful heir to the Red Hall and Park. But he always denied it himself, which was curious, as he and Lady Lacy disliked each other excessively. He was never at the Hall after Sir John married, though he was his sworn friend before, and people said he never went anywhere else where he was likely to meet the baronet or his wife. All the while I was at the Hall I never heard my lady mention his name. There was some secret cause for this mutual dislike which I tried to find out a hundred times, but never could. Yes, sir. He was undoubt-edly a gentleman who stood high in everybody's opinion except my lady's. He was a sort of a lawyer, at least he had been edu-cated for the bar, but he spent most of his time in travelling, sometimes on the continent, and sometimes to outlandish places that nobody ever heard of before. I have known him to go off on one of his long trips—maybe to South America, maybe to China—and be gone for a year or two, and then quietly come back when nobody was expecting him. No, sir. He had no relations that I know of nearer than Sir John.

I don't know why I have told you all this about Mr. Barston. Although he was never at the Red Hall, he was everywhere else. I can't say that I disliked him, though I always felt uncomfortable when he was near me. I could not help thinking that he knew exactly what I was thinking about, and then I was always sure to think of things that I did not want him to know when he was in the same room. It was when I was out with the child that I would see him. Sometimes, when I would be driving out (for my lady frequently sent me with Ellen when she was not disposed to drive herself), Mr. Barston would come galloping up after the carriage, and take the child before him on his horse, and gallop off with her. He seemed to be very fond of her, and she loved him better than anybody in the world, except her mother.

After Sir John's funeral was over, Mr. Barston came home. He had been absent nearly a year, but it seemed that he was now going to settle down. The old place, Oakland, where he lived, was repaired, and he rode over to the village one day to offer me the place of housekeeper. It was after I had agreed to go to the Red Hall, and I could not have accepted his offer if I had fancied the place. He persisted in his arguments when I told him I was engaged to my lady, and offered me "any wages I wanted." I suppose he was more anxious to get me, because he thought my lady would be disappointed. Once, when he met the carriage, he renewed the offer, asking me when my engagement would be at an end at the Hall, but I then told him plainly that I did not wish to make the change. My husband was courting me then, and he hated Mr. Barston so thoroughly, that I had learned to dislike him too. No, sir. He was not a drinking man then; he has learned to make a beast of himself in this country. No, sir. His name is not Willis. His name is of no consequence. It is like enough that Mr. Barston had caught him in some improper conduct—poaching, maybe. I remember one time, as he was handing the child back to me after one of his gallops, he said, "Kitty, I wish you would quit keeping company with that fellow. He is not good enough for you, or for any other decent girl." I asked him what he had to say against him, and he answered, "He is a brute, and has only a brute's instincts; but you won't be advised by me. I see it in your face." And so he rode off. Heigho!

My husband—I was not married then—had been gamekeeper for Lord Morton. I never knew exactly why he left Lavington, though I know he left in disgrace. He blamed Mr. Barston for interfering, as I found out from things he would let drop when speaking of him; and it is very probable that Mr. Barston, who was frequently at Lavington, had given my husband a bad word whenever he had the chance. During Sir John's lifetime there was

some hard quarrel between him and Mr. Barston, which my husband helped to aggravate in some way.   He never told me the
particulars.   I only know that he had kept them apart a long time
after they were willing to be friends again.   I just remember the
lines I spoke of, and may as well repeat them before I forget them
again.   I never could see any sense in them myself.

> "A score and a half score he ne'er shall attain,
> Who holds the Red Hall and the Lacy's proud name——"

I have forgotten it again.   It is something about bloody jewels,
but the principal thing is the prophecy that no Lacy should live
thirty years, and they do say that they have always died young,
and always by some violent death.   There is something in the
poetry about "kinsman's blood;" maybe I'll remember it all before
I finish my story.   Sir Elbert was found dead in his bed the day
before his birthday, when he would have been thirty.   There were
marks of violence, I have heard, but no one ever knew who killed
him.   He was married very young—had married against the
wishes of his relations and friends, and both his sons were born
before he was of age.   His wife died when Sir John was born.

My husband—yes, sir, certainly.   We were married in Scotland,
by Scottish law, as you will hear presently.   I was going to say
that my husband has always hated all the Lacys and all belonging to them.   I really don't know what reason he has, but I am
certain of the fact.

You want to know about my marriage?   Well, sir, we were in
Scotland.   My lady and her bosom friend, Miss Clare Tamworth,
had a cottage near Stirling.   One day, when I was driving with
Ellen, Mr. Barston came galloping after the carriage.   He had
been away a year or two, but the child remembered him, and
clamoured for him to take her on his horse.   I cannot understand
why my lady allowed it.   She always knew it, for the child always
told her.   No, sir; she never mentioned Mr. Lacy Barston's name
to me, or to any one else, so far as I know.   But she might easily
have told me to keep Ellen in the carriage if she objected to her
gallops with Mr. Barston.   However, he told me that day to meet
him at the same place an hour later, and rode off with the child.
I had to go to Stirling to get a brooch which my lady had left at
a jeweller's to be repaired, and while I was in the shop Mr. ——,
my husband, came in.   He was dressed like a gentleman.   I had
left him at Lavington a month before, and had received two or
three letters from him, but did not expect him.   The coachman

had taken the carriage somewhere to get a bolt replaced that had
been lost, and ——, my husband, told me he had come to marry
me, and had arranged everything for the ceremony in a neigh-
bouring street. I was easily persuaded, for I loved him. When
we reached the place—I think it was a magistrate's office—he told
me I must answer to the name the man asked, and to write it in a
book. I don't see why you should insist on knowing the name,
but it makes no difference over here. It was Clare Tamworth.
Yes, sir, he did sign *his* real name. I shall not tell you what name
he signed. The marriage was legal. I asked a lawyer, who certainly knew all about it, and I have the certificate. After we
were married he walked back to the jeweller's and left me there,
bidding me keep the marriage secret until he gave me leave to
tell. I did not see him again or hear from him until a month
later.

My story is almost done, sir. Last summer we went to Clifton,
where Miss Tamworth lived. I used to take Nellie out on the
Downs every fine day between luncheon time and dinner. Sometimes my lady and Miss Tamworth would be with us, and sometimes we would be alone. One day Nellie and I wandered down
to the bank of the river—the Avon. A large ship was going
down the river from Bristol—going out to sea. The tide was
rising, but was not high enough, and the vessel came close to the
bank and got aground. There was a great deal of confusion on
board. Some sailors got into a boat and brought a rope ashore
to fasten the ship until the tide was high enough to float her off.
While I was watching the sailors a gentleman clambered over the
side of the ship and leaped down on the shore. It was my husband.

" Kitty, my dear," he said, " I've come for you. I was going to
walk over from Bristol, but the ship sailed twelve hours before the
appointed time. The captain suddenly decided to go out on this
tide, and I should have missed you if we had not got aground."

I was very much bewildered. I was glad to see him, of course,
and I was only too happy in the prospect of going away with him.

" I'll take Nelly home, then——"

" That is impossible," he answered; " the ship will be afloat
before you could get up the bank. Bring her with you. We can
send her home by the pilot boat. Nellie, do you want to go on the
big ship ?"

" Yes, yes !" replied the child eagerly ; and before I could offer

an objection he took her in his arms and stepped in the little boat.
I followed, hardly knowing what I was doing, and in a few minutes we were climbing over the side of the vessel.

"I have no clothes," I whispered, as he drew my arm through
his; "and I cannot possibly go in this way——"

"Pooh, pooh! I've a trunk full of dresses in the cabin—a regular outfit. This is the lady, captain—Mrs. Butler——"

"And daughter?" replied the captain, touching his cap to me.
"You did not mention the child, Mr. Butler."

"Didn't I? I forgot it, I suppose. Come on, my dear; I will
show you the cabin," and we went down stairs.

All this occurred more rapidly than I can tell you, and I did not
exactly know what I was doing until we were all in our state-
room. While Nellie was engrossed with the strange sights
around her, my husband endeavoured to pacify me with his explanations. He said he had been several weeks in Bristol, had taken
passage in this ship for himself and wife, had bought "my outfit,"
as he called it, and was coming to Clifton for me that evening.
When he found the ship was actually going in the afternoon, instead
of the next morning, he made up his mind to go in her, and write
for me from America. He said "a good Providence" had run the
ship aground just at that spot. I thought so too, then, but now I
think it was a bad devil!

The ship was soon moving. A little tug towed her down the
long river very slowly, because the tide was coming in so strongly,
and it was dark before we were in the channel. The child went
to sleep, and I laid her in one of the berths. It was almost midnight when the pilot went off in the tug. I could not send Nellie—
I could not bear to do it; so my husband bade me write a letter to
my lady which he sent by the pilot.

The next morning we were at sea. I have never known a happy
hour since that day. Nellie was told—*I* told her, that the ship had
sailed away with us while she was asleep, and that she must call
me "mother" and Mr. Butler "papa" while we were aboard, and
that we would take her home whenever we could "get the ship to
turn round." We told her she must not say anything to the captain about her real mother, for fear he would not take us back.
She is a wonderfully *old* child, and she obeyed me implicitly. She
was not much distressed, and if she had not cried for her mother
sometimes in the night I would not have been so miserable. We
reached New York in twelve days and came directly here. My

husband has been getting drunk nearly every day since we came. We have a house not very far from Hawder's. No, sir! I *dare* not tell you my husband's name; he would kill me! I have not dared to write to my lady since we landed, but I have made many plans to get away with Nellie and get back to England. I am certain my husband did not intend to bring her away, and he solemnly swore to me only yesterday that he would take me and her back as soon as the spring opens. If he would only leave off drinking I believe he would do it. He has no business, sir. I don't know where he gets his money. Mrs. Baird is awake.

CHAPTER IV.

JOHN HAWDER'S STORY.

I DON'T think talking hurts me a bit, doctor. You have pulled me through this bout so fast that I feel quite well enough to go out if you would allow me; but if you won't, you can let me sit up here in the blessed sunlight at least. English? Yes, sir! Devonshire, too, the garden spot of the world! The Lacys? oh, yes, I have known them all my life. They are a queer lot, but I can't say they are altogether bad—leastways not all of them. Sir Elbert was a real gentleman, though he was headstrong and violent. He was always very kind to me, and was godfather to my poor brother, who is now in heaven, and I called my boy after him. My father was Sir Elbert's steward, and his oldest son, Master Elbert, was born the same day I was. I remember well enough playing with him and his brother, the late Sir John, when we were all younger than my boy yonder. I was too young to know much about the final quarrel between Sir Elbert and his son, but I heard a good many of them. Sir Elbert was violent and the boy was fierce. He was proud as Lucifer, and when his father struck him that morning, he said, "You are my father, and I cannot strike you back, but I'll leave your house," and that night he ran away. Within a year he died, or was killed in some horrible way, I don't know how, and Sir Elbert did not live long after him. The prophecy! Well, sir, the people used to say there was a prophecy about the Lacys dying young. I don't know it. It was something about "bloody jewels." After

3

Sir Elbert's death his son, Sir John, went to live at Oakland with
Mr. Barston, who was his uncle. He was not very rich, but lived
in a quiet way among his books; and his two boys, as he called
them, that is his son Lacy and Sir John, grew up together. They
were a good deal more like real brothers than the two young Lacys
were, and I am sure they loved each other dearly. Mrs. Barston
was Sir Elbert's sister, and one of the best women that ever lived.
The people called her Lady Mary, though she had no title. There
is another tradition current in the neighbourhood, which says all
the bad of the "haughty Lacys" is monopolized by the men of the
race and all the good is monopolized by the women.

It has been nearly a dozen years since I saw or heard anything
about Devonshire people. My father had a large family, and I
persuaded him to let me come to this country when I was quite a
youth. 1 had been fairly educated, and thought I could make my
own way in the world if I only had room. But I have never been
lucky, somehow, though I have always managed just to get along
and keep my head above water. And now I am thinking of taking my boy to Devonshire, and let him grow up among his own kin.
Oh, yes, sir, I am sure of employment that will yield me enough
for my wants.

You wish me to tell you what I know of Mr. Butler? I would
rather talk about something else. I suppose you have some good
reason for asking, but I don't know anything very good about
him, and have no desire to harm him in any way. You are very
good, sir; but I do not believe you can ever befriend Butler, unless you could make him leave off his drink, and that cannot be
done. I have known him to be perfectly sober for a year at a time,
and then suddenly fall back again into his old habits. He is terrible when he begins one of his spells, but he soon gets stupid and
harmless. The first time I ever saw him was six or seven years
ago. It was in New York. I can tell you about that, certainly. I
was working in one of the theatres, doing odd jobs and getting
very fair pay. I had to stay until late. When I had finished my
duties, I went through the stage door into the boxes, to see the last
of the play, and just as the curtain fell there was a row near me.
One man was fighting two, and that seemed wrong in my English
eyes. So I went in and took one of the two in hand. It only
lasted a minute or two. I polished my man off, and then I saw
some policemen coming, and I slipped back by the stage door.
Before I got through it the single man followed me, crossed the

stage with me, and we were soon in a side street and safe. It was Butler. He was perfectly sober, was well dressed, and looked like a gentleman, and talked like one. The fellow he was fighting had a knife and had cut him a little in the arm, and I took him home with me and dressed his wounds, and then made him a bed on the sofa. He had that scar on his forehead, and it was something that the bruisers at the theatre had said about that which brought on the fight.

When I went down stairs the next morning I found Butler up and dressed. He was trying to get the blood stains off his coat sleeve. I got him a needle and thread, and he sewed up the cuts in his sleeve very neatly: " I learned that at sea," he said. My wife was sick, and Elbert was a baby then. I kindled a fire and made some tea. After he drank a cup he got up to go.

" You're English," he said, " and your name is Hawder. I read it in the Bible yonder before you came down. I am going now, but I want to come to see you again some time. I have nothing to say about last night's work. If I had seen you or any other man beset by two bullies, I should have done what you did. So would any Englishman. I hope your wife will soon be well again. Good-bye."

She didn't get well again. A month later I buried her. When I got back from the funeral I found Butler at my door. I was not in very good spirits, and did not want company, but I had to invite him in. He did not talk much, as he was pretty full of rum. I made up a bed for him again and left him asleep. In the morning he was worse. He had been drinking in the night and was furious. He talked a lot of wild stuff about being at sea, and fights on bloody decks and bags of doubloons. I was not much afraid of him, though he was frightful enough; but I could not leave my baby boy in the house with him; so I took the child out by a back door, and left him with a neighbour when I went to my work. When I went back at dusk he was gone. He repeated this the next week, and I don't know why I endured it as long as I did. Somehow I could not get my own consent to turn him out or refuse him admittance. He was an Englishman, and somehow, he seemed to think he had a sort of claim upon me; perhaps because we had been in the scuffle together at the theatre. And besides, he would come sometimes well dressed, with nice kid gloves on his hands—he has very small white hands—and would behave like a gentleman. He would tell interesting stories about

storms at sea, or about adventures with savages in some tropical
island. One night, I remember, he told how he and a shipmate
had got lost in the bush. It was on the other side of the world—I
think in Australia. They had gone ashore to fill their water
casks. He must have been an officer, as he left the men at their
work and wandered off into the woods with his companion. "We
did not know we were lost until dark," he said; "in those latitudes
the sun goes down like a shot. We did not have much time for
discussion before we knew that we were among enemies. A long
spear came glancing through the bushes and plunged into a tree
trunk by our side, and quivered wickedly in the failing light.
There was only one thing to be done, and that was to charge in
the direction from which the spear came while we could see. So
we tore our cutlasses out and dashed into the dark bushes, shouting aloud in English for our men. Another spear met us and
made an ugly hole in Jack's side. I suppose that hurt cost half a
dozen of the niggers their lives, for we were among them in a
minute, and Jack laid about him like mad! I was as cool as I am
now, and kept up the shouting while I fought. My pistols were
emptied very soon, and no shots were wasted. There seemed to
be a hundred of the black devils, and they would have finished
my history pretty soon, if the men had not come up, and if I had
not been wise enough to keep close to the savages so that they
could not use their spears. Half a dozen pistol shots from the men
concluded the fight. The savages disappeared like a lot of ghosts.
We had to leave poor Jack, who had fought his last battle. My
only hurt was a wound in the head, that was not dangerous."

"Is that the scar on your forehead?" I asked. His face suddenly became ghastly pale, while the ugly seam grew purple. At
last he answered:

"No! And, Mr. Hawder, please remember that all reference to
this beauty spot of mine is forbidden for all time to come. And
now good-night." And he walked out of the house before I could
speak.

He came afterwards, and did not seem to remember my unlucky
question, which I need not say was never repeated. I asked him
on one occasion, when he was telling of some other fight he and
his men had, how it happened that they were armed? He looked
at me with a queer expression, and said "it was customary *down
there*," but that was the last of his fighting stories. When he was
drunk he would talk all kinds of outlandish gibberish, but never

said anything that was connected or comprehensible. I have never known him to laugh, except in such a horrid fashion that it made my flesh creep. My belief is that some dreadful secret is on his mind, connected with that ugly scar, maybe, that drives him to drink as he does.

One of the theatre managers owns this farm, and he offered me enough money to give me a bare living, with this house to live in, if I would come here and oversee his land. I was tired of New York, and tired of Mr. Butler, and my boy was puny and fretful, so I consented and moved here two years ago. Elbert seemed to grow strong and healthy at once, and I was able to have him constantly with me, and as I left no traces, I lost Mr. Butler—or rather he lost me. I never saw him after I moved until last autumn—it was October; the boy and I were in the orchard yonder gathering apples. We were under the big tree by the road side when a Jersey wagon came down the road, and the man who was driving stopped his horse, and asked me the way to Baird's. It was Butler. He had a lady and a little girl with him, and one or two trunks were in the back part of the wagon. He knew me, of course, and I knew him, but he gave no sign of recognition, and neither did I. He thanked me civilly for the information I gave him and then drove on. I have not seen him since, but I heard his voice the other night, when Mr. —— Smith was nursing me so kindly.

Did I know Mr. Lacy Barston? Yes, sir, I knew him well. He was a mere stripling when I left England. Heigho! It is a wonderful relief to change the subject of discourse. Mr. Barston is, or was, the noblest gentleman I ever knew or heard of. No Lacy blood in him, except what he got from his mother, Lady Mary, and he could get nothing but good from her. His father was not rich, and he had very little pocket money, but what he had was mostly spent for the comfort of poor people about Oakland. I remember that he and Sir John were out shooting one day, and Sir John shot at an old horse of Farmer Dawson's in pure wantonness. The horse was too far off for the shot to hurt him, but he was frightened, and tried to leap over a fence and got staked, so that he had to be shot in earnest. Mr. Barston said nothing about it, but he saved up his weekly allowance until he had enough to buy another horse, which he sent to Dawson with *Sir John's good wishes.* I know all about it, because I took the horse and the message, being bound to secresy first. I never saw him out of

temper in my life, though I have known him to endure bad treatment from his cousin more than once, and fairly conquer him at last
by sheer amiability. It was not for want of pluck, sir. He could
have doubled up Sir John in two minutes, and I don't believe he
knew what fear was. He was always playing off some prank, and
his whole life appeared to be one joke. His great delight was to
disguise himself and pass himself off for somebody else. The
last trick I knew him to play was upon Lord Morton, to whom he
got introduced as a French governess. He wrote a lot of letters
from people Lord Morton knew, and took them himself to Lavington, and actually was engaged by Lord and Lady Morton for their
daughter, Miss Ret, now Lady Lacy. It was she who discovered
him after he had deceived everybody else. They did not agree,
for some reason, though there was never any quarreling between
them. Oh no, sir! he only passed himself off for the French
woman for a joke. None of his jokes ever hurt anybody. He
would not harm a fly.

Since I left England I have heard of his father's death, and also
that he had inherited a good lot of money from some distant
cousin. And in the last half dozen years he has wandered all-
over the earth. No one can tell where he is at any time certainly.
He has been in Australia, in South America, and once on a polar
expedition, where he was caught two winters in the ice. Yes, sir,
I think he has been in this country too. Well, yes, sir, I may say I
know he has. Have I ever seen him here? Well, sir, I might have
seen him many a time without knowing him, as he can make himself look like anybody rather than himself. Have I never seen
him to know him? Well, sir, you know if I had seen him in
any other character than his own I would not feel at liberty to
——; thank you sir, I am sure you would not wish me to betray any
confidence. I don't mean, though, that I have been bound up; I
mean—I don't mean anything. I feel a little tired talking so
much; might I go lie down awhile? Thank you, sir.

CHAPTER V.

CAPTAIN STRONG'S STORY.

I AM captain of the royal mail steamer "Austria," belonging to the New York and Liverpool line. I have crossed the Atlantic ninety times, and have seen all sorts of weather. Yes, I have carried all sorts of people, too. Perhaps the queerest lot I ever carried was on my last voyage. The ship left New York at noon on the tenth day of April, in the midst of a blinding snow storm. I remember that everything about the land was white, and that we sailed into bright skies and shook the snow out of our sails before dark when the pilot left us. The wind came cold and strong off the Long Island coast, which lay all white on our larboard quarter, and took the old ship like a race horse out of sight of land. We had but few passengers, as it was too early in the season for the Yankee rush. You know the Yankees don't begin until May. The day before we sailed a nice gentleman came aboard to look at his state room and arrange his trunks. I had a list of my passengers, or rather the purser had, and we looked through the list to find his number, as he had forgotten it. We soon found it —"Mr. John Smith and daughter." He had one of the best state rooms in the ship. The twin room next to it, number six, was taken by Mr. and Mrs. Barston. Mr. Smith seemed to think this was a queer name, and asked me a great many questions about them. But I could not tell him, as I had not seen them. But at sailing time there was no "Mr. Smith and daughter," and I had to go without them. Just before dark, when the pilot boat quitted us, an old gentleman, who had a bright little boy by the hand, handed me a letter, which only contained a line or two. I remember every word of it. "Mr. John Smith presents his compliments to Captain Strong, and regrets that his name must be erased from the passenger list. But his friend, Mr. John Jones, the bearer, has taken Mr. Smith's ticket for himself and son, and the agents have kindly consented to the transfer. Mr. Jones will take charge of Mr. Smith's luggage to Liverpool, as he has very little of his own." Of course I was bound to be polite to the old gentleman, who was very feeble, and I showed him to his state room, number eight. Mr. and Mrs. Barston were already in number six. I think Mr. Barston had had something to drink before he came aboard, and I know he had had something since the ship

left her dock. Mr. Barston kept up steam enough to run the ship
in his own stateroom. His wife, who was a very handsome woman,
stuck faithfully by him and must have had a hard time. She was
seasick, too, poor thing. For a whole week she never got on deck,
and her husband never stopped drinking. He had a bottle of
champagne at breakfast time, and always finished it before he left
the table. He was very polite, especially to old Mr. Jones (who
sat next to him), and would have been good looking enough if it
had not been for a long seam across his forehead that looked like
a sword cut. It was generally red, but when he would take a
tantrum, which was pretty often, it would get purple, and then he
looked like the devil. The steward always had to take him to
his state room from the table, while the stewardess took care of
his poor wife, who did not eat enough to sustain a snipe.

Old Mr. Jones was very regular in his habits. In the morning
he and his little boy, Johnny, had a regular romp on deck. They
had it all to themselves, as none of the other passengers got about
so early. The child was very shy, and I could never get more
than a word or two out of him, and he was always watching his
father as if he wanted to know what he would like him to say. I
picked him up one day suddenly, to show him a school of por-
poises near the ship, and asked him, "Is your name Johnny?"
Bless you, he was only a mite, but he opened his eyes wide and
sharp and answered, "That's what papa calls me!" I hadn't
time to ask him any more, as the old gentleman took him out of
my arms, saying, "He is the best child alive, captain, but is a
little shy!"

After breakfast the old gentleman always went into the second
cabin. You know the second cabin passengers could not come
into the saloon, and could not come abaft the mainmast, but the
first cabin passengers could go where they liked. Mr. Jones was
very fond of pottering about among the seasick passengers and
brightening them up a bit. There was one poor fellow, a Mr.
Hawder, who was very miserable, but Mr. Jones actually got him
on deck a day or two before we saw the Irish coast. He had a
boy with him, too, a bright little fellow who staid by his father
all the time. When Mr. Jones got them up and comfortably fixed
near the funnel, he went down after his boy, and walked about
the deck for some hours. I suppose the children would have
liked to play together, but the old gentleman kept to his own part
of the deck and never let go his boy's hand. It was all well
enough, you know, for him to go among the second class passen-

gers, but he did not intend the child to form any second class acquaintances. Bless you! he was as proud as Lucifer!

I am coming now to the end of my story. We sighted the coast on Sunday, a gale blowing from the nor'west. It was just after dinner and nigh dark. We had had good weather until that Sunday, but it came in with a gale of wind, and by night it was a regular storm. Most of the passengers were huddled in their berths, but when the storm was knocking the old ship the hardest, who should come on deck but Mr. Barston! He had been pretty sober all day, that is, for him. But I have always noticed that a man who gets champagne drunk—I mean a good regular drunk—don't get entirely sober under a week. His wife was not able to be with him, as the rough sea had put her to bed, where she lay helpless and miserable. Old Mr. Jones had Mr. Barston's arm, and they both appeared rather to like the weather than otherwise.

"I think you will find it more comfortable below, gentlemen," I said, as they clung to the rail on the lee side of the gangway.

"Below!" shouted Mr. Barston. "Why, captain, this is glorious! It is the first good weather you have had. I have been caught in a cyclone twice, and could sleep comfortably on deck in this little breeze."

"But, Mr. Jones——"

"Never mind me, captain," said the old gentleman. "I, also, have seen worse storms than this. Mr. Barston was anxious to tell me a story, as he expresses it, and says he can only tell it in the open air."

They seated themselves on the edge of the skylight grating, just under the lee of my cabin. I was studying my charts, and was within a yard of them while they sat there.

"You will remember, then, Mr. Barston," said I, "that you must not talk any secrets, as I cannot help overhearing you."

"All right, captain! My story is only a bit of romance that I am anxious to tell Mr. Jones. I dare say it will put you to sleep if you listen."

But I didn't go to sleep. And when the story was over I half fancied that I should never go to sleep again! I had put the ship head to wind, and felt pretty safe for the night, and only wished to confirm my judgment by going over the charts once more. Mr. Barston had evidently a fit of the horrors, as no man perfectly sane could have said the things he said. I cannot understand to this day how poor old Mr. Jones took the thing so quietly. They sat there, and talked and smoked cigars, raising their voices when the wind howled through the rigging, but neither of them paying the smallest attention to the storm, which was about as bad a storm as I ever encountered.

"Well, Mr. Jones," began the other, "my story is about some English people—boys and girls, and men and women. You are an Englishman?"

"Yes."

"I thought so. But it is not likely that you ever heard of my boys and girls. Let me see! There were two boys, brothers, who lived in England—no matter what part—some years ago! What did you call that youngster of yours?"

"John."

"And that kid of Hawder's is called Elbert, is he not?"

"Yes."

"Well, let me call my two boys Elbert and John. Those names will do to distinguish them as well as any. Elbert was the elder by a year, and was heir to a good name and a fairish estate. But his father spent about eight years in developing whatever there was of the devil in the elder boy, and at the end of that period struck him. On the same night Elbert ran away, and he never set foot in his father's house afterwards. In a year or two his father heard of his death, and not long after died himself; so John was left the last of his race. Do you understand?"

"Yes."

"Elbert walked out of his father's house—a mere child, mind you—and within a mile he fell in with a company of roving players, who took pity on him, and gave him a blanket to sleep on in their tent. By daylight they were off, taking the boy with them. He had a little pocket money, but they would take none of it. During the day they plodded on, aiming to reach some village by night-fall, when they would spread their tent and gather all the loose shillings they could by their performances. One of the actors had a daughter about Elbert's age. Her name was—well, call her Kitty Willis—as Willis was her father's name, and Kitty will do as well as any name to designate her. Elbert told this girl his story—the exact truth—and they two kept the secret. She was kind to him then and always. God bless her! She ought to be blessed, for nobody else was ever kind to him! It seems to me now, as I recall his story, that he came into the world at enmity with humanity, and that poor little girl, the half orphan daughter of a strolling player, set herself against humanity in pitying and befriending him!

"For three months the boy wandered through the provinces, taking some little parts in their plays sometimes, rather tolerated than otherwise, and leading a hard enough sort of life. The other child kept a sort of watch over him, and did what she could to lighten his burdens. He was a mere mite, you know. But it never once occurred to him that he might go back to his father's house and live like a gentleman. One day, three months after he had left his home, the players were in Liverpool, and Elbert was accosted in the street by a gentleman who recognized him—a Mr.——. No matter; he was a neighbour of his father's. Yes—related to him. He —the old gentleman—said the boy must certainly return to his father's house. The boy answered by darting down an alley and escaped. But before he got away the old gentleman had extorted a promise from him that he would communicate with his father the next day. So he kept his promise. He addressed a note the next evening to his father from the deck of the *Hindoo*, a Calcutta liner, and gave it to the pilot at the mouth of the Mersey. He had shipped as a cabin boy, a poor orphan who could read and write a little. Twenty years ago the *Hindoo* sailed probably within a few miles of this very spot. She was spoken just out of sight of land, and she was never heard of again!

"But master Elbert could tell the history of that voyage if you could only get at him! The ship got round the Cape and was crawling along under light breezes in the Bay of Bengal when she met another ship. This was a brigantine, which outsailed the *Hindoo* in the light wind, and was soon within half a mile, and then she hoisted a black flag and began to fire upon the big ship. The boy could not give many details. He could tell of a day's fighting under that burning sun, of decks slippery with blood, of the gallant stand made by a score of desperate men as a hundred fiends at last clambered on board. He could remember the hopeless struggle against enormous odds, and the death of the last man who resisted. He could tell how the pirate captain hesitated a moment whether or not to chop off his head also, and finally concluded to spare him, because he cursed him to his face! He could also tell how the ship was gutted and scuttled, and how he, the solitary survivor of all her company, sailed away from the scene of the strife, under the black flag of the pirate, as her cabin boy.

"The brigantine was manned by men of all nations. The captain

was an American, and his name was Butler. He was the most
hideous mortal that ever lived. He was all brute. But, for some
unaccountable reason, he took a liking to that boy—the waif he
had gathered from the sea—and though he cursed him twenty
times a day, he did not maltreat him. For ten years, in which the
boy passed into manhood, he was the constant companion of that
brute. And when the captain died—must I tell you how he died ?
Well! It was on the other side of the world.

"They had a law on the brig, in fact they had several laws. One
related to the distribution of gains. Every man had the same
share in the gains, which were sometimes honest enough, except
that the ship paid no customs. She was an armed smuggler, and
they had an island on the Australian coast, which was totally inaccessible except at one spot known only to the smugglers. It
was the mouth of a little river, almost concealed by the dense
undergrowth, but affording secure anchorage. It was a famous
hiding place. Here they would land their guns sometimes, and
leaving nine-tenths of the crew, would sail out, their yards all
down, and go on a trading expedition under fore and aft sails.
An officer or two staid with the shore crew and maintained disci-
pline, which was rigid and inexorable. Another law related to
quarrels, which were infrequent. This provided that any serious
quarrel should be settled by the quarrelers. They were landed at
some safe place, armed only with cutlasses, and time allowed them
to settle their differences. The survivor was taken aboard and
no questions asked. Officers were the peers of officers, and they
could not quarrel except among themselves. The men were not
allowed to answer officers, and no disputes were possible.

" Elbert was a lieutenant. He had been promoted, as all officers
were, by the unanimous vote of the men. He had done something
that the men thought particularly plucky in a little fight with
savages. The captain would have prevented the promotion if he
dared, but he was powerless against the unanimous vote of the
crew. But it was possible to tantalize the boy—for he was under
twenty when he was elected—and one day there was a savage
quarrel. You may think it strange, but they quarrelled about
their nationalities. One might think all love or respect for one's
country would die out in such a life, but it did not. Each said
some terribly hard things about the other's birth place, and at last
some words were spoken that brought the steel out of the scabbard. They were quickly disarmed, the brig's head put about,

and the next day they were on the Australian coast, far out of the track of ordinary traffic. A boat was lowered, and the captain and Elbert were landed with their weapons in their belts. As they walked into the bush Elbert recognized the old battle ground where he had encountered the savages a few months before.

"I don't know whether you are enough interested in the boy to care about his emotions, but I may as well tell them. He thought first of his kindred in far-off England, and the thought of them made him more eager to settle accounts with Butler, who had dared to traduce them in traducing his country. Then he thought of the fierce struggle that had occurred under those very trees when he had fought his way from forecastle to quarter deck. Then he thought of a resolution he had formed, which was to quit that accursed vessel that day, dead or alive ! He had collected all his booty, which was mainly in Bank of England notes, and it was belted around his body. He had exchanged a lot of gold for this money the last time the brig had been a schooner, when they were in a civilized port. It was Melbourne.

"A hundred yards from the shore—it was a little bay on the north coast—they came out of the bushes upon a sandy opening, and Elbert unbuckled his sword belt, drew his cutlass, and threw belt and scabbard on the ground.

"See here, Britisher !" said Butler, as he bared his own blade, "have you any objection to jaw a little before we begin ?"

"None in the world, except that time presses. There is a storm brewing, and the brig would be safer a little further from the shore."

"Wa-al!" drawled the captain," we need not trouble ourselves about the brig. I have a proposition to make !"

"Make it !"

"Wa-al ! I bear no malice. If we git to choppin' one another here, I guess we'll both git hurt some. I don't want to hurt you particular, and dam'me if I want to git hurt myself!"

"I do not understand you !"

"Oh, it's all plain enough. Instead of fightin', s'pose we toss up ? whichever wins shall return to the brig. The other stays here !"

"I am not going back to the brig in any event," answered Elbert coldly. "If you will apologize for your insulting words, you may return and welcome."

"And if not——"

"1 will assault you when I count ten. One, two, three, four——"

"Hold hard, Britisher! I cave! There's my hand. What! you won't take it? Wa-al! no matter. I apologize for what I said, and I think you might oblige me by tossing up! You won't? Wa-al, I'll go then. Look here, boy! Don't be fool enough to think I am afeard to fight you. You have seen me tackle bigger men before now. The truth is I am sick of the brig, and I did not want to kill you, and if you had a grain of sense you would go back! They would make you captain! You won't? Wa-al! good bye, and good luck to you! It is not likely that we shall meet again this side of—— whatever place sich good people as us go to! I s'pose you know that bushmen live hereabouts?"

"Yes. I saw a few of them just where you stand only three months ago!"

"Wa-al! that's cur'ous. But I b'lieve you're right; and if you think this is a healthy spot, I don't. You are not likely to come off as well this time as the last, and the best piece of advice I can give you is to keep your eyes skun! Good bye."

"Elbert watched him as he pushed his way through the bushes, picked up his belt and sheathed his weapon, and then creeping on hands and knees, gained a little knoll near the beach, and saw the captain ostentatiously wiping his bloodless cutlass on a handful of broad leaves that he had plucked as he passed through the bush, and stepping into the rocking boat. Half an hour later the boat was hanging at the davits, and the hoarse song of the crew as they hoisted in the anchor came floating over the water.

"The heavens were black, and the wind came in little fitful gusts, as the brig expanded her wings and turned her prow seaward. Elbert climbed a tree on the high ground and watched the vessel, as she rose and fell, slowly crawling away from the coast. Then he fastened himself securely in a fork of the tree with his sword belt, and fell asleep—sleeping as only a sailor *can* sleep amid the roar of the storm, as it swept over land and sea. You hear the wind now? Well, it is a mere zephyr compared with that tropical tornado!

"Now there are two or three things that I must tell you to make my story hang together. First, about the boy. In the ten years he spent in that floating hell he had never once forgotten that he was born a gentleman. All his gains were honest gains, barring the absurd customs. He participated in the profits of smuggling, but he shared not in the profits of piracy, though these were by far the larger. Again, he had never destroyed human life, except in one terrible fight with savages, so brutal that they might scarcely

be called human, and then he fought for his own life. In the horrid conflicts that occurred, though rarely, he simply refused to take
a part, though he also refused to shelter himself while the fight
lasted. He would stand on the deck and take his share of shot
or sabre stroke, though he would not strike back. His life was
preserved by one long miracle—reserved for worse horrors than
any he encountered on the pirate's deck.

"The second point relates to the ship. It would seem incredible
that a vessel should live a dozen years in these days of steam,
preying upon all mankind. But it is nearly certain that no man
lived who knew the true character of the innocent schooner
Peggy, whose marine papers were always straight and regular.
She remained the *Peggy* until she disappeared in the thick
growth of her secret anchorage, and when she emerged, brig
rigged, with her two terrible guns, she was altogether another
ship. And again, whenever she assaulted a strange sail, it was
clearly understood by every man under her flag that it must be
victory or death ; and also, that no witnesses must be left when
the victory was won! When she left the island armed for piracy,
every man was required to be on board, and when she sailed away
from the coast that afternoon, she carried with her every mortal
that knew her except the boy that was peacefully sleeping in the
tree. As for him, his chance of escape from that dreary wilderness was less than it would have been had he been cast into the
sea a thousand miles from land, with an oar to keep him afloat.

"The third point relates to the strange proposition of Butler to
remain in the wilderness, and allow Elbert to return to the ship.
I cannot explain his conduct. It is not credible that he was
afraid, or that he doubted as to the result of the combat. If they
had fought he would have killed the boy, for he was a cold blooded
sworder of no ordinary skill. There may have been some lingering'
ray of human feeling left in his wicked bosom. The boy had
nursed him once when he was badly wounded and mad with
fever, and staid by him, enduring his curses, until the crisis was
past. Or he may have had some plan of escape that I cannot
conceive. The north coast of Australia, in that day, was the
crater of the pit!

"The last point relates to the boy sleeping in the tree top. How
could he sleep, knowing all I have told you? I cannot explain
this either. He had lived a hard life, and had gathered some sort
of philosophy out of it. He had carried his life in his hands so

long that he did not value it very highly. He was young and
strong and hopeful, and he saw his dismal prison floating away
from him. And God had been merciful to him thus far, for his
hands were unstained. Poor, poor boy! if you had known him
you would have pitied him also."

I do pity him from the core of my heart," replied Mr. Jones.

"Do you? Well, well! the boy slept; possibly because there
was a natural reaction from high excitement. When he opened
his eyes the tempest was over, and the streaks in the eastern sky
betokened the approach of day. The sun rose out of the tossing
waves, and Elbert, hungry and thirsty, began to estimate his
chances and form his plans. He climbed higher up the tree and
peered anxiously into the virgin forest, wondering how long it
would be before he would see the long spear of the bushman
glancing among the green leaves. Then he looked seaward along
the line of coast, and he saw two things. First, the hull of a ship,
dismasted and broken, rolling in towards the beach, and second,
the body of a man in the water, bobbing up and down, almost at
the foot of the tree. He descended rapidly, and pausing to plunge
his head in the little stream that trickled over the sand, and to
quench his thirst, he waded out through the surf and drew the
body to the beach, recognizing the unlovely features of his late
captain, swollen and disfigured in death.

" A more careful survey of the bay showed him a boat, bottom
up, drifting towards the shore. The brig had grounded just inside
the eastern headland a mile or more from where he stood. With
the prompt decision of a sailor he stripped off his clothes, and
swam out to the boat, and, with great difficulty, turned it partly
on its side, when he discovered the mast and sail still in place.
Partly swimming, and partly carried by the tide, he once more
gained the shore, where the boat, beating on the shingle, shook
the mast out of the step. Securing this, and drawing it out on the
sand, his next task was to right the pinnace with infinite labour,
and then with patient toil he baled her out with his hat.

"It was high noon when he pushed off from the land, and with a
fair breeze sailed towards the wreck, now hard aground and
motionless. The stern had caught on a tongue of rock projecting
into the bay, and the battered bows were almost submerged when
he clambered on board. Securing his boat on the lee side of the
wreck, he picked his way among the obstacles that encumbered
the deck to the officer's cabin, still out of water. The storeroom

adjoining was locked, but, seizing an axe, he with ready hand beat in its panels. He filled a large bag with biscuit, happily uninjured, and dragged it to the side and placed it in the pinnace. Then with great difficulty he got a small water cask strapped down under the thwarts, and filled it with a bucket, pumping the water from the large cask that was securely fastened near the after hatchway. This took half a dozen journeys from his boat to the cask. He took a pair of pistols from the rack in the cabin, some ammunition, a spy glass, the ship's compass, a pair of oars, and then, with the confident courage of youth, pushed off, spreading his sail, and passing the headland, steered boldly out upon the restless ocean with a mere cockle shell for a ship. As he sat in the stern sheets, munching a biscuit, he looked back at the long curve of the bay, and to the spot where he left the body of the captain, and saw the beach swarming with black savages!

" The breeze was steady and favourable. He rounded the western cape, and, guided by his general nautical experience, he set his course southwest, vaguely intending to land at the brig's island if he could find it, and if not, to get into the general track of Australian liners. When the night came on the breeze died away, and he took down his mast, and securing it by lashing to the thwarts, he stretched himself out in the bottom of the frail boat, rising and falling in the placid swell of the sea, and slept.

"At the end of the second day the sun went down in a bank of cloud, and Elbert, warned by occasional gusts of wind from the west, shortened his sail and kept awake, running as close to the wind as possible. By midnight he was obliged to take his mast down and keep his boat across the waves with his oars. He estimated his distance from the coast at about a hundred miles, as he had been sailing a little south of east for nearly forty-eight hours. But he could not estimate the eastward drift of his boat since the wind had changed, and he waited the return of daylight with great anxiety. Before the dawn came he distinctly heard the roar of breakers, and with manful determination he pulled away from the dreaded sound. The rain came in torrents with the returning light, and then he could dimly see the rocky coast, and when the boat rose on the crest of a wave he could see the line of white water stretching away to the south, and within the quarter of a mile of him. He knew he was in deadly peril, but his pluck did not desert him, and he drew off his boots and prepared to battle with the angry elements. Suddenly, with a hoarse shout, he turned his boat's prow towards the shore and pulled through a rift in the line of foam into smooth water. He had recognized the island. In a few minutes he had secured the boat, and walking up the rocky path, entered the hut which the whole crew had vacated a week before. Here was rest, security and undisputed dominion. He was undoubted monarch of all he surveyed, and sole heir to the island and all upon it.

"Do I make you understand the situation? A few words will make all clear. The wreck was tenantless, and the crew had certainly taken to the boats before the brig struck. All the boats were gone, and it was almost certain that Butler had been one of the crew of the pinnace which had escaped destruction. But there was hardly the ghost of a chance for any other boat. Elbert would have seen them if they had entered the bay, and it was far more probable that they sought the island when they abandoned the ship. The bay was a mere indentation in the coast, affording no secure anchorage in heavy weather, and the only chance left them was to pull away to the east. But in the face of the storm that wrecked their ship they could not possibly escape destruction. They were dashed to pieces upon that iron coast, and probably the captain was the solitary body yielded up by the remorseless sea. All of this was perfectly clear to Elbert as he lay in his hammock under shelter, while the rain poured down from day to day. The hut was rudely fashioned, having a roof thickly thatched with many layers of broad leaves and bits of old canvas, and water-tight over the sleeping quarter where hammocks were suspended when the island was inhabited. Provisions and stores were abundant, gathered from many luckless vessels that had been robbed and scuttled, and during the week of incessant rain Elbert cooked his meals daily, taking such variety as his stores afforded. In the intervals he smoked and reflected.

"The island was nearly circular, rather more than two miles across. Its coast was rock bound and inaccessible on all sides excepting the narrow opening that gave egress to the little river. In the centre, which might be the crater of an extinct volcano, the land was higher and bare of vegetation. From the highest point the entire horizon was visible over the tree tops. Here Elbert repaired every day, when the rain was over, and anxiously scanned the wide expanse of waters, hoping to see a passing ship. But none ever appeared. The island was distant from the great ocean highways. His only hope of escape was by the pinnace,

which was a large boat, entirely seaworthy, and capable of carrying a dozen or more. It is very probable that it was overladen
when the brig was abandoned, as the three boats would not con-
tain the numerous crew, except by close packing, and it was
doubtless capsized in the storm. The other boats carried no sails,
and if overcrowded, would hardly live a minute in the fierce storm
of the tropics.

" There was a large cavern near the hut, in which the valuables
belonging to the crew were stored. There were nearly a hundred
wicker baskets, neatly made, each bearing the name of the owner.
It spoke well for the *morals* of this community of outlaws that
there were no locks upon any of these. A few had become common property by the death of former owners, and these contained undivided spoils, small arms, and such articles of value as
belonged to the furniture of the brig. By their law Elbert was
sole owner of all that the island contained. But he never thought
even of looking into the baskets bearing the names of his late
shipmates, though he knew there was enough wealth in that cave
to satisfy the most extravagant wants he could ever indulge.
From the common stock he took freely all that he required.

"The pinnace was originally schooner rigged, and the main-mast
and sail were on the island. Elbert devoted many days to the
task of fitting her out *de novo*. There was an abundance of spare
canvass and cordage in the cavern, and by contriving a system of
blocks and pulleys he was able to take in both fore and mainsail
from his place in the stern. The jib was more unmanageable,
and he concluded to risk this sail, which was under his control in
a great measure, as he trailed the jib sheets also to the stern.
His plan was to carry as much canvass as the boat would bear, to
make the most of any favourable wind he might have. He had resolved to quit the island, to sail to the southward, and failing to
find a ship, to get round the south western cape and perhaps to
Adelaide or Melbourne.

" In the ten years he had spent on the brig or the island, Elbert
had made but one friendship, and that was scarcely worthy of the
name. There was a taciturn Englishman, who was called Jack
Schollard, because he was " fond of his book," as the rough sailors
said. He talked very little, and read incessantly when the ship's
duties allowed him the leisure. As a fighter he was the most
desperate of the savages around him, and had won his rank of
lieutenant by his prowess. The kindness he showed to the boy

was in lending him books and explaining difficulties which Elbert could not surmount unaided. He spoke most modern languages, and sometimes when he and Elbert were alone he would encourage him to resume the language of civilization in exchange for the slang of the ship. Once, when Jack was sick, he was left on the island while the brig was away on a long cruise, and Elbert was left with him to attend to his wants. These were few and simple, but as his eyes were diseased, he could not read, and he kept the youth reading aloud to him day after day for several months. It was a mine of wealth to the boy, who got a sort of education by a royal road, in spite of the proverb. He never manifested any emotion whatever, though Elbert once and again expressed his gratitude to Jack for allowing him to remain with him, and, indeed, selecting him for his companion on several occasions. Three months before the wreck of the vessel Jack had landed in the pinnace at the very spot where Elbert and the captain had parted for the last time. They had brought some water casks to fill, and while the men were employed at this work Schollard and Elbert wandered into the forest, where they were suddenly attacked by a swarm of savages. In the fight Schollard was killed and Elbert wounded, but the men who rushed into the fray found him astride the body of the lieutenant fighting his maiden battle, and doing a man's work. The natives were put to flight and Elbert carried aboard the brig, and before sunset was formally elected lieutenant. As his wounds healed he quietly resolved to quit the ship forever at the first opportunity. He did quit, as I have told you, and thereby saved his life.

"The only excuse I offer for giving this incidental bit of history is my desire to account for the change that had come over Elbert, transforming him from boy to man. It was a great shock to him to lose the solitary friend he had in the world, for his world was the hated ship! And when he looked over the book basket a day or two before he left the island, I am obliged to say that he dropped some tears of genuine sorrow. Poor Jack! What horror was in his earlier history, turning the cultivated gentleman into the tiger, no man knows! Poor Elbert! The fixed purpose of his soul, when he was left by Butler on that savage coast, was to find the bones of his friend and bury them!

"And now as the youth, whose lip and chin were covered by the silken down of early manhood, steered his little ship between the mimic capes of his harbor and out upon the swelling ocean, he thought he cast out of his life all the memories of his bitter past. He had ballasted his boat with enough provision to suffice him for a month at least, and with a fair westerly wind, his sail close hauled, he sped away on his old southwest course. He was steering from memory, as he had no charts, and only a vague idea of the trend of the coast. His purpose was to sail as steadily as the wind would allow on this course for ten days, and then to turn his prow eastward and seek some port in South Australia. He did not heed the truth that his chances were as one in a hundred, and that a very moderate storm would certainly wreck his frail boat. Oh, the blissful confidence of youthful ignorance! How dire the loss, when this is exchanged for the experience of maturity!

"I can hardly tell you how he slept or how the time passed for six days. Sometimes the wind died away, and then he would lower his sails, unstep his masts, and securing them as well as he could, would sleep, sheltering himself from the sun by an awning he had made while on the island. Such a calm found him on the sixth day, after twenty hours of steady progress, and he stretched himself out about noon and fell asleep. He was wakened by the whistling of the wind as it tore his awning out of its fastenings, and blew it away to leeward. He lay stupidly gazing up at the sky, sparkling with a million stars, until, recognizing his peril, he seized the helm and with a sailor's instinct tried to bring his boat head to wind. In vain! The boat shipped a sea as she rolled in the trough and then turned slowly over. He clung to her side, and as she half righted, rising upon the crest of the wave, he almost lost his hold. But he was again in the trough in a moment, and managed to get into the boat, which was full of water. As he mounted the next wave there was nothing above the surface for the wind to catch, and he was tolerably safe. And so he rode out the storm, which was only a transient gust, and when the sun rose the sea had almost gone down again. Everything was lost from the boat, oars—sails and provisions—and she was no better than so much lumber, buoyant enough to keep him on the surface, but utterly worthless for all else.

"I cannot tell you coherently what happened next. The sun beat pitilessly upon him throughout that seventh day, and when the night brought out the magnificent constellation of the southern cross, with the myriads of brilliant stars that seemed to whisper hope to him, he was almost past the reach of hope. When the day came again he was only partly conscious of the burning sun, and then all was night. Hungry, thirsty, weary and disheartened, his last thought was that the death so swiftly approaching was the truest friend he had ever known!

"As his senses returned he was bewildered by the uproar around him. He was lying in a bunk, in his clothes, still wet, and a man was leaning over him, trickling brandy into his mouth with a spoon. He saw a good-natured face kindling in a smile as he opened his eyes.

"Ah!" said the man, "we are coming round again! Keep quiet now, and swallow just two more spoonfuls. So! now, if you want to sleep again—— but stop! Here, cook! bring a basin of that soup. Can you take a little soup? I thought so! How long have you fasted? Never mind! You will be all right by daylight. More soup? Well, cook, give him another basin and no more, and don't let him talk till I come back. Not a word!"

"Accordingly, as the little doctor bustled away, the first word of the cook, who was a fat Irishwoman, was—

"How did ye get drownded, darlint?"

"What ship is this?" answered Elbert.

"The *Bellony*, darlint; how did ye——"

"Where are we?"

"In port. Port Philip. The divils are all gone crazy about the gowld!"

"What gold?"

"Sure, thin, ye don't live about here! Why, the gowld they are picking up out of the dirt beyant Melbourne. All the passengers and most of the crew are off, and the rest are goin'——"

"How came I here?"

"We picked you up this evenin', just out here in the bay. You was floatin' on a bit of a boat in a dead faint. The ship was nigh runnin' you down, when one of the b'ys see'd yees. It was Pat forninst ye there. The docthor has been workin' wid you these three hours. Ah! whist! here he comes!" and then with an affectionate whine she continued, "ye must just mind the docthor, darlint, an' keep quite! He'll tell you everything in the morn'!"

"The doctor felt his pulse, which was beating with healthful vigour under his fingers, held the light up to see his pallid cheeks regaining their colour, as the soup and the brandy and the assurance of safety all combined to work the rapid cure.

"I was capsized in a sudden squall last night or two nights ago. I don't know which——"

"All right, my lad!" interrupted the doctor. "You must positively go to sleep now and you can tell your story in the morning. Promise me that you will not talk any more until daylight."

"I promise, doctor. But please give me a little more soup."

"Not a taste! You are getting along famously now. You shall have a good breakfast by daylight. Go to sleep!" and he clambered up the staircase to the deck. Elbert turned on his side obediently, but was instantly pounced upon by the old woman as soon as the doctor's back was turned.

"I've brought you a dhrop more of the soup, darlint," she said as she handed him a basin, holding about half a gallon. "The docthor is very good at say; but we are so near the shore now— Holy saints! How the boy does ate! How long have ye starved, darlint?"

"Elbert worked away steadfastly until the basin was empty, and then handing it back to the old woman, he pressed his finger on his lip and pointed to the staircase. In another minute he was peacefully sleeping, while the ship was warped into her dock.

"By the first gray light of the dawn he examined his belt and found his money intact. He rose from his bunk, and, gaining the deck, found the sailors gathered in knots eagerly discussing some subject of universal interest. The Hibernian who had been pointed out to him as the man who pulled him out of the water beckoned him to his side.

"Do ye know where the gowld counthry is?" was his eager question.

"No. I am a stranger."

"There's a dozen of us, all handy boys, who are going to look for the diggin's. Will you go along wid us?"

"Yes. When do you start?"

"As soon as we get our wages. They are buzzin' about it now in the cabin. The captain don't want us to lave, but our bargain is out when the ship is docked, and that's now. Half the boys have gone without their wages."

"Can I go ashore?"

"Sure ye can go when ye plaze. There's the shore and there's the gangway."

"Amid the confusion Elbert quietly walked ashore. His sailor dress was his passport. He joined a gang of half a dozen at the head of the pier and passed from the view of all who knew anything of his previous history. Three days later he was at the gold diggings beginning a new life. And that is the end of my story, and with your permission I'll try for some sleep."

As Mr. Barston rose he turned his haggard face to the light that was swinging at the head of the cabin stairway. Old Mr. Jones supported him. He stopped at the door of my state-room as the ship lurched, and a great wave came aboard and went hissing astern. Mr. Barston fumbled in his bosom and drew out a little box, which he opened, and taking out a large necklace he threw the box on the deck. Mr. Jones picked it up, and then clutched Mr. Barston's arm again. He seemed to have a fit of horrors as he rattled the jewels in his hand.

"Do you know," he said hoarsely, "do you know that I am mad enough to believe that this accursed bauble is the cause of all my trouble? It has been hidden in my bosom for seven dreary years. In all that time, which seems like seven ages, my only solace has been drink. And now, as I feel the old fit coming upon me, I have enough manhood left to tear away this infernal chain at least. Lo! avaunt! and quit my sight!"

As he spoke he cast the necklace over the side. A mountain of dark water received it, sparkling like a hundred glow-worms as it disappeared. With a horrid laugh he threw himself on the deck, his body quivering in convulsions. Mr. Jones knelt by him, loosened his neckcloth, and raised his head and shoulders with the strength of a giant.

"Take his legs, captain, please," said the old man, composedly, "and let us get him quietly to his berth."

"My dear sir, let me call the steward. You can never carry him."

"But I can, captain," replied the old gentleman. "We don't want any steward. He is quite light. Come on!"

That Mr. Jones must have been a stunner in his youth. He tripped lightly down the staircase and through the passage way, carrying more than half of our unconscious burden. When we reached Mr. Barston's room, Mr. Jones coolly pushed the door open and we laid him down on the sofa. His poor wife was huddled up in a corner, and to my astonishment little Johnny was in her arms. He was in his night dress and looked just like a little girl. His eyes were something smaller than saucers.

"I heard her crying, papa," said he, as his father looked in mute amazement at them, "and I heard her calling me. She woke me up, crying and calling me, and I *had* to come."

"You did right, my darling," answered his father, "but I'll take you back to bed now."

"Oh, please don't take the child from me," said Mrs. Barston, moaning pitifully. "Let her stay with me to-night." The poor woman evidently thought Johnny was a girl, and old Mr. Jones humoured her.

"You shall have her again to-morrow," he replied, as he took Johnny in his arms, "that is if you are discreet. But now your husband needs attention. The captain will send the doctor to see him. Good night."

"Let me kiss her, papa," said Johnny. Mr. Jones held the little fellow down to her and he kissed her tenderly, patting her cheek with his little hands.

"Heaven bless you, sir," said Mrs. Barston, as he left. "I will do whatever you tell me."

The next morning the storm had abated, and I put the ship about and ran for Queenstown. As the sun rose we sighted Cape Clear. I announced to the passengers that we should be in Cork harbour in the course of the day, and most of them got on deck. Mrs. Barston was like another woman as she sat on the lee side of the stairway, with little Johnny cuddled up on her lap. The boy was bold as brass and seemed very fond of her. Mr. Barston was doing well, but the doctor kept him in his state-room. Old Mr. Jones was extremely attentive to Mrs. Barston, who seemed to regard him with a sort of reverence. They spent an hour or more in very earnest conversation, and when the tender left us at Cork Mr. Jones and the boy went off in her. He said he would catch the night boat for Holyhead and be in London the next morning. The sight of land appeared to make him young again, and he skipped about as lively as a kitten. As the tender steamed away he was holding the boy in his arms, who was kissing his chubby hands to Mrs. Barston, while Mr. Jones was singing, as loud as he could,

"A wet sheet and a flowing sea,
And a wind that follows fast."

He sang elegantly too.

CHAPTER VI.

THE LADIES.

IF the gentle reader has read all the foregoing, he or she ought to be tolerably well acquainted with the most of the personages that figure in this story. It will be necessary to introduce him or her to two or three others, who thus far have been only incidentally mentioned, and to bring them more prominently into the narrative. Hitherto the author has been obliged to allow the characters to do their own talking, and he has discovered that this is a very unsafe procedure, inasmuch as they rarely know when to stop. It is a remarkable fact, probably known only to authors, that these fictitious people are really more unmanageable than real people. You cannot snub them. You cannot change the subject. You cannot walk off and leave them. They will talk. The author fondly hopes that the change will be acceptable to the gentle reader, who is probably a lady, and therefore antagonistic to talkers on principle.

It is also requisite that the reader, fair as well as gentle, should go back some six or seven years. It is a comfort to know that this also will be easily done, as the honoured sex, of which she is an ornament, proverbially manages this chronological feat with great facility. In fact, the author distinctly remembers several ladies, who were well grown girls forty years ago, who are somewhere in the thirties to-day.

The time, then, some few years before the events recounted in the preceding pages. The place, the fairest portion of the earth's surface—Devonshire—five miles from Exeter, the village of Lavington, always thriving and always pretty, with the spire of the church at the south end, and the gray tower of Morton Priory peeping above the green trees of the park at the north. You can just see the flag on the tower, hoisted to indicate that Lord Morton is there. During a large part of the year he resides upon another estate in Essex, for he is a working member of the Upper House, and one of his sons, Mr. Allan Harwood, is the member for Lavington in the House of Commons. But this is the season when London is deserted, depopulated—a barren wilderness of houses, with only a million or two of its population left.

If you will enter the lodge gates and walk through the park you will be charmed with its beauty. The carriage road follows the windings of a little stream, a branch of the Esk, until you reach the rising ground upon which the house is built. You will have to go around to the western side, where the ladies are upon the terrace. There are three of them, and with honest trepidation the author begins the hardest part of this true history—the description of the sovereign rulers of humanity.

Lady Morton sits in the American rocking chair near the bay window. No fairer specimen of womankind can be found in Her Majesty's dominions. The bloom of youth is not lost but developed into the maturity of the matron. All that was lovely in her beautiful girlhood has ripened into surpassing loveliness at her third climacteric, to which she has now attained. Those honest, bright brown eyes, looking into yours with fearless majesty, are the windows through which you catch a glimpse of the pure woman's soul, full of gentleness and truth. That broad brow, so calm and smooth, without the wrinkles that care brings, or the furrows that sorrow ploughs, betokens the royalty of the wife and mother, whose lightest wish is the undisputed law of her realm. There is a fine curve in her nostril, and a quiet firmness in the lines of her mouth, that indicate the possession of a decided character, yet give no sign of strong-mindedness. You would not think of her as taking part in wordy contests. Her countenance gives no such intimation. Over all, like a veil, there is an expression of sobriety, which has been wrought by experiences through which her heart and her head reached maturity many years agone. Placid, wise and good—too proud to be haughty, and adorned with too true a humility to be servile, she is to her children the ultimate authority in all questions of taste, of propriety, of morals; and to her lord, the light of his eyes and the pulses of his heart.

Her daughter, Ret Harwood, who sits near her in the window seat, may be described in the same words—if you deduct thirty years and their experiences. The likeness betwixt those two fair women is very remarkable. The golden tints in the hair of the younger have ripened into minute threads of silver in the elder. But you see the same calm eyes, gentle and true, in both.

Do you expect any description of their dresses? If so, you are doomed to disappointment. No masculine reader would know anything about it, be the description never so elaborate, and the ladies would probably be shocked at the horrid taste displayed if they could see the attire of those who dressed in a fashion now ten years old. Moreover, the author is lamentably ignorant on this general subject, and would be certain to commit some atrocious blunder if he essayed such a description.

The third lady is something under twenty. She has blue eyes, a profusion of light yellow curls, like floss silk, floating over white shoulders and neck. No signs of sobriety here. She has two rows of pearls that are perpetually visible, when she smiles or talks, which is all the time. This is Miss Clare Tamworth. She is an heiress, an orphan, a Lady-Bountiful at her own home near Clifton, a harmless little flirt, who has never allowed any of her numerous victims to fall deeply in love with her. She has no faculty for sentimental love making, and woe to the wretched wight who attempts sentimental dialogues with her for interlocutor! The men who have deliberately set themselves to win this fair prize have never progressed beyond a sigh or two. She contradicts all established theories. The ready tears spring from her gentle eyes at the recital of a story of sorrow or suffering, but if the *raconteur* should attempt to slip in a love plea while her heart was thus softened, he would be astounded at the readiness with which the sympathizing tears gave place to merriment and mockery. The unanimous verdict of the men who sought her favour was that she was utterly heartless. And, like many other unanimous verdicts, it was false. Hitherto the right man had not come. Woe to the man who should really love her and love in vain! Happy the man who should so love her as to compel a reciprocal passion! As she stood at the edge of the terrace, twining a clematis vine over its frame, she looked like a fairy, free from care, and taking all the enjoyment life afforded, as the humming bird takes its sustenance from the free flowers that adorn the earth.

"Come sit by me, Clare," said Lady Morton, "we must arrange the programme for the week."

"It is all arranged, my lady," replied Clare. "Ret and I made it up last night."

"Subject to your approval, mother," said Ret.

"Let me know what your two wise heads have planned. I reserve the right to amend your plans, remember."

"First, then," said Miss Tamworth, seating herself as directed, "to-morrow is devoted to the Red Hall. This is by special invitation from Sir John, and your veto will not apply here, as your

lord and master has accepted 'for self and friends.' We are to
lunch there at one."

"That disposes of to-morrow," answered Lady Morton, "as the
gentlemen return here to dinner. Have you arranged the mode of
conveyance?"

"Yes. You and Ret are to go with Lord Morton and the rector in that old stuffy coach. I am to go on horseback, escorted
by Sir John. We are to flirt all the way to the Hall and back.
Sir John is to take you down to dinner, of course, and he is to flirt
with Ret during the evening, while I try to enslave the rector."

"I wish you success, my dear. But John is almost as impene-
trable as yourself."

"And that is the very reason why I should assault him! Besides, he is quite passably handsome. I noticed his whiskers in
church yesterday. They are positively elegant!"

"For shame, Clare!"

"That is quite *en règle*, mother," said Ret mischievously.
"You know that the chief glory of episcopacy consists in freedom
from those little restraints which dissenters practice."

"I'll tell the rector that speech, Miss Ret!"

"Very well. But it will accomplish nothing. We have a com-
pact, Johnny and I, by which I am a dissenter at Harwood House
and a churchwoman at Lavington. I made this agreement to
avoid scandalizing his flock."

"What are we to do on Wednesday, girls?" said Lady Morton.

"Clare says she is dying for the sea-coast, mother," answered
Miss Harwood, "and we thought, if you approved, we would
make up a party to the Smuggler's Cave."

"That involves a drive of forty miles."

"Only nineteen, mother——"

"And nineteen to return."

"But you cannot count the return journey, my lady," said Miss
Tamworth. "If we get there we are obliged to come home again.
The rector says we can gather multitudes of shells, and the cave
is a great curiosity."

"We will decide about the sea-coast later. What have you for
Thursday?"

"We leave that to you, madame," answered Clare.

"Why, Clare!" said Ret, "you know we had decided to ride to
Oakland."

"Did we?" said Miss Tamworth. "Well, we must wait for the
invitation, I suppose. My programme ends with Wednesday."

"Mr. Barston is to come on Saturday," observed Lady Morton. "I don't see how you can get an invitation in the meantime."

"We might meet Mr. Barston," said Clare, blushing a little; "and we saw him in London, you know——"

"Well!" said Lady Morton, amused.

"Well, ma'am, he invited us to Oakland then—that is, he gave a general invitation. The rector says it is the prettiest place in Devonshire."

"It is very pretty," answered Lady Morton. "I have not been there since Mr. Barston died. Lacy was a mere youth then. He and John were at Oxford, and I have hardly seen him since. I doubt if I should have known him with his great beard if I had not expected him and looked out for him. But one could not be mistaken in his kind eyes who had ever looked into them."

"Sir John says he is a regular muff," said Clare.

"Johnny says he is a regular Methodist," said Ret.

"Your father says he is a spotless gentleman," said her mother.

"Of course!" replied both young ladies in a breath.

"You must remember, girls, that he is not very rich——"

"And take care not to fall in love——"

"Be quiet, Clare! you know that was not my meaning. I only desired to remind you that you cannot expect Oakland to be very elaborately furnished. One of his quaint sayings is, 'that going in debt is first cousin to stealing,' and he says he has never owed any man anything, and never will. Since he came of age he mortally offended a rich old cousin by refusing a loan from him. The old gentleman wished the house repaired and modernized, and offered to advance the necessary funds. He was not entirely disinterested, as he is Lacy's heir-at-law. But the boy stoutly refused to accept the money, saying he was free born and would not become any man's servant by borrowing. The cousin then proposed to give him the money, or at least to require no security. But Lacy declined, saying a gift involved an obligation only more intolerable than a loan."

The girls listened with great attention to this story. Clare said nothing, but Ret after a little pause said,

"I think he did right, mother."

"Certainly, my dear."

"Captain Callahan tells a queer story about him, too," said Clare. "He says they were in Paris together a few months ago, and Sir John got involved in a quarrel with a Frenchman, who

challenged him. Sir John referred the Frenchman's second to Mr.
Barston, who was the only countryman he knew. They were at
the opera, and on the way to the hotel Mr. Barston recognized the
gentleman who presented the cartel, and after the polite formalities with which those horrid men preface a meeting for murder,
Mr. Barston asked him some questions about Sebastopol. You
know he was there during the war. The other—he was a Captain
Dutilh—soon became interested and told of a hair-breadth escape
both he and his " principal," Sir John's antagonist, had made in
the trenches. They were both wounded, and their men had been
driven out by the Russians, and while they were under a heavy
fire ' some Englishman' had carried them, one at a time, beyond
the reach of bullets. They said they certainly ' owed their lives
to him;' whereupon Mr. Barston mentioned some circumstance
that proved himself the deliverer, and then very quietly said he
would ' take the settlement now.' And the result was the with-
drawal of the challenge and an interchange of explanations. The
curious part of the story was the literal acceptance by Mr. Barston
of the Frenchman's professions. Captain Callahan says he coolly
told Dutilh that, having the choice of weapons, he should choose
cavalry sabres, and Sir John being invincible with that weapon,
would kill his friend, whose *life belonged to him*, Barston, and
therefore the foolish quarrel must be made up."

" Johnny told me about that, mother," said Ret. " He says Mr.
Barston never intended to let them fight at all. He had concocted
some wild scheme to stop the duel when his recognition of Captain Dutilh suggested the other plan."

" Your father has had charge of both these young gentlemen
since the death of Mr. Barston's father, and he has frequently told
me of Mr. Lacy Barston's eccentricities, as he calls them. I have
seen very little of him since his boyhood, but he is a prime favourite
of mine in spite of his pranks. He was a terrible young rascal in
his boyish days."

" He is tolerably given to tricks still," observed Miss Tamworth.
" I have heard of some recent escapades of his, in which his bosom
friend, Sir John, participated; but I have never heard of any
harm following his practical jokes."

" Sir John has improved vastly since they were schoolmates of
my boys. He was passionate and quarrelsome, and his cousin,
Barston, was perpetually getting him out of scrapes. Lord Morton was present when old Mr. Barston died, and heard him give a

solemn charge to his son to take special care of his cousin. 'While he lives, my son,' he said, 'remember that he is your mother's kinsman, and as you revere her memory, be father, brother and friend to John Lacy.' The quaint manner in which young Barston has fulfilled this obligation has amused your father many times, but he tells me that he has faithfully and effectually performed his duty in this matter."

"I suppose the baronet is out of leading-strings by this time," said Miss Harwood.

"He never knew that he was led, I fancy," replied Lady Morton; "but he has always been disposed to rely upon Barston in any emergency."

CHAPTER VII.

The Gentlemen.

IN the village of Lavington the most attractive and most comfortable house is the rectory. It was built by Lord Morton very soon after his inheritance of the barony. He demolished two or three cottages to make room for the garden and lawn, and the young trees he had planted here are grown to a good size. It stands near the church, whose stately spire, at the south end of the town, faces the gray tower of Morton Priory at the north. There is a modest chapel, held by dissenters, midway the main street, and this also was the gift of the lord of the soil, who is himself a dissenter, though the family attend the church when they are in Devonshire. It is a noteworthy fact also that the rector and the Presbyterian minister are close friends, which is not often the case in English towns, more's the pity.

The rector's library was lighted by one large bay window opening upon the lawn, and here were gathered four gentlemen, industriously filling every nook and corner of the room with tobacco smoke. It was a little past noon, and the *debris* of luncheon encumbered the table behind them, as they had drawn their chairs to the open window, and gazed lazily out upon the green lawn while they enjoyed their cigars.

Peering through the smoke, you may see the handsome face of Lord Morton, so much more handsome than any of the others, as

experience, and gravity that grows out of experience, and the sense
of responsibility and fixity of purpose, the result of laborious
thought and kindly interest in humankind beautify the countenance. These overbalanced the fancied advantages of lightly burdened youth. His long brown whiskers have sundry silver threads
in them which are positive adornments. His bold gray eyes, full of
truth and kindness, twinkle like stars at small provocation, because he carries in his bosom a perennial fountain of humour,
which he perpetually labours to smother, and perpetually fails to
do it. He must keep up the dignity of the statesman and legis-
lator. His joyous holidays are the days he spends in company
with his wife and children at Morton Priory, where he gets rid of
a volume of jokes accumulated in previous months of repression.
He attained manhood in early youth by brave endurance of deep
heart sorrows, and his subsequent life has been passed in sunlight.
No one of his four children has the remotest touch of jealousy of
any of the others, and his *friendship*, over and above his fatherly
love for them, is their dearest inheritance.

The rector, or " Parson Johnny," as he is universally called by
his kindred—the name being given him by his father when he
first turned his attention to theological studies— is the next to come
into view. He comes of a handsome stock and shows it. Like
his father, he cultivates a pair of side whiskers, long and silky,
but he has inherited a sedateness of demeanour from some other
ancestor that his immediate progenitor missed. There are certain
indications of his clerical vocation about his attire, and probably
also in his countenance and demeanour. The guileless simplicity
of his character has fitted him most accurately for his calling.
The air of truthfulness and fearless honesty in his eyes, and tones,
and gestures, is the heritage of his race. He is a man of parts,
has been a diligent student, and were it not for a sort of laxity in
his grasp of theological dogmas, in so far as these apply to minor
points, and a sort of readiness to find correspondencies betwixt
his creed and that of dissenters, he might aspire to high prefer-
ment in the church.

Sir John Lacy is in the cushioned arm-chair. He has a habit
of falling into soft spots and of taking special care of his own comfort. With many praiseworthy qualities, he has this sort of polished selfishness that distinguishes well-bred Englishmen from
men of other nationalities. He was a soldier in the Crimean war
—a cavalry subaltern—and he brought back with him an unscarred

body and a good reputation. It could not be said of him that he shrunk from exposure to any danger that came in the line of duty, but he did not volunteer for the mere sake of incurring risks. He fought well and valiantly, when fighting was to be done, and complained fretfully of the privations incident to camp life when the battle was over. He is a little vain of his shapely person, especially when he dons his uniform. He is colonel now of a regiment of volunteer riflemen, and the ultimate authority in military matters at Lavington. He has sleepy looking blue eyes and a profusion of tawny beard, and would be remarkably good looking if he were not contrasted with Lord Morton and the Reverend John Harwood.

You need not waste much time in examination of the other occupant of the library. Nothing striking here; only a plain athlete—Lacy Barston. He also was soldiering; when his cousin went to the Crimea he went with him. Nothing special was said about his prowess, and in fact there was not much chance for distinction in his regiment. "He was a jolly companion and a very safe sabre to have at one's bridle-arm in a cavalry charge." This was Sir John's judgment, and I may remark here that Barston always managed to take that precise position in their short war experience. He was "whimsical, but true as steel." This was Parson Johnny's judgment, and I think he probably knew Barston's interior life better than any other. He was "a gentleman in every pulsation of his heart." This Lord Morton said, and there was no better judge. As he sits apart there, blowing the fragrant smoke through his thick moustache, you would not give him a second look unless you should chance to catch a glance from his deep blue eyes, so earnest, so thoughtful—revealing a capacity for unmeasured jollity, and—if you are swift enough to detect it—a limitless capacity for tears as well.

These are very slight sketches. Will the reader please fill up the rude outlines? or, still better, wait until these gentlemen "pronounce" themselves in the course of the story?

"I must say, Parson Johnny," said Lord Morton, "that you are a capital judge of cigars."

"Do you like the flavour, father?"

"Yes, very much. I believe they are better than my Cabanas."

"That cannot be," objected Sir John; "those Cabanas you gave us in London should be branded *ne plus ultra*. These are very fine, parson, but your father is perhaps the only man in England that can produce anything better."

" What is your verdict, Barston?" said the rector.

" I have a special reason for withholding it in this presence. Be content to know that they are good enough."

" Come, sir," said Lord Morton, " you only excite our curiosity. Favour us with your opinion."

" Not unless Parson Johnny insists——"

" Certainly I insist. Always obey your seniors!"

Mr. Barston took a letter from his pocket, which he unfolded with great reluctance. Glancing over it he hesitated, shook his head, and put it back.

" Cannot do it! It is too cold-blooded!" he said.

" If you don't read that letter," said Sir John, half rising, " we three will throttle you and take it by force! I see it is one of your tricks, but you cannot escape us all!"

" I am too lazy to fight, but I do not doubt that I could evade you. I will read the postscript. This letter is from Parson Johnny, who orders me to read it. ' P. S.—If you are at Harwood House, old Swiss, please get the butler's key and look on the first shelf at the right of the door, and steal me a box or two of father's Cabanas. You had better get one Colorado and one Oscuro. The latter are the better, but father is coming down and he prefers the others——'" He put up the letter and continued, " These are the Colorados!"

" You young rascals!" said Lord Morton, when the laugh had subsided, " do you keep up all your supplies in this fashion?"

" Oh no, sir," answered the rector. " You know my bachelor establishment is very inexpensive. I am pretty well supplied with cigars, anyhow, and this theft was perpetrated wholly in your own interests. I might have written you to bring some ' Colorados,' but it looked so awkward to invite an expected guest to furnish his own cigars. Swiss, did you get a box for yourself?"

" Certainly not," said Barston, indignantly. " As Lord Morton prefers the light cigars, may I ask why you ordered the Oscuros?"

" Why for you, of course. You agreed with me in thinking the dark ones better when we were at Harwood House in the spring."

" My lord," said Mr. Barston, " you cannot trust Parson Johnny. He might send some less honest person into your house, and rob you more shamefully. I hope I need not say that I did not borrow ' the butler's key.' Nothing would induce me to do such a thing."

" May I inquire how you got the cigars, then?"

"I did not get them at all, sir. I just read Parson Johnny's letter to your hopeful son, Allen."

"A nice lot of vipers I have raised!" said Lord Morton, pretending to sigh. "I suppose Allen did not object?"

"On the contrary, he said it was jolly. 'You see, Swiss,' he said, 'it will play two tricks on father at once. First, he is awfully stingy about the Cabanas, and second, it will be prime fun for Parson Johnny to make him run down his own cigars!"

The senior joined in the laugh with great enjoyment. "I have never heard," he said at last, "how Mr. Barston obtained his title. I know you boys have been calling him 'Swiss' since your school days——"

"Let me tell that story, father," said the rector, eagerly, "that is, unless 'Swiss' wishes to relate his own adventures?"

"Not I. You have so vivid an imagination that it always refreshes me to hear your yarns. If you mean the cow story, though, you have no right to call that *my* adventure."

"Well, let father decide. You remember, sir, that we were all at Oxford together, and all freshmen. Barston could have entered the higher class, but he generously declined to start ahead of us. As far as rascality was concerned, his education was already finished. All of the ordinary villanies of freshmen he disdained, but constantly invented new tricks to astound the authorities. He was never caught, and kept up a fine reputation by perfect recitations, exemplary behaviour during hours, attendance at chapel, and general outward rectitude. But at night 'Swiss' displayed his peculiar talent, and the rest of us used to wait patiently for his guidance. One of our special enemies was old Doctor Blixem, who had a favourite cow, and one night Barston unfolded his scheme, which was to put old Blixem's cow on the roof of our dormitory. I can't tell you how he got her up stairs——"

"I twisted her tail," interrupted Barston, coolly. "There's a great deal of fuss made about scientific discoveries, but the fact is, the most of them have been either accidental or else suggested by some corresponding law in nature. There is the steam engine business; one fellow, I remember, is said to have discovered steam power by being half drunk and throwing a 'Florence flask,' whatever that is, into the fire. The flask contained a little wine, and it bubbled up and made steam, and blew the fellow up, or the back out of the fire-place, I forget which. Another chap saw the tea-kettle lid bobbing up and down, and he made an independent steam discovery. Then Mr. Watt made the engine and got the credit. Now, here is the application of power to the stern of vessels—the propeller instead of the paddle wheels. No fellow was wise enough to think of propulsion, but the paddle wheel was universal. Now I venture to assert that the screw propeller was suggested to some boy who screwed a cow's tail to make her go; but when he came to apply his discovery to steamship navigation, he had not the manliness to confess where he got his inspiration. Again, if I do not weary you——"

"Go on, go on!" said his audience.

"Well, the propeller only half does the work after all. Now, an experienced man can not only propel the cow, but can *steer* her. I steered Blixem's cow, and she was awfully green and cranky, and kicked abominably. I am sure I could put that cow up stairs, after a little practice, without a baulk. But I tire you——"

"Go on, go on!" said his listeners.

"Well, gentlemen, I feel indignant when I see the amazing pretension of these inventors! Who has ever tried to steer a ship with the screw? Some villain has got a patent, no doubt, and is now rolling in wealth, for applying an original discovery of mine and Blixem's cow! Proceed with your narrative, Parson Johnny. I have finished."

Parson Johnny indulged in a quiet laugh and went on.

"Anyhow, he got her up and on the roof. There is a balcony about large enough to hold the cow, and there he left her. During the night she lowed dismally, and Barston said she wished to be milked. So he took a bucket up and actually milked her while the rest of us watched on the campus. While thus employed he sang melodiously :

'Come, arouse thee, arouse thee, my brave Swiss boy,
   Take thy pail and to labour away!'

He had and still has a magnificent voice, and old Blixem heard him. The next day the cow was got down with blocks and pulleys, and we were all hauled up for examination. Old Blixem was in a great rage because the cow had been milked, and was intent only upon finding the milker. None of us had any trouble about denying that part of the business, until Barston's turn came, when the doctor said he would not insult so exemplary a gentleman by questioning him, especially as he had heard him singing *in his room* at the very hour when the milking must have been done. We all got off, and of course Barston became the 'Swiss Boy' at once.

"Did it end in this way?" asked Lord Morton.

"Oh, no. Swiss told Blixem the whole story before the term was over, and that was the brightest manifestation of his genius. He said the cow was a very valuable animal, and he thought it would injure her to let her go unmilked, and therefore he did it. Blixem not only forgave him but thanked him."

"Doctor Blixem is a regular trump, sir," said Mr. Barston. "We were fast friends, and he helped me over many a tough place. I could not take so many kindnesses from him, you know, without clearing that cow out of the way. I had to tell him."

"Well, sir," said Lord Morton, rising, "I have several cows at Morton Priory, and they are all at your service. Come, stay there while we are in Devonshire. It will be more cheerful for you than your solitary life at Oakland, and a great favour to me."

"You are very kind, my lord, and I frankly accept your invitation to spend as much time as I can at your house. No other house in England is so attractive to me."

"And no guest will be more welcome than yourself, Lacy. Shall I send for your traps?"

"No need, sir. Parson Johnny will drive me over when I am ready. He must have a drag, you know, to take his big fiddle."

CHAPTER VIII.

The Red Hall.

IT was a bright noon-tide in August when the gay party passed through the lodge gates and caught sight of the tall gray tower of Sir John Lacy's house. This tower had been known in former days as the Lacy Keep, and was more ancient, by several centuries, than the rest of the building, which had been added to the tower, a bit at a time, and without regard to architectural rules. The park surrounding the Hall was almost a wilderness, as the property had been totally neglected during the baronet's minority. But as Lord Morton's carriage, followed by the two equestrians, drew nearer the buildings, the signs of renovation increased. The windows were all open, and the scaffolding of the workmen covered all the main front. The disagreeable odour of paint pervaded the larger part of the house, and was escaped only when they reached the dining room, which was the ground floor of the old Keep. Here there had been no improvement attempted. The walls were wainscoted, and the grim old furniture, all oaken, like the walls, gave an air of antiquity corresponding with the marks of age distinguishing this part of the edifice. The large dining table in the centre was covered with a snowy cloth, upon which the noonday repast was spread when the party entered.

"I bid you welcome to the Red Hall, my lady," said Sir John, with courtly grace, offering his arm, "and I beg you to honour me so far as to occupy the throne, at the head of the table."

"That were an ill omen, Sir John," she replied; "take the head yourself and allow me to sit at your right hand."

"I accept your presence here as the harbinger of better days for the Hall. This is my first appearance since the renovation began. Later in the summer I hope to take more formal possession, when you and my lord will preside at a regular festival. It will be his valedictory, as he relinquishes his guardianship and inducts the heir of all the Lacys into his heritage. Parson Johnny, you may sit next Miss Tamworth, at the end of the table. I have been sounding your praises on our way hither. See that you keep up your reputation. Miss Harwood, my love, be seated. Serve, Thomas!"

It was a recherché little feast. Sir John had brought a cook with him from Paris, and that artist won golden opinions from the hungry party. Green turtle, some chops, a salad, and a little wine. English men and women in sound health extract enjoyment from feeding that other nationalities are strangers to. After the repast, which was prolonged a little by all, Lord Morton dismissed the ladies with great politeness.

"You will have an hour, ladies," he said, "in which to explore. Sir John desires you to investigate every nook and corner——"

"And beware of the paint——" put in the baronet.

"And while you are absent," continued Lord Morton, "I will have to indulge these boys in a smoke. Parson Johnny stole a lot of my cigars, and has a supply with him. My lady, I beg you to keep the keys at your girdle hereafter. It begins to grow serious when they get after my Cabanas!"

"Nobody had the keys except Allen," said Lady Morton.

"I think you had better make no exceptions. Allen, I learn, thought it special fun to rob his poor old father, because he fancied I was particularly "stingy" about my cigars. Certainly these sons of mine have inherited their proclivities from *your* side of the house, as no ancestor of mine was ever caught in such tricks."

"My kindred have always borne a good reputation," replied Lady Morton, with pretended dignity. "You bear the name of one of them whose history is part of the history of England."

"Well, well! I will say no more. If you once get a woman talking about the virtues of her ancestry, there is no telling when she will stop. Allow me to indicate the way. Keep the corridor the whole length of the new building. The staircase is at the end. No danger of paint up stairs. It is all dry. Come, Parson, produce your stolen property. I hope you will give us a sermon upon honesty next Sunday."

Leaving the smokers reeking in the fumes of the vile weed with which they poisoned the pure air, we will follow the ladies in their explorations. At the end of the long hall they found the staircase, and at its foot a little old woman with a bunch of keys in her hand.

"Mrs. Froome, the housekeeper, my lady," she said, dropping a curtesy to Lady Morton. "I am to show you the way."

She tripped lightly up the steps with this introduction, followed by the ladies, who looked with surprise at each other and at the active little body that preceded them. Arrived at the first landing, she faced them again and fumbled among her keys, chatting volubly the while.

"This corridor, my lady, is on the back of the house, and all the rooms on this floor open upon the front lawn. Since Sir Elbert's death nobody has lived here except my grandson, Thomas, and myself. You saw Thomas, the butler, at luncheon."

"Your grandson!" said Miss Tamworth, "why he is fifty years old!"

"Yes. I am ninety-one. I have lived eighty years in the Red Hall. This is the yellow room. It is the principal guest-chamber. The furniture has not been renewed in my lifetime, and is faded a good bit. Mr. Lacy says we cannot have any new furniture at present."

"You mean Sir John?" said Miss Harwood.

"No, ma'am. I mean Mr. Barston. He has ordered all the repairs, and Sir John has only been here once or twice. Mr. Lacy's father was Sir John's guardian, you know, and since he died, Mr. Lacy has been watching over him like an older brother. Isn't it strange," and here she dropped her voice into a confidential whisper—"isn't it strange that Sir John should look exactly like Sir Ranald? I will show you his portrait presently. None of the Lacys have resembled him, and they do say as Sir Ranald was the first of the line. But I beg your pardon for chattering so much."

"Go on, Mrs. Froome, if you please," said Lady Morton, "we are very much interested."

"Well, my lady," resumed Mrs. Froome, "they used to say, ever so long ago, that the last Lacy would look like Sir Ranald. There is nothing about it in the prophecy."

"The prophecy!" said all three of her listeners.

"Yes. Many a time I have heard it. This chamber is Sir John's. You see there is modern furniture here. That is the door of the dressing room. There is another dressing room adjoining, and then comes my lady's room. You can go through the two doors. No fear of paint. It has been quite dry for a week. You can see Oakland from this window."

"The view is charming," said Lady Morton; "but you were speaking of the prophecy."

"Yes, my lady, if you are not tired we will go to Sir Ra- nald's room. It is in the tower just over the dining room." She unlocked the door as she spoke, and passing the other chambers, reached the end of the corridor. Descending two or three steps she opened a door, deeply set in the thick wall, and entered a spa- cious chamber almost bare of furniture. The walls were hung with old tapestry. A large sofa covered with crimson velvet, and two or three arm chairs to match, were grouped together in the centre of the room. The tapestry was of the same colour, and there was a sombre air about the apartment in spite of the bright sun- light that streamed in at the open windows. A faded red carpet covered the floor, apparently more worn by age than by use. At one end of the room a large open fire-place, with great brazen andirons, highly polished. A red fire screen, folded, leaned against the wall near by; opposite, a variety of armour was arranged, some sus- pended upon the antlers of a deer, fastened to the wall, and some hanging from iron hooks. In the midst of the armour, a large gilt frame, the picture being covered with a crimson cloth. The room and its furniture, scrupulously free from dust, had an inde- finable, weird aspect, that sensibly affected the visitors. The old housekeeper seemed to enjoy the effect of this show chamber upon the ladies with a grisly satisfaction, that was positively comical, upon her bright and pleasant countenance. She wheeled the sofa round, facing the light, and when the ladies were seated, she drew one of the chairs in front of them, and evidently indicated by her whole demeanour, as she seated herself, that she was prepared to gratify their curiosity if they chose to question her.   My fair reader, they were descendants of *your* ancestress, Mother Eve. Need I tell you that they did ?

" We always show this room to visitors," began Mrs. Froome, smoothing her apron—" but I don't have much to say about the family to strangers, of course.   But you are kinsfolk, and after Mr. Lacy, you are the nighest kin Sir John has.   I have heard many bits of stories about the old Lacys, and maybe you can tell *me* some things I don't know."

" Indeed, Mrs. Froome, we know very little.   We can hardly be called kindred, however.   Lord Morton's grandmother, I think, was married to one of the Lacys—but I am not sure.   I have never heard a word about the prophecy, and hope you will tell us about it, that is, if there is no family secret that should not be revealed."

The old woman nodded pleasantly, and ambling to the window she pointed to the gentlemen sauntering under the trees a quarter of a mile off.

" They won't be back under an hour," she said, smacking her lips.   " Of course there is nothing to conceal, leastways from you. But to tell you about the prophecy I must begin with Sir Ranald." She resumed her seat, and without more ado furnished the material for the succeeding chapter.

CHAPTER IX.

Sir Ranald De Lacy.

I CANNOT tell you, ladies, in what reign Sir Ranald lived.   I think it was in the time of Henry V.   I know he fought in some French battle, and I think it was Azincourt.   He was a great warrior and a favourite of the king in spite of his religion.   All the Lacys have been Protestants.   It is said of Sir Ranald that he kept his religious views to himself, though he was very intolerant when he could safely indulge his prejudices.   He was called the " Fighting Lollard."   After the great battle of Azincourt the English army overran Normandy, and it was here that Sir Ranald's story begins.

It was at the siege of a French castle where the defenders fought
with great desperation under the Count De Lys. When the English got in at last they still fought from room to room, and finally
the count and his family, driven into the topmost chamber, made
their last despairing stand. Sir Ranald gained this room with two
or three of his followers, and it is said that he killed two of the
count's daughters who were fighting like men, with his own hand,
and cruelly wounded the third, who fought like a tigress over her
father's body. But she was not killed, and when the conquerors
returned to the main army Sir Ranald brought her with him.
There was a great lot of booty gained and Sir Ranald got the lion's
share, all in jewelry of value. To make himself secure in the possession of this wealth he married the Lady Marie, a French priest
performing the ceremony while the lady was thought to be dying
from her wounds. There is a legend which says Sir Ranald bought
the priest to consent by professing to renounce his religion, and
the Lady Marie, who was very bigoted, consented because she
thought she was dying and wished to secure a higher place in
Heaven by saving a notable heretic like the Fighting Lollard,
whose name was a terror in all that region. She did not die, however, but came to England and lived a year in this very tower,
which then stood alone in the midst of the Lacy lands, which in
those days reached to Morton Priory.

Once secure in his own home, Sir Ranald's conversion faded away·
All his retainers were Lollards, and nobody got entrance to the
Lacy Keep but Protestants. There was great strife between him and
his French wife, which culminated in declared hostility when Sir
Ranald had his infant son baptized by a Lollard preacher. He
laughed at her vehement recital of his former vows, and when she
reminded him that the most solemn part of his promise related to
the faith of any children that might be born to him, he said his
promises to the priest were an " agreement with hell," and were
annulled by a more solemn authority. The unhappy lady, who
was of a violent temper, then declared the marriage was null also,
and announced her intention of quitting Lacy Keep with the child
at the first opportunity. Whereupon Sir Ranald imprisoned her
in the room above this, and carried the key at his belt, taking her
daily food to her with his own hands and allowing no communication with her whatever.

You know the country was in a very disturbed state in those
days. The Lollards were persecuted and slain, wherever it could

be done, and this particular locality was the scene of many bitter
feuds. All the nobles nearest the Keep were Catholics, and if it
had not been for other wars that drew attention from this little
corner of the kingdom, Sir Ranald would have found it hard to
hold his lands. Besides this, his old reputation as the Fighting
Lollard stood him in stead, as it was well known that the taking
of the Lacy Keep would be a most costly victory.

I should have told you earlier that Sir Ranald had a half-brother,
though not of the Lacy blood. His mother was the widow of Sir
Anthony Vane, and her son was two or three years older than Sir
Ranald. This man, Sir Hubert Vane, was a rigid Catholic, and
on that account, a favourite of the king. He was also an accomplished courtier, contrasting strongly with Sir Ranald, who was
more of a warrior, and whose religious prejudices were opposed to
the frivolities and excesses of court life. There was a hollow friendship between the half brothers, though each secretly despised the
other. After the marriage of Sir Ranald the courtier visited the
Keep once only, bringing some message from the king, and was,
entertained with all the hospitality due from a Lacy to a guest.
In the few days Sir Hubert spent at the Keep he managed to in-
gratiate himself with Lady De Lacy, and to establish very confidential relations with her, partly on the score of kinship and partly
on the ground of a common faith. It was just at the time that
Sir Ranald began to display the cloven foot of the Lollard, equally hateful to his wife and his kinsman. They parted in anger at
last, each regretting that the accident of birth forbade an appeal
to the arguments they carried in their scabbards.

After the birth of her son, the countess—she called herself the
Countess De Lys—resided constantly in her chamber. I would
take you up to see it but it is not necessary. It is like this room,
but has never since been used except as a lumber room. I suppose no one who ever heard the story of the countess would sleep
in it for the Lacy lands. Sir Ranald spent some hours each day
with her, treating her with great courtesy at all times, steadfastly
refusing to discuss the question of creeds, and steadfastly refusing to release her from this imprisonment. All that he could give
her, except liberty, she had. But when he left her she and the
infant spent the long hours alone, seeing no countenance and hearing no voice but his for weary months. He dared not allow her
maids to attend upon her, as he knew she would fulfil her threat
to quit the Keep upon the first opportunity. But her woman's
wit was too much for all his precautions.

Of course the forced seclusion of the countess was known beyond the walls of Lacy Keep. Stories of that sort are very apt to get out. And it happened that Sir Hubert Vane heard of the birth of the child, of the mother's imprisonment, and, probably, of the cause.

Sir Hubert came to Exeter with a body of men-at-arms. One day, when De Lacy was in the lady's chamber, an arrow came in at the window and fell at his feet. He took it up and found a billet fastened to the barb. It was from his half brother, addressed to his wife, proposing to deliver her from her imprisonment, and appointing the next night for her flight.. The letter also said that the king promised his protection, and that the church would annul her marriage with her heretic lord, but would assure the succession of the Lacy estates to her child. The countess sat quietly by while he read the letter, and no words passed between them. Sir Ranald retired from the room and passed the earlier hours of the night in perfecting his plans to circumvent his wife and kinsman. It was a serious business to defy the king; it was a far lighter matter to slay his kinsman. He concluded at last to question the countess again, and if she refused to obey him, to remove the child. Accordingly, he climbed the stair again, torch in hand, and reëntered her apartment. It was empty. He rushed to the open window and saw the rope ladder fastened to the sill— heard the tramp of horses' feet, at the very base of the Keep. A bow and a sheaf of arrows stood near the window, and catching up the weapon he discharged an arrow into the darkness. He heard it ring against a steel corslet, heard a shriek and a curse. He threw down the bow, and with a Lacy's recklessness leaped upon the window sill, grasped the frail ladder, and in another moment was on the ground, sword in hand. At the same instant the court yard gate was flung open and half a dozen men from the Keep rushed out with torches and flashing weapons. The horsemen fled, all but one, and he was encumbered with the lady. He drew his sword, however, and spurring upon Sir Ranald, met his ready weapon. Before the retainers reached the spot the combat was over. The long sword of the Fighting Lollard had passed through the body of his half-brother and slightly wounded the countess, hanging nearly lifeless upon his arm. Sir Ranald's arrow had glanced from the knight's corslet and pierced the body of his wife.

When the bodies were taken into the Keep the jewels belonging to the Countess De Lys were found in the bosom of Sir Hubert

Vane. He had unclasped his corslet and thrust the precious packet in the breast of his leathern doublet. Before he had time to refasten his armour the impetuous assault of Sir Ranald compelled him to betake himself to his weapon, and he had dealt one blow upon the unprotected head of the furious Lollard an instant before the latter's blade had found the opening in his corslet. If it had not been for his anxiety to secure the jewels he would have escaped the sword thrust. And his blood was the first that stained them since they had become the Lacy Diamonds."·

Lady Morton started.

Yes, my lady, his was the first. They got plenty of stains later.

Such rude surgery as was practiced in that day was soon applied. The wounds were bound up, the lady carried back to her chamber, and the dying knight placed upon Sir Ranald's own couch. Before he died his incoherent mutterings revealed that the jewels were the real attraction that had brought him to his death, and not the poor countess. Fearful of attracting attention, he had come to the Keep with but three of his followers. To one of them he had confided the child, directing him to ride to his camp near Exeter, and he was speedily followed by the others, when half a dozen armed men issued from the Keep. The correspondence between Sir Hubert and the lady had been carried on by arrows, the countess being able to bend a bow equal to a man-at-arms. Those old oaks you see from the west window sheltered the knight and his men. And when Sir Ranald had retired with the intercepted letter, she immediately sent a shaft into the wood bearing a note in which she besought Sir Hubert to deliver her that night. The note was found in his doublet.

The knight died and was buried among the Lacys with due honours. The countess lingered day by day, weeping for her lost child. Sir Ranald's wound was slight, and the day after the combat he was scouring the country in search of his heir, but no trace of him could be found. The men-at-arms that had been encamped at Exeter had disappeared, leaving no clue by which they could be followed. No information could be obtained from the dying countess, and Sir Ranald, baffled and wearied, after three days of fruitless search returned to the Keep in despair. He found his wife speechless and insensible, evidently entering the dark valley; and when the sun disappeared behind the fatal wood the lady's attendants announced to Sir Ranald that she had ceased to breathe.

CHAPTER X.

The Prophecy.

WHILE the women were busied preparing for the burial of Lady De Lacy, Sir Ranald paced his chamber in deep distress. His life had been passed in contention and strife, but since Azincourt, where he had won great renown by his prowess, he had been followed by a series of misfortunes. In the storming of the Castle De Lys he had stained his sword with the blood of women, and the savage cruelty of that day's work saddened his after life. It is very probable that the wounds he had inflicted in the heat of that last struggle in Normandy were given in self-defence, for the legend says the French women were armed cap-a-pié and fought like the Amazons of ancient times, and in this last catastrophe he had certainly slain his wife by accident. There was a proverb extant that declared the "sword that slew woman or priest" was accursed, and Sir Ranald was not free from the common superstition of his age. He lost the king's favour, and his companions in arms shrunk from him. Since the birth of his child and the bitter contention that followed his baptism, his intercourse with his wife had been most unhappy. While she loaded him with reproaches and threatened him with desertion, he maintained the same courteous demeanour, though inflexibly refusing to admit any professor of the Catholic faith within the walls of the Keep. The only exception to this rule was the solitary visit of his half brother, and this had been fatal in its results.

His sorrowful meditations were interrupted by the entrance of an old man with snowy hair and beard. Sir Ranald placed a settle for his visitor and continued his walk.

"Thou art disturbed in mind and ill in body, my son," said the old man; "I pray thee rest upon yonder couch and I will watch while thou sleepest."

"I cannot sleep, Father Ralph," replied De Lacy; "the events of the last few days would seem to banish sleep evermore. I cannot find ground for self-reproach, yet my unhappy fate has heaped sorrows upon me without measure. Bethink thee: my lady slain by my hand; my mother's son died on my sword; my child lost to me beyond the hope of recovery! And in addition to all this the certainty of royal wrath and probable persecution of all

Lollards for my sake. Where wilt thou find shelter if Lacy Keep be garrisoned by royal soldiers?"

"Think not of me, valiant knight. There are many sure refuges for me, even here in Devon, and many true Christians who will still gather to hear my message; but I would fain comfort thee in thine affliction. Remember, it was not thy will that sped the shaft against thy lady's breast; and to her life was well nigh intolerable, else would she not have essayed this desperate venture. The death of Sir Hubert was instead of thy death, and thou wilt carry the scar from his brand upon thy brow while thy life endures; and I have hope of finding thy son when the bruit of these late events is over. Thou hast indeed deep cause for sorrow, but thou knowest there is abundant consolation within thy reach."

Sir Ranald listened with profound respect to the aged pastor. It was a distinguishing trait of the Lollard heretics that their spiritual teachers were universally revered and loved. So many instances of heroic endurance of persecution and privation were found among these wandering preachers that they seemed to bear a charmed life. On his return from France a year or two before, Sir Ranald had encountered a party of Lollard preachers, in custody of a small body of archers, led by a Carmelite monk. It was at night, and the two little troops encamped in the outskirts of a village. Sir Ranald's Protestantism was not suspected, as Lollards of noble birth were comparatively rare; but in the morning the prisoners were all gone, and De Lacy zealously assisted in the search for them—in the wrong direction; and a day or two later the fugitives arrived at Lacy Keep, where they found shelter and security. Father Ralph, who was among the captives, had remained as chaplain of the Keep, beloved by all its inmates excepting the countess.

Sir Ranald paused in his walk, and putting aside the tapestry opened a secret closet in the wall. From this he took a jewel case, and seating himself near the venerable Lollard he drew out a glittering necklace. It was composed of twenty-four diamonds of wonderful brilliancy, each set in a framework of gold shaped like an open lily. The gold work was of exceeding delicacy and beauty, and the precious gems were set in the opening cups of the gold lilies, the double clasp being covered with emeralds of unusual size. There were spots of blood disfiguring the necklace and bedimming the flashing stones.

"Thou seest this accursed bauble," said the knight, "and canst estimate its value better than I. Know, Father Ralph, that the rumour of this toy reached me at Azincourt, and the insane desire to possess it induced my foray, which ended in the fall of the Castle De Lys. Perhaps the possession of these jewels inspired the owners to resist to the death, and certes, the foul greed that possessed me in that fierce fray was begotten of the fiend. I need not tell thee that it is hateful to mine eyes. And now I pray thee take it into thy keeping. It has been in the custody of its rightful owner, the mother of my lost heir, and now it belongs to him. Take thou the charge and tell thy faithful son, who is now wandering in Scotland, the story, that he may assume the charge after thee. I repent me now that I consented to his departure from the Keep."

"Better to entrust both jewels and story to Hester. She is a wise maiden. The dangers that threaten me and her brother will not reach her; and it is through her agency chiefly that I hope to find the child. Thou wilt remember also that the accident of gentle birth is in her favour, though I have learned, and thou also, I trust, that no birth is gentle save the new birth. Howbeit the Lady Hester Langley can gain entrance into houses where Ralph the Lollard would ne'er be welcome."

"Thy daughter is even now in the chamber above," replied the knight; "do as seemeth good to thee. Tell her the sad story and give the jewels to her keeping. Canst thou not exert thy skill and give me an hour of sleep?"

"Doubtless," replied the Lollard. He took a vial from his vest, and with steady hand dropped a small quantity of liquid into a cup of wine. "Drink this, noble sir, and betake thee to thy couch. Slumber will steal upon thee anon, and I will watch here while thou sleepest. I have rare entertainment at hand—even a true copy of a Gospel, which yonder benighted monk, from whose power thou deliveredst me, had with him. Strange that he should extract lessons of cruelty and idolatry from such a source!"

Sir Ranald drank the composing draught, and unbuckling his sword-belt he stretched himself upon the couch. The Lollard drew the taper behind the knight's helmet, casting the couch into shadow, and producing his precious parchment was speedily engrossed in its contents. The deep breathing of Sir Ranald soon proved the potency of the preacher's drug. The noises of the Keep sunk into silence, excepting the clash of armour as the sentinel turned in his monotonous walk upon the outer wall. As the night drew on the wind rose, increasing in volume until it grew into a furious storm. The thunder roared and rattled, the lightning gleamed, the rain lashed the walls of the tower, but the sleeper slept and the student read, each unconscious of the warfare of the elements. The diamonds were lying in the open case, also shaded by the helm, but to each flash of the lightning, as it came in at the lattice, the jewels responded with a shower of rays, like sparks from an anvil. So prompt was the response, so vivid the answering flash, that the preacher's attention was attracted, and he laid aside his manuscript and watched the gems with eager curiosity. Although far above the current superstition of the time, the Lollard was somehow impressed with the idea that something weird and uncanny attached to the jewels, and he stretched out his hand to close the case. At the instant there was a long, blazing flash of lightning, accompanied with a terrific roar of thunder, that seemed to shake the solid Keep to its foundation stone. The old man glanced at the couch and saw Sir Ranald starting up, his countenance looking ghastly in the glare of the lightning and his hand pointing to the opposite side of the chamber. Turning his eyes in the direction indicated, the Lollard saw a sight that seemed to freeze the life currents in his veins.

The tapestry was drawn aside, the heavy folds held in the white hand of the Countess De Lys. She was attired in a long white robe, a dark crimson spot staining the right side. An arrow in her right hand, with blood stains on its barb and feather, all visible in the momentary glare of the lightning, was pointed at the couch occupied by her lord. A fold of white linen was bound upon her forehead, and her long black hair fell over her shoulders. Her pallid lips moved, and while the Keep vibrated and the subsiding roar of the thunder formed a hideous accompaniment, both knight and Lollard heard each sentence she uttered:

> " Empurpled with blood drawn from kinsman's vein,
> The curse-cumbered jewels their stain do retain
> Till the salt waves of ocean shall wash out the stain!
> Who hireth Red Keep, of the Lacy's strain,
> A score and a half score may never attain,
> Till the tower and the last of the Lacy name .
> Shall pass from the earth amid tempest and flame!"

The words issued from her lips in a dull monotone, and as she concluded, another blinding flash illuminated the chamber, and again the Keep shook under the crash of the thunder. Her black eyes glared upon the appalled listeners an instant longer, and then the tapestry fell into its place, and they were alone. Sir Ranald fell back upon the couch, and the Lollard, drawing an inkhorn from his pouch, rapidly wrote down the words of this weird prophecy while they were still ringing in his ears. When he had finished he placed the parchment in the box with the necklace, which he closed and deposited in his pouch.

The knight collected his confused faculties, and rose from the couch while the preacher was still writing, and, after a brief pause, motioned the old man to follow him. Taking the taper in his hand he led the way to the stair, and the two ascended to the death chamber above. The body of the countess was upon the bed, cold and lifeless. The knight laid his hand tenderly upon her brow, and could scarcely believe the testimony of his senses when he felt the cold, smooth surface, and saw the unmistakable tokens of death. The bloody arrow, which had been drawn from her side, was lying on a settle, near the bed. Hester Langley was kneeling at the bed foot, her face resting upon her arms in peaceful slumber.

"What thinkest thou, good father?" said Sir Ranald. "Did we see that vision but now, and hear those fearful words, or are we both crazed?"

"I cannot answer thee, noble sir," replied the Lollard. "I have written down the words I heard, or thought I heard. I cannot think we have both been deluded by the same wild dream. What sawest thou?"

"I saw my wife standing in the chamber below, with the shaft in her hand. I heard the words thou hast written. I saw them overlooking thee while thou wast writing. If I dared to yield to my most earnest longing I should spend the remainder of my days in solitary vigils, like those benighted worshippers whose creed we abhor! Surely there remain for me no more deeds of knightly prowess. The hand that sped yonder fatal shaft is bereft of its cunning. The ear that hath heard those words of doom is deaf henceforth to the sound of trump. Naught remaineth for me but the swift fulfilment of her grewsome word. 'A score and a half score.' There are three or four dreary years between me and that attainment."

Ladies, the story of the Red Lacy is almost ended. Two years later he married the Lady Hester Langley. As nothing was heard of his first-born son, at his death, which occurred a year after his second marriage, Ralph Lacy, the infant son of the Lady Hester, was the acknowledged heir of Lacy Keep.

CHAPTER XI.

THE LACY DIAMONDS.

I SHOULD have said at the beginning, that I repeat all this long story just as I heard it. The Lady Mary, Mr. Barston's mother, told me the most that I have told you, and have yet to tell. The Red Lacy, as Sir Ranald was universally named, relinquished all his warlike habits, and lived the life of a hermit, very zealous for the Lollard faith, and at the last a preacher of note among these persecuted people. It is said that he was killed by a kinsman of Sir Hubert Vane, who was hunting heretics by authority of Henry V. in the last year of his reign. The knight was found at the edge of the dark wood yonder with a cloth-yard shaft through his body.

Twenty-five years later a gay cavalcade appeared beneath the walls of Lacy Keep, then occupied by Lady Hester Lacy and her son. At the head of the brilliant array was a young knight, who demanded possession, as the Signior Henry De Lacy, the first born of the fighting Lollard. The claim was haughtily rejected by the lady and her son, Sir Ralph. The new claimant then demanded the jewels of the Countess De Lys, offering to relinquish his claims to the Lacy lands if these were surrendered. In those days the value of the diamonds was very far greater than that of all the lands. This also was refused, and the new comers prepared to assault the Keep. The fight was prevented by the appearance of Sir Ralph upon the wall, who demanded a parley. The resemblance between the two knights was apparent as they stood face to face, each scowling upon the other. The object of the parley was to propose a settlement of their rival claims by single combat. This was so accurately in accord with the sentiment of the time that the proposal was immediately accepted, and Sir Ralph rode forth from the court yard sheathed in armor, with the fatal necklace glittering upon his plumed crest. Their lances were laid aside by common consent, and they rushed upon each other with sword and dagger. The elder born was killed, and the other, sorely wounded, was carried into the Keep to die. The knights who had accompanied Sir Henry informed the lady that his widow and twin sons were in London, and before Sir Ralph died he urgently entreated his mother to yield the Keep and lands to them, the rightful heirs. These half brothers also were laid side by side in the cemetery which now belongs to Morton Priory, and they are the last of the old stock interred in Devonshire.

The next step in this catalogue of deaths was the sad fate of the twin brothers, Halberd and Hugh. They had entered the service of the rival houses of York and Lancaster, and in the wars of the Roses they met at St. Albans' under shield, and Sir Halberd fell. His brother, who did not inherit the Keep, escaped the Lacy curse, and lived to see Henry VII upon the throne of England and two generations of the elder branch laid in early graves. In all the contests the jewels were somehow the bone of contention between rival kinsmen, and so continued until they passed out of the family nearly a hundred years ago. They were secured by will to a Lady Lacy in the reign of George III, and she married a Sir Mark Denham after the death of her first husband, and so the jewels are gone. I have heard that the Denhams took them to America, and there is some legend about their death in a wild part of that country, where they were seeking the diamonds which had been lost. I do not know the particulars; but I am thankful to say they are gone. There are the gentlemen on the lawn.

"Ladies," said Lord Morton, "if you intend to dine at Morton Priory you will have to begin your return journey at once. I have ordered the carriage."

"We will join you immediately," replied Lady Morton. "Mrs. Froome, we have been deeply interested in your story, and some day I may tell you the sequel. At present we must leave Lacy Keep——"

"Look at Sir Ranald first, my lady," said Mrs. Froome. She drew the curtain from the picture, and the three ladies looked with curiosity and with a certain trepidation at the face of the Red Lacy. It was a sad countenance, not repulsive as they expected, but positively handsome but for a scar upon the forehead which the painter had probably exaggerated.

"It was painted after his second marriage," said Mrs. Froome. "He was called the most *debonnaire* of the English knights at Azincourt. I like to look at him. But there is not the least resemblance to Sir John. Do you see any?"

"Not the slightest!" said the three ladies with a little shiver.

Before they descended, Miss Tamworth and Ret made an exchange of apparel. That is, Miss Harwood assumed the riding habit and Clare took her place in the carriage. The old time story they had heard was still on the minds of the ladies, and of course was also on their tongues.

"Do you remember, Herbert, any story about the Lacy diamonds?" said Lady Morton, as they rolled through the lodge gates.

"Ah!" answered Lord Morton, "Mrs. Froome has been at her old tricks! Yes, I have heard her story at second hand. My dear friend and cousin, Sir Charles Harwood, told me the old legend. He had learned it from Barston's mother, the Lady Mary, as she was called; and since his death I have heard it substantially from her. She was the sister of the late Sir Elbert Lacy, John's father, Miss Clare."

"Yes, I know. But you have some more recent history of the jewels, have you not?"

"Yes. They came into my family and now belong to Lady Morton. They were left by will to my grandmother, and my father was her heir. The testatrix was the second wife of Sir Mark Denham, and the diamonds were claimed by his son without any shadow of right. My father thought of emigrating to America, and these jewels with other valuables were taken there."

"You seem reluctant to speak about them," said Miss Tamworth. "I hope you will pardon my question, if it was indiscreet, and forget it. How beautifully Ret rides! You can see her there through the glade. She is flirting with Sir John abominably!"

"Dismiss your fears," said Lady Morton, gayly, "Ret will keep within bounds. She would require a week to get even with you. My dear, Clare has heard so much about the diamonds that she is devoured with curiosity to hear more. Do you object to continue the story?"

"Not at all. It is rather sad in some parts of it. This Denham, the son of Sir Mark, and a younger son, by the way, went to Louisiana in search of the jewels, accompanied by his son. They were hidden in a grove, and he had somehow got an inkling of the locality. However, he became involved in some political plot and was hanged, with his son, on one of the trees in the identical grove. The jewels were there for a whole generation. By a very remarkable concatenation of circumstances I also learned something about the probable locality, and found them."

"Did the old fate attend them? I mean was there any 'kin blood' shed in the effort to reclaim them?"

Lord Morton started.

"I had forgotten about that legend!" he said. Yes, there certainly was. A near kinsman of my own, then unknown to me, tried to kill me, and very nearly succeeded! He was undoubtedly searching for the diamonds when the fray occurred, and so was I."

"Did you kill him?" said Miss Tamworth, timidly.

"No. Heaven be praised! I wounded him severely. We fought with swords. In that country at that time it was customary to carry arms. We both had sword canes. He assaulted me, and in defending myself I wounded him. He was killed by a rifle bullet, however, at the end of our encounter. The shot was probably fired by an Indian whom he had maltreated."

"And the diamonds?"

"Were dug up afterwards. Lady Morton wore them on her wedding day. I have never seen them since."

"I will show them to you some time, Clare," said Lady Morton. "At present they are in London."

"Were they not injured during their long burial?"

"No. They, with other valuables, were enclosed in a box that was covered with sheet lead and perfectly impervious. We have passed the equestrians, who are lagging behind us."

"My Lady," said Clare, "pardon me just this last time! I saw Ret when she was presented, you know. She had a lovely brooch and earrings. The former was in the shape of three lilies, with the diamonds in the bells of the flowers. The earrings were single lilies, exactly matching the brooch. Are these part of the famous Lacy diamonds?"

"Yes and no! They were included in the inventory which Lord Morton received, but I have since learned that they were added by Lady Denham, who was very rich. The original jewels were only those of the necklace, and they are larger and finer than those you saw."

"Well, I am truly glad of that! They are so lovely! and it is a comfort to think that the horrid curse don't attach to them!"

The gentlemen laughed at this sally.

"Would you not wear the necklace, Miss Clare?" said the Rector. "Suppose they should be left to you by will——"

"Never!" said Miss Tamworth, with a little shudder. "You may laugh as much as you please. But I believe every word of that story, and I would as soon put a snake around my neck as the Lacy diamonds."

CHAPTER XII.

TWO HAPPY FELLOWS.

A T the Rectory in Lavington there was a cosy chamber known as "The Swiss Boy's Den." Mr. Barston, whose habits were somewhat erratic, was the proprietor of this apartment, which was kept in scrupulous order. In one corner was a most elaborate collection of fishing tackle. In another, two or three guns and some curiosities in the shape of outlandish arms. Along one entire side of the room were some book cases well filled with volumes which Barston had culled from the large library at Oakland. His father had been a great student, and Lacy walked in his footsteps. Oakland was also a bachelor establishment and the ostensible home of the "Swiss," but Parson Johnny pleaded so piteously for companionship that Barston had by degrees grown into the habit of living with him the larger half of his time. He was swallowed up in legal studies, and was making famous progress.

On the morning succeeding the visit to the Red Hall, Barston was seated at the table in his "den," deeply engrossed in a formal looking letter which had just arrived. The Rector was out visiting a sick parishioner. There was a glow of contentment on the handsome countenance of our hero—there, it is out! The author did not intend to announce him so early, but his gentle readers have already discovered that Lacy Barston is the hero of this story. It is hoped, however, that the identity of the heroine is not so apparent. The author will be very cautious and envelope her in mystery as long as possible. While Barston was thus engaged, the hall door was closed with a bang, and coming up the staircase three steps at a time, Sir John Lacy burst into the den.

"Swiss! I have been looking for you. It is jolly to find you here. I have something to tell you! Botheration on your letters! You can read them after. I am too happy to wait!"

"My letter contains good news, Jack. I also am happy this morning."

" Shake hands then, old fellow! We are two jolly dogs together. May I tell my story first?"

" Certainly," answered Swiss. " Here, take this stuffy old chair. Put your long legs over this one. So! Now fire away while I hunt a weed."

" Never mind the weed, Swiss, but listen. Just get behind me so as not to see my blushes! Oh, Swiss! I think I have got her!

" Got whom?" said Barston, moving behind him.

" Ret, Ret, Ret Harwood! My beauty, my darling, my darling Ret! Oh, Swiss, if I should be mistaken I am lost forever!"

The bright glow passed away from the joyous face behind him, and a cloud of unspeakable agony settled down upon the broad forehead. Then lifting his blue eyes to the ceiling, as if in piteous appeal for strength to endure, and then smoothing his thick beard over his quivering lips, and with the dauntless air of a tried warrior, he came round in the light and faced his happy friend.

" Let me hear your whole story, Jack," he said steadily. " Maybe I can judge better than you what the chances are."

" I can hardly tell you!" said the excited baronet. " I only know that I love her so desperately that she must be mine! You know we went to the Hall yesterday? Well, she came back with me on horseback. Oh, how she rides—like a Centauress, Swiss! Well, she found I was spoony and did not repulse me! I ventured to say two or three things about settling at the Hall, and about the future Lady Lacy—and, and, I *can't* tell you all the foolery I talked. But she listened, Swiss, and listened kindly. I told her lots about you and your goodness—and——"

"And what?"

"And that I thought you would make love to Clare if you were not so confoundedly proud of your ' poverty,' as you call it, and so determined not to marry a rich woman!"

" Did you?"

" Yes. She says Clare would be a priceless treasure to any man if she were penniless. Those were her very words! Well, I dined at the Priory, you know. And after dinner we had music. And then a promenade on the terrace, and I talked some more foolery, and she listened! Oh, Swiss, if I were not so far gone, if *everything* were not at stake, I should feel confident."

" What do you intend to do, Jack?" said Barston.

" I can't do anything until I talk to Lord Morton. And, Swiss, who is there in the world to take my case in hand but you! You,

who have stood by me—brother, friend, father almost. You, who
have delivered me out of troubles scores of times, saved me from
the consequences of my follies—stood between me and death more
than once! And now, that I am menaced with something worse
than death, to whom can I go but to you!"

As he spoke he rose and laid his arm on the shoulder of his
kinsman and hid his face upon it. The warrior forgot his wounds,
though they were bleeding, and laying his hand on the head of his
agitated cousin, his kind eyes filling, he answered him,

"Dear Jack, you can rely upon me. What man can do I will
do for you. I cannot imagine any reason why the course of your
love should not run smooth. It shall if I can make it so, God
helping me!"

The young men resumed their seats, and Sir John remained
silent, a little ashamed of the emotion he had displayed. His
companion rested his head upon his hand and meditated.

"Jack," said he at length, "let us understand one another. I
never had any serious thoughts about Miss Tamworth. It is not
my poverty—but you have not heard my news."

"No! what a selfish fellow I am! I forgot you had good news
too. What is it?"

"This letter," replied Barston, handing it across the table, "is
from Parchment. It announces the death of my grand uncle, Miles
Barston, and my inheritance of his estate. I am not poor now."

"Why that is the old Indian who wanted to repair Oakland."

"Yes. He died suddenly. Parchment authorizes me to draw
upon him for any amount up to fifty thousand pounds. He says
the estate will yield much more."

"I congratulate you, Swiss, with all my heart. If somebody
would only die and leave me such a lot of tin I should feel more
confident about my wooing."

"For shame, Jack! How can you say or think anything so un-
gracious either of Lord Morton or his daughter!"

"I only meant that I should feel myself a better *parti*," replied
Sir John, a little abashed. "I have no idea of my own pecuniary
condition. Lord Morton has had charge of my interests since
uncle died. I shall not have to give a list of my possessions to
him, fortunately, as he will have to give the list to me shortly."

"You will have a good estate, I fancy," said Barston. "There
has been a long minority, and both my father and Lord Morton
have managed judiciously. I know the mortgages are all paid off."

"I don't care about estates! If I owned this entire island I would cheerfully give it for a kind word from Ret. Must I tell her that I was mistaken about you and Miss Tamworth?"

"Yes! No! don't say anything about it. It is damaging to a young woman to be talked about in that way. When I get spoony I'll tell you in time. Where are you going?"

"Back to the Priory. Won't you come with me?"

"Not to-day. I must ride in another direction. Did you know that I had Roland down here? Yes; Parson Johnny sent for him yesterday, and he is dancing about in the stable yonder, dying for a good gallop. I am going down to the coast. You know I have a piece of land there. Here are my riding boots, too. How kind and thoughtful Parson Johnny is. Do you know, Jack, that he is about the best man alive?"

"No I don't, but I do know who is. It is Lacy-Barston, and I am ready to maintain it on foot or horseback, with lance or sword, with cudgel or fist, or any other way you choose. There lies my gauntlet!" He dashed his glove down on the floor, shook his cousin's hand warmly again, then picked up the gage of battle and ran down stairs.

Barston followed him more deliberately. Sir John's horse was at the door. As he mounted Barston called to him to wait until Roland was saddled, as their way lay together to the end of the village.

Roland wasted an enormous amount of equine energy as his rider curbed him, making him shorten his strides so long as they were in the street.

"It's a bright day, Swiss," said the baronet, "everything looks jolly. Roland is mad for a canter. There is a good lot of happiness in the world, Swiss, after all."

"Happiness, Jack, is said to be a flower or a fruit that can never be graffed. It comes only from one root, and cannot be cultivated except about the root."

"And the root?"

"Is Duty. You may meditate upon that bit of philosophy as you ride. I promise you I will. Good bye."

"Stop, Swiss! I don't know so much about your philosophy and your roots, but I do know if there are two real happy fellows in England they are here, just about to part. Away with you!"

CHAPTER XIII.

EBENEZER.

ROLAND snorted with delight as his rider turned out of the long street, and shaking his rein loosely, started away over the downs in a mad gallop. They were great friends, Roland and Swiss, and had passed through some rough experiences together in the Crimea. That both of them came out of that little adventure without a scratch, was one of the marvels of the age to all who knew their history. On the part of Barston the perils he encountered and evaded were not by any means selected. He had no dare-devil recklessness about him. But there was a calm philosophy, perfectly genuine, that superficial people called fatalism, which made him totally indifferent about *results* when he was working out a definite purpose. He omitted no needful precautions. For instance, he had a thick steel plate seven or eight inches in diameter securely fastened over his left breast, completely defending his heart, and he always wore it under his vest when he went into battle. "You see," he said in explanation, "those Cossack fellows with their confounded long poles might poke one suddenly, and it is not on the sword arm side." There was always a method about his "whimsicalities," of which he had any quantity.

All the country between Lavington and the coast was perfectly familiar to him. He rode through shady lanes, sometimes cutting off a mile by leaping a hedge and riding across wide fields, where the odour of the hay cocks was like the breezes from the Spice Islands. It was high noon when he reached a farm house half a mile from the little arm of the channel that washed his land. A boy with a long cut across his face, filled with white teeth, met him in the lane.

"Sarvant, Master Lacy," said the youth, pulling at a lock of flaxen hair in lieu of a hat; "be ye goin' to the 'ouse?"

"Not now, Tommy. Are you all well? So, Roland!" and he dismounted. "Here Tommy, mount!" and catching the boy under the shoulder he swung him into the saddle. "Now ride gently, Tommy. Put Roland in the stable and give him a mouthful of hay, and an hour hence some oats. Tell your mother I hope to find a curd when I come back. I am going down to the water. It is now twelve and a half. I expect to be back by two o'clock."

As the boy trotted down the lane Barston crossed a stile into the meadow. At the other side the ground fell away, and in the descent to the coast became more broken and rocky. A small stream ran along the edge of the meadow, and Barston followed its windings, through stunted bushes and over rough stones, until the sea burst into sight as he cleared the covert. At this point the streamlet plunged over the rock, falling eight or ten feet, and then by a succession of small cascades reached the belt of sand which the tide left uncovered. The head of the first fall was fully sixty feet above the sea level. Swiss clambered down the face of the rock and with cautious footsteps at last reached a wild platform about half way down, where the water was collected in a little pool. All around was the solid rock, and the large, flat stone at the bottom of the pool had been worn smooth by the floods of ages. At the times of heavy rainfalls, a furious torrent roared through this rocky defile, and all the earth was washed from the rocks, which stood in fantastic shapes on every side. It is probable that no mortal foot had ever reached this nook of the earth except Lacy Barston's. It was almost inaccessible either from above or below.

He threw his felt hat on a projecting crag, and drew off his long boots, and then stretching his body face downwards on the broad flat rock at the edge of the pool, he gave some slight vent to the agonies he had been suffering for hours. No human eye could see him here; no human ear could hear his groans. The plash of the rill tumbling from the rock above him, and the gentle murmur of the stream as it passed out of the pool and rippled on towards the sea, were the only sounds audible to him. And here hidden, torn by conflicting emotions, the quaintness of his nobility was manifested. He spake aloud, holding strange converse with himself and One other, and the only Auditor he had.

"Put off thy shoes!" he began his monologue, "for the place where thou standest is holy. Oh, my beloved! How sweet has been my dream! And now I know full well that I must dream of thee no more. Father! It was a heavy load thou laidst upon my brain, and heart, and soul! My mother's kinsman! And yet if the charge had not been solemnly put upon me I could not have escaped. My Ret! My beautiful, my pure Ret! Mine no more!"

He stood erect, his beautiful face calm and gentle, his kind eyes looking around this wild prayer place. A great round boulder as high as his head was on his right hand, and above it a long gray stone was lying amid the debris of the last flood. He clambered upon the boulder and raising the monolith, the young giant stood it upright on the larger mass. There was a fissure in the top of the boulder, and the end of the stone he had reared up, slipped into the crack and wedged itself tight by gravitation. As he stood by the side of this rude pillar he held up his hand reverently and said:

"If thou lift thy tool upon it thou hast polluted it. To this spot will I return whenever I am in sore distress and while this witness stands. I will remember the hills from whence cometh my help. Hitherto hath the Lord helped me. Ebenezer!"

Half a dozen hours before Sir John had announced to him that they were the two happiest men on earth. And while he spoke his own heart was running over with happiness, while Barston's was waging a grim combat with despair. But now this athlete had conquered despair, and looked forward with cheerful courage to the future, and the pang that had rent his heart had been wonderfully healed, and at this very moment the heart of his kinsman was torn with agonies that could find no expression in words.

"This place is my Proseuche. No temple made with hands can equal it in grandeur. No closet of man's contrivance can match it in privacy. And I alone know the way to it from the hill-top and from the beach. Now, Master Barston, keep in mind the lesson learned here to-day. Watch over Jack. The devil told you while you were galloping over the downs that you were a better fellow, and worthier of Ret. Sister Ret! It must come to that, my boy. If the devil had not lied, and if you were every way worthier, so much the more are you bound to teach Jack how to equal you. It is part of the charge. And the main lesson you must remember is the weakness of nature and the strength of grace. So take the motto-word 'Ebenezer!' I must go up there once more."

He climbed the boulder again, and stood by the side of his pillar. There was an odd mixture of superstition and of simple reverence in the man. "It would take a power equal to the lift of a ton weight to withdraw this stone from its socket," he said, as he bent over and kissed its rugged summit. "And now for a dip in the bright sea. 'Ebenezer!'"

Going down the rock from point to point with the assurance of one familiar with the pathway, he reached the narrowing belt of yellow sand. As he looked out upon the water he saw three things. First, the cluster of rocks a mile out towards the sea, known as

"The Smugglers' Cave;" second, half way between him and these rocks a boat drifting in shore, her sail swaying from side to side as she ran up into the wind now and again; third, a swimmer coming in from the rocks, evidently after the drifting boat, but gaining nothing, though he was putting forth all his strength.

" Heaven be praised !" said Barston, as he ran down the shallow bank, "there is time enough if I do not waste my powers. ' Ebenezer!'" and he clove his way through the advancing tide, running like a mill race, with the vigour of a trained athlete.

CHAPTER XIV.

THE SMUGGLERS' CAVE.

BEFORE Sir John Lacy reached the Priory he met Lord Morton's carriage. The two young ladies were within. He had been so filled with his story, and so engrossed while he talked with Barston, that he forgot the appointment of the previous evening. It had been arranged that he should take them—Ret and Clare—to the Smugglers' Cave, and his errand to the village was to engage Barston for the fourth seat.

" And you have forgotten everything," said Miss Tamworth reproachfully.

"I confess my fault," replied Sir John. "Don't scold, please, but listen. Both Swiss and I had matters of high import to discuss, and he has gone on horseback ahead of us. We shall find him at the farm house, no doubt."

" What farm house ?"

" At the Ripple Farm. It is Barston's property, and is near the very spot. We will take the next turning and save five miles by avoiding the village. I can leave my horse at Oakland, which is not far distant, and join you in the carriage. Take the first turn to the left, William, and I will catch you at the lodge as you pass." So saying he galloped ahead and was soon lost to view.

" He is a nice youth," said Clare. "I had arranged a pretty speech for Mr. Barston and shall forget every word of it now."

" Never mind, dear," replied Miss Harwood, "you can compose another. I never knew you at a loss. If we meet Mr. Barston on the coast we can bring him back with us."

When the Baronet joined them again he looked so contrite and humble that he was forgiven at once. "It was all owing to my confounded selfishness!" he said. " I was so intent upon my personal gain that I hardly listened to the good news Swiss told me. His grand uncle is dead, Miss Harwood, and Barston gets a big lot of money."

"Indeed! That is good news. Father will be glad to hear of Mr. Barston's good fortune."

" So will everybody else that knows him. He took it very coolly himself. I don't think he expected it either, as he and the old gentleman did not part on very good terms, the latter being displeased because Swiss would not accept a loan from him. He was a peppery old fellow, and told Swiss ' he was very independent on a very small foundation.' "

" What did Mr. Barston reply ?" asked Clare.

" He said ' his independence was the bulk of his capital, and a debt incurred without certain means of repayment was a theft.' "

" Which is true," remarked Miss Harwood.

" Bosh!" said the baronet; " such a theory carried out would destroy the credit system."

" And abolish the bankrupt courts," retorted Ret.

" There you go!" said Sir John; " that comes of having a brother in Parliament. I suppose Herbert rehearses his speeches to you before delivery, and you will know as much as a blue book. Hasn't he been tinkering at the bankrupt courts lately ?"

" Indeed I don't know. It was Father who told me about the bankrupt courts. From the little I understood I thought they were a necessary evil, though."

" Here is the Ripple Farm," said Sir John, " and there is Tommy Dawson. Hillo, Tommy! has Mr. Barston been here to-day ?"

" Yes, sir," answered Tommy, opening his gash; " he left his 'orse and went down to the water 'cross the meadow. He is coomin' back at two o'clock, and mammy is fixin' a curd for him."

" All right. Drive on, William; we shall find him at the Ripples. That is the little fishing village, ladies, whence we are to sail for the cave."

But Mr. Barston was not there. Sir John soon secured a trim little boat, and, rather vain of his nautical skill, declined all offers of assistance, put off with his fair freight and reached the Smugglers' Rocks in safety. They landed, and leaving the sail free, Sir John secured the boat by bringing the anchor on the rough pier and sticking the fluke in a crevice in the rocks. Then passing around to the sea side of the miniature island they were soon engrossed in their explorations.

In less than an hour after their arrival Sir John noticed the rapid encroachments of the tide and warned the ladies that they would soon be forced to embark or to take refuge in the cave proper, which was ten or fifteen feet above high water mark. It had been voted inaccessible upon the first survey, and they declared their readiness to return. Sir John led the way to the landing, and they beheld with dismay the boat adrift and far out of reach, wind and tide both carrying it towards the shore. The anchor had slipped from its fastening, and was probably retarding the boat's progress as it occasionally touched the bottom. The gravity of the situation was instantly apparent to the baronet, and he maintained a cheerful demeanour with great difficulty.

"Ladies," he said, "you must return to the other side of the rocks and I must swim after the boat. Do not delay, for seconds of time are now of enormous value. If the tide advances before I get back you can climb the rocks. Be brave and hopeful, and if I do not return, Miss Harwood, you will know that I have given my life a forfeit for imperiling yours! Not a word, but do quickly as I counsel you!" He threw off his coat and waistcoat while he talked, placing them high up on the rocks near him, and the terrified girls hastened to obey him while he struggled out of his boots. A minute later he was riding with the tide and making too much progress to *last!*

Our friend Barston with measured strokes neared the boat, and with his muscles in full vigour grasped the gunwale. With his hands once upon the boat's side the trick of the gymnast stood him in stead, and in a moment he was lying panting in the bottom of the rocking boat. Small rest served him. He had detected the trailing anchor before he reached the boat, and his first task was to draw that in. Then catching the sheet he drew the sail close aboard, putting the tiller down, and went with race-horse speed across the course of Sir John.

"Keep up a minute, Jack!" he shouted; "I must tack once."

"Never mind me, Swiss! Go to the rocks and take off the women. I can keep up here an hour."

Swiss made no reply, but putting the boat about passed within ten yards of the baronet. Another short tack brought the boat beyond him to windward, and then letting the sheet loose, Barston drifted down upon him. Getting his arms around his slip-

7

pery body, he got his shoulders, then his waist, above water, and finally dragged him into the boat by main strength.

Sir John was exhausted. He had put too much steam on at the start. While he was getting back his powers his companion talked to him.

"It would slightly surprise the ladies, Jack, for me to present myself just now. My apparel is on the main land, yours is on the rocks. When you are equal to the task I will relinquish your boat to you again and take to the water. By-the-bye, one more tack will bring us to the rocks. How do you feel?"

"I believe I can breathe, Swiss. How does it happen that you are always near when I am endangered?"

"It is my charge, Jack. None of your nonsense now! Can you howl?"

"Yes."

"Well, howl out loudly. The girls will hear you now."

"Howl yourself."

"I won't. I don't wish them to know I am here; I should die of shame! Howl, you villain, and relieve their minds!"

"Courage!" shouted Sir John. "Scream if you hear."

A very musical squeal, in duett, came floating over the water.

"There, Jack, take the tiller. Are you all right?"

"Certainly. Where the deuce are you going?"

"Ashore," replied Swiss, as he plunged head foremost over-board. When his head emerged he went on: "Before you can get into your duds I shall be near the land. The wind and tide both favour me. Don't mention me to the girls. I will meet you at Ripple Farm."

When Mr. Barston reached the shore he saw the little vessel gliding from behind the Smugglers' Rocks, the broad sail full and the baronet astern with his hand on the tiller. Her head was turned towards the shore, and Barston drew his body up the face of the rock and was speedily hidden behind the stunted bushes that grew in the crevices; but while he was not visible he was audible, and if the boat had been half a mile nearer its passengers would have heard a voice of wonderful power and sweetness carolling out:

> "A wet sheet and a flowing sea,
> And a wind that follows fast!"

"I have two things to do," said Swiss, as he reached his Pro-scuche—"first, to return thanks to the Helper!" and he stood reverently a few minutes in silent devotion; "next, to dress and go to Ripple Farm; and I may add, thirdly, to eat Mrs. Dawson's curd before the ladies get there, lest she have but one! One curd between two healthy young women, at two o'clock, P. M., would be a hollow mockery! Besides, I saw a lunch basket in the boat! Perhaps they don't like curds either; or if they do, they don't know anything about Mrs. Dawson's! Heigho! It is a clear case. I shall have to do without the curd until I *know* they won't have any. It would be dreadfully underbred to eat it!"

The air of lofty indifference with which Mr. Swiss regarded Mrs. Dawson's spread, was very comical. There was a curd of about ten inches diameter and two inches thick. There was a little pitcher of yellow cream. There was a dish of golden Porto Rico sugar that had never been passed through refiners' hands, and was therefore saccharine. Swiss licked his lips in his mind's eye while he resisted the old dame's entreaties to partake of her dainties. He put her off with various evasions until Lord Morton's equipage appeared in the lane. Mr. Barston assisted the ladies to alight, kept a grave face as he glanced at their wet shoes and skirts, for the sea had caught them before the boat reached their perch on the rocks, and listened very politely while both of them together recounted their adventures. The story was not very coherent, but Swiss understood it all.

"Mrs. Dawson will allow us to dry our feet at her kitchen fire, I am sure," said Miss Tamworth.

"And she will divide between you goddesses some nectar and ambrosia she has been saving for you," said Barston, leading the way into the kitchen. "Behold the feast, and fall to!

"Not one taste!" said Miss Harwood, decidedly. "Tommy announced to us two hours ago that this curd was not prepared for goddesses at all. Allow us to return the invitation; 'fall to' yourself."

"Never! Curds are my daily food. I am tired to death of curds! And this is raw Porto Rico sugar! Terribly indigestible stuff no doubt."

"Oh, how nice it looks!" said Ret.

"Nice! Do you know what you are saying?"

"Certainly. I always take raw sugar with curds."

"Do you indulge in curds, Miss Harwood?"

"Whenever they are abundant and not bespoken," said Ret. "Please eat it up, Mr. Barston, if you *can*. I don't believe anybody could eat that monstrous curd all at once. We had sand-wiches in the carriage."

"Lawks, my lady!" said Mrs. Dawson. "I have three more curds——"

"Mrs. Dawson," said Swiss, "it is unjustifiable homicide for you to keep them another minute. If you will produce them I will show these ladies that *one* honest man can manage one curd. Jack will eat another, and we will see what they can do with the other two."

When the party quitted the Ripple Farm Mrs. Dawson had not the vestige of curd on her premises. William sat on the box and nibbled sandwiches.

CHAPTER XV.

Ah! Che la Morté.

THE windows were all open looking out upon the terrace at the Priory. It was after dinner, and the candles were illuminating the room where sat Lady Morton, her daughter, Miss Tamworth, Lord Morton, Sir John Lacy and the Rector. The author has been oppressed, since he introduced the ladies, with the conviction that he must describe their dresses at least once, and the present occasion seems opportune.

Lady Morton wore a pearl coloured silk, trimmed with two flounces, pinked out and headed with broad cross cut folds of pearl coloured China *crêpe*, caught and crossed at intervals with narrow folds of pearl satin. Her overskirt was of China *crêpe*, trimmed with folds of satin and rich fringe. The low body was trimmed with Grecian folds of *crêpe de Chine* bordered with fringe. Her fair neck was surrounded with rich lace, held in with very narrow black velvet.

Her daughter wore a dress of apricot *poult de soie*, trimmed upon the lower skirt with a deep flounce of white *point appliqué* lace. Her overskirt, sleeves and sash embroidered in a delicate flower design, scarlet, green, black and white, bordered with lace, was remarkably striking. Her square open bodice, embroidered to match, displayed a square of tulle laid in folds upon the neck.

Miss Tamworth was dressed in a black *gros grain*, with a flounce eight inches deep, the plaits of which were laid in clusters all one way, with a space the width of the plaits between. This space was occupied by three pointed straps of black velvet, the middle one the deepest. Tunic overdress of black cashmere, trimmed with a broad band of black velvet and looped up on the sides but not on the back. She wore a butterfly bow at the back, Hungarian sleeves, and overcoat sleeves of black silk.

This accurate description, the author flatters himself, is a triumph of taste and ingenuity. That the costumes were perfectly stunning cannot be doubted, and the author has no uncomfortable dread of making a mess of this business, as he has copied *verbatim* the three descriptions from *Demorest's Monthly*. What the ladies looked like, thus attired, the fair readers will judge for themselves. It is hoped they will approve. If not, they will please remember that Madame Demorest is responsible, and *not* the writer, who, unhappily, does not understand a word of the jargon.

"Come Ret, come Parson," said Lord Morton, "we must try those selections from *Trovatore*. Are you in accord, Parson?"

"Twang, twang. Yes, sir," responded his son.

"Well, commence, my dear. *Andante!* One, two, three, four, now!" and tossing his violin into place he led off. Lady Morton, mistress of the instrument, played the piano accompaniment. The rector with his violoncello added to the firmness of the foundation, while his father played the plaintive melody with exquisite grace and feeling. The listeners were charmed, and unanimously demanded an *encore*. As the first notes of the prison song, "Ah! che la morté," were sounded, a voice joined in from the terrace,

> "Ah! I have sighed to rest me
> Deep in the quiet grave,"

and the wail was so life-like and genuine that all the listeners were visibly affected. Mr. Barston stepped into the room through the French window as the song concluded.

"Why, Swiss!" said the rector, "I never heard that song with such power before. Do you really want to die?"

"Not immediately," replied Barston. "But to confess the truth I was affected when I began to sing, and perhaps my voice trembled a little."

"What was it, Swiss?"

"Why, I discovered that you were playing in two flats instead of four. That high B took all the skin off my throat. I did not know it until it was too late to stop."

This was a very lame and impotent conclusion. All of his auditors laughed excepting the rector.

"Why did you not come to dinner, Mr. Barston?" said Lady Morton; "we waited for you."

"The ladies promised to visit Oakland to-morrow, Madame," replied Swiss, "and I had to ride over to warn my retainers. They will expect luncheon, and the experience I had of their prowess to-day at Ripple Farm, coupled with my knowledge of the state of the Oakland larder, made it doubly necessary to prepare——"

"Why, Mr. Barston!" said Miss Tamworth, "we had nothing but curds."

"And bread and butter. Mrs. Dawson looked aghast when she removed the dishes. There were four curds—all of good dimensions."

"And Swiss had the big one and ate every bit of it," said Sir John. "In fact, I believe he had engaged all four of them for himself. Mine was quite small and I just nibbled at it. Swiss looked so cross that it took away my appetite."

"Come out on the terrace, Swiss," said the rector; "I would not stay here and listen to such slanders."

When the young men got beyond earshot the rector put his arm through his friend's and gave an affectionate squeeze.

"What ails you, Swiss?" he said simply.

"Don't ask me any questions, Johnny. I am slightly unstrung, but I shall be better anon."

"Don't tell fibs, Swiss. You are not slightly unstrung but thoroughly miserable about something. Out with it. Maybe I can help you."

"Alas! no. If kind sympathy were all I wanted I know yours would be freely given; but, Johnny, I will just say one word, and that is, I cannot tell *you*, of all men, what distresses me. Let that suffice, dear friend, and don't torture me with questions."

The rector looked amazed, meditated a moment, and blushed. Swiss saw the colour mounting up to his temples, in the moonlight.

"Your song was not all sham, Swiss, was it?"

"No. I am ashamed to own it to you even. But it would be a great lie *now*. The manhood that longs for death is little worth. In a few days I shall find the path I must take. I am confused now. Did you read Parchment's letter? I sent it to your study."

"Yes. It cannot be that which troubles you."

" I don't know. I think I should suffer less if I were poorer. The old gentleman has left a large estate. I must go to Calcutta, I think, as he had extensive interests in India which require looking after. I am thankful for that prospect. Let us talk about something else. It is not at all jolly for a fellow to be moaning over his own troubles. Johnny," he added suddenly, " if I have to go away, promise me that you will watch over Jack."

" Certainly, Swiss. I should do that anyhow without a promise. You must tell me what special dangers to avert."

" I need tell you nothing. We have been boys together, and we know each other's faults and foibles. I know yours so well that I can transfer Jack to you without fear, if you will only feel that you have a charge, as I have always had. Jack is a good boy, has good impulses, but he is easily misled. My work has ever been to counteract evil influences, to watch for them, and to thwart the devil on every side. If you appeal to Jack's honour you will always get him. Let him see the right and he will avoid the wrong."

" Swiss, dear friend, tell me, have you gotten rid of ' *ah! che la morté ?*' There is an intonation that reminds me of it while you talk."

Barston stopped in his walk and raised his big eyes to the glorious sky. The full moon was climbing over the tree tops on the eastern edge of the park. The rector watched his calm face anxiously, until Barston turned his eyes to his and answered, with inexpressible sweetness,

" Dear Johnny, I know that my grief is entirely and thoroughly selfish. I hate selfishness enormously. Don't you think I shall root it out? I *know* I shall. But in the process there are some poor little plants that I have been cultivating, and watching, and watering, and loving, that must be rooted out also. It will hurt me a little, but will not kill. When I was singing that lying song I *did* think of possible tigers or cobras in India, but that is gone. I cannot think of any lines more utterly mendacious than—" and here he burst into song—

> " Ah! I have sighed to rest me
> Deep in the quiet grave!"

" Let us go in, Parson. Those amiable ladies are sharp eyed and sharp eared. If you have blundered on the truth, with your slow masculine reasoning, how much more infallibly will feminine clairvoyance analyze inflections in a fellow's voice. The next horror to positive misery is the pity it invokes. Let us go in and be hilarious."

"That is deceit, Swiss."

"On the contrary, it is genuine philosophy. I cultivate jollity upon principle. I must go to London on Saturday. When we meet again the clouds will be gone, and we begin to dissipate them to-night. Come in."

"Poor Swiss!" said the rector, "you must grant *me* the luxury of sympathy. If you would allow me I might gild the edges of your clouds a little."

"Bad policy, Johnny! Don't waste gilding on such bad material. I happen to know that the sunlight is behind them, and sooner or later they will vanish. It is the Sun of Righteousness, Parson, with healing in His beams."

"Swiss," said the rector, "I was called out this morning to see one of my flock. It is old Willis. I think his days are numbered. If you would see him you might comfort him in many ways, chiefly by giving him cheerful views of the country beyond the dark valley. There are things he would say to you which he will not say to me. What do you say? My profound conviction is that a sure place to look for the rays you speak of is in just such ministrations."

"Thanks, Parson," answered Barston, "I will visit him to-morrow. But my creed is not Episcopal, you know."

"Pooh! what do I care for your creed? All creeds are alike when one faces death. I mean the minor fripperies that separate evangelical sects. I am entirely willing to risk Willis in your hands, and I engage to endorse every word you say to him."

"Come in! I am going to have 'Trovatore' over again. Your father can easily transpose to A flat, and we will make Miss Clare sing Leonora's part. *Allons!*"

CHAPTER XVI.

WILLIS.

"MY name is Lacy Barston," said that gentleman as the door of Mr. Willis's house was opened, in response to his knock. "May I come in? Mr. Harwood, the rector, told me Mr. Willis was sick. Are you his daughter?"

" Yes, sir," answered the handsome girl he addressed; " walk
in, sir. Father is sitting up to day. He feels better."

Swiss followed her into the little sitting room at the end of the
passage, and found the invalid, propped up in an arm chair at
the open window. His daughter placed a chair for the visitor,
and taking up some needlework, which she had apparently laid
down to admit him, resumed her seat at a little distance, furtively
examining the new comer as she bent over her sewing. She had
clear, cold eyes, watchful and keen, and a decided air of self-possession and composure that attracted Barston's attention.

" I am glad to see you down stairs, sir," said he, as the girl announced him—" Mr. Lacy Barston, Father."

" Thanks," answered Willis, feebly. " I think I feel better
down here. The doctor bids me throw physic to the dogs, which
I am quite ready to do."

" The rector invited me to call upon you," said Swiss, turning
the full blaze of his gentle eyes upon him; " and it will give me
great pleasure to serve you in any way."

" A little less than kin but more than kind," muttered the sick
man. " That is a poor travesty, too. I am sensible of your kindness, sir, yet hardly know how to avail of it."

" Mr. Harwood knew I was going to London in a day or two.
Perhaps he thought I could render you some service there."

" No, unless you might——. But I hesitate to trouble a gentleman like you with petty commissions."

" I beg you will dismiss your scruples and entrust me with any
business that I can do. It will be a kindness to me, as I desire
occupation above all things."

" Well, sir, there is a manager in London—his name is Tompkins—who may be found at No. 10 Burnet street, Strand. He
owes me certain moneys. I do not know how much, but, much
or little, 'twill be acceptable. It is my proportion of the gains of
his last tour through the provinces."

" How can I tell if he makes the proper settlement?" said Barston, entering the name and address in his note book.

" He is honest. You will only have to tell him that Joe Willis
is ill and in need. He will pay you if he has the money. We
have been together for three years—players, sir, but

> " ' All the world's a stage
> And all the men and women merely players.' "

" And at which scene are you now performing?" said Barston,
looking pitifully at the wan face of his interlocutor.

"The lean and slippered pantaloon at least, and perhaps a little lower. But the last scene-shifting does not appal me so much. I am in doubt about Kitty there, and cannot decide as to her future. There is something in your face and manner, sir, that emboldens me to ask you to watch over her——"

"I need no one to watch over me, Father," said Kitty, gently but decidedly.

"Foolish girl! the world is full of snares and pitfalls. This gentleman is the son of the Lady Mary, of whom I have told you. I am a native of the village, Mr. Barston, though I have rarely seen it for more than a dozen years. Kitty was born here, but has been the companion of her father through all his wanderings. When I become a 'grave man' I pray you to think occasionally of my daughter, and shield her from harm if you can."

"I will. When I return may I see you again? Thank you. I have been a medical student and have some little knowledge of diseases. I think you will be feeble while you live, but that you will live longer if your mind is tranquil. Have you any other considerations that cause you anxiety besides those that belong to earth?"

"I can hardly answer you. Perhaps I rely somewhat upon the record of a blameless life, and so find tranquility."

"It is a safe dependence, my friend. I have no other hope than that, except it be the record of a death also. It is the blameless life and the blameful death, *united*, that make the unanswerable plea."

"The rector said as much," answered Willis. "He left a book for me to read that interests me greatly. It is here," and he produced it.

"'The Pilgrim's Progress,'" said Barston. "My dear sir, I leave you in good company. My deliberate judgment is that no uninspired book can compare with 'Bunyan.' When I return we will discuss it."

"I cannot take kindly to this theory of imputation, on either side of it," said Willis thoughtfully. "Adam was too far remote from me to damage me, even if the transmission of guilt were right."

"Did your father have any pulmonary trouble?" said Barston.

"Yes. He died of pulmonary disease."

"And therefore you sit there feeble and fainting. All the doctors of all schools will tell you that physical ailments descend from sire to son. There are many analogies in nature's laws. Why should not moral ailments be transmitted also?"

"I have not thought of that! It may be so. But if true, it adds to the difficulty of the converse proposition—the righteousness!"

"Ah! brother mortal, that is inherited also; read rare old 'Bunyan.' No other man has so clearly stated the case. You will be pleased with the quaintness of his utterances. Read the allegory, and if you find him incomprehensible apply to the rector for explication. I almost know 'Bunyan' by heart, and as I grow older, and meet with works of greater pretension, I admire him the more."

"It is pleasant to hear *you*, sir," replied the sick man; "when may I see you again?"

"To-morrow," said Barston, rising and pressing his hand. "Good bye. Miss Kitty, you may read to your father if he tires. He is happy in having a woman to minister to him, especially as that woman is his daughter." He shook hands with her at parting, and walked rapidly in the direction of the rectory, where Roland awaited his coming. Half an hour later he was cantering through the lodge gates of the Priory, whence an equestrian party was about to start for Oakland.

"I am puzzled with this new charge," said Swiss to himself, or to Roland. "Here is an old fellow in the last stage of *Phthisis Pulmonalis*, if my medical lore is not at fault. The girl evidently knows it, and she is entirely resigned, apparently. She is as self-reliant as——Ret Harwood. But there is a wide difference between them. Ret walks the earth like a born princess, endowed with a majesty that is unselfish and beneficent. The other seems to rely upon constant watchfulness. Ret's face reflects a thousand emotions. The other manifests no emotion whatever. I foresee that Kitty will furnish me occupation when her father dies. Cold, distrustful and wilful. It would have been far more pleasant to watch over Ret. But there comes in the innate selfishness. Innate! Selfishness was a prime ingredient of the forbidden fruit.

"Two or three things to be done, Master Barston. First: convince yourself that Jack is a worthier fellow than yourself, and then instruct Ret and her father. It is not difficult if you will only be honest. Second: get Parchment to use some of this new money in paying the mortgage on the Lacy lands, and see that you do it so secretly that Jack will not even suspect you. There is a test for your wit, my boy. I suspect Parchment won't do. Some other legal limb must be found. Parchment would interpose some stupid objections, and Lord Morton would pump him dry. Third: old Willis and his money. It is not probable that Mr. Tompkins will have a large balance. You must make him owe Willis, say fifty pounds, and let him remit it himself. If you take it Willis will question you, and lying is out of your line of business.

"If you attend properly to these little matters, you may perhaps spend Christmas in Calcutta. If all goes well, Jack will be out of your charge by that time, and Willis will also be beyond the reach of your ministrations. Then you may spend a year of moderate mourning, and educate your heart to cultivate new affections. Don't be ass enough to conclude that all nature is antagonistic because you have to root out your foolish love. O, my princess! if I might have won thee! But that is positively your last groan, my boy. Accustom yourself to think kindly and as becomes a brother of Jack's wife. There's another stinger for you to throttle. It is worse than old Blixem's pet problem, which you solved by forty-eight hours of patient application. This is a matter for forty-eight years, if you live so long. So go at it.

"Roland! I sometimes fancy I should like to be with you in the Crimea again. But it was very poor amusement to be chopping up those Russian fellows. Yet how you used to enjoy it, Roland. I have known you to leap clear of the ground, you old rascal, with sabres flashing around you, and the din of the bottomless pit driving men mad. Do you remember getting that scar on your neck? That was a Cossack lance. The poor fellow that carried it carried his right arm home in a sling, sir.

> 'Away with melancholy,
> Nor gloomy changes ring.'

"The chap that made the music for those jolly words must have had a queer idea of congruity. The Dead March in Saul is no worse. There is the house, and there are the ladies. Jack is assisting Miss Harwood to mount. Parson Johnny is escorting Miss Tamworth. Roland, you shall have the honour of trotting beside Lady Morton's bonny bay. Most excellent lady! I love and revere you! You keep ever before me the memory of my mother. A large part of my last dream has been the hope of transferring that title to you. Bah! Good morning, ladies. You honour me by trusting my punctuality. It is precisely one o'clock. My lady, may I escort you to Oakland?"

CHAPTER XVII.

ONE YEAR LATER. MR. BUTLER.

THE will of Miles Barston, Esq., contained several stipulations. One provided that five thousand pounds should be expended in repairs at Oakland, and even indicated the sort of improvements he desired. Another, after enumerating certain Indian possessions, directed the legatee, Lacy Barston, to proceed to Calcutta (where the testator died), and to dispose of this property under very accurate instructions. The amount of money invested in Indian securities was considerable, and the wisdom of the old man was manifested in the directions he left for their disposal. When Barston embarked upon the return journey, he was possessor of rather more than one hundred thousand pounds that the East Indian part of his inheritance had yielded.

The ship *Orion* had very few passengers from Calcutta, but she called at Port Philip and took up a few more. She also took a new mate, replacing an officer who had died in Calcutta. The new man, whose name was Butler, was young, but proved himself a thorough seaman, to the satisfaction of the captain, who was compelled to dispense with his ordinary caution and to accept the only sailor he could find in the port with sufficient knowledge to navigate the ship. Butler was very taciturn and reticent—would give no other account of himself than that he had deserted from an American vessel a year earlier to engage in the hunt for gold. He had found some, too, and when the bargain was concluded he entrusted a weighty bag of gold dust to his captain, to be returned to him upon the arrival of the *Orion* at Liverpool. The ship from which he deserted was the *Bellona,* and he only did what every other sailor on board had done, namely, relinquish his wages already earned and join the crowds then flocking to the newly discovered diggings. He was not an officer—only an able seaman. The story was corroborated by the authorities of the port in the main, and the offence was very materially modified by its universality at that particular time. Butler was sober, expert and vigilant, and rather a favourite with Captain Hardy after they had been a few weeks at sea.

Mr. Barston was attracted also by something in the mate's manner or appearance, but the attraction was not mutual. The seaman, who was tolerably affable with the other passengers, was silent and gloomy whenever Barston was near. Sometimes he affected not to hear when the latter addressed him, and he always spoke in monosyllables when obliged to answer. It was a remarkable example of instinctive repugnance with no visible cause. Swiss was puzzled. He had never encountered such unmistakable dislike before. Once there was a sudden squall, common enough in those seas, and in the confusion attendant upon an unexpected order to shorten sail, the mate clambered up the mizzen shrouds in his zeal to aid the sailors, and was dashed down by a blow of the flapping sail. Barston, who was holding himself erect by the leeward rigging, foresaw the catastrophe, and starting forward caught the mate as he fell and drew him under the bulwark, pretty much as an elephant would pull down a bullock. Butler started from his encircling arm with a muttered curse, darted up the ladder again, and fairly secured the sail by skill, strength and pluck combined. But for Barston's interposition he would have been swept over the bulwarks and lost beyond a doubt. Instead of softening in his manner, however, the mate was more repellent than before.

Swiss had a habit of "not giving up things," as he himself expressed it, and he pursued the sailor with his friendship throughout the long voyage. To an onlooker the contest was very amusing. Barston, quietly persisting in polite inquiries as to the mate's health, the ship's progress, the portents of the heavens and the like. Butler, with sleepless vigilance watching the possible drift of each question, and answering with the fewest words possible, and finally wriggling out of the conversation by some pretext connected with his official duties.

"I thought you were a Yankee, Mr. Butler," said Swiss one day, catching the mate when engaged in securing a boat at the davits. He could not quit the job until completed, and Barston pursued his advantage.

"Did you?" replied Butler.

"Yes. But I discovered my error when I heard you speak. There are certain intonations that are not indigenous out of England. You are not only English but Devonshire."

Butler glanced at him half in terror and half in anger, but made no reply.

"I have given some attention to this matter of dialects," continued Swiss, meditatively. "If I had time I half fancy that I could fix a man's birthplace very accurately by his speech alone. Now Captain Hardy is undoubtedly Yorkshire. Mr. Moody, the first mate, is as certainly Lancashire. Beautiful Devon has a lingo of its own."

"I see no difference," muttered the sailor.

"Ah! that is because you have not given the matter your attention. Devon is the garden of the earth. Perhaps climatic influences may affect the voice, as they certainly affect the physical organism, and it may be true that the delicious air of Devon softens the intonations. I don't know any of your name there, but I would wager that you were born not far from Lavington."

"Here, Tom," said the mate desperately, "splice this infernal ratlin. I must go to the maintop." A sailor relieved Mr. Butler, who was at the masthead a minute later.

"This chap puzzles me enormously," said Mr. Swiss, lighting a cigar and walking aft; "there is something about him that seems to recall old memories, and now I am convinced that I have somewhere and sometime encountered him or some of his breed. I wonder if I ever harmed him or his? I have a great mind to ask him. But I must not be hasty. My little encounters with Mr. Butler relieve the monotony of this tiresome voyage amazingly. I shall tackle him systematically every day, until I find out why he recoils from me so decidedly."

Mr. Barston's benevolent intentions were frustrated very unexpectedly the next day. He found the mate standing near the wheelhouse, and, putting on his customary innocent expression, he asked him if he knew the coast near Exeter.

"Mr. Barston," replied the sailor coldly, "all reference to my birthplace pains me. I have avoided you because I knew you were from Devon. You said you took me for a Yankee. But no Yankee that I have ever met can match you in curiosity!"

"I sincerely beg your pardon," answered Swiss penitently; "what you say is true. I have annoyed you, I know, though I meant no unkindness. Pray forgive me, and I will trouble you no more. There is the hand of an English gentleman! Take it, man, and let us be friends!"

"And strangers," answered the other, grasping his hand.

"As you will," replied Barston. "I am ashamed of myself for troubling you, and apologize honestly for the past, which was, after all, only a clumsy proffer of friendship. Say that you will forget it."

" Ay, ay !" said Butler, composedly. I harbour no malice. You caught me the other day when I was going to Davy Jones! I think you made a mistake !"

" Now," said Swiss, as the mate left him, " here is another problem for me to work out, and it's a stinger ! The rascal has tied me up hand and foot, and I cannot investigate him without denying my very nature. There was something thoroughbred in the way he called me a Yankee! I have a presentiment that Mr. Butler will be a whetstone for my wits for some time to come. What am I to do ? I will die before I give up the task of finding the key to this mystery; and I will die before I tackle him again, either secretly or openly ! I must wait the developments of Providence, and watch !"

When Mr. Barston stepped ashore at Liverpool the problem was still unsolved. It is quite probable that he rather enjoyed his perplexity, and promised himself pleasant occupation in the future while he accumulated facts and recalled memories. " If I can only get enough conditions the equation will be easy," he thought. The next day he was in London and in consultation with Mr. Parchment about the investment of his Calcutta money, and the next found him gliding over the rails towards Lavington.

The train arrived in the night and Swiss went to the inn. He had not announced his arrival in England, and no one expected him. A sleepy waiter showed him his chamber and asked for orders for the morrow's breakfast.

" Is Mr. Harwood at the rectory ?" asked Swiss.

" Yes, sir."

" Well, I shall breakfast with him."

" Shall I call you, sir ?"

" No; I always waken at the right time. Good night !"

Poor Swiss was the victim of memories. It was just a year since he sailed for India. During the voyage, and during his residence in Calcutta, his mind was occupied with new interests. But now he fell back upon the life he had left in Devonshire. There had been some changes whose reports reached him in the east. Ret Harwood was Lady Lacy, that was the first—Jack's wife. This is the short sentence he had been repeating three hundred days and nights, like a school boy. Each time he said it with new emphasis, and it always hurt. It was a hard lesson, but he had it now pat—Jack's wife. He wondered if Jack appreciated the fact, and he said " of course !" and then he knew he was lying. He tried to think of Lord and Lady Morton, of Allen and Parson Johnny, but he came back to the old lesson, "Jack's wife," and then he suddenly remembered the Proseuche!

"Ah!" said he, turning wearily on his side, "to-morrow, if Roland is alive and well, I shall visit Ripple Farm. It is curd time, too!"

Willis died soon after he left last year. There was Kitty to look after. He would go there to-morrow on his way to breakfast. Kitty first—that was duty. Breakfast next—that was necessity. Finally, Proseuche—that was strength. And so he fell asleep.

He was wakened by the roar of a train coming into the station, and found the sun looking into his window. While he dressed he heard the 'bus drive up to the inn door, and the clatter of luggage, and the voices of porters and passengers. He thought he recognized a voice, but was not certain, and could not see from his window any of the talkers. When he went down the new comers were lounging lazily in the coffee room, but were all strangers. He paid for his lodging, and leaving directions to send his luggage to the rectory, he marched out on the path of duty. A short walk brought him to the trim little cottage where Willis had lived. He knocked once and again, the door being ajar, and at last, no one appearing, he pushed it open and entered the sitting room. Kitty was there, looking very pretty in her black dress, and her beauty probably somewhat heightened by her blushing face and beaming eyes, as she extricated herself from the encircling arms of Mr. Butler!

CHAPTER XVIII.

BAD NEWS.

"PARSON JOHNNY," said Swiss as he sipped his coffee, "this Mocha is good. I have brought you a bale, however, that has been highly praised. I invested a lot of tin for it in requital of your teachableness. Do you remember how long it took me to make you give up those poisonous Chinese weeds and take to the fragrant berry?"

"I have not given up tea, Swiss. I always drink it at the Red Hall. By the bye, you have not asked for Ret. She has a little

8

daughter. There goes another cup! Sally broke one yesterday. How did you drop it?"

"The coffee was hot, Johnny, and that is mendacious! I was so startled by your news that I dropped the cup. Ret's baby! By the three kings of Cologne! I adopt the child this minute!" This was the extent of Mr. Barston's profanity. "How old is the child, and is she like her mother?"

"One question at a time, Swiss. How old? Let me see, this is the eighteenth. The prodigy is three weeks old. Resemblance? Well, I have not studied her features very carefully, but I think they look like a small lump of pink putty."

"What an old heathen you are! But no matter. Give me another cup of coffee. Here, make it in the egg cup, as you are so stingy about your china. Why don't you get married, Parson, and live decently? It is not canonical for a man to be moping over broken cups and saucers!"

"Why don't you get married yourself, Swiss?" retorted the rector. He looked anxiously at his friend's face as he spoke.

"Now that is a very sensible question," replied Barston, thoughtfully. "I will give the matter very serious consideration. I brought a hundred thousand with me from India. I must either marry or give some of it away. It is too much for a bachelor. By the bye, perhaps I can set up a couple I encountered this morning. Kitty Willis and——"

"Kitty Willis!" said the rector, "that must be a mistake, Swiss. She has no masculine friends."

"Ah, but she has. The gentleman came from Australia with me. His name is Butler. I saw him hugging Kitty in her own house. Do you happen to know any Butlers in this vicinity?"

"Yes, two or three. Father always brings old Saunders down here with him. Mr. DeVere has a very stylish butler, who looks positively gorgeous on state occasions. I dined there recently, and was struck with his manly beauty. Such legs, Swiss! Then Mr. Bottomry, who made such a lot of money on cotton, has a gorgeous butler, that he took with the property when he bought Denham's estate. None of these know Kitty——"

"What rubbish you are talking, Parson! Now listen to some sensible observations. This Butler joined our ship at Port Philip. I heard him talk, and discovered by his accent, first, that he was Devonshire, and second, that he was Lavington——"

"You are talking rubbish now, Barston; Lavington has no idioms."

"Indeed!" replied Barston. "Well, I certainly had no intimation of his birthplace, yet I pronounced him Lavington out at sea, and he acknowledged that I was right. You need not laugh. There is a certain sound in words ending in R peculiar to Lavington."

"For example?" said Mr. Harwood.

"Contour, uproar, far, spar, bar, tar——"

"Very good, Swiss. I notice that *you* twist your tongue half a dozen times round the terminal letter—but who else?"

"Why, Jack Lacy."

"Well, any others?"

"Yes; mother always did."

"Any other?"

"Yes; Mr. Butler."

"Who finishes your catalogue. Now, Swiss, I'll give you a little solid learning. That unfortunate twist in your tongue was inherited from the Countess De Lys, the ancestress of yourself, your mother, and Jack. It is merely a Gallic shibboleth. Mr. Butler probably was similarly unfortunate in having a French ancestor. You never heard me, or Allen, or Father, or Ret talk in that absurd fashion."

"No," answered Barston dryly, "you are all new comers. You have brought with you the lazy drawl of Essex. I don't remember just at this moment any other examples, but no doubt there are plenty within reach. I wish you would look after that Butler a little. I have an uncomfortable presentiment whenever I think of him. I don't know any harm of him, however. He is a good sailor, a glum sort of fellow, but sober, self-contained and silent. There seems to be large capacity for evil in him."

"Come back to the mutton, Swiss. Your own matrimonial plans are more interesting to me. Now, I will venture——"

"Look you, Johnny, I will answer you once for all, seriously and positively. The woman does not live whom I can ask to marry me! You need not look shocked. Just rest content with this assurance. I were a wretch to think of it!" And he strode over the rector's carpet with the tread of a giant, his smooth brow and placid eyes openly contradicting his dilated nostrils and quivering lips. "Some day I will perhaps tell you a story, Parson. If I ever tell it you shall be my auditor. I have never whispered a syllable of it to any man excepting One, whose human sympathy and whose divine compassion are both engaged in my behalf. And I am sure I should have gone mad long ago if He had not heard and helped."

The rector rose, and putting his arm round the burly waist of his friend, walked silently by his side. Presently they stopped by a book-case, and the rector produced some cigars. As they lighted them he touched the bell and a servant entered and removed the breakfast remnants. Then they drew their chairs to the window, and throwing open the sash they filled the outer air with their fumigations.

"Swiss, my dear brother," said the rector tenderly, "I am about to lighten your sorrows by telling you something——"

Barston started, and looked upon him with dilated eyes.

"I know how to make you forget *your* troubles," continued Mr. Harwood; "it is only to excite your sympathy. Know, then, that I also am greatly afflicted."

Swiss studied his distressed countenance with great concern but made no reply.

"What I tell you, Swiss, I have gathered in fragments, by observation and inference. I have not spoken to any one about either——"

"What do you mean by 'either?'" said Barston.

"Either trouble, for I have two. The first is not entirely personal. It relates to Ret, however——"

"Don't torture me with your horrible rigmarole. Say what you have to tell."

"I hardly know how. Jack is going astray and is fast breaking Ret's heart. I don't know what he is doing. I have only been able to detect restraint and anxiety, but have not dared to ask any questions. Perhaps I overrate the trouble, but I know that my sister is unhappy and that her husband neglects her cruelly."

"How long has this been the case?" said Barston.

"Always. They went to the continent for the honeymoon. The restraint and anxiety were visible to me when they returned. I sometimes think my Mother suspects it, but am not sure. Ret does not dissemble, but she makes no sign. My inference is that Jack gambles. He is in a bad set. Callahan is at Exeter with his regiment, and he and a lot of his fellows are at DeVere's every week, and Sir John always meets them there. They play every night, and for high stakes, I fear. Old Mr. Bottomry, who has the reputation of lending money upon good security, asked me some questions touching the value of the Red Hall and lands only a week ago. I don't believe he would have made the inquiries without an object, and I suppose Jack is trying to borrow money from him. I was at the Hall yesterday and learned—not from Ret but from Mother—that Sir John had been absent a week. One would think that nothing short of urgent business would take him away at such a time. Ret is very much engrossed with her baby, and did not appear distressed; but, Swiss, that marriage has proved a failure. Alas! it is a horrible failure!" and the rector covered his face with his hands and groaned aloud.

"Johnny," said Barston steadily, "it may not be so bad as you think. It may be that God has brought me home in time. You were right about my sorrows; they are all gone. And now I have positive, clearly defined work before me, which I hope to perform."

"What is your purpose, Swiss?"

"To restore Jack's honeymoon! I want wisdom and grace. Oh! Johnny, I am sorely distressed! I see, better than you can, how Jack has been misled—led captive by the devil of play. It is the outbreaking of an old leprosy. I got him away from Baden last year almost by violence. He is the most desperate gambler I have ever seen or read about. And you, dear friend, have been brooding over this all this time. Why have you not consulted Lord Morton?"

"Ah, Barston, how could I distress my Father——"

"It would have been better and wiser; but now let us keep this miserable secret between us. If I cannot restore Jack to paths of rectitude no one else can. Heigho! Out of the depths have I cried unto thee, O Lord! Heavenly wisdom is the prerequisite here. If any man lack wisdom, let him ask of God, who giveth liberally. That is a faulty translation, Parson; it is not 'liberally,' it is far more. The word is 'simply;' that is, God giveth *simply*—as if all His perfections culminated in His character of the Giver. What blind moles men are to yield to despair! Courage, Johnny! I have a Proseuche!"

CHAPTER XIX.

COLONEL SIR JOHN LACY.

WHILE the two friends were discussing the matters recorded in the preceding chapter, Sir John Lacy was rapidly riding towards the Red Hall. He had spent the previous night at Mr. DeVere's with two or three officers from Exeter. The rumours of heavy play were founded on fact, and Lacy had lost large sums, and his friends had given him very significant hints of their desire for settlements. At the time of his marriage Lord Morton, who had been his guardian, announced his intention of paying the mortgage upon the Lacy estate; but the solicitor who represented the holder of this claim had declared it satisfied, asserting that some transactions between him and Sir Elbert Lacy were still unsettled, and enough money remained in his hands to free the Red Hall from encumbrance. Mr. Parchment was very much dissatisfied with the report he received, but he could extort nothing from his brother solicitor beyond the bare acknowledgment that the mortgage was paid. The ten thousand pounds which had been devoted to this object Lord Morton then settled upon his daughter. It was all gone before the happy pair returned from the Continent, and poor Ret came home disenchanted. Her expostulations seemed to cause her husband such exquisite pain that she shrank from their repetition until the last of the money was gone. He was repentant and full of plans of reformation, when they were fairly settled at the Red Hall, until he met his old associates, Callahan and others, a few months before Barston's return.

The rector was right in his surmise about the mortgage. Mr. Bottomry had a lien upon the Red Hall equal to the amount Barston had secretly paid, and it was Sir John's application for an additional loan that had induced the old money lender's questions to Mr. Harwood.

The baronet had recently been elected colonel of a regiment of volunteers. It was at the time when the formation of rifle regiments was the popular amusement of Englishmen. There was a review to come off to-morrow on the downs near Lavington, and Sir John was going to the Red Hall for his uniform.

And something else.

This inveterate gambler had arrived at the point reached by all fools who fall into that vortex. He thought he had learned how to *win*, and if he could only get a few thousands to start with he could soon reclaim his losses. He had seen Mr. Bottomry that morning, who declined making further advances upon the Red Hall unless "Lady Lacy's dower right were vacated." He would lend upon *other* property, such as jewels, but the ten thousand he had already lent was the utmost extent he would go upon Sir John's signature alone.

" Now," thought the baronet, as he cantered over the turf, " if I can persuade Ret to sign the paper, or get her to lend me her diamonds, I shall be all right again."

He threw his bridle into the hand of his groom and entering the hall met Mrs. Froome the housekeeper. The old lady was perpetually on the watch for dismal portents.

" How fares my lady ?" said he.

" Better, Sir John. She is sitting up in her chamber. Walk up, sir."

" Presently, Mrs. Froome. I came away so early that I have had no breakfast. Can you send me a chop and a cup of tea ?"

" Certainly, Sir John. Where shall I serve ?"

" In the library, please. I want to look over some papers. Can you ask my lady for the safe key ?"

" Yes, sir; but—but hadn't you better step up yourself? It will take a few minutes to cook the chop, and my lady might think——"

" Oh, certainly. I have been away two days. I'll be down in a few minutes, Mrs. Froome," and he went up the great stairs.

" Dear me!" muttered Mrs. Froome; "he said the identical words : ' How fares my lady ?' When the Red Lacy came in that fearful night that was his question. I vow he looks like the picture, too !" So saying she bustled off to the kitchen to order Sir John's breakfast.

The pallid face of Lady Lacy flushed slightly as her husband entered the chamber. She was in a reclining chair near the open window. Miss Tamworth was by her side, holding the sleeping babe upon her lap.

" Good morning, Ret. Good morning, Miss Clare. I am glad to see you sitting up, my dear. Is that the heiress of Lacy? What a jolly little mite it is! I had forgotten the review, Ret, which comes off to-morrow, you know. I wish you were well enough to drive over to the downs. Miss Tamworth, *you* can go, certainly."

" Not without Ret, Sir John. We shall have to wait for the next time. Take this chair."

" No, thank you. I am going to get a chop in the library. I left DeVere's before they were up, and the ride has given me a famous appetite. My lady, lend me the safe key, please; I want to look over some law papers."

" The key is in the jewel case. There it is, near the head of the bed. It opens with a spring. You know the secret ?"

"Oh, yes; open sesame! *Comme ça!* Here it is;" and he held up the key. I will bring it back after breakfast. There is Mrs. Froome's signal—tinkle, tinkle! The chop is ready and so am I Ladies, *au revoir!* Miss Lacy," and he touched the cheek of the infant timidly, "I wish I dared to take you in my arms. What a jolly little pink mite it is!"

And stepping gingerly over the carpet, with the air of a man who respected the sanctity of a sick room, the baronet withdrew.

After satisfying the cravings of his vigorous appetite, the young husband and father set himself resolutely to the investigation of his "law papers." These consisted of copies of mortgages and various memoranda of indebtedness, with a statement of his sources of revenue. With knitted brows Lacy pursued his un-customary toil with figures and estimates, and finally put away the documents with a sigh.

"If I could only get clear of that cursed mortgage to old Bot-tomry, and wipe out the I. O. U. that Callahan and DeVere hold, I should be passably comfortable." He muttered this as he walk-ed restlessly to and fro, swinging the safe key on his finger. The only place to look for lost property is in the hole it was lost in. That stands to reason. Ecarté! The devil never invented the equal of that game. But I think I have discovered the way to win. And this shall be my last trial, by Heaven!"

He sat down and covered his face with his hands, as if to shut out the light, and after some minutes he started up again; he was greatly disturbed as he resumed his march and his self-commun-ings.

"Here is the case. I *must* get back that money! And I must have Ret's diamonds to start with. They are worth twenty thous-and pounds. I will borrow ten on them, and win back my lands and money, and then replace them. I cannot discuss the matter while Miss Tamworth is there; and the case is lying waiting for me. I touched it when I got the key. I can touch it again when I put it back. After all, the jewels are mine by a double right. They are the old Lacy heir-loom, and I am the legal owner of my wife's personal property. And I am only *borrowing* them. It really looks like a change of luck already begun to have them actually under my hand."

This was very cogent reasoning.

When he went back to his wife's chamber he found her alone. Her chair had been wheeled round away from the window and she seemed to be sleeping. He went noiselessly to the corner where the iron box stood, and opening it replaced the key. The little case was there, and seizing it with unsteady hand he allowed the iron lid to fall into its place with a snap. The sound aroused Lady Lacy, and thrusting the jewel case into his pocket he approached her hastily.

"I have put the safe key back," he said, avoiding her eye.

"Have you?"

"Yes. I must go back to DeVere's to dinner. He has invited a lot of fellows from Exeter—all officers of the regiment—and it just suits me, as I can wear my uniform, you know. The review comes off quite early——"

"Mother will be here this evening. I thought you would be home to-night. She has promised to stay all the week."

"Well, I shall have the pleasure of dining with her to-morrow, and every other evening. This is my last night away from home. Dear Ret," he continued remorsefully, "you were out of luck when you took so good-for-nothing a dog as I. What a poor selfish wretch I have been! But I will do better hereafter." He stooped over her and kissed her forehead. "This time I am tied up to these fellows, but I shall be clear of all entanglements after to-night. I must go before Lady Morton comes, I fear, as I have to see old Bottomry on business. Will you make my excuses?"

"Yes, if you must go."

"I think I must. Here is Mrs. Froome. When you go down, Mrs. Froome, please tell Burgess to put the military saddle and holsters on Saladin. I must get my uniform. Good-bye, my lady, until to-morrow."

"Good-bye! Will you return early?"

"I hope so. Yes, certainly." And so they parted.

An hour afterwards the handsome young soldier was cantering gaily down the road, his long sabre hooked up to his belt. He had met Lady Morton's carriage, and exchanged greetings with his mother-in-law, giving her encouraging accounts of Ret's convalescence. "What a beautiful boy he is!" thought Lady Morton as the carriage proceeded, "if he were only more stable. Perhaps paternity may sober him. I hope so for Ret's sake. People get along without very excessive love now-a-days!" and she mused upon the short, undemonstrative married life of her daughter until the carriage stopped at the grand entrance to the Red Hall.

It was near the close of the afternoon when Sir John turned out 'of the main road and rode down a shady lane. Mr. Bottomry's house was a mile or two off by the lane. The baronet remembered a short cut across the meadow, and selecting a low place in the hedge he spurred his horse to the leap, and as he struck the soft turf on the other side of the hedge he reined up Saladin to avoid the shock, as another cavalier galloped up to the spot he had just cleared.

CHAPTER XX.

SWISS.

" JACK!"
   " Swiss!"

" Where are you going? Where are you from?" said both together, as they shook hands with great vigour.

" I am *so* glad to meet you, dear Jack," said Barston. " I have been to the Ripple Farm, and came through by Bottomry's. Were you going there?"

" Yes," answered Sir John doubtfully. " What in the world did you want of Bottomry? Surely *you* don't want to borrow money?"

" No, indeed, I am rolling in wealth. I should like to see *you* borrowing from anybody else than Lacy Barston. So! You were on your way to this old rascal, were you? What do you want with money, Jack, and how much do you want?"

" Too much for you to lend me, Swiss," answered the baronet gloomily.

" That answers only one question. What is your present need?"

" Don't ask me, Swiss. Please let me go to Bottomry now. I pledge you my honour that I will never go there again."

" You won't go this time either," answered Swiss, positively. " I have just left Bottomry, and you are out of his debt. Here! I have bought your mortgage, Jack, and I would tear it up before your eyes only there are certain legal formalities to observe. Meantime, you owe *me* ten thousand pounds."

" Swiss!"

" Where are you going, Jack?"

" To DeVere's."

" Well, I called there this morning, too, and have an invitation to dine and sleep there. If you go, I go."

"Oh, Swiss, I don't want you to go. Just give me this one night. I cannot tell you any lies. Those fellows have won so huge a lot of tin from me that I am desperate. I was going to borrow a little more from Bottomry and then win back my losses."

"Poor Jack," answered Barston pitifully; "why, you foolish boy, you can *never* win from Callahan and DeVere. If you had all of Bottomry's money *they* would have it before morning. I know them thoroughly. They are unprincipled sharpers, and if they don't positively cheat, they at least have a way of winning that is infallible. Did I ever deceive you, Jack?"

"Never, Swiss."

"You can't win, Jack, because you are a gentleman. Those fellows are not troubled with *that* obstacle. They are blacklegs!"

"Fie, Swiss! You should not say so."

"But I should, Jack, because it is true."

"You should not say so in their absence."

"I will repeat it, Jack, in their presence to-night if I go back with you," answered his friend quietly.

"You would have to fight them, Swiss."

"Very likely. If any of their brother officers overheard my remarks they could hardly avoid it."

"And then?"

"And then I would fight them with cavalry sabres and cut off their fingers," replied Swiss coolly. "It would spoil their skill at ecarté. Don't you believe I could do it? You have seen me handle the implement. Here, hand me your sabre. So, Roland!" and taking the weapon he rode up to the hedge. "See here, Jack, here are five buds, watch them!" Waving the bright blade above his head as it flashed in the sunlight, he went through the ordinary exercise, counting at each stroke.

"One, two, three, four, five! There are the buds on the turf. I have the same wrist that I brought from the Crimea. Do you remember that poor Cossack that wounded Roland?"

"Yes, Swiss. He thrust his spear into Roland's neck because you would not let him get at me, and then you laid his shoulder open."

"Exactly! If he had been playing ecarté with you I should have taken his fingers. Come, Jack, brother, come home!"

"Impossible! My regiment parades to-morrow, and I have promised DeVere to spend the night with him——"

"But I bear you his permission to spend it with me instead," answered Barston. "I told him I had just arrived from India, and he could not deny me. I could not ask him about your debts to him, Jack," he continued simply, "because that would have been indecorous, and because I knew you would tell me. I will pay him. Come home!"

"Barston," said Lacy, with glistening eyes, "I cannot take this money from you. You cannot humiliate me so, can you? Don't you see how sorely you hurt me?"

"Jack!" said Swiss, his loving eyes blazing—"dear kinsman, bethink you! In all the world I have no kindred but you and your baby. When Parson Johnny told me of her birth I vowed she should be my heiress. I have brought a hundred thousand pounds home with me. I left as much in England. Why should you not have it now? It is yours if you outlive me, and it is your child's anyhow. To whom could I leave this useless money? and how much more sensible and pleasant to share it with you now, while none will know it but ourselves and God. Humiliate you, my brother! Why, Jack, you put me to shame, because you compel me to remind you that I have placed my life between you and danger more than once. Do you think more of my money than of my blood? Oh, Jack, you need not be told that I am ready to imperil life and fortune for you and yours, now and always."

"Swiss," said Lacy, "suppose our cases were reversed. If *you* had been foolish and weak and had involved yourself in ruin; suppose I had two hundred thousand pounds, would you take my charity and live in idleness and peace?"

Barston winced. His entire life had been one of sturdy independence. His slender patrimony had barely sufficed for his simple wants until his eccentric kinsman had left him his fortune, and yet no eloquence could persuade him to accept a penny from the old Indian while he lived.

"Jack," he said, at last, "your question is unfair. I am so constituted that I *could* not have fallen into similar circumstances. For example: I could not play ecarté at all. I couldn't bear to keep the money if I won; it would scorch my fingers! Again, I could never have been deceived and cheated by such shallow knaves as Callahan and DeVere. But, brother!" and here his great eyes kindled again, "if you had inherited money, and I were in need, surely I would take freely from you what you would freely offer me; especially, if you had no mortal nearer than myself to share with you."

" But you will marry, Swiss——"

"Never! my heart is in the grave!" replied Swiss passionately. " Oh, Jack! my heart is hard as the nether millstone—dead as a ton of door nails! and if you deny me the brother's right to help you, to live for you, to deliver you from the devil's clutches, as in the present emergency, to restore you to your wife with the burden off your heart—oh, Jack, do you not know that she is withering under the same burden!—if you deny me now, I swear to you the blessed sun shines in vain for me!"

" I am conquered, Swiss! God helping me, I will nevermore touch a card! I will do precisely what you say, dear kinsman, true friend, loyal gentleman! Shall I go directly home? You do not doubt me?"

" Doubt you, Jack! Surely not. You may go to DeVere's if you like. I will trust you in the very jaws of the pit, now that I have your promise. Will you let me settle with those villains, or will you take some of *your money* to-morrow and do it yourself?"

" Better let me do it. I will ride back now. Where are you going? Won't you come with me?"

" As far as Lavington. I must see Parson Johnny to-night. To-morrow I want to see my heiress. Ha! Roland, over we go! Come on, Jack! Saladin leaps like an antelope. Here, put up your sabre again. I forgot I had it."

" It looks very stupid, Swiss," said Sir John, " for me to be riding over the country in all this finery."

" Behold!" answered Barston, " the orb of day is sinking behind the western hills. An hour hence he will be hidden beneath the tossing waves, and then we will ride on in darkness and your finery will be invisible. By the time the moon appears you will be within striking distance of the Red Hall, and when her light appears above the tree-tops of the Dark Wood you will be filling your wife's heart with joy in telling her of your late resolve."

" And of my brother's faithful love——"

" None of that nonsense, Jack. Just tell her that you have reflected and decided to do right. Don't bother her about your pecuniary affairs. Women don't know anything about such matters; and besides, she might tell Lord Morton, and make all sorts of mischief. I think you and I can arrange everything. You know my father was your guardian, and no doubt he owed you a lot of money——. What are you laughing at?"

"It sounds so funny to hear you lying, Swiss!"

"You're another!" said Barston. "Here's my road and there is yours. Oh, Jack! if I could only tell you how happy you have made me. The last vestige of pure emotion that is left me is my love for you! Good night! God bless you, old Jack!"

"Good night! God bless you, old Swiss!"

CHAPTER XXI.

The Power of Prayer.

"PARSON JOHNNY," said Swiss, pushing his chair back from the table, "this business of feeding three or four times a day is altogether unworthy of intellectual beings."

"It depends a little upon physiological science, Swiss," answered the rector. "If the brain is the thinking part of your organism, the doctors say it requires supplies of phosphorus, which you get from food."

"Very well. I accept the explanation. I wonder if there is any phosphorus in curds? The old lady had two to-day, and I am afraid I ate both of them."

"Where did you find Jack?"

"In Bottomry's meadow; I went first to my Proseuche——"

"What in the world do you mean, Swiss?"

"Don't you know? Well, Paul found Lydia at one of those places 'where prayer was wont to be made'—that is, '*Proseuche.*' Some of the patriarchs had them. Jacob had several; Bethel was one. Samuel had one, where he reared the great pillar, Ebenezer. No doubt Paul had one——"

"You mean Saint Paul, I presume," put in the rector.

"Yes. I also mean sinner Paul. He bore both titles. Concerning his saintship, he says he is less than the least of all saints. Concerning the sinnership, he says he is the chief of sinners. I opine that the Proseuche was more precious in view of the latter."

"Go on with your story. I cannot stop to argue with you now."

"I suppose not. I went to the curds next. Then to DeVere's. I found Callahan there, and found that Jack had been there some days. I also learned that he had gone home for his uniform, and that he had some business with Bottomry. So I went there. I, also, had a little business with Bottomry, which I despatched. Jack not arriving, I concluded to meet him *en route*, and taking a short cut across a meadow, I found Sir John leaping the hedge just as I was putting Roland at it."

" Go on, Swiss," said Mr. Harwood, with kindling eyes.

" There is not much more to say, Johnny. He was overjoyed to see me, and very soon told me all his story. He thought he was terribly involved, and was consequently somewhat cut up. But the poor boy never did know much about figures. Confidentially, parson, those rascals have been cheating Jack's eyes out of his head, but with careful management he will come out all right. When we compared notes he found out he was better off by ten thousand pounds than he thought!"

" Indeed! The notes you compared were bank notes——"

" Your wit is positively stunning, parson. What I say is that Jack owed ten thousand pounds less than he thought when I met him. The little he owes those blackguards I'll lend him, and he has done with cards forever."

" Are you sure, Barston ?"

" Yes, positively certain. I trust his promise, and while he lives I shall never leave him again. Yesterday I projected a trip to the Arctic circle. I wished to verify some isothermal charts. To-day I trample upon all the demands of science and devote myself to Jack. He is safer under tutelage, and he will allow no one to bully him except old Swiss."

" You have never seen him since his marriage until to-day," said the rector. " I remember that you sailed as soon as the preliminaries were arranged. Jack has your room furnished at the Red Hall. It is the great room—Sir Ranald's."

Barston's pleasant face clouded. A troop of thoughts galloped through his mind, all of them painful. He tried to think of Ret and her child as rejoicing in Jack's peaceful life, but he could not. Something oppressed him, and he longed for some secret place where he might hide himself and groan, and as he glanced out at the pure moonlight he actually thought of getting his horse again and seeking his " munition of rocks."

" Parson," he said suddenly, " you know Episcopal preaching usually consists of moral essays twenty minutes long. Suppose you vary the performance and give your flock something didactic ?"

"What can you suggest, Swiss?" replied the rector, good-humouredly.

"The potency of prayer. Let us discuss it a little and you can write a sermon in an hour. There are only two or three points."

"With all my heart. I should like to have you for my curate, Swiss. Begin!"

"First, then, the condition of the creature, when normal, is dependence upon the Creator. Elaborate that. You will find some good hints in John Owen on the one hundred and thirtieth Psalm, if you don't mind stealing some old thunder. You will be pretty safe, as no man among your auditors will detect the theft unless I am there."

"That is very good, my reverend friend. So much for the duty. Now for the encouragement."

"It is not so easy. If you make your argument upon bare revelation there is no difficulty. There are multitudes of texts containing the promise of success. I need not quote them to you. But there is a little book, by Godwin, called 'The Return of Prayers,' which has some wonderfully clear arguments set forth in quaint style. This, also, is a safe place from which to steal ideas, as the book is not at all popular."

"I have the book and have read it with great pleasure and profit. John Owen, also. It is quite likely that I have already used them both without quotation marks. But you have not suggested what I am waiting for. I want some distinct line of argument that will meet the current unbelief of humanity. Men repeat prayers, day by day, with some vague apprehension of the duty, and still more vague expectation of profit. How can I argue to make this expectation distinct and positive?"

Barston rested his head on his hand and mused. The rector's question was a hard one, and the ready answers that came into his mind were not arranged in order for didactic discourse.

"Let us light our cigars, Parson, and walk out in the moonlight," he said at length. "Perhaps I can shake my ideas into shape as we walk."

"With all my heart," answered the rector. "We will walk the entire length of the street, and then our cigars will have vanished. As we return we will stop and see Kitty Willis. I should like to ask her some friendly questions about this new arrival—what do you call him—Mr. Butler?"

Miss Kitty answered their knock in person. They found an

old dame in the little parlour, who, Barston learned afterwards, had been living with Kitty since her father's death. Kitty was an expert sempstress, demure and diligent, and she resumed her work, blushing a little at the remembrance of her morning interview with Mr. Barston ; but she was so perfectly composed that the rector found it difficult to ask her his " friendly" questions.

" Mr. Barston tells me," he said, after the ordinary greetings had been exchanged, " that his vessel brought a friend of yours from Australia—a Mr. Butler ?"

" Yes, sir," replied Kitty.

" Have you known him long ?" continued Mr. Harwood.

" Fourteen years, sir."

" Is he a native of Devonshire ?"

" Yes, sir."

" Do you know any of his kindred ? The name is new to me in this locality."

" I have not lived here very long, sir. You know my father came only a year before he died. I did not become acquainted with Mr. Butler in Devon."

" Has he not spoken of his family to you ?" persisted the rector.

" Not much, sir. I believe he is not on good terms with his relations. I met him first in Yorkshire fourteen years ago, when we were both children. He afterwards went to sea, and has not been in England since, until to-day. There are some reasons why reference to his English life is disagreeable to him, and I have not felt at liberty to distress him only to gratify an idle curiosity." All this was said very steadily, and the rector was rather discomfited. Swiss thought he would like to be somewhere else, but he came to Mr. Harwood's assistance.

" It is something more than idle curiosity, Miss Willis," he said gravely, " that prompts Mr. Harwood's questions. He is much interested in your welfare, and as the rector of the parish, it is his duty to watch over you. You may also remember that your father requested me to shield you from harm if any threatened you. The obligation is binding upon me. I do not assume such responsibilities lightly, nor do I relinquish such charges without good reason. If you cannot satisfy us about the moral character of Mr. Butler, we are both bound to seek information from other sources. You are inexperienced, and may be misled by your feelings. We need not tell you that we have no motive in our interference but your good."

9

"You and the rector are both very kind, sir," answered the girl, "but you may rely upon my discretion in this instance. It may be that Mr. Butler will volunteer to satisfy one or both of you in due time. It would not be proper for me to suggest this to him. You and Mr. Harwood will decide for yourselves whether or not you are called upon to investigate him." This was said with so much composure that her visitors felt that their work was done for the evening. They accordingly bade her good night and retired.

"It appears to me, Swiss," said the rector, when they were again in the street, "that Miss Kitty rather got the better of you in that discussion. You looked very crestfallen as you left her."

"Sympathy, my dear Parson," answered Barston. "If you are so easily daunted by a woman's sharp tongue in all your pastoral visits, I pity you."

"I don't think I ever encountered one like Kitty's. She is the pluckiest girl in the village. What in the world did you take me there for ?"

"I believe you mean 'what in the something else,' only you don't like to express your real sentiments. *I* did not take you. You took me."

"But it was some suggestion of yours about this Butler that got me into the mess. What is amiss in the man ?"

"I cannot tell," replied Swiss, thoughtfully. "My instinct, which I dare not distrust and cannot contradict, bids me beware of this Butler. I am attracted to him, interested in him, and at the same time repelled. I am not at all sure, however, that Kitty is not a full match for him. What a tigress she is! It is a curious fact that she exerts the same double influence upon me—half attractive, half repulsive. Her cold self-possession is a perpetual challenge !"

"I suppose I may as well tell you, Swiss, that I have caught you in a fraud. All that matter you were trying to get out about the power of prayer I read in print. It was published in the *Christian Visitor* about a year ago. I remember it was signed 'Proseuche.' Now, you read the thing there, and have imbibed the sentiments, and have tried, in your blundering way, to put them forth as your original thinking."

"Was it a good paper, Parson ?"

"Very. Far better than your dilution of it."

"Well, Parson," said Swiss coolly, "some of these days your sharpness will be the death of you. *I* wrote that paper !"

"Did you, old Swiss!" replied his friend, squeezing his arm. "You don't know how much comfort you have given me! I almost know it by heart. My poor Swiss! you must have passed through deep waters to have thought out that article! But you have made me so confident that I almost think I can get whatever I ask for——"

"So you can, Johnny, with certain limitations. I got Jack to-day because I prayed first. He was going to destruction; and when I left him he was on the high road to prosperity and peace. If we don't get the exact form of the thing we pray for, we get more and better. Here is the station, and the London train will start in five minutes and will take me. I must see old Parchment to-morrow. No use to expostulate, my boy. I have to go. I stole four of your cigars, so I am supplied with all necessaries. There is the bell, by the three kings! Good night, Parson."

The rector watched the train until it was lost to view behind the hills, and then slowly returned to the parsonage. At the door, a groom holding a horse accosted him with startling intelligence.

"Oh, Mr. Harwood, please mount Saladin and ride at once to the Hall! Sir John has been thrown, and I am afraid he is dead. I have sent the doctor, and Jennings went to the Priory for Lord Morton. Ride fast, sir, please!"

————

CHAPTER XXII.

A LETTER.

LONDON, 31*st August*, 18—.

"MY DEAR JOHNNY: How can I go to Devon? I cannot. There is no possible occupation for me there. It seems like a year since Jack died, and it has only been two weeks! I dare not go back. Indeed, I am not at liberty to go. Do you remember Spencer at Oxford? He has been on two exploring expeditions, and to-morrow starts on the third. His destination is the Antarctic circle, and I have enrolled myself among his crew. He said Providence had certainly sent me to him, as he lacked a man with my smattering of scientific knowledge, my smattering of medical lore, and my invincible *physique*. Oh, Johnny! it is true that Providence sent Spencer to me, for I should have gone mad under the terrible shock, if this long voyage and its duties had not been presented. I long to get away from the earth, and this comes nearest to it. It is the wildest goose-chase that any poor lunatic ever projected. Yet Spencer is so full of it, so sanguine, so determined, that I have caught the frenzy. When this reaches you I shall be on blue water.

"Parchment has my will. I have made you my executor, Johnny. If you have to assume the duties of the office, dear friend, before another summer comes and goes, will you not believe that I have found rest? Ah, what a full answer that would be to all my prayers since they began at my mother's knee!

"I ought to say something to you for you to repeat to Lady Lacy. I was with Jack last. The substance of our conversation I told you that fatal night. But she will probably wish to know every word he spoke. Alas! I cannot recall anything. I only remember his beautiful face, full of affection, when we parted; and I think I may say his mind was free from trouble, as he and I had fully arranged matters before we separated. All the future looked bright to him, poor boy!

"But there is one thing I may say to you, and to Lady Lacy through you. I have been denying it to myself for three or four years, yet I knew all the time that it was true. Jack had organic disease of the heart. In the year or two I spent in the hospitals I gave my special attention to this class of diseases, the more because there are other ailments that simulate the symptoms. But there are certain *infallible* signs, and Jack exhibited them. I stated his peculiar symptoms to Doctor Holly, who pronounced them *fatal* without hesitation. Knowing this I have been somewhat prepared for the shock of his sudden death, and should now be comparatively calm in the midst of my sorrow were it not for an awful conflict of thoughts, purposes, memories and regrets that overwhelms me, and which is as appalling as indescribable. If I live a few years I hope to unfold them all to you, but now my only refuge from madness is the salt spray of old ocean.

"I have mentioned the fact of Jack's disease for two purposes. First, he has been in the jaws of death from his boyhood, and you and I have always been on the verge of the present distress. The circumstances might have been infinitely worse. Suppose he had

died before I met him? Suppose the excitement of his late
engagements with DeVere and Callahan had been too much for
him, and he had died in the midst of ecarté! Second, it is very
probable that he died and then fell from his horse. You tell me
there was no scar or bruise upon him. I believe this must have
been the case, for he was a thorough horseman, and was certainly
not thrown. I have seen him in a cavalry charge shake his feet
clear of the stirrups and stick to his horse as if he were part of
him, while the mad brute was dashing frantically over a field
flashing with a thousand sabres. He could not have been thrown.
It is true that Saladin may have fallen with him, but there would
have been some bruise or scar to betoken it if he had. It is possible
that Saladin may have fallen in his frightened gallop to the Hall.
There is a wide ditch between the stables and the Dark Wood,
I remember, and this may account for the earth stains on his
saddle.

"Make such use of these suggestions, in your talks with Lady
Lacy, as your own excellent sense will indicate to be best.

"I must say a word about Butler, and I desire to write with
great caution here, because I have nothing but my instinct to
plead as a reason for my profound distrust of the fellow. I know
absolutely nothing of his previous history. You heard Kitty tell
of her earlier acquaintance, and she told very little. And now
hear and heed! By some sort of intuition I seem to know that this
man's life has been marred. There is some hideous episode in his
history that will stain it evermore. He is silent, watchful, suspicious, resolute, passionate. Once and again I have been impressed with the conviction that he is of gentle breeding. At sea
I have watched him in perilous circumstances, and he has always
been prompt, cool and efficient. If I were engaged in a desperate
venture, where pluck, endurance and cool ferocity would win, I
should feel safe with Butler at my side. I would not hesitate to
entrust uncounted money to his honesty, and if he were my
enemy I should dread no blow in the dark. He is not that sort
of a man. Yet I should feel assured that a conflict was inevitable, and that it would be *à l'outrance* when it came. Sometimes,
and indeed most times, I find that I rather pity than dislike him,
yet I always recoil from him and the thought of him with inexplicable horror. There *must* be some reason for this! Watch
him, Johnny, for Kitty's sake. Do him no injustice because of
my vague distrust, and, on the other hand, suffer him to do no

wrong by disregarding my warning. He has plenty of money.
When he came aboard he was from the gold diggings, and he
had been very successful. The captain told me that Butler had
given a large bag of gold dust into his charge when he joined the
ship.

"Another word about Kitty. She is handsome and good, I
believe. But this new-comer must be an accepted lover. I saw
him with his arm around her waist while she rested her head on
his breast. She is not the sort of woman to assume such a position unless matters were pretty well settled betwixt them. She
is wonderfully self-reliant, and will baffle you if you are not cautious and persistent. But don't let that fellow get her until you
know more about him.

"And now, my dear Harwood, I have purposely left to the last my
answer to your remark anent our last conversation. I have thought
two or three times since I began this letter that I would leave
that portion of yours unanswered. And then I thought I would
content myself with general reflections, without noticing the *argu-
mentum ad hominem*. But this would be disingenuous, so away
with it! I will endeavour to give you my exact thoughts, albeit
they are beclouded and somewhat erratic.

"First, then, I hold to my original proposition. Man must
needs pray always. When he does not he contradicts a primal
attribute of his nature. Second, this being normal, and enstamped
by the Creator, it is one of Nature's forces, as potent and as real
as centripetal attraction. There may be other and counteracting
forces, but these must needs be abnormal, and the consequences
of the fall, and, therefore, transient. You know the late discussion touching the viscous flow of the *mér de glace* in the frozen
north. It is well established that the ice field continuously moves
toward the sea, and is constantly giving off the icebergs, and
constantly being renewed from Nature's grand laboratory in those
stern solitudes. My friend, the operation of this invisible force
illustrates the operation of the prayer power. It belongs to the
relation subsisting betwixt Creator and intelligent creature. Now,
advancing a step, consider how the higher relation of father and
child augments the strength of the argument and the vehemence
of the force! One step more brings you to the relations growing
out of the covenant, ordered and sure! And thus you are shut up
under the inexorable logic of the case. The symmetry of the
scheme of Redemption would be impaired under the contrary hy-

pothesis. No logical argument can be constructed against this statement that may not be answered by an appeal to the lapsed condition of the race. By the ordinance of the Creator, man is as really a praying animal as he is a breathing animal.

"Leaving this inductive process, take still higher ground, and heed the testimony of Revelation. There you will find the facts stated in the simplest form, and without limitations. 'Ask, and ye shall receive, for every one that asketh receiveth.' You ' know the force of the original word. It is 'because' this is the law of heaven's jurisprudence that the asker receives, the seeker finds.

"I am now prepared to meet your terrible question touching the disastrous failure of my prayers in Jack's case. I did not fail, Parson, even in the details! I prayed for success in my projected efforts for Jack's deliverance and restoration, and I got the answer. My poor boy was saved, and his heart was quieted and happy when we parted. His future looked unclouded to him, and I believe he passed away in the sunlight. It is we who are left that mourn.

"And here I would stop if I dared, but I dare not. It is here that my thoughts are in chaos! I cannot bring order out of the confusion, but it will come anon. You hint that a mysterious Providence has suddenly reversed my prayers, and given me mourning for joy—the spirit of heaviness for the garment of praise. Dear friend, it is not so. Personally, I am enveloped in clouds and darkness, for I am sorely smitten; but behold! through rifts in the dark cloud I do constantly see the deep, blue vault of heaven, blazing with myriad stars, and by their light I discern days and years of happiness and peace for me, Lacy Barston, that would have come to me never save through the portals of this dread calamity! It is not possible for me to write coherently here, and you must wait until we meet. Meantime, remember me, and reciprocate the affection of

"Your friend,

"LACY BARSTON.

"*To the Rev.* JOHN HARWOOD, *A. M.,*
Lavington, Devon."

CHAPTER XXIII.

ANOTHER LETTER.

LAVINGTON, *5th September,* 18—.

"MY DEAR FATHER: I left mother and Allen with Ret this morning, when I came away from the Hall, and I rejoice to tell you that she is quite well and composed. It has been a terrible shock, and I marvel that it did not kill her, in her weak condition. The dear little baby has proved a messenger of peace, and she seems to have grown into all the crevices of her mother's heart. We have missed you more than I can tell you, and we all look forward to the end of the week with joyful anticipation. Nobody can fill the vacuum your absence makes, Father.

"The funeral of your poor old gamekeeper brought me to the village to-day. I have been to see him every day since he was hurt, and am charged with many grateful messages from him to you. The last time I saw him alive he said, 'Please your' reverence, Master Johnny, ask my lord if he won't give my place to you lad, Butler, when I am gone.' He then told me all the incidents of his fight with the poachers, which I will recount to you.

"It occurred on the same night that Jack was killed. Old Blake was in the wood near the Lacy lands, watching for the rascals that have been stealing your pheasants. It was quite early in the evening when they came—three of them. It was moonlight, and he recognized them and imprudently called out their names. It was Groves and his two sons, and they are a thoroughly bad lot. As they were three to one, they assaulted him, and would probably have murdered him outright if Butler had not suddenly appeared. One of the sons had a knife and wounded Blake slightly and gave Butler an awful gash on the forehead. It is cut into the bone and will disfigure him for life. But notwithstanding this wound he caught up Blake's gun, shot one of the boys in the legs and knocked the father down, and then helped Blake secure the third. It was a plucky fight. You know Blake was fatally hurt afterwards by the accidental discharge of his own gun after he reached his cottage. The doctor bound up their wounds, but he says nothing can obliterate the ugly scar just over Butler's eyes. Young Groves swore positively that he did not inflict the wound, and Butler said he could not swear that he did. The three Groves are committed for trial, however, and will be transported.

"I hardly know what to say, my dear Father, about old Blake's suggestion. I have delivered his message to you, but you will expect me to say something about this new candidate. Indeed, he may hardly be called a candidate, as he has said nothing about the matter to me. He is a stranger, resolutely silent about his past, though he is a native of Devonshire. The only person who knows him here is Kitty Willis, and she decidedly declines giving any information on the subject. Barston told me that he joined his ship, the *Orion*, at Port Philip, presenting no credentials, but showing marked ability as a seaman, and Captain Hardy gave him some official position, whose duties he performed faithfully and well. Swiss does not like him. He says he has come through a bad experience of some sort. You will understand, and Swiss particularly reminds me, that he *knows* nothing against the man, but says he "recoils from him instinctively." I ought to say here that Barston is a gentleman of such pure nobility of soul, and of such delicate sensibility, that his instincts are almost sure to be just. I wish you knew my dear friend as intimately as I know him. But he may be in error in this case. I think there is a promise of marriage betwixt Butler and Kitty Willis, and this is in his favour, as she is a young woman of good sense, and would not be likely to make an ill choice. Perhaps, if you should decide to make him your gamekeeper, he might marry Kitty and live in Blake's cottage. Dr. Holly says his wound is not dangerous, though he escaped death by the breadth of a hair. The cut looks as if it had been inflicted by a tomahawk.

"Dr. Holly also says, rather positively, that Sir John Lacy died of heart disease, and that a post-mortem examination would prove it. His theory is that Jack fell dead from his horse. Barston wrote me the same thing just before he sailed last week on his mad cruise, which is very curious, as they certainly had not compared notes. You know Barston studied medicine before he went into the law.

"About the matter of DeVere and Callahan. To think that I have been concealing from you, O wise Father, all that I feared about Jack's intercourse with those fellows, and that you knew all the time! Well, sir, I went to DeVere's to-day and saw both him and Callahan. They were very polite and sympathizing. As soon as I could, I asked about the state of Sir John Lacy's indebted-

ness to them, and they both, with great show of indignation, said
they held no obligations of his. I endeavoured to question them,
but was put off with polite lies. I infer that Swiss paid those
I. O. U's. If you put the question to Parchment—but you cannot
do that, of course.

"Dear Father, I wish you would please disinherit me. I do not
know exactly what forms are necessary, but I very earnestly desire to vacate my inheritance in favour of Herbert. I do not want
to be Lord Morton. I don't like parsons to have titles anyhow,
and I mean to be a Lord Bishop when low churchism gets into the
majority. This matter has been on my mind for several years,
but I have never spoken to you about it, because I could not bear
to think or speak of the possibility of outliving you. And now,
having said so much, I will stop.

"My best and kindest friend, I have another word to say. Since
Ret's calamity I have seen a great deal of Miss Tamworth, and
have discovered that I could love her if you would allow me. I
have for some years admired her more than any other woman in
the world except Lady Morton; but I thought Swiss loved her, and
have therefore repressed my own desires for his sake. Dear
Swiss! But it has suddenly occurred to me that I was mistaken,
and in the midst of much confusion of thought and many doubts,
I find my blood coursing through my veins with accelerated rapidity whenever I think of Clare. If you tell me I may have her,
there will be nothing to do but get her to have me. I will not
think about her—that is, I will endeavour to keep my thoughts in
subjection—until I get your kind permission. This is my highest
idea of filial obedience.

"There has been a great deal of a mild sort of flirting betwixt
Miss Tamworth and me. It may be that she is merely keeping
her hand in with me, as no other eligible is at hand just now. She
certainly flirted desperately with Barston, but he is so cold-blooded
a fellow that I could not get jealous. Perhaps her intent was to
provoke me to jealousy. I am so utterly ignorant of feminine wiles
that I cannot decide the point. But in serious matters, such as
mission work among my poor parishioners, she exhibits so much
zeal and such remarkable sense that I am constrained to admire
her on that account. She would make a most capital parsoness.

"This reminds me that I want a school house, father. I do not
expect to make a very heavy draft upon you. I have a good lot
of money of my own. But this Methodist chap—I beg his par-

don, he is a Presbyterian of the free church, I believe—I mean the Reverend Mr. Macdower—is getting up a regular mission school. If you don't build me a school house he will get ahead of me, and by securing the children, will make the next generation in Lavington dissenters! He is one of the best fellows in the world, and we are excellent friends on the sly. He had the impudence to ask my aid in establishing his school, and I have partly agreed to join him in the enterprise, and to furnish some of the teachers from my flock! The school could thus be non-sectarian, and as you are not troubled by any allegiance to the prayer book, you can contribute with a clear conscience. As for my money, I cannot decide how much I can spare for dissenters until I know how my matrimonial schemes will turn out. The locality we have in view is rather south of Lavington than in the village proper, and the pupils we expect are the children who work in the mills. There are two or three hundred of them, and they belong to nobody but the devil and Macdower, and I propose to enter the lists against him. He has a dozen godly men and women who are eager to begin this mission work, and I can probably gather as many more. Miss Tamworth specially favours the scheme, and will prove a most efficient worker. Two or three hundred pounds will build the house, and Lord Morton owns the land we have selected.

" Before I close, dear father, I would just mention the fact that your supply of Cabanas at the Priory is nearly exhausted. There were only two boxes left the last time I was there, and there is only one now—that is a box of Colorados. The other one was dark. I suppose you will be better satisfied to have enough to last until Christmas, and if you will send some, say a thousand, to me, I will send them (or part of them) to the Priory. It will perhaps be more convenient to keep a few at the parsonage, and I would suggest one box of Colorados and five boxes of Oscuros. You had twenty-two boxes of dark cigars at Harwood House last May; I counted them. I mean twenty-two *after I left.* Allen is a great rascal, and may have 'conveyed' some of them since.

" Your loving and dutiful son,

" JOHN HARWOOD.

" *To* LORD MORTON,
" *London.*"

CHAPTER XXIV.

NELLIE.

MR. BARSTON returned in safety from his Antarctic explorations. He claimed the discovery of an entire continent. He called it "Spencerland," in honour of the commander of the expedition, who was too intent upon his scientific investigations to care for honours. He and Barston constructed a set of isothermal charts, an extensive map of certain inaccessible coasts, which were closely beset with ice floes eleven months and twenty-nine days in each year, and brought back to England valuable specimens, geological and vegetable—the former being small chips from the aforesaid coast and the latter consisting of lichens and minute slips of the saxifrage genus. They also presented to the Royal Geographical Society, of which Mr. Spencer was a member, elaborate treatises upon sea currents, tides and ice drifts; and these papers were duly read, and discussed, and printed, and filed away in the archives of that venerable society. It is probable that one man in every million of her Majesty's subjects read every word of this highly entertaining and instructive literature. There were many adventures, some hair-breadth escapes from ice nips, months of heroic endurance while "frozen in," all of which might furnish material for a romance, but which do not concern the present veracious history. Mr. Spencer, by way of a change, then sailed for the West Indian Archipelago with the especial object of investigating hurricanes, cyclones and other meteorological phenomena of that turbulent region. As neither he nor his vessel has been heard from since, it is probable that he is not yet ready to report progress. Mr. Barston did not accompany him on this expedition, and as the reader is more interested in him than in Mr. Spencer, the latter will, with this brief notice, pass out of the present narrative.

But the gentle reader has not yet done with Mr. Swiss. He spent several weeks in London, editing the aforementioned scientific papers. Then he went to Lavington. It was in the early spring, and Lord Morton was in London. Lady Lacy was at the Red Hall, and Swiss, who had not seen her for nearly four years, was full of eager curiosity, and was also conscious of some trepidation as the swift train approached the pretty village. The reader has already discovered that his whole life was bound up in hers, and that all his capacity for loving was employed in loving her. The rector was also in London, but Mr. Barston went directly to his old quarters in his friend's house. It was rather lonely, but Swiss was a philosopher. The morning after his arrival he went out on an exploring expedition, first to Kitty Willis's house, but she was not at home. "She had gone to the Red Hall in Lady Lacy's carriage," the old woman informed him. Then he mounted Roland and rode to the Ripple Farm.

Tommy, Widow Dawson's son and heir, was waiting in the lane. The gash across his countenance was still unhealed, and the white teeth, which should have been sunburnt from constant exposure, still glistened within the gaping chasm.

"Glad to see you back, Master Lacy," said the boy. "Mother heard you were in Lunnon, and we've been expecting you every day."

"I am glad to see you, Tommy," answered Barston, shaking his hand. "How is your mother?"

"Main well, sir. Must I give Roland a bite?"

"Yes, and I will get a bite too, I hope. I am going to lunch on bread and milk."

"Better nor that, sir!" replied Tommy, with a grin that threw the upper half of his head into a right angle with the lower jaw.

"My dear dame," said Swiss, as he entered the cottage, "Tommy has raised my expectations! Are curds possible in April?"

"Curds are possible at Ripple whenever *you* come, Master Lacy," said the widow. "Lawks! I can make 'em at Christmas! August is the nat'ral month for 'em, but I can make August weather by the kitchen fire. Will you have it now, sir?"

"When I come back, please. I am going to the beach for a sea dip. Do you know that I have been breaking the ice nearly every day for two years to get my salt water bath? I have been to a country where August is midwinter, and where midsummer does not melt the ice. Towels? thank you. Within the hour I shall be ready for the curd."

"I wish you would go round by the road, Master Lacy. Some day you'll break your precious neck among the rocks."

"Never fear, dame. I am very cautious. Don't tell anybody that I scramble among the rocks. That which is easy for me would be perilous for Tommy."

When Mr. Barston returned from the beach the luncheon was ready. He always insisted upon his seat at the kitchen table, though Mrs. Dawson had a "best room," which was regularly aired and dusted but never occupied.

"Mrs. Dawson," said Mr. Barston, "I thought of going to the West Indies the other day, and one thing I had decided to do was to buy a cask of Porto Rico sugar. I have an idea that I could select the best on the island. Out of this cask a barrel belongs to you."

"Thank'ee, Master Lacy. Does sugar grow there?"

"Yes, also cyclones. My friend, Mr. Spencer, has sailed in search of the latter."

"Are they good to eat?"

"No, they are an unwholesome sort of diet, I fancy. I have heard nothing about Oakland and nothing about Lavington. Can you give me any gossip?"

"No, sir. William was here yesterday. My lady has engaged a nurse for Miss Ellen. Did you know the little baby was named Ellen Barston?"

"No, indeed," said Swiss, startled.

"Yes, sir. She is named for your baby sister. Sir John had so named her, though she was not christened when he died."

"Who is the nurse, Mrs. Dawson?"

"Kitty Willis."

"Ah! How did it happen?"

"William says Lord Morton and the rector recommended her very highly. Master Lacy, I have found out something."

"Indeed! What is it, dame?"

"Do you remember when old Dobbin was killed? Well, sir, William says *you* bought the new horse and not Sir John."

"Pooh, dame, it was all the same. What does William know about it?"

"Sir John told him," answered Mrs. Dawson, severely. "You sent Hawder's boy with the horse——"

"And the jackass told Jack, and Jack told William. What a coil about nothing!" replied Swiss. "Tell me some more recent gossip."

"Don't know any more, sir. Lord Morton's gamekeeper——"

"Old Blake?"

"No, sir. Young Butler."

"By the three kings!" said Barston, starting up, "things are growing complicated! What were you about to say, dame?"

"Nothing, sir—only Butler is an ugly brute! William can't abear him. Kitty is a pretty, decent girl, and ought to have a better spark than that drunken rascal."

"Softly, dame. Butler is rather handsome. Indeed, if he were dressed in modern costume he would pass for a thoroughbred. As for his drunkenness, that must be a mistake. I was two months and more aboard ship with him and he never touched rum."

"Well, sir, he touches it now. I don't want to harm him if he would let that gal alone. He goes to the village every other night to court her, and now that she is at the Red Hall he will go there. It is more convenient for him. He lives in Blake's cottage, which is near the Hall, you know."

"Tommy, bring Roland," said Mr. Barston. "I think I will ride round by the Priory road and call on Mr. Butler. Dame, the curd was faultless. May I light my cigar here?"

"Lawks! Master Lacy."

"That means yes. Puff, puff. Good bye, dame. Tommy, you expect a shilling?"

"No, sir!" answered Tommy, mendaciously.

"Well, shut your jaws! Here is half a crown. Ho! Roland!" And mounting the restless horse he held him quiet with an iron hand. "Dame," he said, "perhaps it would be better to keep all that gossip for my ears alone for the present. There is some mystery about these people. Let us not excite their suspicions. I am going to unravel the mystery this time, by the three kings! Away, Roland!" and with a snort and a mighty bound Roland darted from the door, while Tommy looked on with admiring eyes. Then, as the horseman disappeared behind a little clump of trees, the boy turned his gaze upon the bright coin in his hand, while the upper half of his cranium lifted itself two or three inches.

"'Ere's the 'arfcrown, mother," he said, regretfully; "he allers says a shillin', and allers gives me 'arf a crown or a florin. Put it in the stockin'. Now he's come they'll chink in faster. By Christmas I'll have a small fortin!" How prone is humanity to forecast the future!

As Roland turned into the high road, Barston saw a landau that had passed the mouth of the lane a few minutes earlier, now half a mile away. Peeping above the top, which was thrown back, he saw the flutter of ribbons in the jaunty hat of the occupant. Then as he drew nearer he recognized the horses and then the livery on the broad shoulders of Lady Lacy's coachman, William. With beating heart he shook his bridle, turning his heel to Roland's flank, and in a moment he was beside the carriage, peering anxiously in the face of Kitty Willis. William checked his horses.

"Hooray!" he shouted. "Welcome home, Master Lacy!"

"Thank you, William. How is my lady? Well? And this is Kitty Willis—and—Nellie Lacy, by the three kings! Stand, Roland!" And leaning forward he held out his arms to the child, while a tempest of emotions swept over his face.

The child gazed into his gentle eyes with steady scrutiny for a moment, and then holding up her little hands was caught to his breast, while her rosy face was hidden in his flowing beard.

"My darling! my darling!" muttered the strong man as he drew his horse apart. "Ret's baby! Jack's baby! Oh, Merciful! *My* baby evermore!" And scarcely conscious of his own thoughts or purposes he spurred Roland again, and galloped away with the child clinging to his neck, crowing with delight.

Perhaps the story thus far told has been so clumsily related that the gentle reader has failed to see through Lacy Barston's soul-windows, and therefore cannot account for many of his acts and speeches. To the author he looms up in grand proportions, and the steadfast nobleness of his character shows through all his whimsicalities. Naturally impulsive and passionate, his life has been one long practice of self-denial and self-restraint. In his early youth his dying father, recognizing the inherent force of his character, had charged him to watch over his kinsman, John Lacy, through life, and this burden, which was a solemn obligation in young Barston's mind, had doubtless coloured his entire life. And now that death had relieved him from this charge, he had comfort in remembering that he had never uttered one unkind word, though frequently sorely tried by his restless ward. Somehow he had come to regard Sir John as the representative of his own father and mother, and therefore entitled to whatever he might claim of him. Otherwise he would never have relinquished the only woman who had ever attracted him. And God had been good to him in tempering the quaint relations he sustained to his cousin with a brother's love, making endurance and forbearance easy duties. He had seemed to step into his father's office, and Jack being gone, the great unselfish love he had cherished for him was now suddenly transferred to the infant nestling in his bosom.

"Do you know me, baby?" he said at last, pulling up his horse.

"No. What name?"

"Cousin Lacy. Can you say 'Cousin Lacy,' Nellie?"

"Tousin Lacy. I love Tousin Lacy!" and she parted his beard with dimpled fingers and kissed him.

And so the child passed into the core of his heart, taking her place there with all due authority, and reigning with despotic sway while its pulsations continue. She is there to-day, exacting, wilful and loving.

CHAPTER XXV.

THE GAMEKEEPER.

WHEN Barston relinquished Nellie to her new nurse he turned from the high road, and passing through a grassy lane entered the broad domain of Morton Priory. Half a mile from the highway was situated the gamekeeper's cottage. He had no definite plan beyond seeing the gamekeeper, and deciding for himself as to Butler's character and habits. The memory of old Willis and of the wistful expression of his face, when he entreated him to watch over his daughter, was the most prominent impression upon his mind. He endeavoured to analyze his feeling of repugnance, which was always uppermost when he thought of Butler, but he could not make up a reasonable case. The reports he had heard from Mrs. Dawson he took *cum grano salis*, making allowance for prejudice and for possible jealousy on William's part. Kitty was attractive enough, and, in Barston's judgment, far too good for any man in a subordinate position; as for allowing her to throw herself away upon a drunkard, that was not to be thought of. There was also an unaccountable suspicion in his mind that Kitty was hardly good enough for Butler, whose rough manners had always seemed to Barston to be assumed for a purpose. While he was still busy with these reflections, he reached the stile leading to the cottage, and seated upon it he saw his quondam shipmate watching him composedly as he approached.

He wore a gray shooting jacket and trousers, his nether limbs being covered with long leathern gaiters buttoning above the knee. A felt hat, cocked up over his brow, half concealed his eyes.

10

As he straightened himself with indolent grace, there was in his manner a consciousness that he was on his own premises, and there was nothing servile in his salute when Mr. Barston checked his horse at the stile. Two things shot through the mind of the visitor. First: that Mr. Butler was vastly improved in appearance; second, that he was on guard.

"I heard that you were here," said Barston, with direct honesty, "and I rode in to see you."

"How can I serve you, sir?" replied Butler, quietly.

"By telling me the truth. You need not look insulted——"

"I am not in the habit of lying, Mr. Barston."

"I did not mean to imply that you were. I should like to ask you a few questions, if you do not object."

"Proceed, sir," said Butler, reseating himself upon the stile.

"I scarcely know how, by the three kings!" returned Barston; "but the truth is always safe. I have heard—nay, I have seen, that there is such an understanding betwixt you and Kitty Willis as should only exist betwixt those who intend marriage."

"Well, sir?"

"I have reasons for what I say about this matter. When her father died he requested me to protect his child from harm. On that account alone I have sought you to-day."

"You mean that my courtship may harm her?"

"Possibly. Or rather, that your marriage with her might harm her. I do not know. Hang it, man!" he continued, with a little outburst of temper, "why are you so infernally glum and mysterious? If you are an honest man, a sober man, and the girl likes you, it would be a great pleasure to me to aid rather than hinder you. Who *are* you?"

"Lord Morton's gamekeeper," said the other, "passably honest, perhaps. Passably sober—sometimes——"

"Who *were* you? There is the true difficulty! You come upon us here a waif from the ocean. For aught I know to the contrary you may have been a pirate. Why the—— deuce can't you enlighten me enough to quiet my conscience? Look you! We have been together in peril, and if there were not some horrible reason for your reticence, there would have been confidence betwixt us. What black spot is in your past that you should be constantly on the watch against friend and foe?"

Butler rose slowly, and throwing his leg over the stile slid down into the lane.

"Waif, drunkard, possible thief, possible pirate!" he said, counting the epithets off on his fingers. "Hadn't you better add 'possible murderer,' and so complete the catalogue?" and he dashed his hat upon the grass and faced his persecutor with pallid countenance, on which there was no sign of fear. Then Barston saw on his forehead a long purple seam, an inch above his eyes, the more noticeable because of the ashy hue of the rest of his face. Barston threw his bridle on Roland's neck and dismounting drew near his interlocutor, his soul filled with tender pity.

"I have wounded you sorely," he said gently, "and I am very sorry. Let me atone for my fault by befriending you. If you are crushed under some hideous memory—for so my instinct teaches me—I pray you let me comfort you. God is more merciful than we think Him. Do you not remember that He allowed me to avert an impending death once——"

"Ay!" answered Butler; "and I also know that I owe Him no thanks for that! The peace I have failed to find on earth might have been mine a thousand fathoms down under the sea!"

"You shock me!" said Barston; "such dreadful words should never issue from mortal lips. No calamity has befallen you that is not common to man, and no calamity is incurable while life endures. Will you allow me to aid you?"

"I require no man's aid," said the other; "if you really wish to do me a kindness, let me alone. As for the young woman, it is likely enough that she incurs less peril under my protection than she would under charge of a gay young gentleman like you."

"You are not speaking your true sentiments," replied Barston, with dignity. "The tokens you give of gentle breeding are unmistakable. I implore you to confide in a man of your own class, and let me extricate you if I can from the past, and assure your future. Mount my horse and ride to Oakland. I will get another in the village and follow you."

"You accused me of drunkenness but now," said Butler, picking up his hat and reseating himself upon the stile. "Most men would say you were either drunk or mad to make such a proposition to me."

"Perhaps. But you know that I am neither. Will you come?"

"A thousand times no!" said Butler. "Is it not possible for you to leave me to myself?"

"It is not possible," answered Barston, gravely.

"Well then," said Butler, with a defiant air, "let us understand each other. There can be no quarrel between us, first, because you have saved my life; and second, because I am not insensible of your kind intentions. I will say nothing about your conceit as to my true condition. I know that you are a whimsical gentleman, and you may take up some new conceit to-morrow. But I notify you that I will thwart you in every way, as I have opportunity, unless you consent to walk apart from me. It may be that I shall apply to you some day and remind you of your generous offers. In the meantime be on your guard. I am on mine."

"Pooh!" said Barston, "the contest is unequal. I have no vulnerable spots. I cannot walk apart from you if I would. My home is here, and this girl's welfare was put under my charge. I cannot relinquish it until I know more of you. If you will at least quit drink——."

"I cannot. One must sleep sometimes."

"Rum is a poor soporific. You have taken to it since we met on shipboard."

"Yes," said Butler, wincing a little.

"And you have got a new mark since we parted. Doubtless it also is due to rum?"

"What a devil you carry in your tongue, Mr. Barston," said Butler, with a ghastly attempt at a smile. "You are very thoughtful of Kitty's welfare. Heaven pity the unfortunate woman *you* may chance to marry!"

Barston mounted his horse. He had thrown away his cigar when he met Nellie, and he proceeded to light another while he pondered the last speech of the gamekeeper.

"That strikes me as a very sensible observation, Mr. Butler," he said at last. "The truth is, matrimony is a very risky business on the part of women. Men who are not brutes are very apt to be fools, and I really do not know more than half a dozen amongst my acquaintances who are fit to assume so grave a trust. We shall meet again, and I hope you will be in a better mood. It occurs to me now, as we are about to part, to ask you if you have none bound to you by ties of blood who might suffer in seeing you degraded—no mother, no father——"

"I am alone in the world," said Butler, turning his back upon him as he crossed the stile. "My mother died before I was old enough to know her, and all I remember of my father is a scowling face and bitter tongue. My chief solace now is in cursing his memory!"

Barston watched his retreating form until it disappeared in the cottage door, and then rode soberly down the lane.

"The fates have dealt hardly with him," he thought, "and I suppose the mournful tones of his voice awaken my sympathy. It is the most inscrutable mystery altogether. I am not sure that I came off victor in yonder encounter of wits. The fellow is plucky as a dog! He got that crack on the crown in some devil's business or he would not have winced so when I referred to it. He boldly challenges me to the contest, and I purpose to begin my part by taking Kitty to Oakland. If I get her there he will have to do his courting under difficulties. I will offer her the place of housekeeper, at high wages, to-morrow."

Mr. Butler unlocked a cupboard, took out a bottle and a glass, and seating himself near the window poured out half a tumbler of brandy. As he sipped it he watched the horseman riding down the lane.

"Mr. Barston is a troublesome customer," he thought; "he has inherited his mother's sharp wit and his father's invincible pertinacity. What a handsome fellow he is! If he were not so undeniably thoroughbred I vow I should be jealous about Kitty! He will be apt to begin operations against me without delay, and I must get the start of him somehow. I must ask Kitty. She will know if he has any weak points. Something must be done to get him out of the neighbourhood. Is there no way to get this devil's brand from my face?" and he ground his teeth in an agony of rage. Then he emptied his glass, and taking a double barrelled gun from the corner, he left the cottage, and crossing the meadow, struck through the woods in the direction of the Red Hall.

CHAPTER XXVI.

SWISS IN TROUBLE.

LADY LACY'S carriage conveyed her, with Miss Tamworth, Nellie and her nurse, to Morton Priory the day after the foregoing occurrences. There had been an amicable contest between her and her parents ever since the death of Sir John, touching her continued residence at the Red Hall. The elders were more eager to have their daughter resume her old place in her

old home, because of the incumbrance in little Nellie, who was the
tyrannical mistress of both houses, but Ret had steadfastly declined "for the present," and had always cogent arguments to
present against the arrangement, drawn from the requirements of
the estate, which she was bound to administer in Nellie's interests. Another plea was furnished by Miss Tamworth's constant residence at the Red Hall as Lady Lacy's guest. She had
never left her since Nellie's birth, and the thought of separation
did not enter the mind of either.

The park was putting on its spring attire and was truly beautiful. The evergreens, standing in clumps near the house, had
gotten rid of the rust of winter, and the deciduous trees, with
their young, green leaves, were bursting into new life under the
delightful sun of Devon. The conservatory runs along the
southern side of the house, and on this bright morning the double
sashes were open and the wealth of fragrant bloom was within
reach of the lawn. Lady Lacy had never yielded her proprietor-
ship of the conservatory, and half an hour after their arrival she
opened the glass door in the drawing-room communicating with
the conservatory and entered her ancient domain. She had taken
but a few steps when she was startled by the sound of voices. The
speakers were hidden by the dense foliage of two huge lemon
trees, and as she retreated she heard a sentence or two.

"You must come and live at Oakland, Kitty——"

"Impossible, Mr. Barston."

"But you *must*. Everything depends upon it. Are you so mad
as to wreck your own happiness——"

Lady Lacy passed back into the drawing-room and closed the
door, hearing no more of this interesting colloquy. Miss Tamworth was at the piano, and Lady Morton standing near her.
While Ret was still stunned and trying to collect her thoughts,
the glass door opened behind her and Mr. Barston entered with
Nellie in his arms. Kitty, with flushed face, followed, and Ret
was lost in admiration of the cool effrontery of our friend Swiss,
who approached her with his hand extended.

"I rejoice to see you looking so well," he said, glancing at her
black dress. "My dear little Nellie met me on arrival and bade
me come in this way. I hope I have not startled you!" he added
anxiously, noticing her perplexed look.

"Yes you have, a little. How long have you been here?"

"I arrived but now. My lady, I feel that I am indeed at home once more when I receive your welcome. Ah! Miss Tamworth, you look as charmingly innocent as if you had no broken hearts to answer for. I have been in England but a few weeks and have met half a dozen victims of your flirting powers already! Nellie! have you not told your mamma that you met your cousin Lacy yesterday?"

"Oh, yes," answered Miss Tamworth. "Nellie gave us glowing accounts of her ride yesterday. As you have made a conquest there so expeditiously, I think *you* must have been learning some flirting lessons among the Esquimaux damsels."

"I have not been among them," replied Barston, "and I have not offered 'delicate attentions' to any lady since I saw you last. The renown you have acquired as a heart-breaker has seemed like a constant challenge to me, and so I come to prove your prowess."

"Indeed, you have come in vain," said Clare, lightly. "I shall not waste any efforts upon you. I happen to know that you are sworn to celibacy."

"I?" said Swiss, in surprise; "you are greatly mistaken. For thirty dreary months I have lived among rude men. No woman's presence to humanize, no woman's voice to soothe. In the midst of appalling horrors, day after day, when all the days were nights, I have watched the gorgeous constellations of the Southern Pole, and longed for the returning sun. The ice, spread around me in almost limitless floes, or standing in cold splendour, huge bergs, glittering in the moonlight, was not more desolate than my lot, deprived of gentle woman's influence and sympathy. And in that long imprisonment there was no waking hour when the ladies, in whose presence I stand to-day, were not present in my thoughts. And I think I may truthfully add, there was no hour of sleep when they failed to gild my dreams."

"If it were not for the air of earnestness you put on," said Miss Tamworth, "I would compliment you on that pretty speech. Still I am sure you have professed to be proof against feminine wiles. The rector has quoted you——"

"Ah!" said Barston, "Parson Johnny has misunderstood me, perhaps. He has not been wretch enough to accuse me of——"

"Nothing worse than confirmed bachelorhood. But that freezing account you have just given of your late surroundings has awakened all my curiosity. I shall require a full chronicle of your adventures."

" Mr. Barston has kindly come to entertain us to-day," said Lady Morton. " John and his father will be here to dinner."

" Yes," answered Barston, " I left them at the Rectory. Parson Johnny will drive out here to luncheon. Lord Morton and he arrived in the early train, and I had the pleasure of taking breakfast with them. I was too impatient to wait for them. Nellie, I will take you on Roland's back again after luncheon;" and he gave the child to Kitty, who retired with her through the conservatory.

Lord Morton and the rector arrived shortly after and were received with great *empressement* by the ladies. Sundry parcels, brought down from London, containing articles of feminine adornment, no doubt, attracted the ladies on the instant, and following the servant who bore them to some interior chamber, these charming women gloated over ducks of bonnets until luncheon was announced, when they gloated over cold beef and salad.

" Do you return to the Red Hall before dinner?" said Mr. Barston, addressing Lady Lacy.

" Yes. The carriage is ordered at two o'clock. Nellie must be at home before dark."

" May I take her, then, on Roland? There are some law papers which Mr. Parchment told me I ought to see. They are in the safe——"

" And Mrs. Froome has the key. Certainly you may take Nellie, if she will not encumber you."

" Then I will go at once, if my lady will excuse me."

" On condition that you return to dine and sleep," answered Lady Morton.

" Your room has been waiting for you, Lacy," said Lord Morton, "for years, and you have never occupied it."

" Many thanks! I cannot accept, positively, until I see those legal documents. It may be necessary for me to take them to London at once; but it will be a great disappointment to me if it should so happen. Nellie, my darling, get your wraps!"

Miss Tamworth and the rector followed Barston, leaving Lord and Lady Morton with Ret at the table.

" My dear," said Lord Morton, " I am greatly perplexed about that boy and I require the aid of your sharper wit. Sit still, Ret! I want your judgment, also."

" Of whom are you speaking?" said his wife.

" Of Lacy Barston. I had to wait an hour for John this morning, as he had a vestry meeting, and while he was absent, Butler, the gamekeeper, called. It seems his visit was intended for the Parson, but he said he greatly preferred telling his story to me. He is courting your nurse, Ret."

" Yes, sir."

" Well, he is terribly jealous of Mr. Barston! When he blurted out this statement I was disposed to get in a passion, but something *real* about the fellow's appearance kept me cool. He says Barston is pursuing the girl constantly. Did she drive on the Exeter road yesterday, Ret?"

" Yes, sir."

" Butler says Barston waylaid her yesterday, and also that he went to Lavington this morning specially to see her. Was she there this morning?"

" Yes, sir."

" Then he saw her, no doubt. As John and I walked down from the station we met him, and he said he had just seen your carriage. I cannot tell what to think. I did not ask John, but have been brooding over the matter all the morning. The girl is the daughter of an actor, who died here a few years ago, and has some smattering of education. But Barston could hardly think seriously of marrying so far beneath his station! There is no accounting for infatuation, however. The whole story is complicated. Butler says Barston offered Kitty any wages she would demand if she would quit your service and enter his! It will require something like an earthquake to shake my confidence in Lacy Barston's integrity. But I am thoroughly annoyed and perplexed. Enlighten me, wife!"

" Come, Ret!" said Miss Tamworth from the door. " It is going to rain. I ventured to order the carriage at once."

They rose from the table, and as Ret arrayed herself in bonnet and wrappings her mother stood apart, meditating. Lord Morton waited anxiously for her reply, which came at last.

" Ask John! Tell him all about it. I feel certain that he will be able to explain everything. Don't you think so, Ret?"

" Alas! no. Good bye, Mother, Father!" and as they kissed her they noticed the tears in her gentle eyes.

CHAPTER XXVII.

SWISS EXPLAINS.

A T the Red Hall the Keep, which was the nucleus of the system of buildings that made up the residence, was a huge square tower, rising two stories above its surroundings. The ground floor was the dining room, and the next floor was Sir Ranald's room. This had been somewhat modernized by Sir John, and a stone portico added to the Keep, giving entrance to the dining room and also to a stairway leading directly to the library, as this ancient chamber was now called. This had gradually grown to be the main entrance, and when Lady Lacy arrived, just in advance of the shower, she ascended at once to the library, where she found Mr. Barston seated at the table and poring over musty looking deeds and leases. He rose at her entrance and placed a chair for her, and after some allusion to their good fortune in escaping the rain, which was now falling, he resumed his study of the papers while she sat quietly by.

" Cousin Ret," he said at last, " if you will allow me to claim kindred, I find enough in these papers to make it necessary for me to return to London. There is a flaw in your title that must be mended."

" I do not understand you," she answered.

" It is easily remedied," said Barston, placing the deeds in his pocket. " You will entrust me with the papers ?"

" Certainly. What is the nature of the flaw ?"

" The death of Elbert Lacy, of which there is no doubt, has never been legally proven. The inheritance of the Lacy estate is really in Nellie, in equity, and it could doubtless be established by Chancery proceedings. I expect to arrange it less expensively."

" I am glad you have mentioned the matter, as I have wished to consult you about it since—for some time. Pray, whose interests conflict with Nellie's ?"

" None. That is, without some slight rectification the lands might pass to—to—another, who has no sort of right to them. My legal knowledge is so superficial that I wish to consult Parchment."

" And who is that other ?" persisted Ret.

" Oh, no matter. You see there was a will three generations back, and there has been no will since. Lord Morton would probably know about it. My father was Jack's guardian;" he winced as he uttered the name, and his voice faltered a little, but he went on, "and when he died he gave me some general directions, which I have tried to follow."

" I see I must speak plainly, Mr. Barston. *You* are the heir-at-law——"

" Not I!" replied Swiss stoutly. " What an absurdity! Who has put such a wise notion into your head?"

" No one. I have read all those papers and some others. Mr. Barston," she continued, earnestly, " I owe you a great deal of money and I am going to pay it!"

" What astounding bosh you are talking!" said Swiss, rising and approaching her.

" I am talking sound sense," she replied, firmly, " and you know I am right. I owe you ten thousand pounds, which you paid to Mr. Bottomry, and some more—I don't know how much, but you will tell 'me—that you paid Mr. DeVere, and I am not going to allow you to deprive yourself of your legal rights to these lands, sir! They are yours, under your grandfather's will, not Nellie's!"

" Now, by the three kings of Cologne!" said Barston, stamping his foot, " see what comes of a woman's dabbling in law matters. I was inaccurate just now when I said my knowledge was superficial. I know enough law to be certain that I have no rights here."

" Very well, sir. Waiving that point for the present, will you please explain about Mr. Bottomry and Mr. DeVere?"

" Explain!" stammered Swiss. " Certainly—that is—there is nothing to explain. Seriously, madame, you have no right to make ducks and drakes of Nellie's inheritance."

" Did you pay any moneys to those gentlemen in behalf of my husband?" said Ret, with deliberation.

" Well, really, this is very irregular, and I may add very uncomfortable," said Barston. " I may have had some transactions with the gentlemen you name, but I cannot be expected to remember all the little details." ·

" Did you pay Mr. Bottomry ten thousand pounds?"

" Perhaps; but it was not Nellie's money, and allow me to say it was not yours, that Mr. Bottomry claimed. According to your own wild inference it was my own ·debt I paid, as Mr. Bottomry held a lien upon the Lacy lands."

"I must pay that money, sir."

"Cousin Ret, listen to me a few moments," said he, with calm desperation. "You are young and may marry again."

"Never! never! You are cruel to say so!"

"Oh, forgive me if I pain you. I would gladly die to shield you from pain. And now I make all my explanations at once: It was my right to pay Jack's debts, for I loved him. Judge how I loved him when I yielded *you* to him! You! you whom I have loved all my life! Ah! Ret, do not answer me, but listen. Let me spend my life in comforting yours!"

"Oh, how cruel!" she broke in, passionately, as she rose from her chair. "You who have been so kind and good until to-day! Who would have thought that you could wound me so deeply!"

"If loving you with every pulse of my heart——"

"You insult me, sir!" she answered, her eyes flashing. "How can you, who have been a noble gentleman hitherto, persecute me thus shamefully?"

Barston looked steadily at her beautiful face with an astonishment that would have been comical had it not been mixed with dire distress.

"Will you please——"

"There is nothing to explain which you do not already know, sir," said Ret, moving to the door. "Oh, Mr. Barston, I should be filled with indignation if I did not pity you!" and she swept out of the room. In a moment she burst in again, and running up to where he stood, stunned and silent, she said, "the memory of your friend and kinsman should have sheltered me, sir, and saved me from this pain, and you from such baseness!" He looked stupidly at her, without reply, wondering if she had gone mad. "A poor defenceless girl! Oh, Mr. Barston! I almost hate you!" and she bounced out like a shot, and this time did not return.

Roland was standing under a ruined arch near the portico, sheltered from the April down-pour. His master pulled his hat over his brow, buttoned his coat, and while the parting words of Lady Lacy were still ringing in his ears, he mounted and rode away from the Red Hall, never heeding the storm that swept over the earth, so engrossed was he with the storm of passion, dismay, remorse and sorrow that tortured his own bosom.

The arch was the remnants of an old sally port, and was undoubtedly a part of the ancient outer wall of Lacy Keep. It was

built of massive stones, and on the inner side adorned with gro-
tesque carvings of saints and angels. Besides the main arch
there were some fragments of the wall still standing, and the
entire ruin had been carefully preserved through later generations
of the Lacys, and was, in fact, the show ruin of the neighbourhood.
It was overgrown with ivy, and there were sundry hiding places
in the remains of the wall. Out of one of these, near the arch,
the scarred countenance of Mr. Butler peered, overspread with
a sardonic grin, and affording a sharp contrast to the pious expression on the stone faces in the arch, as he watched the horseman galloping away. It also afforded a very strong contrast to
the lovely face of Lady Lacy, watching *him* from her chamber
window.

CHAPTER XXVIII.

A MONOLOGUE—MASCULINE.

"'A DEFENCELESS girl!'" said Mr. Barston, as Roland
sped down the avenue; "'a defenceless girl,' she said.
It appears to me that she made a very respectable defence. By the
three kings! how beautiful she looked, while her eyes were blazing! How lovely, when they were drowned in tears! So she
'almost hates me!' I suppose if I had stayed a little longer the
almost would have grown into the altogether. 'Insulted!'
'wounded!' and by Lacy Barston, who has been worshipping her
with blind idolatry for a dozen years. By Lacy Barston, who
would bite off his tongue before he would insult a woman.
'Cruel!' and I have a reputation for such a degree of milk-
soppishness as would not hurt a fly!

"What *could* there have been in my words or manner that
roused such a devil in this gentle girl? I only told her that I
loved her. I am sure I should have endured it better than that
if the proposition were reversed! What a tigress she is—my
darling! She has rejected me point blank! Scouted me and
my offer with bitter reproaches! But she cannot prevent me
loving her," and he ground his teeth—"and I intend to love her
while I live—and afterwards, please Heaven!

"I was too abrupt. What a simpleton I was to blurt out a

declaration to this 'poor defenceless girl' without proper warning! I should have dangled after her five or six months, made
pretty speeches and written poetry! Oh, Ret! I thought you
had more sense. Alas! it was not that. She dislikes me personally, and she was outraged because I did not respect her
widowhood. She would have been better pleased if I had gone
about helping her moan over Jack! Why, the poor boy has
been nearly three years buried, and she spoke of him with the
coolest composure! But I have not seen her since he died, and
it would have been more decorous in me if I had gone over the
usual condolences! How is a fellow to know all these conventionalisms who has never had any practice in the humbug?

"It is clear that the difficulty is just there! For she said something about 'the memory of my kinsman' shielding her from my
outrageous proposal.

"I may as well face the situation. Second marriages are an
abomination. Suppose I had married Ret and lost her—could I
ever put another woman in her place? Never! never! My soul
recoils with unspeakable horror from the bare thought! Nay,
the thought of taking any other woman on the earth gives me a
regular fit of the horrors. I could never do it! And no doubt
Ret—I beg her pardon—Lady Lacy, cherishes the memory of her
husband as I should cherish her memory if I had suffered similar
bereavement.

"And so I have been led thus far astray by my blind and selfish passion, and have pained and shocked my beloved with brutal recklessness! Yonder reprobate said, 'Woe to the woman I
married,' and he was right! All my thoughts of comforting,
defending, protecting her, were unlimited bosh! I should have
made her life miserable! To think of linking such sweetness and
beauty to my rudeness! Ah! if Mr. Butler had only foreseen to-
day's experience, he need not have threatened me with 'thwarting
my plans.' I must leave the field to him. But I'll warn Parson
Johnny, by the three kings!

"I must go to London to-night and make Parchment fix these
title-deeds. The poor little defenceless vixen cannot prevent that
at least. I do not know how to prove Elbert Lacy's death, but
Parchment can manage it. What admirable wisdom the sharp
little woman displayed in that contest about the Lacy succession,
and she has gotten all her knowledge of the case from these musty
parchments. But Bottomry! How did she know about Bot-

tomry and DeVere? It is pretty certain that the rascals did not tell. Johnny has been prating, no doubt.

"It is raining like blazes, and I never knew it! I wonder if it was raining in this fashion when I left her ladyship, and if so, I wonder if she enjoyed the prospect before me—three miles to the nearest shelter. I will not believe it; she would not turn a dog out in such a storm as this.

"Just a year ago, in the blaze of the Polar moonlight, I climbed the high peak on the coast of Spencerland. I found the large saxifrage in the sheltered valley, and I kissed it—for her! and when I gained the summit of the black rock, where no mortal foot had ever stood before, I carved her name there with the spike of my Alpenstock, and it is there still, 'RET,' and I thought I should tell her of it some day, and of the peril I foolishly dared, merely for the sake of putting that inscription there! And afterwards, on my solitary tramp over floes and hummocks, how often I turned and looked back at the bald crag that bore her name.

"If she knew it she would go there, climb where I climbed, and chop out my inscription with a tomahawk!

"I wonder if any other fellow has been prowling about here or has met her in Essex? By the three kings! that would be a jolly business. She don't know anybody here but DeVere and Callahan. Is it possible that a puppy so unmitigated as DeVere could catch her fancy? Pooh! I'll not believe it. I cannot understand why I am not more demoralized, unless it is because she said 'Never! never!' when I suggested matrimony. If she had a liking for any other man she is the soul of truth and would have said so; and I would cut his throat! It is not that.

"One of two things must needs be true. I have cancelled the possibilities on the two sides—all but these:

"First, she must have been so devoted to Jack that the thought of marrying again is utterly abhorrent to her. Let us try that equation! Jack, poor boy, was not the sort of fellow to awaken an undying attachment. He was handsome, brave, truthful, indolent, and selfish. I may say so to myself alone, for I loved him. He thought he was madly in love, but he wasn't. Had he loved her he could not have gotten into the toils of those shallow knaves. Parson Johnny has told me enough to satisfy me that her married life was not happy. How did she come to marry him? Well, he was handsome, impetuous, was endorsed by Lord and Lady Morton, and Ret was fancy free. The marriage was very natural, and the subsequent repentance natural, too. I dismiss that proposition, therefore. It is not that.

"Second, for some sufficient reason she must hate me. What have I done or said? Could she, in her Harwood pride, resent my interference in that gambling business? No doubt Parson Johnny has told her, as I blabbed very freely to him; otherwise she could not have known about Bottomry and DeVere. When she was discussing the payment of that money her eyes flashed like the Cossack spear-heads when Jack and I rode down upon them! Oh, what eyes! and she keeps a lot of tears just under the lids to drown a fellow after she has scorched him pretty nearly to death, and beguiled him into a love declaration! But she is too sensible to hate me for that, and if I had allowed her to squander all that money in repayment the resentment would have died for lack of fuel. I dismiss that proposition also. It is not that.

"I wonder if I am conceited enough to think myself invincible? It was not conceit that prompted my sudden avowal just now. She looked so charming, and I have waited so long! It has been almost four years since I saw her, and I have been courting her diligently, in my thoughts, which no mortal could know, and I was foolish enough to think she might know with her quick wit. And there is that darling baby! I *must* have Nellie! She said this morning, "Oo may kiss me, for I love oo; but your beard 'cratches me!" I did kiss her, and Ret will kiss her, not knowing that she is so near to kissing me. It is a very unsatisfactory sort of proxy business, but it is better than none.

"My lady, do you think you have done with me?" and here he spoke through his set teeth. "If you do, you are greatly mistaken! But I must wait. If I had been allowed to select the circumstances of our late encounter I could not have arranged matters better. I leave her with a very plain declaration of love. She dismisses me with a very clear declaration of hostilities. I have these deeds, and I intend to fix them so that she cannot discover anything more than she has already guessed about the Lacy inheritance. If she insists upon paying that Bottomry money she may do it. It is all one. Nellie will get it anyhow. Since I sailed with Spencer my income has accumulated, and I am no poorer to-day for that outlay; and then she will remember that interview, and when she reflects upon her cruel words she will repent; and if she begins to repent she will be vanquished! But I'll not have her that way, either, by the three kings! She shall love me!

"And so I'll be off again to salt water. One day with Parchment, that is to-morrow, and then I'll take the first ship I can find. Where shall I go?"

"Porto Rico first. I must get some sugar. I have a half promise to Mrs. Dawson. Besides I want some for myself. These grocery rascals sophisticate their wares, and it will be jolly fun to watch all the manipulations, and to be certain of the purity of one hogshead at least. Then I shall go to Cuba. I want cigars, and I intend to see them made with my own eyes. I'll get a lot for Parson Johnny, too.

"There is Lavington, Roland; you sleek old villain, I am going to give you a long rest. I have three or four hours before train time for a bath, a dry suit, a letter to Parson Johnny and a smoke! Ah, Ret, my love! The prospect of leaving thee is appalling! But when I see thee again I shall leave thee no more, and I leave thee now only to be more sure of thee when I return."

CHAPTER XXIX.

ANOTHER MONOLOGUE—FEMININE.

WHEN Lady Lacy parted from Swiss so abruptly she ran into her chamber and locked the door. She threw her hat and shawl aside, and as she passed the window she saw Barston leading Roland from under the arch. She was a little shocked, as it was no part of her intention to send him away in the rain, and while she tried to think of a pretext for detaining him, he twisted his hand in Roland's mane and vaulted into the saddle. He passed her window like a flash, giving her a glimpse of his grave face as she drew back behind the curtain. It struck her suddenly that he was handsome. Then she saw the mocking face of Mr. Butler peeping out of the dripping ivy, and it occurred to her that *he* was hideous. Then, as the tramp of the galloping horse died away, she sat down and cried.

Of course!

You know how it is, reader. It makes no difference whether you are gentle or not.

"It is perfectly outrageous!" she began, clenching her little hands until the nails imprinted themselves upon her palms. "To think that I, of all the women in the world, should have been subjected to such an affront! Oh, why did I not scratch his big eyes out! How dared he do it!" and she sprang from her seat and began to stride about the room. "I had almost forgotten about his villainy when he began to talk about loving me. Me!" here she stamped viciously. "And it has only been a few hours since I heard him making love to that brazen minx, poor Kitty! No doubt he has been persecuting her with the voice of an angel and the heart of a fiend! Oh, how can he do it, the hypocrite? I cannot bear to think of it! What does that ugly wretch look so satisfied for? It is his work, telling his horrid lies about gentlemen! Ah, me! I heard him myself! Oh, Lacy Barston, I have no faith in mortal man! But that's a story! My Father and Johnny are true as steel! And Allen and Herbert! And I have been thinking these years that Lacy Barston was all that was noble and good! Ah! the deceitful wretch! to dare to talk to me of marriage!

"If it had been possible for me *ever* to think of such a thing I almost believe I could have learned to like this false villain! Oh, how thankful I ought to be that he was unmasked so thoroughly!

"I declare I have no patience with Father's cool way of discussing the matter! He seemed to think there was some satisfactory explanation. Oh, these men! Didn't I *hear* him?" As she passed the mirror she paused and glanced at the reflection of matchless loveliness—more lovely and attractive because of the distress in face and attitude. "What *can* he see in Kitty, I wonder? He is infatuated. Perhaps, he is a lunatic! A nice business to ask me to marry a lunatic!" and here she cried a little more.

"If he had not been thoroughly wicked he would never have ridden off in the rain! How it *does* rain! He is such a tiger of a man that he don't care for anything! I wonder what he will say when I meet him again? How shall I tell Mother what he just said to me? I cannot tell her! She would abhor him if she knew. I'll tell nobody!

"And there's Nellie, never tired of talking of him. He is not content with a moderate amount of wickedness, but wants to steal my child's heart. If I thought he really wished to marry Kitty! Oh, what an absurdity! he has never had such an intention! There goes that ugly gamekeeper! and he looks as triumphant as Satan! You are a fine gentleman, Mr. Barston, to choose such a rival as that! He is going to the housekeeper's room. I wish Mrs. Froome would give him a regular dressing! If he is courting Kitty I will get Father to give him more wages and let them marry. It would be a triple kindness! Certainly a kindness to these two, and a mercy to that poor misguided man, who must be half drowned by this time. Drowned! He *can't* be drowned. Ah, he don't know that *I* know of his exploit when we were at the Smuggler's Cave! To think that he has actually saved my life! Because John told me that he could never have caught the boat, and when Mr. Barston got to him he was nearly exhausted! How came he there? Was he watching over *me?* Oh, dear! he said he '*relinquished*' me to John! My head will burst if I think any more about him!

"Mother did not seem at all shocked, though she was perplexed by Father's story. She said, 'ask Johnny;' as if Johnny *could* explain away that dialogue I overheard in the conservatory. If he could—oh, if he could! It wounds me so deeply to relinquish my good opinion of John's cousin! And then, if he never dared to speak to me again of love, I might come to forgive him in time.

"Did anybody ever see a man ride like this lunatic? He bounded from the ground as if he had wings on his feet, and tore away on that mad beast like the Wild Huntsman! I almost expected his horse to blow flames from his nostrils."

She poured some water in a basin and bathed her face, washing away the traces of tears. She moistened her handkerchief with eau de Cologne, and bound it round her temples. And she sat down to think.

"Johnny says I don't reason, but 'intuit' things. Let me try one point at a time. That is the way these wise men do. First: The gamekeeper's story. I believe he is really in love with Kitty, and if so, jealousy is the next step. It comes easily. His first charge related to Mr. Barston's meeting with Kitty on the Exeter road. But Nellie was the attraction there, perhaps. Naturally he was eager to see *John's* child, and Kitty's story of that encounter was very straight and simple. He could not have made love speeches with William listening. That is out of the question. So Butler probably told a story about *that*. Then, if he told stories about one thing he would do the same about another. I don't *believe a word* of that rascal's story. Why did his face wear such a triumphant grin just now? Shall I go ask Kitty? Never!

never!" and she drew herself up with haughty grace, while the blood rushed to her cheeks and temples.

"Second: Can there be any explanation of what I heard in the conservatory? He said, 'Kitty, you must come to Oakland and *live* there.' And then he said something about wrecking *her* happiness. He did not mention *his* happiness. Altogether he did not talk like a man in love. The mere words may be explained, as they were not enforced with *tones*. It was a far different tone he used in the library just now, when he said 'he loved *me* with every pulse of his heart!' If he had not been talking such foolishness, his voice would have *forced* me to believe him!" and once more the crimson hue overspread her face and neck.

"Suppose there had been no Kitty in the world, and he had said all *that* to me! What could I have said? Alas! I cannot tell. He is such an obstinate wretch that he would not have listened to my objections. Of course such a thing is too absurd to think of! A young, rich, handsome man, who knows everything and can do anything he pleases, and who could marry almost any girl in England, to throw himself away upon a poor widow! Why, Clare Tamworth would be a more suitable match, a hundred times! And he could get her easily if he tried. I vow I will quit thinking about him!

"I am glad we are going to Carlisle next week! Clare is set upon that visit, and I am longing to get out of this neighbourhood for a few weeks. And it is not probable that any persecutors will follow us there, unless he should conclude to court Clare—the perfidious wretch! There, I am thinking of him again! But it would be so ridiculous to overhear him telling Clare that he loved her 'with every pulse of his heart!'

"The most reasonable thing to expect is, that Johnny will come over here in a day or two, with some story in defence of his beloved Swiss. If we can only get away before he does!

"But Mr. Barston is so devoted to Nellie that he might come to Carlisle to see her. Suppose I leave her here with Kitty? That would be a real sin, for if he had a clear field, me away, and nobody to take care of that poor girl, nobody can tell what might be the consequences! With that voice of his and those big eyes, that look so honest and gentle and loving, that horrid man could delude a saint!

"I don't think I *can* quit thinking about him. He shocked me so dreadfully with his fierce way of talking that I am entirely unstrung. A pretty way he has of making love! To say such dreadful cross things to a poor woman, and then to rush out of the house and gallop off in that insulting manner. If I harboured resentment, I should be delighted to hear that he had taken cold and was dangerously ill. Ah!" she said, with a charming little shudder, "how wicked I must be even to think of such a thing. This is a fine return for saving my life!

"It seems like yesterday when this great giant was a boy and full of boyish pranks, leading my brothers into mischief and always standing between them and harm. I can recall a hundred tricks, but not one unkindness, and no one ever accused him of falsehood; yet if these accusations were true, he would be both cruel and false! What would Johnny say to such charges?

"What an irritable, ill tempered man he must be! Instead of explaining his misbehaviour he must tear away in a towering rage, and that after such violent professions of love and devotion. If he ever dares to renew his professions I——"

CHAPTER XXX.

THE RECTOR EXPLAINS.

THE rector dined at Morton Priory on the day whose events are recorded above. The rain continued far into the night, and he, nothing loth, remained at his Father's house. Two days after, he, with Lord and Lady Morton, were at the Red Hall whose inmates were busy with preparations for a visit to Scotland. Miss Tamworth appeared to have charge of all the arrangements, and Lady Lacy was preoccupied and silent. Her languor disappeared, however, when the rector suddenly said:

"I have a message for you, Ret, from Swiss."

"A message?"

"Yes; I have the letter here somewhere," and he fumbled in various pockets. "Ah! here it is. I'll read what he says. Um! um!"

"Read it all, John," said his mother.

"Oh, no ; Miss Tamworth might come in. Where is she, Ret?"

"In her own room. She is preparing for our journey to-morrow, and will not be here for an hour."

"Well, then, I'll read it all. There are no secrets in it, but it would look odd to Miss Clare——"

"Never mind Clare," said Ret, snappishly; "read while you have the opportunity."

The rector looked at her with surprise, but obediently began to read :

" 'My dear Parson'—he's in London, you know—that is, he was. Nobody can tell where he is now. 'My dear Parson, I have two or three things to tell you to-night. First, about Kitty——' "

" Ah !" said Lady Morton, " that is precisely what I am most eager to hear."

"Indeed !" said the rector; " what makes you so interested in Kitty, Mother ? Ret is the proper person to——"

" Will you please read the letter ?" said Ret, with perfect outward composure.

"Certainly. Where was I ? Oh! first about Kitty. I must stop here, Ret, to explain about Kitty—Mother wishes to know. Well, ma'am, Kitty was left to Swiss by her father."

"Left to Swiss ! What rubbish are you talking, Parson ?" said Lord Morton.

" It is all right, sir. When old Willis was in his last illness I sent Swiss to see him. Ah, if you only knew how Swiss can talk ! The old man told me afterwards that he was an angel ! And he told the truth—only Swiss is better than an angel ?"

" John, how dare you talk in that fashion !"

" Far better, Mother. An angel cannot have human sympathy, and Swiss is filled with it. An angel could not make any man or woman love him to distraction, and Swiss can."

"Including Kitty ?" said Lady Morton quietly.

" Ma'am !"

" I say, has he inspired Kitty with this distracting attachment ?"

" I don't know what you mean, Mother. Swiss is a gentleman, and it would not occur to him to try his powers of fascination upon Kitty Willis."

"Indeed ! Well, sir, that is just what is said of him."

" Who is responsible for the slander ?" replied the rector hotly. " Mother, *you* did not believe it, surely !"

" I have suspended my judgment in the case until I could hear from you. Your Father said he would ask you."

" I forgot it," said Lord Morton. " The story is a short one, Parson. The gamekeeper, Butler, told me that Mr. Barston was persecuting Kitty with his attentions——"

"Attentions !" said his son, aghast. "My dear Father, how

could you be deluded by so monstrous a story? Kitty is a good girl and is good looking; but Lacy Barston, the scholar, the accomplished gentleman, the bright Christian—humble as any, yet more haughty in his ancestral pride than

'Haughty Gunhilda's haughtier lord!'

Really, I am ashamed to discuss so absurd a proposition. The man is an ass or a rascal! Here, listen to Swiss: 'First, about Kitty. I saw her three or four times, and urged her to take the housekeeper's place at Oakland. The old woman with whom she has lived so long would also take some position there, to shelter the girl from evil tongues. I had a long talk with Butler, and almost concluded to withdraw my opposition, when I remembered her father's earnest appeal to me to watch over his orphan child. Johnny, I am afraid Butler is bad—wholly bad. I fancy he is a man of good blood and I fear he has lost his place in society by the commission of some horrible crime. I must tell you the whole truth, and I do it most reluctantly. I have nothing to support my opinion but vague instincts, yet when I challenged him to unfold his past, he put me off with dreadful words about his father, whose very memory he abhors. Yet with all this distrust and repugnance I am strangely drawn to this miserable man, whose life I saved at sea. He almost cursed me for doing it! Now that I am away, I pray you investigate this case. If your mother or sister, or both, would undertake it, out of pure compassion for a motherless girl, it would be far safer in their hands. In my clumsy efforts to aid and shelter her I have made her hate the very sight of me, and I have positively failed to accomplish any good. If I had any influence over her it is lost——!"

He was interrupted by his sister, who rose from her seat and pointed through the window at a man on the lawn. It was Butler.

"It seems to me, Father, that your gamekeeper should make some explanation, and he happens to be here. No time like the present." She spoke with composure, though her face was flushed and her little hands clenched. The wrong she had done in her thoughts to poor Swiss filled her with sorrow, and with her repentance she remembered the diabolical grin she had seen on Butler's face when Barston, laden with her reproaches, left Lacy Keep.

"Yes," answered her Father promptly, and passing through the window he held up his finger to the gamekeeper, who approached at his signal.

" Mr. Barston has explained all that was mysterious about his interviews with Kitty, and your insinuations were false." This was said with severe dignity, and Johnny expected to see the other confused and apologetic.

" Indeed!" replied Butler, with a sneer. " Your lordship is easily satisfied. Or, perhaps, you may think this gay young gentleman is justifiable in filling a poor young girl's mind with wrong notions."

" What do you mean, man!" replied Lord Morton; " do you persist in charging this gentleman with wicked intentions——"

" That is as your lordship pleases," said Butler coolly. " I have told no lies, and I am as incapable of that vice as your lordship——"

" How dare you!" said Lady Lacy, suddenly appearing at her father's side. The gamekeeper removed his hat, yet returned her haughty glance without wincing.

" Your ladyship will pardon me," he said, " but I do not understand. I am on my defence, it seems, yet I do not yet know whom I have offended."

" Go in, Ret," said Lord Morton. " Butler, I would not do you an injustice, yet you have done a foul wrong in this matter. Had I not known Mr. Barston so well I should have been misled by your cunning story. I can make allowance for jealousy——"

" Pooh!" said Butler. " Excuse me, my lord. I cannot be held responsible for your inferences. Mr. Barston has been very officious in his interference with my affairs——"

" Speak with respect of your superiors, sir."

" I do not recognize them in Mr. Barston or his associates, such as Mr. DeVere. If your lordship is displeased I will retire. I have no apology to offer for anything I have said or done."

" I give you warning to quit my service——"

" No warning necessary, my lord," responded the other. " I am paid up to yesterday and I will vacate your premises to-night. Will Lady Lacy allow me to say a word to her nurse?"

Lord Morton turned into the room, but Ret was gone.

" There is no reason for denying you if she is disengaged," said Lady Morton. " If you apply to the housekeeper she will inform Kitty that you wish to see her. I think it would be right, however, to say what you have to say in Mrs. Froome's presence."

" I do not object, madame," said Butler. " I only wish to explain to Kitty my changed relations, and the cause. I also wish to be the first to announce her deliverance from persecution. Ha! ha! pardon me, your reverence, but I cannot help laughing to think how your zeal and Mr. Barston's have resulted."

"I wish you would come to the Rectory to-morrow," said the rector gently. "If you will allow me to befriend you and Kitty it will give me great pleasure. There are things you might say to me that you would not reveal to others——"

"You mean, to explain 'my antecedents,' as the Yankees say? Thank your reverence! You are too low church in your views to favour the confessional. If I go into that business I will apply to Father Tom, who will probably let me off more lightly."

"What a devil the man is!" sighed the rector, as the other passed out of sight around the angle of the house.

"Swiss is right," said Lady Morton, decidedly. "This man is well born and has been driven by crime from his proper station. I think, also, he is wholly bad! Herbert, my dear, I thank you for dismissing him. Where is Ret?"

CHAPTER XXXI.

THE LETTER.

WHEN Lady Lacy returned to the room from the terrace in obedience to her father's command, her mother and brother were standing in the window, interested in the discussion between Lord Morton and Butler. She espied the open letter on the table, and with the superb grace of a tigress she noiselessly caught it up, and after glancing hurriedly at the others, she silently passed out of the room. Gaining her chamber she locked the door, and falling on her knees upon a low ottoman under the window, she spread out the sheets on the table and began to read. It is possible, and under the circumstances not indecorous, for the gentle reader to peep over her shapely shoulder. Although the rector has already read a portion of the letter, it will be more satisfactory to the reader, probably, to have it all together.

LONDON, *1st May.*

MY DEAR PARSON:

I have two or three things to tell you to-night. First, about Kitty. I saw her three or four times, and urged her to take the housekeeper's place at Oakland. The old woman with whom she has lived so long would also take some position there to shelter the girl from evil tongues. I had a long talk with Butler, and almost concluded to withdraw my opposition, when I remembered her father's earnest appeal to me to watch over his orphan child. Johnny, I am afraid Butler is bad—wholly bad. I fancy he is a man of good blood, and I fear he has lost his place in society by the commission of some terrible crime. I must tell you the whole truth, and I do it most reluctantly. I have nothing to support my opinion but vague instincts. Yet when I challenged him to unfold his past, he put me off with doubtful words about his father, whose very memory he abhors! Yet, with all this distrust and repugnance, I am strangely drawn to this miserable man, whose life I saved at sea. He almost cursed me for doing it. Now that I am away, I pray you investigate this case. If your mother or sister, or both, would undertake it out of pure compassion for a motherless girl, it would be far safer in their hands. In my clumsy efforts to aid and shelter her I have made her hate the very sight of me, and I have positively failed to accomplish any good. If I had any influence over her it is lost, and I begin to think I am a general failure. Perhaps if she is in love with this fellow she may be able to control him, and deliver him from evil habits, and all my obstinate interference may have been so much resistance to the orderly march of beneficent Providence.

"Nevertheless, I cannot shake off the responsibility her father put upon me, except by transferring it to the excellent ladies I have named. If they will assume the trust, my cares are at an end. Use your eloquence, Parson, in Kitty's behalf.

The second matter relates to Lady Lacy. When I saw her last we had some controversy, touching transfers of certain property. Will you please deliver this message? Tell her I hold to *every word* I said to her with a tenacity as relentless as death. There is nothing possible or conceivable in the events of Providence that can change *any part* of my opinions or desires as related to her. Yet I cannot contend with her, and will obey her commands as accurately as possible. The title to the Lacy lands now stands in her, with no chance of litigation as against her, except such litigation should be begun by Lacy Barston. If she insists upon this litigation, I beg to refer her to Mr. Alfred Parchment, who is my solicitor, and her's also, I believe. You know, or rather *she* knows, that the whole question rests upon the interpretation of the will of Sir Harold Lacy—three generations old.

" Speaking as a lawyer, I should say here that a serious obstacle in the way of settlement is found in the difficulty of proving
Elbert Lacy's death. While I have no doubts on that point, it would
still be proper to demand security from any holder of the Lacy
lands who should propose a transfer of title. *My* title depends
solely upon the extinction of the Lacy line, and I cannot eject her
by legal process until I *prove* the line extinct. To do this I must
prove Elbert dead, which would be (legally) both difficult and
expensive. As a matter of pure economy, I prefer leaving her
in peaceable possession.

" Another point relates to certain money transactions between
Sir John Lacy and Lacy Barston. I am the holder of a mortgage
upon the Red Hall and lands for ten thousand pounds. It was
transferred to me by Mr. Bottomry. Parchment would not allow
me to cancel this mortgage two or three years ago, as I desired,
and if your sister still wishes to pay it, I am bound in common
honesty to warn her that the document is defective, as Sir John
had no (legal) right to transfer, while his elder brother's death
was unproven.

" Still another point relates to other money transactions, for
which I have no legal vouchers. It pains me no little to recur to
these matters, but my lady is obdurate, and *noblesse oblige.* I will
make a fair statement of these when I return, and will abide by
her decision.

" When I return ! I cannot now say when this will be. I am
writing in the cabin of the *Dixie,* a side wheel steamer that will
go down the river an hour hence, bound for ' Nassau and a market.' She is laden with sundry commodities very much in demand
in the southern half of the Disunited States, and is commanded by
Frank Hazard, who was Spencer's first officer and my good friend.
I am only a passenger this time. I expect to investigate the condition of affairs in the Confederate States, as the *Dixie* thinks of
going to Charleston for the market which may not be found at
Nassau. She also thinks of returning with a cargo of cotton, if
the blockade of the southern ports is not too strong. Some one
has asserted to me that New Orleans sugar is better than that
from Porto Rico. I hope to satisfy myself by personal inspection
on this point. If I get into the Southern States and *out* again
with a whole skin, I purpose a short visit to the West India
Islands. Cuba for cigars, mainly for you and your father, and
Porto Rico for sugar, mainly for Mrs. Dawson and her landlord.

"By the bye, Johnny, please ride Roland down to Ripple occasionally and look after the old lady a little. Roland knows the way. And give Tommy an occasional half crown; it is the tip he expects from Roland's rider. You will recognize Tommy by his mouth. Nature has been bountiful to him in that regard, and no animal except an alligator can rival him. If you tell Mrs. Dawson you love me, she will give you a curd of astounding elegance.

"And now, dear friend, I am admonished by the noises above my head that my time is nearly up. I also hear the singing of the steam, and Hazard tells me the last boat will quit the ship in half an hour. You will wonder what strange freak has taken me away from England. I cannot explain to you now, though I may do so hereafter. I will only say that I have been nourishing a scheme for many years, looking to the acquisition of a certain possession more valuable than all my inheritance. I thought I was tolerably near the attainment, but have suddenly learned that I must wait—I cannot tell how long. But I am resolved to pursue this object until I die, unless it shall be revealed to me that sin is in the pursuit. It does not seem so to me now. If you were to ask me how I fell into so egregious a blunder as to think I was near possession, I cannot tell you. I do not know. It is mysterious, perplexing, humiliating. And my restless spirit longs for the restless sea.

"When I get upon blue water my mind is usually clear. At present I am stunned, stupefied as one who has been feeding upon opium must feel. The course of Providence has been inscrutable to me. Obstacles confronted me from the first inception of desire for this prize, which has been the solitary object of my life, and longed for with a passionate longing that is inexpressible. It is so much a part of my life that I think my life would end if the longing died. And as the stately march of Providence removed the first obstacle, a second, more insurmountable, took its place, and compelled my acquiescence. I thought it was gone forever, but I was mistaken, and when this also was taken away it seemed to wrench from me memory, consciousness, hope, faith, and all the attributes of manhood. Then I fled to the sea again, and on its broad bosom I found peace at last and the old hope revived. It would avail nothing to tell you what new plans I laid, and how I approached with steadfast steps the attainment once more. It was too soon, and the coveted possession, almost within my grasp as I thought, eluded me.

" And as I go forth again, with a purposeless energy that seems akin to madness, I am only conscious of one unshaken determination, to hold fast to my pursuit, and wait.

"I am upheld in this resolve by the profound conviction that the prayers of my whole lifetime cannot be wasted. And the success which I shall win at last will fully atone for all the disappointments I have hitherto endured.

"Anchor atrip! Farewell, dear friend.

"LADY BARSTON."

As she read the concluding lines Lady Lacy covered her face with her hands, and while the tears dropped through her slender fingers upon the open letter she murmured:

"Oh dear! oh dear! what *shall* I do! He thinks me cruel, heartless, proud, unreasonable, and yet he loves me, he loves me!"

Later in the day the rector applied to his sister, with troubled countenance, for consolation.

"Ret," he said, " I walked down to the Dark Wood since Butler was here, and I have lost Barston's letter! I am *sure* I thrust it in my pocket when that fellow was talking to Father, and then I forgot all about it until I returned from my walk. I have turned all my pockets inside out! I have been down to the Wood again, but it's gone! There was a long message to you in it!"

"Can you not remember it?" she answered, with deceitful composure.

"No! It was something about title deeds and law matters, and there was a great lot of bosh in it about some wild goose chase upon which he has set his heart. I thought you might help me to understand what the lunatic is driving at. I'll go back to the Wood and take another hunt for it."

"Very well, Johnny," said Ret, sympathetically. "If you fail to find it you can tell me the main points, and I can guess the rest. Make haste back."

And when the perplexed rector passed through the ruined arch, on his hopeless errand, the heartless vixen drew the letter from her bosom and nefariously kissed it!

Gentle reader, these feminine characters give an enormous amount of trouble. One may honestly endeavour to describe their tricks, but their motives are beyond human scrutiny.

CHAPTER XXXII.

CLARE'S SYMPATHY.

SO little has been said hitherto about Miss Clare Tamworth, that the reader must be somewhat doubtful about her mental exercises, as she has kept so quiet and undemonstrative. It is possible that Lady Lacy has a positive identity in the minds of all who have patiently read the foregoing pages. In the hope that his duty as a faithful chronicler has been discharged in her case, the author leaves her to work out her natural destiny, while a little more direct attention is bestowed upon her chosen friend and companion.

The playful accusation of our friend Swiss was founded upon fact. This amiable young lady was lover proof. Barston had really met with two or three doleful swains in London, whose best powers of fascination had been tried upon Miss Tamworth in vain. One of them, the Viscount Lappermilk, was specially discomfited. He was an Oxford man, and Barston had befriended him there in his hopeless digging among Greek roots, and won his gratitude and confidence, and he unbosomed himself over a dinner at the club in this wise:

"Miss Tamworth, Swiss, is a wegular stunnah! She has lots of tin, too. Don't twy for it, ol' fellah, you cawnt go in and win. I twied; and weally, I got so spoony that I forgot the tin. But she is equally beyond the weach of delibewate appwoaches or the passionate wush. I twied both."

Although Lord Lappermilk was himself rather impecunious, he was the son and heir of an earl, and would inherit a very fine estate some day, and Swiss frankly told him that he should waste no energies in pursuing so coy a damsel. "She has won honour enough, Lappermilk," he said, "in throwing you over. I shall not give her the chance to repeat the exploit upon me."

"She did not exactly throw me ovah!" replied the Viscount. "When I made the wush she said it was pwetty, and she had wead it in a book. I assured her that I spoke my weal sentiments and was wegular spoony, and she wung the bell and told the flunkey to 'bwing Lord Lappermilk a glass of iced water.' As she chose to take it in that way I thought I would not pwess the mattah. But she is without a heart, Swiss."

To disprove this slander is the purpose of the present chapter. When the Reverend John Harwood started for the Dark Wood the second time, he met Miss Tamworth near a belt of shrubbery beyond the ruined arch.

"My dear Miss Clare," he said, "I have lost a letter that I am most anxious to recover." ·

"Can I aid you in your search?" said she.

"Yes! Perhaps you may find it in the shrubbery. I think I passed through this edge of it as I went to the Wood. I am going back there. It is from Swiss."

"Where is he?" inquired Miss Tamworth. "I miss him dreadfully."

"He is on the sea by this time," answered the rector, with a pang of jealousy. "If you are so much interested in him I am glad he is gone!"

"On the sea! What unexplored regions does he seek this time?"

"I think he is going among the Yankees. It is some sort of piratical expedition. The letter tells, if we can only find it. I'll be back in fifteen minutes," and he walked hastily away.

When she entered the little grove of evergreens Miss Tamworth diligently examined the ground at each step without finding the lost letter. It is not probable that her search would have been successful if she had examined every square inch of the plantation. She was slightly startled to see Butler standing in the path when she raised her eyes. Kitty was just disappearing in the direction of the Hall.

"Will Miss Tamworth do me the great kindness to listen five minutes——"

"Not here, certainly," replied she, as she turned to follow Kitty.

"I beg your pardon," persisted Butler, "if you will look across the fence here you will see the gardener within call. What I say to you must be said secretly if at all!"

"What do you wish?" said Clare, with calm dignity.

"I wish you to believe me. First of all, I am a gentleman of good name and the rightful owner of a fair inheritance. I can offer you no proof but this;" and he pulled off his leather glove an stretched out his hand, white and small, with long tapering fingers· "I thought I might rely upon the instinct of a well-bred lady to recognize one of her own class even in this disguise." This was said with steady composure. "I was Lord Morton's gamekeeper an hour ago, but have been dismissed, mainly because I intend to marry yonder girl."

"Kitty Willis?" said Miss Tamworth. "You surprise me. I know nothing about the matter. Supposing you are telling the truth about your own station, which I do not dispute, I cannot see the propriety of the match you propose. It is not probable that your family——"

"I am thankful to say that I am alone in the world. None of my kindred, near enough to call for affectionate interest, remain upon the face of the earth. Besides, the girl is better bred than you suppose. Anyhow, I am bound in honour to marry her, for I promised when we were children a dozen years ago, and I have never yet failed to redeem my word; and she is dearer to me than any other woman can ever be. I only wanted to ask you to be kind to her."

"I am not aware that I have been unkind to her."

"Far from it, madam. On the contrary, I am emboldened to make this appeal to you because you have been specially kind. If you will consider what is involved in orphanage and poverty—at least such measure of poverty as makes this place and her wages important to her—and think of the torture inflicted by mistaken kindness on the part of the rector and his friend, Mr. Barston——"

"I cannot imagine what you are talking about," said Clare, impetuously; "What do you mean by saying these things?"

"I mean that her pastor thinks the discharged gamekeeper is not good enough for her, and tells her so. I mean that Mr. Barston told her two days ago that I was a brute, and unfit to marry any decent girl; and I mean that I would rely more upon your gentle charity and your quick wit to shield her while I am absent than upon anything else. Mr. Barston——"

"Will not trouble you or Kitty very soon. He has gone on a piratical expedition."

"What say you?" said the other, a paleness overspreading his face. "What horrible words are these?"

"I suppose it was only the rector's joke," she said, a little shocked at the effect of her words; "but Mr. Barston has really sailed for America."

"On board the *Dixie*, I'll be sworn! Do you know, Miss Tamworth, that I should have sailed in that ship if she had delayed her departure only one more day? and finding Barston aboard, I swear I would have scuttled the ship to get finally rid of him!

What a narrow escape for us both! for I cannot quarrel with Barston, for two weighty reasons; one, he saved my life once——"

"And the other?" said Clare, as he paused.

"No matter about the other; one is sufficient. I am greatly relieved to know he is out of England. Miss Tamworth, I thank you for your kindness in listening to me. I ask no promise from you; I only remark that I desire to remain unknown and unsuspected for the present, and only you and Kitty know that I am anything more than Butler the drunken gamekeeper. If you could be told all of my story I should be certain of your sympathy." He brushed his hand across his eyes as he spoke. "How much of my present distress is due to my own misconduct, and how much to the flagrant wrong doings of others, I cannot say, and you would hardly care to hear. Adieu, madam. It is not probable that we shall ever meet again!" and suddenly opening a wicket in the fence and crossing the garden, he passed from her sight forever.

"Poor man!" said Clare; "this is decidedly romantic. ' He must be a gentleman, or else the prince of dissemblers! Anyhow, I sympathize with him in his distress, and will keep his secret. I shall have opportunities to question Kitty when we get to Carlisle. I must also find out why the rector takes so deep an interest in Kitty. Here he comes, without his letter." As Mr. Harwood approached she recommenced her search, flitting in and out among the trees like a well grown bird of paradise.

"How kind of you," said Parson Johnny as he joined her, "to hunt for that tiresome letter. "Never mind it; some one will find it, probably, and return it."

"Mr. Butler was here just now," replied Clare, "and I saw Kitty also, just after you left me."

"Indeed! Well, if they should happen to read it they will scarcely approve of all Barston's sentiments. He speaks of them both in it."

"Do you remember what he says?"

"Yes; that is, I remember the general drift of his remarks. Swiss thinks Butler is a scamp, and so do I. He confronted my Father to-day in a manner that was rather insolent, considering his station. Swiss thinks that the fellow is better bred than he appears."

"So do I," answered Miss Tamworth.

"You do? well, that settles it. But Barston also fears that he has committed some crime by which he lost caste. He will not allow any one to question him about the past. I noticed that you called him *Mr.* Butler just now."

"Did I? He reminds me of some one I have known, but I cannot tell whom. What does Mr. Barston say of Kitty?"

"A great deal. He knew her father, and has always taken a great interest in her. Butler is courting her—indeed they are so far agreed that they will marry, no doubt. This makes us eager to know more about him for the girl's sake."

"Probably you had better let them alone. Here is Ret; let us ask her. Ret, what do you think of Butler?"

"I think he is a rascal. I was looking for you. The dressing bell has just rung. Come in."

"You Harwoods are a hard hearted, suspicious, obstinate set," said Clare impetuously. *I* believe Butler is a good sort of man, and if he wants to marry Kitty I mean to help him. There! You need not look so astounded. I have been allowing you to have your own way so long that you are well nigh ruined. When we get to Carlisle I am going to conspire with Kitty to circumvent you. Come on, Ret."

"Did you find your letter, Johnny?" asked Lady Lacy, as they entered the hall. "Well, never mind it, dear."

CHAPTER XXXIII.

Two Years Later.

THE events which have happened during this unrecorded interval do not affect the course of the present narrative materially. After various adventures Mr. Barston found himself in New York at the end of two years, and secured passage to Liverpool by the Royal Mail Steamer *Scotia*. The only circumstance to notice was his accidental meeting with a countryman in New York, one John Hawder, whom he had known in his boyhood. Hawder's father was steward of the Lacy estates, and the younger Hawder had emigrated to America several years before. He was a widower and had a child, born in the new country, and the sight of our friend Barston was a bright spot in their dull lives. From Hawder he learned that Mr. Butler, whom he recognized by his description, had been in New York a year or two previously, indulging in evil habits without stint. Barston hoped to learn something of his early history from Hawder, but he knew only some fragmentary portions of his story that did not enlighten Barston, but rather confirmed him in his distrust of the game-keeper. Hawder was about starting to take charge of a farm in the interior of New Jersey, and knowing that Swiss would see his kindred in Lavington, he gave him a post-office address to leave with them. Barston rarely forgot anything, and this address was useful to him later.

Shortly after Barston's departure from England Lady Lacy and her friend, Miss Tamworth, went to Paris, thence to Switzerland, where they spent the summer. There was no intelligence from Mr. Barston for nearly two years. He was in the Confederate States a large part of the time, and postal communication with the outside world was attended with difficulties. He finally escaped in a blockade-runner, bound for Nassau, but being chased by Federal cruisers, was driven into the Gulf, and finally found shelter in Kingston, Jamaica. Mr. Barston being unoccupied, assisted in the ceremonies attending three tornadoes and one small earthquake, and then sailed for Port Rico. Here he invested some sovereigns in sugar, which was duly shipped to London, and forwarded thence to Lavington. The rector received a brief letter from his friend, who wrote very hurriedly on the eve of his departure for New York, and only advised him of this shipment, and requested him to have two barrels filled from the hogs-head, sending one to the Red Hall, with his compliments, to Lady Lacy, and the other to Ripple Farm. He promised to write at length from New York, but as he sailed by the first mail steamer after his arrival he did not fulfil his promise.

One bright morning the Reverend John Harwood was caught round the waist on the main street of Lavington by a stalwart man, with bright eyes and enormous beard, rudely shaken up and actually hugged, to the great astonishment of two small boys, pupils in the rector's sunday school, who had just been patted on their heads and made recipients of sixpence each.

"My dear, dear Parson!" said Swiss, "my heart is filled with joy at seeing you once more!"

"Welcome home, my dear Swiss," answered the rector warmly, "I am truly happy to see you again. When do you embark, and for what port?"

"I have done with the sea, Johnny. Have you any cold meat and bread at your house? I am famishing with hunger."

"That is jolly! I have not had breakfast yet. Come on! I heard the train just now, but did not hope for this pleasure. I am forlorn here now. Father is in London, Ret is in Scotland. If your next ship does not sail for two days you can get a glimpse of them all."

"Get out with your quips, Parson," returned Swiss. "I tell you I meditate no new flights. My confident expectation is to spend the rest of my days on this blessed island. You ought to be above assaulting a starving man. Do you know whether you have any chops in your larder?"

"Certainly, plenty of them! *Soyez tranquille!* Within ten minutes your cravings shall be appeased. Where is your next ship going?"

"To Kamschatka! I want a chaplain, and will take you. Here is the rectory. Have you got a rectoress yet? Why have you not written to me these years? How d'ye do, Bridget?"

"Wilcome home, Mr. Lacy," said that hard featured female. "The master tould me yees was coming, and ye'll find your room in order. Breakfast is all ready, sir."

Mr. Barston, who was entirely humanized within an hour, plied the rector with questions. The Ripple Farm people were prosperous and unchanged, except that Tommy had increased in stature. Mr. Harwood had been there about once a week, and usually partook of curds. Mrs. Dawson had received her sugar and the Red Hall barrel had been forwarded, but Lady Lacy and her household were at Stirling. Nellie had grown, and being petted by three uncles and two grandparents, was totally ruined, but more charming than ever. Miss Tamworth was still unmarried, and, in the Parson's judgment, was a confirmed man-hater. Lady Lacy was in excellent health, but wore habitually the chastened expression that came with her widowhood. Johnny's profound conviction was, that poor Ret's heart was buried in the cemetery of the Lacys. Swiss thought he would try to dig it up, but was somewhat discomfited by the rector's gloomy views.

Mr. Butler had been remarkably erratic in his movements. He had disappeared for a year or more, very soon after Barston sailed in the *Dixie.* Then he had been visible again in Lavington, and was usually attired in well made gentleman's costume. His habits were possibly better. The rector had met him once or twice and endeavoured to converse with him, but pumped nothing better than monosyllables from him. About Kitty he positively declined to talk at all.

Kitty was a model of propriety and reticence. All the efforts Mr. Harwood had made to ascertain the state of her mind had been unavailing. She listened with great politeness and attention to his moral essays, but declined to criticise them. Lady Morton and Ret had talked very kindly to her, and she expressed great thankfulness, but did not say a word as to her intentions. Miss Tamworth steadfastly opposed this kind interference, and the rector said " She patted Kitty on the back, in a figurative sense, and in a most exasperating manner."

" The truth is, Swiss," said the rector, " I am beginning to think that we have no right to annoy this girl any more. If she is not able to take care of herself I am very much mistaken. Mother says it is indecorous to proceed any further."

" That settles the point, Parson," answered Swiss; " you are always in peril when you run counter to the views of a good woman. And in this special case Lady Morton is doubtless the best judge. Did this fellow look like a gentleman ?"

" I think he did and does. I cannot forget that he filled a subordinate position in my Father's household, yet his manner is perfectly unaffected and natural. There is a certain roughness in his demeanour which might pass for eccentricity if one *knew* him to be thoroughbred. He has not been educated, I think. In one of my talks with him I quoted a line from Virgil, familiar to any schoolboy, and he said, coolly, ' I don't understand Latin.' If he had not been of a good breed he would, perhaps, have concealed his ignorance. My judgment is that he has been intractable and violent in his youth, refusing to submit to lawful authority, and has grown up to manhood without restraints, and is now hardened. He talks grammatically and with a good selection of words usually, though at times he indulges in regular sea lingo, as if that were his native tongue. Altogether the man bothers me horribly."

" I am delighted to hear it," said Barston, " and assure you of my genuine sympathy. I have never before encountered a man who was able to keep me in constant suspense as to his status. But I feel authorized to withdraw from the contest, and shall interfere with him no more. Indeed, if his habits are passably decent, it will afford me great pleasure to aid him in any way, for Kitty's sake. It would not be a kindness to help him to ruin."

" What have you been doing, Swiss, in these two years ?"

" A multitude of things, my friend. I have been in many hospitals, trying to comfort wounded, sick and dying men. I have been allowed to take last messages to bereaved wives and mothers. I have learned many lessons of heroic endurance, the like of which I shall never see again on earth. I could not fully appreciate the sentiments of the men who resolutely faced untold horrors and who nourished a constant expectation of final success in the very face of death. Our fellows in the Crimea did about as good fighting as men could do, but there was no such manifestation of devotion to a *sentiment* there. You have told me nothing about Roland."

" The old rascal defies the march of time. He is here, ready for a gallop whenever you please."

" I will renew my acquaintance with him. I must go to Ripple this morning. We'll lunch on curds. Returning, I invite you to dine with me at Oakland——"

" I accept."

" Then at nine-twenty I purpose taking the up train——"

" Are you mad, Swiss ?"

" Sane, parson. But I must travel to-night."

" Whither ?"

" Towards the bleak north. To Stirling! I am dying for a sight of Nellie! You will please give me full directions where to look for the child——"

" Better than that, my friend. I will go with you ! I, also, am dying to see—Nellie !"

CHAPTER XXXIV.

STIRLING.

A MONG Miss Tamworth's possessions was a certain parcel of land in the outskirts of Stirling. A few acres, cut off from a farm which yielded her a small rental, were devoted to a cottage and the needful outhouses, all enclosed by a hedge and shaded by stately trees. It is probable that she spent a few months here, annually, only because of its proximity to the romantic scenery of the lochs, and at the date of the present chapter she and Lady Lacy were busily engaged in preparations for a visit to the Trossachs, Loch Katrine, and possibly to Edinburgh. All this country was new to Lady Lacy, and she looked forward to the excursion with bright anticipations. The Wizard of the North has invested all that portion of Her Majesty's dominions with special interest, and Ret studied with great eagerness the map of their projected journeys, noticing the succession of historic localities, and promising herself unmixed pleasure at every step of their progress. Later in the autumn they were to spend a month at Clifton, where Miss Clare professed to live, though for six or seven years she had been almost constantly a member of Lady Lacy's household. These present and proximate visitations were tacitly accounted a sort of return call, with the understanding that they would then resume their former relations, Miss Clare accepting Lady Lacy's hospitality for an indefinite time. These young women, who had been together from childhood, were sisters in affection, and each was necessary to the happiness of the other, sharing each other's secrets almost universally, but each having one little nook in her gentle heart hidden from all mortal scrutiny.

"Ret, my dear," said Clare, with elaborate indifference, "I think it very probable that your reverend brother will be here to-day or to-morrow."

"Indeed! He said nothing to me of such an intention."

"Yes, he did. He said he desired to accompany you to the Trossachs, and you told him we should go this week."

"Well. He is a good boy, my dear, and will not be troublesome."

"All men are troublesome, Ret, especially in travelling. It is true they make a great parade, getting tickets, attending to luggage, calling cabs and the like. But you can have all these things done by your maid, or if you really need a man, you can always get a railway porter, pay him a shilling and get rid of him after the service is rendered. You can't pay the rector a shilling and send him off!"

"May I tell him your views," said Ret, amused.

"Oh, certainly. But I have already told him."

"How did he like your sentiments?"

"My dear, all men are conceited. He said he was entirely satisfied to take the position, so long as I made no exceptions. But there was a pleasant smirk on his face, indicating his confidence in his own attractions. You can't get the conceit out of them by the plainest statements!"

"If he should come and accompany us it will be for the sake of escorting you, and I believe you are secretly delighted to have the poor boy dangling after you—you hard-hearted wretch!"

"Indeed, you are partly right," answered Miss Tamworth, tossing her head; "he is better than most of the danglers, in that he takes himself off for a quiet smoke about every hour, and one gets short intervals of rest. Ret, I want to look at the Lacy Diamonds!"

"That reminds me——" said Lady Lacy. "Kitty!"

"My lady?" answered Kitty from the garden.

"You are going with Nellie to drive presently. Go to Stirling to the jeweller's—here is his card—and get my brooch. You had better pin it in your collar for safety, securing the guard-chain; cover it with your scarf, Kitty. Here is a half crown. He only had to repair the guard-chain."

"Yes, my lady. The carriage is here now. Shall I go at once?"

"Yes. Now, Clare, you will have to wait Kitty's return. The earrings are up stairs."

"And the necklace——"

"Ah! that is not here. My dear, you have seen these gaudy toys a hundred times."

"I have not seen that necklace for half a dozen years."

"Nor I," answered Ret. There was a cloud upon her fair brow which the quick eye of her friend noticed. She drew near, put her arm around her neck and kissed her.

"Forgive my thoughtless folly, my love! I fear I have given you pain! Ret!" she continued, vehemently, "I do sincerely believe there is some dreadful curse about those diamonds! There! I have hurt you again! Shall I quit talking about them?"

"Yes, dear, if you don't mind," said Ret quietly. "There goes the carriage. Look at Nellie! She is driving!"

"Yes, and if that great monster, Mr. Barston, comes back he will teach her to swear at the horses! What an amiable lunatic the man is!" She was looking out the window and did not see the little glow that spread over her friend's face. "Nellie says the last time she rode with him she held the bridle, and he only talked to that wild beast he rides. Nellie says the horse stands dead still when he bids him. Ah!" she continued, with a little shiver, "what a life the poor woman whom he marries will lead!"

"Suppose you undertake him, Clare?" said her friend, with a little grain of spite.

"Never!" replied Clare. "Nobody knows where he is or where

he has been. It is quite probable that he has two or three wives already in the outlandish countries he has visited. He looks like a regular Bluebeard."

The innocent object of this vituperation was at that moment inspecting the horses in the stable of the "Castle" inn. He selected a steed and was soon cantering down the street, seeking the road that led to Miss Tamworth's cottage. A short distance from the town a lane deflected from the highway, and led along the margin of the beautiful Forth, and while Barston paused at the junction of the roads a carriage approached from the opposite direction, and he drew his horse aside to give it passage. A child in the carriage tossed up her arms with a cry of delight at the sight of him.

"Cousin Lacy!" she said, "take me, take me!"

"My Nellie! My darling! Will you come for a gallop with me?"

"Yes! yes!" said Nellie, struggling to reach him.

He took her in his arms, and restraining his restive horse he directed Kitty to meet them at the same spot an hour later, and then turning down the lane was out of sight in a minute.

"I thought you would have forgotten me, Nellie," he said, when he drew rein after a gallop. "Why, you dear little witch, you have grown a foot since I saw you."

"Yes," said Nellie, "I grow a little every day. Mamma says I may have a little pony when I grow two more feet. But I like to ride Roland with you."

"How did you know me so soon, Nellie?"

"I saw your eyes."

"Well, other people have eyes."

"Other people don't have *your* eyes," answered Nellie, positively. "Your eyes say, 'I love Nellie,' and Nellie loves you— *darely!*"

Swiss covered her upturned face with his flowing beard.

"You shall have a pony before you grow another inch, baby. I saw one in Mexico that will just suit you. I'll go back for it if need be."

"Don't want you to go back. I can ride Roland with you."

"Then I'll get you a Shetland. Or maybe you would like a donkey? There are some beautiful donkeys at Clifton."

"Don't think I like donkeys," said Nellie, doubtfully.

"You had better cultivate the liking, baby. Donkeys are very numerous. But we will try for the Shetlanders."

"Mamma says we are going to Clifton soon," observed Nellie. "We might have a donkey first."

"Very well. There are plenty of donkeys on the Downs. Now we will take another gallop. This brute is not like Roland."

When Mr. Barston reached the rendezvous his horse was minus a shoe and limped painfully. He relinquished the child to Kitty, catching a glimpse of her countenance, which wore a troubled expression, and he thought she looked wistfully at him.

"What is it, Kitty?" he said, kindly. She placed the child on the seat, and stepping out of the carriage came near his stirrup.

"I beg your pardon, Mr. Barston," she said, "but I know you are a lawyer, and I know you will tell me the truth. Please tell me what makes a marriage legal in Scotland."

"An affirmation before witnesses—almost any form of statement will be binding. But——"

"Excuse me, sir, please. Suppose two people are married before witnesses by a magistrate——"

"They are as firmly married as if by the Lord Bishop of London——."

"Suppose," said Kitty, again interrupting him, "suppose they use feigned names? Suppose they call themselves by other people's names?"

"Well," said Barston, reflecting, "if their identity can be established that does not materially alter the case; but there are other consequences, such as possible prosecution for fraud. It is never safe to tell lies of any sort."

"Thank you, sir," replied Kitty, returning to the carriage. "I have a friend who is very anxious to know the law, and I felt sure you could tell me. Are you going with us, sir?"

"No. My horse is lame. I must return to the inn and get another. Besides, Mr. Harwood is in Stirling and we will go together. Good bye, Nellie!"

Arrived at the "Castle" Mr. Barston found two things: a note from the rector, who had gone to call on Mr. Macdower, the brother of the Presbyterian minister at Lavington; a telegram from Mrs. Dawson, saying Tommy was seriously hurt, and begging his honour to come to Ripple Farm, if possible, at once.

CHAPTER XXXV.

A COMPAGNON DE VOYAGE.

"THESE are hard lines," said Swiss; "it is a just punishment forlying. I told Johnny I wished to come here to see Nellie! I *have* seen Nellie, and nobody else! They are going to the Trossachs and the Lochs, and I thought I might go with them. Tommy is the only son of his mother, and she is a widow. I wonder if the whelp has dislocated his jaw! Poor boy! what a wretch I am to talk in this fashion. Well! The only atonement is to start by the first train. Mrs. Dawson would never telegraph unless the case were serious. Landlord! Have you a time table? When does the first train south leave Stirling?"

"In twenty minutes, sir."

"I am called away suddenly. Mr. Harwood will not be back in time. Give him this despatch. Stay. I will leave a note for him. While I write please get me a cab, and put my portmanteau in." He sat down at the table and wrote a hurried note, enclosed the telegram in it, sealed and addressed the envelope, paid his bill, got into the cab, and reached the station one minute before the train started. And while Nellie was recounting to her mother her morning adventures, the hero of them was gliding along, forty-five miles an hour, towards Devonshire.

The porter who seized his portmanteau and rug when he dashed into the ticket office, met him as he came flying out again.

"This way, sir! Smoking? Yes sir! First class, of course, sir! This carriage, sir! All to yourself, sir? No, sir! One other gent, sir. All right, sir! Potmanto under the seat, sir! Thankee sir!"

The other gent was in the opposite corner. He had his rug over his shoulder, concealing the lower part of his face, while his wide-a-wake hat was pulled down over his brows. He seemed to be asleep.

Barston merely glanced at his fellow traveller to see if he was smoking. The train had come from above, and had only been two or three minutes in the station. Probably this was a passenger from farther north. Swiss noticed his well-shaped foot, his well-fitting habiliments, and one white hand, ungloved, holding the rug over his breast.

"Gentleman, anyhow," he muttered. " This compartment is label-
ed smoking, so I need not apologize if I blow a cloud. I wonder
if he is asleep?"

He was soon enveloped in blue smoke. At the next station a
boy clambered up to the window, with a supply of yesterday's
"Times." Barston bought a paper and read steadily till there was
nothing left but advertisements. He did not care to talk, as his
mind was preoccupied, but he looked over at his companion once
or twice, but could not see that he had moved a muscle. At last
they rattled into the station at Glasgow.

"Tickets, please!" said the guard; "all right, sir! Ticket, sir!"
and he passed into the carriage. The sleeper put out his hand as
the guard approached.

"Lavington!" said the guard; "all right, sir. This carriage goes
through, so both you gentlemen can keep your seats."

"Indeed!" thought Barston. "I wonder if my *compagnon de
voyage* is going to sleep all the way. He wakened very opportunely
just now, though I cannot see that he has moved anything but
his arm."

An hour or two later the train went roaring through a long tunnel, and as they again emerged into the fading sunlight, Barston
glanced at his silent companion. He had half turned in his seat,
and the rug was pulled up on his shoulder and across his breast,
its folds covering his chin. The hat was still lower over his brow,
and nothing was visible of his face excepting his nose, and a
thick moustache under it. He had roused himself sufficiently to
make these changes while they were in the darkness of the tunnel.

Barston began to be interested. He was too thorough a gentleman to evince any curiosity, and too thorough an Englishman to
volunteer conversation. It was clear that the other did not desire
an interchange of civilities, and his quiet was certainly not all sleep.

Through another long tunnel, and in Egyptian darkness. The
train was running slowly, approaching a station. Barston detected
the odour of spirits, and heard the gurgling, as the stranger imbibed. Then there came the flash of a Vesuvius, and Swiss saw
by its glare the white teeth of his fellow voyager holding his
cigar. A puff or two and all was darkness again. As the train
drew out of the tunnel Barston was attracted by the lights in the
station, and when he looked again the other had changed his seat
and was now on the same side with himself, his back to the engine.
The rug had fallen away and was spread over his knees, but his

hat was cocked over to the right and his hand was supporting his head. Nothing was visible now but the lurid tip of his cigar. Two youngsters got into the carriage as the train stopped. One took the seat between Swiss and the quiet traveller, the other in the opposite corner. The guard came in, inspected tickets again, and as he departed gave his final instructions.

"You two gents wot just got in change at Brummagen. This carriage goes through to Exeter."

"Lost my matches, by Jove!" said the one in the corner. "May I trouble you for a light, sir?"

"Ya-as! I guess you may," replied the stranger, with a decided nasal twang.

"That is intended for Yankee," said Swiss to himself, "but it is overdone, by the three kings! Now, I *will* watch this fellow if I keep awake all night!"

Watching was not needed very long, however. The new comers talked a little, sometimes to each other and sometimes to Butler.

"You are from America, sir?" said he who had obtained the light.

"Ya-as."

"I think that is a lie," said Swiss to himself.

"Is the war still going on, sir?"

"Ya-as."

"How long have you been in England, sir?"

"Came a week or two ago, I guess."

"From *North* America, sir?"

"Ya-as. Noo Yawk."

"I say, Dick, this gentleman can probably tell you something about Horace. He is from New York. Did you happen to know a young man name of Scroggins—Horace Scroggins?"

"Guess not," replied the American gentleman.

"That is very strange. He went to New York, I know."

"Wa-al, there are about a million inhabitants in that village," responded the other. "I calkilate 'twould keep a man busy to get acquainted with 'em all in a life time."

"I think you would have noticed Horace, though," said the young man after a little pause—"or his wife. She is lovely! She was a nurse-maid in his mother's house, and he ran off to Scotland with her and was married there. And he went to America from Glasgow. None of his family would have anything to do with him after that marriage."

"Small loss to him," said the other fiercely, forgetting his nasal twang. "What need he care about friends or family? Nurse-maid! I have known nurse-maids a thousand times better than your stuck-up countesses."

"Butler! by the three kings!" said Swiss inaudibly. "No mistake about the trill of those r's. What a rage the fellow is in. I begin to understand a little. He has been marrying Kitty, and that accounts for his attachment to nurse-maids. Poor Kitty! That accounts for her eager questions, also. Why should he marry her under a feigned name? I need not watch any more. I'll go to sleep."

He wound his watch, wrapped his rug around his nether limbs, and propping himself up in his cushioned corner, was speedily ·walking with Ret by the margin of murmuring rivulets, and amid the warblings of birds, while she listened with eager attention to the long, long story of his love.

He was wakened at last by the stopping of the train, and as the porters rushed by with swinging lanterns, he heard them cry out the name of the station next to Lavington. Mr. Butler was in his corner, awake and watchful.

"My friend," said Barston, with kindly accents, "I know you."

"Do you?" replied the other.

"Yes. You married Kitty yesterday, at Stirling."

Butler started. "What devil are you in agreement with," said he, "that you know all I do as soon as it is done?"

"Come," replied Barston, "let us lay aside this useless antago-nism. You have married the girl and I hope you will be kind to her. Do you object to the interest I take in your wife, and in you for her sake?"

"What do you purpose now?" said Butler, after a pause.

"Nothing that you do not approve. If you will allow me to help you in any plans you have laid, I shall be glad to do it. What do *you* purpose?"

"I am going to America. Mr. Barston, I have tried to hate you, but I cannot. You have thwarted me once and again, but I have known that you were kind in it all. Now that I have married Kitty, it is not likely that you will care to trouble me more. I have no definite plans. If a time should come when you can aid me, I will apply to you." He ground his teeth as he continued. "Those cursed Harwoods have made themselves odious to me. All of them! And if I can damage any of them hereafter, I warn you that I shall do it!"

"We cannot be friends, then," replied Barston quietly. "Their enemies are my enemies. If you were not under the blighting influence of some wrong, accomplished or intended—some horrible crime, I fear—you would recognize and admire the nobleness of Lord Morton and his family. We are near Lavington. Let me say one word to you. I am a lawyer. Your marriage is certainly legal, but you run the risk of compromising your wife, at least, by marrying under a false name !"

"Who dares to say so ?" said Butler haughtily. "It is false! I married under my own proper name. It is true that I persuaded Kitty to call herself by another name. But what do you know ?"

"Nothing—only that feigned names were used. No matter! It might save you trouble hereafter if you correct the registry and give Kitty's real name. It is no business of mine, and I only warn you for your own sake. Your station in life may——"

"Don't talk to me of names and stations. If I go to America and stay there, perhaps I can make another name. I have been there. There is a vast empire in their far west, where a man may go and possibly forget his previous life. All of mine is one long, dismal curse !"

"Listen to me," said Barston, as the train glided into the Lavington station. "I am attracted to you by an influence that I can neither understand nor resist. If you have done wrong, surely atonement is possible. If you have been wronged, I will stand by you with name and fortune until you are righted. Only confide in me, and let me befriend you if it is possible."

"It is *not* possible !" replied Butler, with cold despair in his tones. "I am partly criminal and partly the victim of the wickedness of others. I am *not* a lawyer, but I think it very likely that your laws would take my life from me for a dozen violations of them! and yet my crimes are so covered that no witness of any of them lives upon the earth! I wish I had never encountered you. But for you I could live upon my hatred of the race! We part here. God bless you, if there is such a Being, which I don't believe !"

With a horrid laugh he pushed the door open, stepped out upon the platform and disappeared, leaving Barston aghast at his words and manner.

CHAPTER XXXVI.

THE RECTOR'S SCOTTISH FRIEND.

THE Reverend John Harwood had certain mission work in Lavington, in which he was aided by the Reverend Andrew Macdower, a minister of the Free Church of Scotland, who had a flourishing congregation in that village. It was not exactly ecclesiastical work, and Mr. Harwood did not officially engage in it, as the gulf between the church and dissenters was too wide to be bridged, and the rector did not care to engage in a task so unpromising as that sort of architecture would prove. The pious antagonism between the church people and "the others" was latent in Lavington, partly because Lord Morton was a dissenter and partly because the rector, though a staunch churchman, was too liberal in his views to lead an assault upon the works of Nonconformity.

Mr. Macdower was a scholar of rare attainments, and as Mr. Harwood was also a book-man, they readily fell into a warm friendship. They had amicable battles over their sectarian differences, while their creeds were identical in almost every particular. For a wonder they agreed in politics, both being staunch tories, the rector going a little beyond the Scot, of course, and both being annually lectured by Lord Morton, who was a liberal. It is worthy of note that the scribblings they both indulged in upon political questions were published in papers far distant from Lavington.

On the day of his departure for Stirling, Mr. Macdower called upon him and charged him with messages to his brother.

"You must hunt up Aleck, Mr. Harwood," he said; "you'll find him weel up in modern science. It would pain me to think you had been to Stirling without seeing him."

"It shall be my first business when I get there," said the rector. "While I am absent I rely upon you to watch over the mill school. Don't allow the children to get astray in the mazes of dissent. If you choose to instruct them in your Westminster theology I shall not object, provided you don't dilute it with your modern rubbish."

"Ay, ay," responded the other theologue; "if we can only get the rising generation weel instructed in the Shorter Catechism there will be little left of your bloated Establishment twenty years hence!"

When Barston was galloping on the bank of the Forth, Mr. Harwood was exploring Stirling Castle. This was soon disposed of, and as his engagement with Swiss was an hour later, he went in search of Mr. Alexander Macdower, magistrate. That worthy was at home, and received his visitor with the courtly grace of a Scottish gentleman.

" I've heard so much of you, Mr. Harwood," he said, " from my brother Andy, that I seem to know you. You are welcome to Stirling, sir, and I suld be happy if you would make my house your home during your stay."

" I thank you, Mr. Macdower, but I leave to-day. My sister is in the neighbourhood, and I hope to accompany her through your lake country. I left your brother in good health, and have messages to deliver about sundry matters. He desires me to say, first, that the last speech of Mr. Gladstone's is a failure."

" And you can just tell him that he has no' made an original discovery in yon direction. I have heard abune a dozen ignorant cadgers say the same thing !"

The rector laughed. " That is a capital answer, and I shall not forget it. We parted in a fight and he had the last shot. He thinks the Westminster Confession contains all the theology that man needs to steer clear of rocks and quicksands."

" He is no' far wrang," replied Mr. Macdower; " may be ye had better tackle Andy on some ither subject."

" Do you swallow the entire Confession, Mr. Macdower ?"

" I dinna say that ! The Confession is no' inspired, ye ken, but it is a safe body o' divinity. It says some things aboot the creation that may be a little dubious. May I offer your reverence a wee taste o' Scotch whusky ?"

" Many thanks, sir, but I must decline. My limited knowledge of that beverage induces me to dislike it thoroughly !"

" Weel," said the Scot, " *de gustibus non est disputandum*, ye ken. If ye canna appreciate Scotch whusky your education has been neglected."

" It tastes," said the rector with a shudder, " like turpentine diluted with peat smoke."

" There was a chap from your country," replied the magistrate, " that I married the morn, who tuk a nip without blinkin' !"

" Married !" exclaimed Mr. Harwood. " Oh, I forgot your Scottish law. Do you find the warrant for Scottish marriages in your Confession, also ?"

"Nay. It is a ceevil contract, ye ken, and is binding if performed by a magistrate. I am weel aware that you churchmen look upon it as a sort o' sacrament."

"Not quite," replied the rector, " but we think it is more than a civil contract. And so do you, I am sure. You say it was a countryman of mine whom you made happy this morning?"

" I didna' say anything aboot the happiness. The leddy was no' ill-looking, but she had that composed appearance which indicated a decided wull of her ain. She will be apt to rule yon chap in spite of his beard, and he has plenty o' that. I didna notice her much, as I was attracted by her diamonds. Hoot, mon! but she had a brooch on her neck worth twa thousand punds, I should say!"

"Indeed!" said Mr. Harwood, rising and drawing on his gloves. " Was it a single stone?"

"Nay! It was composed of three stanes. They were held by delicate gold work in the shape of lilies. The diamonds were set in the mouths of the flowers."

The rector sat down again.

"Do you happen to remember her name?" he asked, gradually getting himself in hand, as he instinctively felt that an astounding revelation was imminent.

"Ay! I remember Sir Walter's lines :

"Tamworth tower and town;"

it was Miss Clare Tamworth."

" I have a curiosity to taste that whisky," said the rector, "if not too troublesome."

The host produced a decanter and glasses with a celerity that was admirable. Mr. Harwood poured out about a gill, and with a polite bow to the magistrate, swallowed it. While he coughed and choked, the Scot allowed a similar quantity to glide down his throat, a drop at a time.

" Ye'll never learn to drink Scotch whusky," said he, discontentedly, " if ye bolt it in yon fashion. It is a cruel waste o' raw material!"

" Raw enough!" muttered the poor rector.

"Pardon me, my dear sir!" said Mr. Macdower suddenly, " I didna see that you were ill! Your cheeks are the colour of your cravat! Tak' another drop o' the dew."

" I am getting better, I thank you," said Mr. Harwood. "Did you say whom it was that the lady married?"

" Ay! a Master Lacy. I dinna mind his baptismal appellation. Some outlandish name. He was in an unco' hurry to catch the southern train."

" I must go, I think. This gentleman was an Englishman——"

" Ay! from Lavington, he said. Must you go, sir? I am proud to have made your acquaintance, sir," and as the rector descended the steps he muttered, " deil tak' the mon! that shot o' raw whusky was too much for him! He is no' accustomed to it, he said, yet he tossed it off like a wild Hielandman!"

The Parson found Barston's note when he returned to the " Castle Inn." When he opened the envelope the enclosure fell out. It was a telegram from Mrs. Dawson, Lavington, Devon, to Mr. Lacy Barston, Stirling, Scotland. " Tommy is very seriously hurt, perhaps dangerously. Can your honour come to Ripple Farm immediately? He asks for you anxiously." Barston's note was as follows :

" MY DEAR JOHNNY—The enclosed telegram will tell you all that I know. I start immediately for Lavington. It is a very sore disappointment, but we cannot resist Providence. Please explain to the ladies the cause of my hasty departure. If Tommy is not fatally hurt I will return in a few days. Leave the plan of your proposed route at the inn, or telegraph me at Lavington. I feel like Moore's 'Peri,' who got a glimpse of paradise and then had the door slam'd in her face!—Affectionately yours,

" LACY BARSTON."

"This is wholly inexplicable!" said the rector. "I am bewildered. Treachery? It is impossible! I would not believe Swiss guilty of wrong if I *saw* him doing it. I should think it an optical illusion. But he has married Clare Tamworth, or I am mad! or that Scotch rascal was drunk! The wisest thing to do will be to see her and ask her what it means. Married! And I have come here solely to ask her to be my wife! Are there *two* Clare Tamworths?"

The unhappy Parson got into a cab, and drove to Miss Tamworth's cottage as rapidly as the Scotch cabby, inspired by an extra shilling, could make his horse go. The ladies were at luncheon. As Miss Tamworth came forward to welcome him, he was the three lilies blazing in her collar. The reader need hardly be told that Kitty ran to her patroness at once with the story of her marriage, and Clare took the brooch and pinned it in her own dress for safety. As the rector glanced at the jewels, he remembered some quaint rhyme he had heard in his young days, and shuddered.

Ret, the dear, sensible woman, placed a chair for Johnny next to Clare, and taking her luncheon as fast as she could, excused herself and left them at the table. She thought Johnny wanted Clare and she almost thought that Clare wanted the rector. Her goodness can be better appreciated when it is remembered that nothing had been said about Barston's non-appearance, and she was devoured by a raging desire to know how he would greet her at their next meeting. Miss Tamworth was too full of Kitty's secret, just revealed to her, and also possessed by a secret consciousness of the rector's attachment, and all her faculties were employed in maintaining an air of utter unconsciousness, of course. So she forgot Barston's existence. Lady Lacy never mentioned his name at all. And the Rector was piously whispering to himself that "there was certainly some curse about those infernal Lacy Diamonds!"

CHAPTER XXXVII.

MISS CLARE'S EXPLANATIONS.

THE Reverend John Harwood sat moodily sipping pale ale, while his companion nibbled daintily at a cake. They were a very handsome couple, having considerable liking each for the other, and it is a horrid shame to leave them playing at cross purposes. Each looked conscious. Parson Johnny was thinking of the speeches he had composed between Lavington and Stirling, and which he had thought out, very much as he "thought out" his sermons, with due reference to the orderly sequence of the argument. And, oddly enough, he was reminded of a funeral discourse he had recently prepared, to be delivered on the Sunday following the obsequies of a dying parishioner, and which was totally lost for the nonce, in consequence of the fellow's unexpected recovery. It is true that he still had the sermon, but there was no certainty that it would be available when his parishioner did die, as the circumstances might be entirely different.

Miss Clare was burdened with Kitty's secret. There was enough romance about the whole story of her marriage to cover all the objectionable features. The bridegroom had enjoined present secrecy upon Kitty, alleging family reasons, and this fact, coupled with Mr. Butler's *distingué* appearance in his fashionable attire, satisfied Miss Tamworth that his claims of gentle breeding were well founded. Kitty herself was considerably flustered, and her story of the unexpected meeting with Butler, and the sudden proposition, the hurried ceremony, and the assumption of a feigned name (which Kitty did not reveal)—her subsequent interview with Mr. Barston and his assurance of the legality of the marriage—all these were jumbled up in inextricable confusion. Moreover, Miss Clare somehow associated this rapid change of relations, and the status of wifehood, with the rector's appearance upon the scene, and wondered what *she* should say if Mr. Harwood made kindred proposals to her.

"What has become of Mr. Barston?" she said, at length. "We expected to see him with you."

The rector handed her the note which Swiss had left, and watched her furtively while she read it.

"He would make a very indifferent sort of Peri, I imagine," she said coolly, refolding the note. "Is Tommy the young man we saw at Ripple Farm? I mean the one with a mouth."

"Yes. I think he has a mouth," replied the Parson.

"You are so charmingly lively this morning," said Miss Clare with some asperity, "that you must have attended a funeral recently!"

"On the contrary," said Mr. Harwood, "I am just from the scene of a wedding!"

Miss Tamworth started.

"And the bride wore a brooch very similar to that you have in your collar!"

Miss Tamworth blushed. Matters were growing serious.

"I am overwhelmed, Miss Clare. I beg your pardon, madame. I meant to say, that this whole business was so totally unexpected, and the secrecy and haste, and all the circumstances, shocking to my mind, that I may be pardoned if I violate ordinary rules of politeness. I called at the magistrate's, Mr. Macdower's, by accident this morning, and he told me of the marriage and the names of the happy pair. Indeed, his description of the brooch convinced me that the bride came from this house, and I did not need to hear any names! I suppose I have no right to complain—but I cannot but feel that I have been treated with little consideration."

"I am very sorry to hear you say so," said Miss Clare, brushing away the tears that started to her eyes.

"Forgive me if I pain you!" said the miserable rector. "It was far from my purpose. I would have thought, however, that you held truer views of the marriage relation than to regard it as a mere civil contract, to be certified by a magistrate!"

"It was not my doing, Mr. Harwood. If I had dreamed that you would so regard it——"

"Oh, Clare!"

"Mr. Barston says," she continued hurriedly, "that the marriage is entirely legal. I had not thought of what you suggest, but I know you are right, and I think I may promise to have the ceremony duly performed in church when we go back to England. It will be only a week or two——. What is it, Nellie?"

Nellie, who had suddenly burst into the room, clutched a good wedge of cake and filled her little mouth. Then she climbed up on her uncle's knees, kissed him, filling his whiskers and bosom with crumbs, and when she had bolted the cake stated her business.

"Where is Cousin Lacy? He said he was coming wid you, Uncle Johnny."

"He has gone to Lavington, baby," replied the rector. "Here is his note; take it to your mamma."

Nellie took the letter and slid down to the floor. She took another wedge of cake, and deliberately munched and swallowed, apparently at the constantly recurring risk of strangulation, intently regarding her uncle and Miss Tamworth as if she would read their secret souls. They were both conscious of certain discomfort under this watchful scrutiny. Then she shook the letter at them, gravely nodding her pretty head, and fairly overwhelmed them with her parting observation:

"I know what it all means!" she said with calm triumph in her voice and manner—"Donkeys!" and she stalked majestically out of the room.

"I cannot say that Nellie is very complimentary!" observed Miss Tamworth.

"No! but so far as her last observation applied to me she was very nearly right! It appears to me that I must look very much like a donkey. I certainly feel like one, and shall look out for thistles as my regular fare hereafter." He brushed the crumbs from his dress, rose from the table, and took his hat and gloves.

"Are you not going to remain with us to-day, Mr. Harwood? You know we go to the Trossachs to-morrow."

"Alas!" said the rector, "I must forego the pleasure I had promised myself. I must give up this excursion and return to Lavington and try to find comfort in the performance of my stated duties. It would be utterly false in me to pretend that this morning's business was of so little moment to me." He spoke with quiet dignity and composure, and Clare began to grow angry.

"Really, Mr. Harwood!" she said, "I cannot see that you have cause for this distress. A marriage has been celebrated, and the gentleman most interested says there are weighty reasons for the informality and secrecy. All the forms required by law have been observed, and the people are married—hopelessly, if you like. If you and Ret, with your inveterate Harwood obstinacy—pray pardon me!—will still nurse your opposition——"

"Say no more!" interrupted the Parson. "If you think I have no cause to complain I am thankful! It is so much relief at least. Will you please make my excuses to Ret? It will only be necessary to say that I find my clerical duties call me home at once. Good bye! I hope I need not say that I wish you all the happiness that is attainable in this world and the next!" He took her hand, pressed it and was gone.

She watched him walking rapidly down the path until he turned into the highway. Then she ran up into Lady Lacy's room with streaming eyes. Ret was on the sofa just finishing the fourteenth perusal of Mr. Barston's note, which she slipped into her pocket with a guilty blush as her friend entered.

"Why, Clare! My dear, dear Clare, what has happened? Where is Johnny?"

"Gone away, inebriated, I think; that is, I hope he is! He drank enough of that pale ale to make three men drunk! He has been doing nothing since you left but drinking ale and talking like a lunatic! I think it is awfully horrid for a clergyman to get into such a state! He is off to Lavington, telling some preposterous story about his clerical duties. A nice state he will be in to perform clerical duties! He will have delirium-thingamy on the route, no doubt. Oh, Ret! I could tear his eyes out, and cry out my own!"

"My dear!" said Ret, with wondering anxiety, "tell me what it means! what did Johnny say?"

"Say! Who could tell *what* he said, with his tongue so thick with ale. He has gone, I tell you—gone after that precious Peri! Ha! ha!" and she laughed hysterically through her tears.

"Clare!" said Lady Lacy, "you distress me very much. Can you not give me a coherent account of your interview?"

"Indeed I cannot, Ret! I hardly know how it began or ended. Mr. Harwood took me to task like a raging hyena, only because I happened to know about a certain matter, told me in confidence! *He* found it out by accident, and why he should have raved at poor me so venomously, I cannot imagine! He would not allow me to say one word, in defence or explanation. Here, Ret! take your brooch! I verily believe those horrid Lacy Diamonds are haunted!"

"This mystery is very vexatious, observed Ret!"

"Oh, those horrid men!" said Miss Tamworth, with a vicious shudder. "Ret, my darling, let us go into a nunnery! We shall thus get rid of Parsons and Peris and live at peace! Your brother is the most ill-tempered man I ever saw! I am not at all certain that he did not swear!"

"I am sure you are not telling stories, Clare," replied Lady Lacy, "yet if anybody else should tell me that Johnny was intoxicated, and in a rage, and indulging in profane language, I don't think I *could* believe the statement. I never knew him to be in a rage in my life! and as for swearing! Oh, what would Mother say!"

"There, there!" said Miss Tamworth—"you need not trumpet the matter all over the world! Of course he did not swear! I was joking about that. Heigho! I don't feel much like joking, either. You did not believe that nonsense about the ale. I only meant to say that he did not eat any luncheon. Something has happened to upset him, and he has gone after Mr. Barston to get comfort. The Peri! Ret! how do you suppose he would look with wings, flopping about the gate of Paradise! What in the world do you suppose the lunatic means, by his 'glimpse of Paradise?'"

CHAPTER XXXVIII.

PHRENOLOGICAL.

MR. BARSTON had a friend in London, who had been his preceptor, in his medical studies, and who was a man of very extensive information and experience. In the scanty time between the receipt of Mrs. Dawson's telegram and his departure from Stirling, Barston managed to write a despatch, beseeching Dr. Cardon to meet him at Lavington, to "attend a very serious surgical case" in the neighbourhood. Doctor Cardon had the same sort of appetite for surgical cases that a child has for sugar-plums, or a critic for the gore of authors, and Barston cunningly worded his despatch so as to make the feast as attractive as possible. The train from London arrived at Lavington at the same hour with Barston's train, and he met the doctor on the platform, in the station.

"My dear doctor," he said, shaking his hand, "this is kind of you. I am much interested in the poor boy, and was not willing to trust him in less skilful hands. Leave your luggage with the porter——"

"Luggage!" answered Dr. Cardon, while he collected various cases in a pile—"luggage! You did not tell me what sort of a case it was, so I have brought *all* my instruments!"

Barston had enough *esprit de corps* to know that the doctor would entrust those precious cases to a porter about as soon as a young mother would leave her baby in charge of a gorilla. Accordingly he assisted the doctor, while they were being transferred to a cab, handling the nicely polished boxes with great tenderness. When they arrived at the inn Barston proposed that they should leave the instruments in the cab while they partook of breakfast.

"Not a bit of it!" said Dr. Cardon, "bring 'em in! Who can tell whether that brute of a horse will bolt or not?"

When they were bowling along the Exeter road under the level rays of the morning sun, the doctor asked Barston to "describe the case." Mr. Barston knew nothing beyond the fact that Tommy was seriously hurt, and the surgeon made himself as comfortable as he could, in his corner of the cab, and fell asleep. He dreamed of dislocated limbs and of amputations, of delightful hours in hospitals and dissecting rooms, of saws, and knives, and tourniquets, and when the cab stopped at Ripple Farm he awoke, refreshed and cheerful.

It required very little time to get the facts. Tommy had projected a visit to Jenny Potter, the daughter of a fisherman on the coast. As Master Lacy could go down to the beach over the rocks Tommy thought he could do likewise, although forbidden, and missing his footing, he had rolled down to the beach, and was brought home on a shutter. Some bones were broken, and Doctor Holly had repaired the damage in that direction. Tommy was a mere bundle of splints. He besought his mother to send for Mas-··

ter Lacy, when he was first brought home, and she had yielded to his urgency, and telegraphed to Stirling. Since the despatch was sent Tommy had been in a stupor, and, when Dr. Cardon arrived, he was totally unconscious.

With practiced hands the doctor felt the ribs and spine of the patient. These were unhurt. One arm was broken and a small bone in one leg, and Dr. Holly had done all that was needful in setting and splinting and had "left the case." His brother practitioner rather objected to interfere, although assured by Mrs. Dawson that he had left Tommy that morning, saying he could do no more.

"Do you know where he went ?" asked Barston.

"Yes, sir; he has gone to Mr. Bottomry's."

"It is only a mile or two," said Barston. "I will go after him and bring him back. Roland is here; is he not, Mrs. Dawson ?"

"Yes, sir; but there is no one here to saddle him."

"I will find some one," answered Barston, moving to the door. "Doctor, wait for me half an hour or so." ·

While Swiss was absent Doctor Cardon opened some of his cases a d "polished off" several ferocious implements with a chamois skin. Mrs. Dawson looked on with dumb horror. She had a vague idea that Tommy would be taken apart and set up afresh when t'other saw bones arrived. Within an hour Dr. Holly's gig rattled up and he and Barston reappeared in the sick room.

Dr. Cardon's reputation as a surgeon was so well established that Barston's apologies for bringing him were unnecessary. The other was very glad to divide the responsibility of the case with a gentleman of Dr. Cardon's fame. Mrs. Dawson withdrew at a hint from Barston, and as he was a *quasi medico*, both of the "regulars" begged him to remain at the consultation.

"You will have the advantage of a very instructive clinic, Barston," said Cardon. "Do you remember the fellow in the Vienna hospital, who was brought in reduced to a pulp ?"

"Yes."

"Well, this case is very similar. The boy has had an ugly knock on the head."

"Several of them," observed Dr. Holly.

"Yes, doctor," replied the London surgeon, "and you have dressed them all as skilfully as mortal man could do it; that is, all except one."

. "I examined the cranium very carefully," said Dr. Holly. "I have shaved his head, you see."

" Yes; and one strip of adhesive plaster is over the right organ of alimentiveness."

" Pardon me ! " said Dr. Holly, stiffly. " I do not know the locality you name !"

" Ah !" said Cardon, " you miss a great deal, doctor, by rejecting phrenology. Now in my first examination of this youth I was very much struck with the splendid development of his masticating organs. · Look at this process ! It is a jaw that would crush gravel stones! and his mouth is big enough to take in a sucking pig at a bite ! Now nature never does things by halves. Knowing this fact, and believing in phrenology, I was enabled to discover an injury that escaped you, and no wonder, as you don't believe in phrenology !"

" I am still entirely in the dark !" said Dr. Holly.

" Of course! Don't be restless, Barston. The boy is just as comfortable as an unborn infant. He is comatose, owing to a small fragment of bone pressing upon the dura-mater!"

Dr. Holly started.

" Allow me to finish my explanation," continued Cardon; " when I found this maxillary," touching Tommy's jaw lightly with his finger, " and this mighty opening for the reception of nutriment, I immediately inferred that nature had a corresponding development of the organ of alimentiveness, and as the right lobe was fortunately in view, I looked in the proper spot, and the development was wanting !"

" Very possibly !" said Dr. Holly, dryly.

" Very impossibly, my dear sir !" returned Dr. Cardon. " It would have been abnormal ! Not finding the organ well marked on the right side I examined the left. If you will take the trouble to look, doctor, you will perceive a decided protuberance on this side ! Come look, Barston !"

" I thought that was a bump !" said Dr. Holly.

" So it is, my dear sir, vulgarly so called. I call it a phrenological protuberance !"

" I mean," said Holly, testily, " that I took it for a contusion."

" Ah! my dear sir, the contusion is on the other side, and has made a depression which was totally indistinguishable except by the aid of phrenological science ! See! I remove the plaster, with your permission. Now, doctor, please place your finger here. Ah ! have I your permission to do a little trepanning ?"

" Undoubtedly," said the other, overwhelmed. The London doctor, smacking his lips, clutched his glittering weapons, and deftly sawing a small hole in Tommy's head, picked out sundry splinters of bone, and rapidly dressed the wound.

"I am going back to London by the first train," he said coolly, as he repolished his implements and restored them to their velvet couches. "Really, Barston, this has been a very interesting case. Nothing more is needed. The young man will be entirely conscious presently, and he could not be in better hands than Dr. Holly's. My dear doctor, it was simply impossible for you to *guess* at that little injury, and I assure you my discovery is all due to phrenology. The youth, in his fall, struck that spot on a round stone. The blow splintered the bone but did not cut the skin; and then there are so many severe bruises and wounds on the contiguous surface that they would very naturally attract all your attention, not being interested in phrenological investigation. I would merely suggest that it would be well to sustain nature with generous fare. He will recover rapidly, and his appetite will be ravenous. Notice the fine swell of the sound organ, doctor, on the left lobe! He is waking."

"Master Lacy," said Tommy, feebly, "I won't climb down them rocks hany more! May I 'ave some curd?"

"Certainly," said Dr. Cardon, with his chest expanded and his eyebrows raised in a triumphant arch. "Certainly; that is, with Dr. Holly's permission."

Dr. Holly was exterminated. Dr. Cardon carefully repacked his cases on the floor of the cab, and with a fifty pound note in his pocket and a benevolent smile on his face, departed. Barston followed him to the cab to get his final instructions.

"The old woman will see the boy fed," said Dr. Cardon.

"You mean his mother?"

"No, I mean Dr. Holly! Barston, this fee is absurd. But I accept it, partly because you have had the benefit of a superior clinical lecture. How did your patient get such a tumble? How high is the bank above the beach?"

"About a hundred feet, I suppose."

"Well, his skull is thick or he would never have incurred such peril!"

"Pooh, doctor!" answered Barston; "*I* have been up and down there forty times."

"Very likely. When I have *your* skull to trepan I shall use a chisel! Don't let the youth stuff himself too liberally at first. There will be febrile symptoms anon. Dr. Holly will manage judiciously."

CHAPTER XXXIX.

Tommy.

DURING the day Barston sat by Tommy's bedside, encouraging him with cheerful talk whenever he was awake. Tommy was conscience-smitten, because he had been warned against the dangerous pathway, which he knew Mr. Barston habitually traversed. The instinct that had prompted Swiss to essay the passage at first would be described in Western American parlance as " pure cussedness ;" but, knowing the route, in all its parts, it was not unsafe to Barston, who had the eye and hand of a mountaineer, and who was an expert in all athletic exercises. To poor Tommy the attempt was almost certain death, and he had escaped fatal injuries by clutching at the stunted vegetation and breaking his fall (and his bones) as he sped to the shingle beach.

" You see, Master Lacy," he said, after Dr. Holly left them, " I thought it would save such a long tramp. Jenny—I'm sparking Jenny, sir—lives just below the hill."

" But you must not try that route again, Tommy. How old are you ?"

" Twenty last Christmas, sir."

" What does Jenny say to your courtship ?"

" She likes it main well, sir."

" And what does your mother say ?"

" I 'aven't asked her, sir. I thought maybe you would tackle mother."

" I will talk to her. Suppose your mother has some serious objection to Jenny——"

" She can't, sir! Jenny makes 'eavenly dumplin's, sir. I was goin' to get dumplin's when I fell down the rocks. And puddin's, too. Mother gave me some of her new sugar to put on the dumplin's, but the paper got mashed when I fell."

" Well," said Barston, " you must not talk too much now. Are you comfortable ?"

" No, sir. My leg hurts, my harm pains me, and my 'ead feels all up in a knot like. I'm main hungry, too."

" After to-day you shall have plenty to eat. You will be feverish to-day, the doctors say——"

" Doctors !" said Tommy; " are there two ?"

"There *were* two. But Dr. Cardon has gone back to London. I am going to stay here until you are better, or I will ride down every day if I go to Lavington. See if you cannot go to sleep, and I will go talk to your mother."

"Master Lacy!" said Tommy, "before you go, please tell me what that Lunnun doctor did to my 'ead."

"He sawed a little hole in it!" Tommy snapped his eyes and shivered. "He wished to see if you had any brains. You thought you could go over the rocks because I did it? Haven't you seen me go up the long ladder at the barn, with my hands, without touching the rungs?"

"Yes, sir."

"Can *you* do it?"

"No, sir! nor nobody else only you. I'll never go near them rocks again!" said Tommy, solemnly.

Barston found Mrs. Dawson in the big kitchen. She was intent on hospitable cares, expecting her landlord to dine at Ripple. Since her boy had been aroused from his stupor her mind was considerably relieved, though she was still doubtful about the damage to his limbs.

"You may dismiss your anxiety, dame," said Barston, seating himself by her side, "Tommy will get well, but will require some nursing. What do you think of getting Jenny to help you?"

"I dunno, Master Lacy," she answered; "does Tommy want her? I think he might be satisfied with his old mother!"

"He has not asked for her. But it would be a relief to you, I fancy. You know he cannot move about for weeks. What sort of a girl is Jenny?"

"Oh, she is a good enough sort of girl," replied Mrs. Dawson, discontentedly. "Tommy has been courting her, I s'pose. But he is only a baby, and she is a slip of a girl."

"They are both tolerably well grown babies. It struck me that Tommy might take Ripple Farm on a sub-lease from you, if he had a wife, and as he would not marry any girl that you did not recommend, perhaps it would not be amiss for you to have her here for a week or two and study her temper. I think she is a pretty, modest girl, and would probably make a good wife for Tommy. Nobody can have Ripple while you live, and I will not consent to any arrangement that does not leave you mistress. It will be more pleasant for you to have Tommy for your foreman than any other. I see some eggs there looking fresh as daisies. If you would allow me to say what I would like for dinner——."

"Indeed, Master Lacy, you would take a load off my mind. I have been trying to think what in the world I could get for you."

"Bacon and eggs! I am going to the village, and will send up a fish. Then a curd, and a mug of your home-brewed would make a dinner for a king. I had a substantial breakfast and will abstain from luncheon, and so at three o'clock I hope to dine. I expect to buy the fish from Jenny."

"Well, sir," said the dame, "you might ask her to bring it up. She will be ready enough to come, no doubt; and if she could stay two weeks—you might ask her mother—maybe Tommy will get tired of her by that time, or she get tired of him; if you think children like them ought to be courting."

"Tommy will be twenty-one next Christmas," observed Barston. "As for the courting, you can manage all that when you get the girl here. I am so ignorant of that business that I cannot give any advice. But the doctors agree that Tommy will be feverish and restless, perhaps for some days, and you require help to nurse him properly. I can easily find some other girl in the village if you don't want Jenny."

"Oh, no, sir; let her come."

"I could send her mother, probably," said Barston, reflecting. "Probably that would be better. She has more experience."

"And she has half a dozen brats, besides her man! No, sir. Better send Jenny. I am curious to see the girl anyway."

"Have your own way then, dame," said Barston, with an air of resignation. "But don't tell Tommy. Let us surprise him."

"That was a bit of diplomacy," said Swiss to himself, as he descended the face of the cliff. "As a general rule you are safe when you oppose obstacles in the way of women. The dear angels like to overcome difficulties. I wonder if I shall have to manage Ret in that way—if I ever get her! Here is my Proseuche!" Yielding to the conceit, which he did not attempt to analyze, he drew off his boots and sat down at the foot of the great boulder. Here he rested, with his face upturned to the bright sky.

"I have all things, and abound!" he said at last, lifting his hands towards the heavens, "and every expiration should be a psalm of praise. Yet I feel that some trial is before me still. Oh, Merciful! give wisdom and strength as I shall need!" and then, with passionate earnestness, as he stood upright, "in Thy time and in Thy way give me my darling, my Ret!"

And as he passed on downward, from crag to crag, the pleasant plash and murmur of the little streamlet followed him, fretting over its rough bed, dropping in tiny cascades, spreading out in miniature lakes, or gliding swiftly over long reaches of smooth rock, it sang the same monotonous song, a succession of echoes of his last word—" Ret, Ret, Ret!"

Jenny was in the porch of the cottage, behind the rough bench that held her scaly merchandise. She knew Master Lacy, and put her apron to her eyes as he approached.

"I want the best fish you have, Jenny," he said, "and I want you to take it to the farm. Where is your mother?"

"Here I be, your honour," said Mrs. Potter, waddling into view, and dropping a fat curtesy. Two or three chubby children followed her, and a baby somewhere in the interior squalled dismally. "Whist, babby! Run in, Jenny, and rock him!"

"Ah, Mrs. Potter, I am about to ask a favour. Tommy Dawson is hurt, you know——"

"Yes, sir; my Sam helped carry him home. Is he hurted bad, sir?" Jenny lingered and the baby squalled.

"Not dangerously. He will get well——" Jenny threw up her hands and ran in, and the baby subsided; "but," continued Barston, "he has broken some bones, and will be abed for weeks. Can you spare one of your children to help his mother nurse him? What a splendid sole! I must have that for dinner! Can you send it to the farm?"

"Surely. Would Jenny do, sir? The others are na old enough. And Jenny sells the fish, too. I can ill spare her."

"I will pay her a pound a week, dame," said Barston; "or rather I will pay you."

"Weel!" said Mrs. Potter, who came from the canny north, "I canna' gainsay your honour. Ye'll count the day i' the wage?"

"Certainly. And here is a week's pay in advance. Can she carry the sole with her?"

"Hoot, ay! The gowd is bright and bonny! How much? What your honour pleases, just. I'll no chaffer wi' you aboot the fish. Tak' it at your ain price, sir. If I had it in Lunnun 'twould fetch half a crown."

"There is the half crown, dame. Take good care of that baby. I think he will make a great singer when he is grown!"

"Ay, ay! My Sam is a gay singer, though he's a bit hoarse wi' the salt water. I'll send Jenny as soon as she gathers some cla'es. Gude mornin' to your honour! Are ye gaun to walk abune the cliff? The tide will be in by noon."

"I am going out to meet it," answered Barston. "The sea and I are old friends. Good day, dame!"

"I was a fule to say aught aboot the half crown," said Mrs. Potter, as Swiss departed, "if I had held my auld jaw he'd a gin me three shillin'! Here, lassie! Awa' wi' you. Gather up some duds and gang to Ripple. Ye're to abide there twa weeks to help his mither nurse your Jo. Ye'll no want that blue gownd!"

"Oh, mother! I'll be there two Sabbath days!"

"Aweel—tak' it alang, lassie. But gin you do ony dirty wark, dinna spoil your cla'es! Ye look weel pleasit to leave your puir auld mither an' the bairns."

"Oh, mother, you did not fall down the cliff and get hurted," said Jenny; "besides, mother, a pound a week——"

"Go 'lang wi' your clatter, lassie. Ye need na just chatter aboot the pound. I'll put it awa' for you again your weddin'."

After Swiss dined he looked in upon the wounded youth. Jenny was seated at the head of the bed, blushing a little, and knitting a little, and talking in a low tone. Tommy's nose and chin, which had escaped abrasion in his fall, were separated by an interval of about ten inches, owing to the chasm made in his countenance by his pleasant smile.

Swiss lighted his cigar and strolled out towards the main road. A great oak stood near the stile, and under its shade he sat and smoked. A cloud of dust came down from Lavington, and a horseman with it, and as he drew rein at the stile and the dust blew away, Swiss saw the rector, whose comely countenance was shadowed by gloom and anger and deep distress.

CHAPTER XL.

SOME REVELATIONS.

AS the horseman approached, Barston began to sing in a plaintive minor—

> "Who travels along this road so late,
> Compagnon de la Marjolaine,
> Who travels along this road so late?
> Always gay!"

"But that last line is false. He looks as glum as a sexton! What a funereal aspect! My dear Johnny, is aught amiss? The ladies! Nellie! Speak, man! Your silence is portentous!" As he spoke he threw the gate open, and the rector rode in the lane and dismounted.

"Nothing the matter, Barston," he said, not noticing his friend's extended hand. "Nothing amiss, except with me!"

Barston peered anxiously in the rector's troubled face, secured the horse by throwing the bridle over a bough of the tree, and sat down on the stile by Mr. Harwood's side.

"Can you tell me, Johnny?"

"Yes; if you need to be told. Oh, Swiss! how cruelly you have wounded me!"

"I?" said Barston, astonished. "I! cruel, and to you?"

"Yes, cruel! Where was the need of your secrecy, your deception? I cannot believe it of you, Swiss, although I know the miserable truth."

"What do you mean, Johnny?" said Swiss, patiently.

"I mean your work in Stirling! Your cunning device to get rid of me, sending me to the castle! and then your abrupt flight after you had thoroughly befooled me, and made me turn myself into a donkey! The very child could see it! *She* called me a donkey! And before your—your—wife, too!"

Barston's eyes dilated.

"This marriage, Swiss! It is horrible every way! What do you put on that astonished expression for? Do you know nothing of a secret Scotch marriage in Stirling yesterday?"

"Yes. I know of a marriage. It was not exactly according to conventional rule, but I know it is legal. Too late to resist the fates, Johnny! I suppose it *had* to be."

"And why did you not tell me? What fiend prompted you to deceive your friend? Oh, Swiss, I could not have so used you, if my life depended upon it."

Swiss took out his pocket-book and rapidly wrote several rows of figures upon a blank leaf. He then tore out the leaf and handed it and the pencil to the rector.

"Will you oblige me by casting up that sum?" he said, politely. "I am anxious to know the total."

The rector glanced at the paper a moment, and then wrote the addition at the bottom, beginning with the left hand figure. Barston gravely examined the sum, nodded his head, and threw the paper on the ground.

"Excuse me, Parson!" he said, gently, "but I noticed that you added from left to right. Is that your usual habit?"

"Certainly. I always add *all* the figures at once. It is easier and more accurate. That is, more certainly accurate."

"The best writers upon psychological phenomena," said Swiss, oracularly, "agree that the mastery of figures is a proof of sanity. Now, the ability to add sums of five figures, and five rows of them at *one* operation of the mind, must demonstrate the normal condition of the mental faculties. It is true that there have been cases well authenticated, in which this wonderful mastery of mathematical problems was manifested by idiots! But, so far as I know, this power has never been shown during temporary derangement. It would contradict the most firmly established theories of psychology. The mental organism may, however, be permanently deranged in some of its parts. And analogy seems to teach that as a man may be blind, and yet hear, so he may be able to cypher, and yet insane! However, a more satisfactory solution of the mystery may be found in a different form of mania, such as *delirium tremens.* "Johnny!" he continued, suddenly, "excuse me, but have you had anything unusual to drink lately?"

"No! certainly not! What do you mean by this exhibition of lunacy? Stay! Yes, I had! That Scotch wretch that married you gave me some stuff that he called "Hieland jew." I verily believe it poisoned me! I have not been in my right mind since, and I have a constant taste of turpentine in my throat."

"Ah!" said Barston, greatly relieved, "slightly inebriated; well, we are progressing. And now to dispel the mists from your poor mind. First: I am not married to any Scotch wretch!"

"Who said you were? Are you married to Clare Tamworth?"

"Whew!" said Swiss, with a prolonged whistle. "Why, Johnny, I should as soon think of marrying the dev—elopement of matured maternity, known vulgarly as Satan's grandmother."

A flash of joy spread over the rector's face! "Oh, Swiss, I know you are not lying! I must be drunk, I suppose! Still, the comparison is not flattering to Miss Clare!"

"I mean no disrespect to her, Parson," answered Swiss, coolly. "I only mean, you blind, inebriated mole, that I do love another darling, precious, peerless woman. If I ever marry, I shall marry her. Miss Tamworth! Why, you deceitful villain, do I not know that you are dying for her yourself! How dare you talk such bosh? But it is not you, it is Scotch whiskey—the 'Hieland jew'—that speaks. Oh, Johnny, do you not know that my soul is wrapped up in Ket?"

" Ret! Swiss, what can I say, dear brother? What joy it would give me to call you brother indeed. Ret! Alas! Swiss, her heart is in the tomb."

" Is it?" said Swiss, indifferently. " Well then, I will go into the tomb after it. It is too precious a heart to stay in such an unwholesome locality. But, Johnny, you must not tell. If I get Ret, it must be by my own prowess. I had to tell you."

" I will not say a word, Swiss," replied the rector, slipping his arm around his friend's burly form. " Now, tell me what that marriage means?"

" Kitty and Butler were married, I presume," answered Barston. " For some unknown reason Kitty assumed some other name."

" And Butler, too," said the rector.

" Did he? Well, I met Kitty afterwards. I had been taking a gallop with Nellie. Kitty plied me with eager questions touching the validity of Scotch marriages under feigned names, and I inferred that she had ' gone and done it.' By the bye, I noticed Lady Lacy's brooch on her breast. When I got back to the inn I found Mrs. Dawson's telegram. I left it for you, and you know all the rest."

" Donkey!" said the Parson, reflecting. " That is exactly the word. If I had not been drunk, or a donkey, I should have known better than to abuse that angel! I don't know what I said to her, and I am afraid to look her in the face again !"

" You mean Kitty?" said Swiss, puzzled.

" Kitty be blowed!" said the rector in wrath ; " I mean that dear, injured, insulted Clare! Swiss, I was a regular brute. I scarcely saw Ret at all, and after saying the rudest things I could think of, I told Clare I would not go to the Highlands with her, as I had clerical duties calling me home ! Oh, what a precious donkey !"

" Don't be calling young ladies such hard names, Parson," said Barston. " Your qualifying adjective hardly atones for the uncomplimentary noun. Besides, it is specially mean, as she is not here !"

The rector gazed at Barston's sober face vacantly.

" What did you mean, Johnny, by Butler's assumed name? did he take *my* name ?"

" Yes."

" Did you *see* it ?"

" No. Macdower, that is, the magistrate who married them, said it was Clare Tamworth and Lacy—something. He could not remember your patronymic ; said it was outlandish."

"That is queer, too," said Barston, thoughtfully. "One of my breed had a castle in olden times within five miles of Stirling, and the ruins of ' Barston's Hold' are still there."

"I am not sure that Macdower did not reverse the names," said the rector, trying to recall the interview ; " perhaps he said something—Lacy."

" Where are you going ?" said Swiss, as the rector led his horse from under the tree.

"Back! To Lavington now, to Stirling to-night, to the Trossachs to-morrow, and I shall give no sleep to my eyelids until Clare forgives me."

" And your clerical duties ?" said Swiss, slyly.

"I leave them in your hands, Swiss. If you will put on a gown you may preach for me. Not in the church, however; but you may invite the congregation out in the churchyard, and give them some of your latest vagaries !"

"I am afraid they have had some of them at second-hand, Johnny, already," said Swiss, with cool impudence.

"That is true," said the candid Parson, " but I always had quotation marks in the written sermon, Swiss. Good bye, you dear old rascal ! I love you dearly !"

As the rector galloped away, raising another cloud of dust, Barston reseated himself on the stile and lighted a fresh cigar.

"It is a queer story," he muttered ; " what design had the fellow in taking my name ? and he swore with such a loyal air that he had *not* assumed a name ! How could I be deceived by his bare assertion ? I remember his haughty manner, too, and thought he looked so thoroughbred while he was lying ! Bah ! I must not trust my instincts so implicitly hereafter."

He leaned back against the trunk of the huge oak, pulled his hat over his face and smoked, his mind filled with a thousand conflicting thoughts. A step aroused him, and looking over the hedge he saw a pedestrian coming up the road. Barston was concealed by the trunk of the tree, and he sat quietly until the man passed him, walking with springing step in the direction of Lavington. There was something in his gait that attracted Barston, and he gazed after him, fascinated. As Butler, for it was he, disappeared where the road turned, Swiss slipped down from the stile and threw his cigar away; his eyes were ablaze and his face pallid as he muttered :

"Elbert Lacy! by the three kings !"

CHAPTER XLI.

The Rector's Chase.

THE horse that bore the rector so rapidly from Ripple Farm could not speak English, and he therefore did his swearing in snorts that were perfectly intelligible, whenever Mr. Harwood dug the spurs in his flank. There was no need of haste either, as no train would leave Lavington for two hours. When he arrived at the rectory, he busied himself with preparations for his return journey, and partook of a substantial dinner with good appetite. At last the hour of departure came, and as the train passed out of the station, he began to regret that he had not insisted upon bringing Barston with him, to beguile the tedium of the journey.

. "There were so many things to consult him about!" he thought, "and he could have talked to me about Ret, and listened to me talking of Clare. Poor fellow! He does not know how hopeless his case is, and I could not bear to tell him. I have tried forty times to get Ret to talk of him since he saw her, but could never induce her to mention his name. She has no idea of his mad passion either, and as soon as he blurts it out, which he is sure to do, she will take care that he has no second opportunity! I could not even get her interest awakened in that lost letter, in which he sent her a lot of messages. I must certainly warn him before he sees her, and tell him the exact truth about her sentiments. He looked so serene when I hinted that she cherished Jack's memory so tenderly, that it would be cruel to enlighten him. Poor Swiss! He has forbidden me to speak of his hopes to Ret, but I can at least sound his praises to her. It is a good thing that she is so patient a listener, anyhow.

"I wish I could feel as serene touching my approaching explanations to Clare! What can I say? Swiss thinks that dreadful whiskey was to blame. Suppose I adopt that hypothesis? It is worth a trial! I'll do it."

Then the rector fell asleep and dreamed that he had Barston and Ret before him at the altar. He went all through the marriage service, Mr. Butler giving the bride away. When it was all done and he approached to congratulate Ret, behold it was Clare! He had made a mistake, and got the wrong lady! While he stood stupefied, and wondering how the error could be rectified, Nellie

came waddling up the aisle and stood before him, nodding gravely
and regarding him with her peculiar, steadfast gaze. Then pointing to Clare and to him alternately, she said, " Donkeys !" and
waddled out of the church. He was thoroughly miserable, and
looked at Mr. Macdower's coming up through the floor of the tran-
sept as a very natural proceeding. And when the Scot, with his
eyes twinkling, offered him a bottle of "jew," he felt impelled to
accept the detestable draught. Before he swallowed it, however,
the church door banged, the bell rang, and the old sexton bawled
in his ear—" Ticket, please !"

" Where are we, guard ?" he inquired, shaking himself awake.

"Brummagen, sir ! Ticket, sir ! Thankee sir, all right !" and the
door banged and locked.

" That sort of dreaming won't do !" said the rector, " that Scotch
rascal had almost got the stuff down my throat ! I believe it
would have choked me, even in a dream."

In the gray morning light, the tall chimneys of Glasgow appeared. The rector had decided to reverse the route that the ladies
projected, hoping to meet them, as he could not overtake them.
They were to stop at the " Queen's Hotel " in Glasgow, and he was
rejoiced to find upon inquiry that they had not arrived. By the
first train for Loch Lomond he was off again, and when at length
he was on board the little steamer, and gliding over the surface of
the loch, he felt sure that he had them before him. Arriving at
Inversnaid, he learned there was a coach due from Loch Katrine,
later in the day, and it was possible that the ladies might arrive,
and proceed to Glasgow that afternoon. He decided to wait.

It was hard work. The boots, who was supposed to know everything, informed him that the coach would arrive in two hours.
One hundred and twenty minutes to be employed in some way.
He would climb the mountain behind the inn. It was called Benjamin something. The view from the summit would certainly
repay him for the toil, and the time would be sped at least. It
was a small affair, but would occupy sixty minutes, anyhow.

Fifteen minutes' brisk walking brought him to a halting place,
and he was quite content to sit on a fragment of rock and rest
awhile. He seemed to be rather farther from the summit than
when he began the ascent. But the placid sheet of water, spread
out at his feet, was very beautiful, and as the great body of the
loch was hidden by a projecting crag, he would surmount that, and
then enjoy a wider view. Panting, after a prolonged scramble, he

sat down again and took a large drink of lovely scenery. The summit of this Benjamin was still provokingly·distant, and he began to doubt his ability to reach it and return within two hours. He looked at his watch. The two hours were gone!

The rector never knew how he quitted Benjamin. But when he reached the plateau, a hundred feet above the inn, he saw the little steamer speeding down the loch, bearing Ret and Clare, both of whom he clearly recognized, seated upon the deck!

"Gone! Dear me!" said Mr. Harwood.

This mild expletive was very unsatisfactory. But the good Parson never thought of using any of the more emphatic phrases wherewith men usually vent their wrath. No escape from Inversnaid was possible until morning. The rector meekly accepted the inevitable, and forced himself to say: "It is all for the best!" At the same time he would have paid twenty-five pounds cheerfully for any decent pretext for tears.

Like a sensible man, he went directly to the source of relief, in so far as relief from disappointment is attainable beneath the skies. He went to work. And the best sort of work to bring comfort and placidity is the work of composition. The rector shut himself up in his room and wrote a sermon. His text was, "Tribulation worketh patience." It was scholarly, rhetorical, evangelical. And he went to bed after it and slept soundly.

When he reached Glasgow he learned that the ladies had spent the night at the "Queen's," and departed for Liverpool that morning. He took the first train and followed them, not knowing anything about their intentions, except that Clifton was their objective point. They were a day ahead of him now and the chase was getting hopeless.

"Lime Street Station, sir?" asked the guard, when he surrendered his ticket.

"Yes," replied the Parson. He did not know anything concerning Lime street, but he was indifferent about stations.

"All right, sir. This carriage goes to Lime street."

In due time Lime street was reached. The rector crushed his hat against the door frame when he emerged from the carriage. His neckcloth was awry, and he looked dilapidated and seedy as he walked down the platform, a porter following with his portmanteau. He glanced about incuriously at the throngs hurrying out of his train and at other throngs hurrying into another train on the opposite platform, and peace entered his soul as he saw his sister and Miss Tamworth entering a carriage within twenty yards of him.

"Hillo, sir!" said the porter, as Mr. Harwood bounded across the rails, contrary to all rule, "that's not the way! I'm blest if he a'nt gone for the down train! He's been and 'ad something 'eavy to drink! Beg parding, sir, but this is the wrong way!"

"On the contrary, my friend," replied the rector, with beaming countenance, "this is the first step I have taken in the right way for a week! My dear Ret, I have been chasing you three days. Miss Tamworth, I have not seen the sun shine since we parted. And there's Nellie! Porter, put the portmanteau under the seat. Here's a shilling."

In two minutes the train slipped noiselessly out of the station, and in five more it was roaring through a long tunnel. While they were in the darkness Mr. Harwood touched Miss Clare's hand and whispered:

"Only forgive me this time!"

When they came into the light again, Nellie requested her uncle to take her on his knee. She inspected him intently, and endeavoured to adjust his neckcloth. He was hilarious, and totally unconscious of crushed hat and travel stains. Lady Lacy asked him a string of questions touching his sudden flight to Lavington and his sudden return. His replies were confused and unsatisfactory. Did he go to see Tommy Dawson? No, but he had been to Ripple and seen Swiss. How was Tommy? He really forgot to ask. How long was he in Lavington? Only an hour or two. What in the world were the "clerical duties" that made such a journey necessary? He stammered something about postponing them. And then Nellie asked:

"How you get your hat mashed, uncle?"

While this was progressing, and while the abashed Parson was trying to get the kinks out of his hat, Miss Tamworth was slyly watching him. He had left her sorrowfully, indignantly, majestically, and he had returned in such a jolly mood that he was positively chuckling with delight, with a hat in the condition usually called "shocking bad." Kitty, who had caused all the trouble, was sitting demure and silent in the corner of the carriage, and the rector had greeted her with a kind smile when he entered. There was only one solution of the problem in Clare's mind:

"Delirium thingamy!"

The rector was devoured with anxiety to explain to Miss Tamworth his "brutal" conduct at Stirling. If he could only get five minutes alone with her! And he stole furtive glances at her through Nellie's curls, trying to see some token of forgiveness in her grave face.

Miss Tamworth was perplexed to know how to keep out of the Parson's reach. She saw very plainly the "mania" in his eyes, and would about as soon accord "five minutes alone" to a laughing hyena as to the jocular Parson. After his trials of the preceding days the revulsion was great, and it is a marvel that he behaved as decorously as he did.

Nellie was excited and restless. She fell asleep on his shoulder when tired out, her golden tresses mingling with his brown whiskers. He would not allow her to be disturbed. They were a very quiet party. When Nellie's nap was over, she announced a proposition that was startling, but which all her hearers thought was very just.

"When we get to Clifton, uncle," she said, "there will be some Donkeys there!"

CHAPTER XLII.

The Donkeys.

THE Reverend John Harwood spent two days at the hotel in Clifton. Miss Tamworth's inheritance was scattered all over that town and Bristol, yielding her a handsome revenue. Her ancestral residence, Vincent Lodge, was nearly a mile from the town, and the rector walked out in that direction on the third day after their arrival. Before he had traversed half the distance he met the ladies and Nellie, who were on their way to Clifton Downs. It was a lovely morning, in which the dying spring was giving place to the incoming summer.

"I have purposely avoided the Downs," he said, after the exchange of greetings, "until Miss Clare would condescend to introduce me. May I join you in your walk?"

"We were coming for you," answered Lady Lacy, taking his arm. "Nellie, walk with Clare while I talk to your uncle."

This was not the precise arrangement the rector desired. Like a blundering masculine, he would have "changed partners" at the start, but his quick-witted sister knew better. She had already decided how to give him his opportunity.

, " I am very much interested in that poor boy," said Lady Lacy.
" Surely you heard something about him at Lavington ?"

" Not much, Ret. I met Dr. Holly, who told me the boy had
broken all his bones and mashed his head in a fall from the cliffs
at Ripple. I think he said they had mended him."

" They ?"

" Yes. Swiss took his old preceptor with him, Doctor Cardon.
You have heard of him ? It is that fellow in London who saws a
man up into small pieces and then sews him up again as good as
new. Ret, it is not polite to turn Miss Tamworth over to Nellie."

" Never mind Miss Tamworth. You shall escort her presently
—as soon as you tell me all you know about Tommy."

" I think that is all. Holly says they did something to the lad's
skull—put a pan on it, or something of the sort. He is all right.
Needs nursing, and Swiss has quietly settled himself down to do
it. He is a glorious fellow, Ret."

" Tommy ?" said Ret, innocently.

" No, Swiss." He paused a moment, reflecting, then added :
" Ret, of all the specimens of unselfish, manly, truthful, kind and
wise men that I have ever met, Swiss is the best! Nobody under-
stands him except his poor friend, Parson Johnny, and he will go
to his grave unappreciated by an ignorant world."

" Well," responded Ret, her cheeks aglow with the exercise in
the sweet air of the Downs, " after that ante-mortem panegyric
you may take Clare. Nellie, come walk with mamma."

Miss Tamworth had caught the same ruddy hue, from a similar
cause. She put her dainty glove on the Parson's offered arm, as
Nellie and her mother hastened ahead in a regular romp. The
hour was early, and the Downs were depopulated.

" You must listen to me patiently, Miss Tamworth," he began,
with grave precision. " I have to explain my misconduct the other
day, and throw myself upon your mercy for pardon. I was not
myself."

" I suppose not," was the grim rejoinder. " I hope you had a
satisfactory reason for getting into that state. You have had a
reputation for very peculiar abstemiousness, which would be seriously damaged if your parishioners should see you——"

" Upon my honour, Clare," answered the rector, anxiously, " I
did not know what the horrid stuff was. Swiss says I was inebriated !"

" Of course !"

"That Scotchman gave it to me. I was faint and sick. How could it be otherwise when he told me he had just married Clare Tamworth!"

"*What* do you say?"

"I say, Mr. Macdower told me he had married a lovely lady that morning to some Mr. Lacy! He said she wore a diamond brooch composed of three lilies. I have seen it on your neck a dozen times. He said her name was Clare Tamworth!"

"And you believed him?" she answered, withdrawing her hand from his arm. "You thought I—I had contracted a secret marriage! What have I done that you should think so meanly of me?" and she put her handkerchief to her eyes.

"Clare!" said Parson Johnny, "come sit down here. Can you make no allowances——"

"None!" she answered, taking the indicated seat, and slyly watching his troubled face through the flimsy kerchief.

"I had come from Lavington with enough courage mustered up to ask you to be my wife. I thought I would tell you how sincerely I admired and loved you. I had gained my own consent to ask you to forego all the brilliant prospects that were before you, and to marry a poor country Parson, who had nothing to plead but an honest affection—nothing to offer but a life-long devotion. And when the magistrate told me, with cold precision, that you were married——"

"You did all you could to get delirium thingamy!" said Clare, uncovering her eyes; "and when you joined us the other day at Liverpool with your hat mashed——"

"That was an accident, Clare," answered the discomfited rector. "I struck my hat against the car."

"And your eyes blazing with excitement," continued the lady, not noticing his interruption, "looking so wild that I was positively afraid of you——"

"That was joy at seeing you again, Clare. I love you, and I cannot make my eyes tell lies! I can scarcely refrain from clasping you in my arms, even now!"

"You had better!" retorted Clare with a little scream; "where are you going?"

"Anywhere? I see that you can never love me, and the wretchedness I suffer away from you is more tolerable than the agony of being near you, and keeping silent upon the only subject that interests me. Do you think I would be brute enough to

annoy you with protestations that are so distasteful to you! You
have had a lot of fellows hanging around you, and talking bosh
so long that you have no appetite for earnest, heartfelt, unchange-
able devotion! Ah! if you could only have loved me! But I am
dumb!"

"None of the 'fellows' ever said such cross things to me as you
say!" replied Clare, piteously, dropping a tear or two. They keep
a supply of them, reader, those angels, and drown a poor thick-
skulled man with a spoonful at their good pleasure! "Pray
don't leave me here alone! Ret is out of sight and hearing! Any
one of the 'fellows' would have offered me his arm, instead of
flying off in a rage! Before I said 'no,' too!"

"It is not necessary to *say* no, Clare. You can look no, and
act no without speaking."

"Dear me!" she said, with a sigh, as she took his arm again;
"one must regulate all one's looks and acts, too! How long have
you—been—imagining yourself in love with poor me?"

"I don't know when I did *not* love you, Clare. I thought you
liked Swiss——"

"Mr. Barston!" said she, with another charming little scream.
"I should as soon think of marrying the——Great Mogul!"

"Why that is what *he* said about you!" said the rector, with·
delicious simplicity.

"Sir!"

"I mean—I thought you had married him! That Scotchman
said a Mr. Lacy something—so I went to Lavington and asked
him."

"And he said he would as soon marry the Great Mogul?"

"No. He mentioned some other dignitary. I forget. Oh,
Clare, will you promise to keep a secret?"

"Yes!" she answered, eagerly. That is their way, reader, those
angels! They will promise anything to hear a secret.

"Well, poor Swiss loves Ret! He charged me most sternly
never to mention it. And I have told you, you see, at once. But
I love you so—there—I am done!"

"You may go on!" she answered, leaning a little more on his
arm, "I suppose I ought to hear all you have to say."

"But I have said all. I love you! I love you! Ah, if you
could only say so to me! Could I make you love me, Clare, by
any self-denial, any endurance, any patient waiting?"

"In two or three years," said Miss Tamworth, slowly and

shyly—"I might—like you a little. Men are such horrid, cross, impulsive, unreasonable things, that I—— Let go my hand, sir! I hear somebody coming."

"Do you love me a little *now*, Clare?" said the rector.

"I don't know! If you don't get delirium thingamy any more, and dash off, leaving me heart-broken with your cruel words, I will try to forgive you this time."

"Do you love me a little?"

"Just a little grain, perhaps. Ah! there is somebody."

"Oh, mamma!" said Nellie, rushing into view, "here are the lovely donkeys!" and she pointed at a string of those attractive quadrupeds, just appearing upon the Downs.

"Thank fortune!" said the relieved rector, "she don't mean us."

"What conspiracies are you two plotting?" said Lady Lacy. "You have been an hour down there!"

"I have been trying to get a sister for you, Ret," answered her brother; "ask Clare if I have succeeded."

"My darling!" said Lady Lacy, slipping her arm round Miss Tamworth's waist. "Come away for a run! I am so happy!"

Clare kissed her hand to the rector as she tripped away, and, turning her blushing face to Ret, whispered,

"So am I!"

The rector took Nellie on his shoulder, and went to meet the donkeys. The leader had made up his mind suddenly that the Downs was not an attractive locality. He laid his ears back, and planted his fore feet firmly in the sod, refusing to move. His driver belaboured his flanks with a switch of about two inches in diameter without effect. While Mr. Harwood waited for the quadruped to alter his mind the ladies approached.

"I would recommend that picture to your serious consideration," said Miss Tamworth. "You can judge how the Harwood obstinacy looks!"

Mr. Harwood took the bridle from the hand of the driver, patted the vicious little brute on the neck, and persuaded him to follow. He placed Nellie in the saddle, and the donkey finding she was a light weight, consented to amble gently along. The rector nodded triumphantly as he moved away.

"Learn a lesson yourself, Miss Clare," he said; "you see what can be accomplished by kindness. Pet the Harwoods a little and you can lead them where you will!"

CHAPTER XLIII.

NELLIE LOST.

TOMMY DAWSON recovered slowly. Dr. Holly kept him abed perhaps a little longer than was necessary, partly because he wished the bones to "knit" well and partly because Barston paid the guinea punctually at each visit. The patient did not murmur; he was fed judiciously, and Jenny was flitting in and out all day. Swiss rode down daily, sometimes from the village and sometimes from Oakland. The rector wrote to him twice a week, and on Saturdays Barston met him at the station as Mr. Harwood came down regularly to attend to the "clerical duties" of Sunday. By the earliest train on Monday he was off again, pining for "the air of the Downs."

When Tommy was fairly out, hobbling about on crutches, Mr. Barston went to London to make purchases. He was adorning his home elaborately. New furniture arrived at the Lavington station in quantity, and the ladies of the Union Mission, half churchwomen and half dissenters, exchanged harmless gossip about Oakland and its lord. That he was setting his house in order was plain, and the natural inference was that he was about to "settle down."

Settling down usually means matrimony.

"It is certainly some London lady," said Miss Liston. She was the daughter of the Honourable Marmaduke Liston, who was cousin to Lord Lappermilk. Mr. Liston lived very economically on his small income, and hoped for the time when dear Lucy would make some gentleman happy, and leave him the whole of his scanty revenue for his personal use. As she was thirty, and indeed had been thirty for an indefinite number of years, Mr. Liston manifested commendable perseverance in hope. Miss Lucy was a devoted churchwoman, and thought the rector was lovely.

"I don't believe it is any lady," said Miss Nevill. She was the young sister of Major Nevill, a gouty old bachelor, living on half pay. He had been in the Crimea and knew Mr. Barston. "Brother says Mr. Barston is too sensible a man to marry. He thinks he is only fitting up a bachelor establishment."

"He was at Spurgeon's Tabernacle last Sunday," said Miss Bul-

lion, the banker's daughter; "probably he is going to marry some
dissenting damsel out of that flock."

"More likely he will start off for the Albert Nyanza or the
mountains of the moon," said Miss Dora Bullion, "as soon as he
has furnished his house. I believe he has been everywhere else."

"Mr. Macdower says he was over in America, where they are
fighting," said Miss Oswald. She was a member of the Presbyterian flock, and was supposed to have designs upon her pastor.
"And he was part surgeon, part missionary and part hospital
nurse. He brought letters to Mr. Macdower from one of his
cousins in North Carolina."

"Madame Laplace says he was in Paris last week," said Miss
Frippery. She was the fashionable lady of Lavington, whose
whole soul was swallowed up in dress. "She met him in the Passage de L'Orme, where she buys her millinery. He was buying a
hat, trimmed with *real* lace; it was a Leghorn; the flowers were the
most expensive he could buy. Madame says it was totally out of
style for any grown person. She saw him write on the back of his
card, 'For my darling,' and he dropped the card in the box. He
took it away with him, so she could not tell what address he put
upon it. It cost a hundred francs!"

"A hundred francs!" said the rest in chorus.

"Only four pounds, you know," said Miss Frippery. "I think
that was quite moderate, considering how rich he is. Of course
it was for a present; for his darling! *That* seems to me to settle
the question of a bachelor establishment!"

Little Nellie got the hat by express and was airing it on Clifton Downs at the very moment that the amiable ladies were discussing it.

Why did not Barston go to Clifton? He had not been invited,
and he was shy.

The rector was so engrossed in his own courtship, that he did
not think often of his friend. When he did, he supposed he was
still occupied with Tommy. On Saturdays he could not talk
much, as he always had his sermon to write. Sunday was filled
up with church services and needful pastoral visitations, and Monday carried him back to Clare. The letters he wrote to Barston
were brief, and the charming egotism of a happy lover made him
blind to everything outside the walls of his paradise.

Miss Tamworth liked Mr. Barston very much; but she liked the
rector more. If the thought of having Swiss at Clifton occurred

to her, she did not entertain it long. The consequence would be to take Parson Johnny off now and again. Mr. Barston could not *always* gallop about the country with Nellie, and there was nobody else to entertain him but Ret. Ret did not fancy him. She had not heard her mention his name for years. And when she tried to make him the subject of conversation, Lady Lacy maintained a cold and dignified silence. There was some bad feeling between them, perhaps growing out of the Lacy inheritance, of which Clare had heard some gossip somewhere—probably from Lord Lappermilk, who investigated rent-rolls of marriageable females on principle. It would be horrid to bring an uncongenial companion there to annoy poor Ret. So Miss Clare reasoned.

"Poor Ret" thought of Mr. Barston, too. Notwithstanding the rooted dislike which Miss Tamworth had detected, Lady Lacy spent many hours in the perusal of some old letters. She had three of them, all written to the rector. The first was written immediately after Sir John Lacy's death. The second was written on the eve of Barston's last voyage. The third was the short scrawl, left at the "Castle Inn," at Stirling. The gentle reader has seen them all.

Following the suggestion so kindly dropped by Miss Clare, we may account for Lady Lacy's conduct in this regard. She was too good to nourish enmity without just cause. She was too good to set an evil example of non-love to her neighbour; so she always locked herself in her room when she perused the letters. Her object, of course, was to detect the hidden villainy in Mr. Barston's character. And her innate goodness of heart always made her eyes humid when she read these epistles (and she always read every word of all of them), and she always blushed when she put them carefully away under lock and key, being ashamed of the rascality they unfolded, and sorrowful for the general wickedness of mankind. It was very remarkable, and altogether inexplicable also, that she usually concluded these exercises by wringing her hands, and saying—

"Oh, if I only could be certain that Mr. DeVere was telling lies! and that Mr. Bottomry was telling lies! I think I could die happy!"

As this little accomplishment distinguished the two gentlemen she named, it is to be hoped that her pious desire will be gratified before this truthful narrative is finished. And as the reader will be curious to know what special instance of mendacity Ret was anxious about, that, also, shall be revealed in due time.

The peculiar relations subsisting betwixt Ret and Swiss were known to themselves alone. Neither of them had ever mentioned the interesting conversation that occurred at their last interview. To Swiss it was full of mystery. To Ret much of the mystery was now explained. But there was no proper opportunity afforded for the explanations that would have broken down all the barriers separating these loving hearts. Lady Lacy rose from the perusal of the letters each time with the conviction that Barston loved her still, and that he would never relinquish her. Why he delayed the renewal of his suit she could not imagine, and she expected each day that Nellie went out with Kitty, to receive a glowing account of a gallop with "Cousin Lacy" when she returned. But Nellie got only donkey rides on the Downs.

Thus matters stood one bright day in the summer. The ladies and Mr. Harwood went to Bath to explore that ancient city. Kitty was left with Nellie, to spend the day at Vincent Lodge, or on the Downs, or in a drive, or, in fact, according to Miss Nellie's fancies, whatever they might be. The carriage was to meet the last train from Bath, in the late afternoon.

It was a late dinner hour when they returned. Lady Lacy inquired for Nellie. She had gone out with Kitty, soon after noon, and had not returned. They had gone to the Downs. The coachman saw them there at three o'clock. He had been to Clifton, and was walking out to the lodge to prepare for his drive to the station in Bristol. Nellie was on a donkey and Kitty walking beside her. It was growing dark, and it was time Nellie was asleep. The rector volunteered to go in search of them, and no one opposed his departure. When he came back, nearly two hours later, the whole household was thoroughly miserable.

He had been all over the Downs, but could find no traces of them. Some policemen had seen them, and the donkey boys had seen them, but all the accounts terminated about the same hour that the coachman named—three o'clock. He was recalled, and closely questioned, but no new information was elicited.

The rector was terribly alarmed and anxious, but he strove to keep a cheerful countenance, for Ret's sake. Miss Tamworth went to bed, prostrated and heart-broken. Lady Lacy was the only calm individual in the house, and she put direct questions to Parson Johnny as to the extent and direction of his search. Then he told her that he had had a dozen men scouring the country within four or five miles of the locality where the child had last been seen. It was at the foot of the observatory, on the cliff, where the donkeys had been dismissed, and Kitty and Nellie had walked leisurely down towards Clifton. One man had brought the information that a woman and child, answering the description given, had been seen going down the zig-zag, a little later.

"I assure you, sister," said the rector, "that this pathway is entirely safe. I went from the top to the bottom myself, and if Nellie went down there, she went safely. Besides, if there had been any accident I should have heard of it. Half of Clifton knows of the child's loss by this time, and the search has been thorough."

"What do you think has become of her, Johnny?" said his sister, steadily. "Do not be afraid to tell me your exact thought."

"Dear Ret, I am totally bewildered! While I am confident that no serious harm has happened, the mere fact that I don't know where to look for her, demoralizes me entirely. I cannot suggest the next step. Oh! if I could only get Swiss!"

"Go to Clifton, brother, and telegraph for him instantly," she replied. He started up, and seized his hat. "Stay," she continued, "you are more excited than I. Here are some blanks. I will write the despatch. Jane, tell the coachman to bring the carriage to the door as speedily as possible," and she sat down at an escritoire and with a firm hand wrote the telegram. "Pray see that it goes at once, yourself. If Mr. Barston gets it to-night, he can be here in the morning. There is the carriage! away with you!"

Throwing her an admiring glance, Mr. Harwood hastened to the carriage, which drove down the gravelled road at a rapid rate. As the sound of the wheels died away, Ret fell on her knees and prayed as she had never prayed before. And when she lifted her wan face, wet with tears, there was a touch of comfort in her countenance.

"If mortal man can find her, *he* can. If wisdom and courage and undying energy can accomplish anything, he will bring her back. And if he does! If he restores my baby to my arms again, I will deny him nothing that he can ask. I will be his slave while life endures, if he wants a slave. And if he asks me to be his wife again, I will marry him! I will do it, if I am convinced that he *stole* them!"

CHAPTER XLIV.

ANOTHER VOYAGE.

MR. BARSTON was enjoying *otium cum dignitate* in the library at Oakland. He had dined solus, and rather late. Too much coffee after dinner made him wakeful. So he sat and smoked, and read a treatise upon magnetic clairvoyance, in very choice French. It was a new book, and he was so much interested, that he did not notice the entrance of the servant, who coughed and spluttered and did all he could to attract his attention.

" If you please, sir," he said at length—" Mr. Macdower is in the hall."

" What!" said Barston, starting up—" bring him in at once ! Why did you keep him waiting there?"

"Thought you were gone to bed, sir. I'll show him in, sir," and he vanished.

"My dear Mr. Macdower—why, what is the matter ? A telegram ! shall I read it ?"

"Yes. It will explain my unseasonable visit."

Barston unfolded the paper, with a vague presentiment of evil, and read:

" From John Harwood, Clifton, Bristol, to Rev'd Andrew Macdower, Lavington. Find Lacy Barston instantly and say that Nellie is lost, and Lady Lacy begs him to come immediately. Get this message to him at any expense, without delay."

Barston read it twice, carefully.

" How did you come, Mr. Macdower?"

" In a cab."

" Gibson, put some things in my portmanteau. Here ! You may as well put these cigars in—all of them. Stay ! leave me half a dozen. Will you have one, Mr. Macdower ? No ? Gibson, if the portmanteau is not ready in five minutes," and he looked at his watch, " I shall go without it. Will you take my place here, Mr. Macdower ? I must take your cab."

"No. I must return. What is your purpose ?"

" There is a train that passes Lavington at one o'clock. I am going to Bristol in that."

" There is a seat in my cab. Here is the portmanteau. We have no time to spare. Come on."

" Cabby," said Barston, as he entered the vehicle, " if you set us down at Lavington station within forty-five minutes, you shall name your fare."

" Fifteen shillins, sir !" said cabby.

" Here is a sovereign. Earn it !"

There were five minutes to spare. Barston obtained his ticket, lighted a cigar and waited. The south train glided into the station precisely at one o'clock. The porter ran along the line of carriages, followed by Barston, looking for a smoking compartment.

" Not one smoking carriage, sir ! Not even second class."

" Then I shall ride third class to the next stop at least," replied Swiss. " Here is a carriage, and a gentleman in it enjoying his pipe. In we go," and the train plunged into the night again with a shriek.

Our friend smoked and meditated. It would be bright daylight when they reached Bristol. What was the first thing to be done ? The odour of his neighbour's pipe was not agreeable. Therefore, the first thing was to get him to put it out, and take a cigar instead.

" My friend," he said, politely, " your tobacco is so strong that the fumes affect my head ! No doubt the quality is excellent. But if you will oblige me by substituting this cigar——"

" Ay, ay, Master Barston !" said the other. " I've had some of your cigars before to-night—on the coast of Spencerland and under the equator !"

" Why, Mobby! I left you first mate on board Spencer's ship —how long ago ? I am glad to see you again."

" I'm cappen of my own ship now, sir," said the sailor, shaking hands with his old shipmate, " leastways of a tugboat, and two-thirds owner, too. I'm done with long v'yages."

" Where is your vessel, Mobby ?" inquired Barston.

" On the Avon, sir, at Bristol."

" We have had some rough experiences together, Mobby," said Mr. Barston. " Do you remember the high peak where we wintered ?"

" Ay, ay, sir !" replied the sailor, " and I remember seeing you on top of it, in the moonlight, poking at its bald head with your Alpenstock."

" Yes! I cut some letters there. He will be a good climber who erases that record ! When did you leave Bristol ?"

" Yesterday. I towed a new steamer out to the Channel—the

Pallas. She is going directly to New York. She is a fine ship. Got aground in the Avon. Had to wait for the tide. That river is worse than the currents we used to get in the high latitudes. Do you remember the old berg, sir, that went out to sea that night, ploughing its way through the floe? We went out in his wake, you know?"

"I remember," answered Barston, thoughtfully; "we had all thought that old berg our great enemy. We were between him and the rock, and we feared the power of the current. You see he was our friend after all, opening egress from our ice prison. We parted from him at sunrise, and stood out to sea!"

"Yes, sir; that was Providence, you· said. Well, Providence got the *Pallas* aground yesterday just to oblige a chap who had left his wife and babby."

"Ah!" said Barston.

"Yes, sir! It was a rum go, altogether. When the ship grounded my cable was taut. I found she would not come, so I jumped ashore to help the boys shove her off the bank. You see I knew how them currents ran, and the ship's officers were chattering like a lot of Frenchmen. While I was working about, this chap slipped over the side and got his wife and babby. They were on the bank."

"Surely he did not expect them to be there?" said Barston.

"No, sir; it was a reg'lar surprise. But he took them aboard with him, and the *Pallas* was soon afloat again. It was all plain sailing then, and I left my mate to take her to the channel, as I had to go to Exeter. Are you going to Bristol or Clifton, sir?"

"Yes; to both places."

"Well, sir," said Mr. Mobby, fumbling in his pockets, "the babby dropped a trinket on the bank. Leastways I picked it up where she had been standing, the little hangel! She was as purty as a picter! I thought you might find some of her people, maybe. Would you mind taking the toy?"

"You had better keep it, Mobby. It is not likely that I could find any of the child's kin. My stay is very uncertain. You will perhaps hear something about it when the ship returns. Is it very valuable?"

"It is only a bit of coral, sir. Here it is! Little Nellie will miss it——"

"Little what!" said Barston, taking the bracelet, and devouring it with his eyes by the dim light of the lamp in the car roof.

"Yon chap called her 'Nellie'——"

"What was he like?" said Barston, with bated breath.

"Oh, he was a swell chap. Had on fine toggery and kid gloves. Had a cut on his face that spoiled his beauty. But his wife seemed very fond of him. I saw her hanging on his arm after they got aboard. She was afeard the child would be scared at the ship. But not a bit of it! She was bold as brass! Her father took her up and said, 'Nellie, do you want to go on the big ship?' and she clapped her little hands and said, 'Yes, yes!' The little hangel! I've been thinking of her twenty times to-day."

"So have I," replied Swiss. "I think I know her."

"Do you? Well, that's jolly! You will keep the bracelet then, sir?"

"Yes. Did you hear nothing about the woman and child being missed?" inquired Mr. Barston.

"No, sir; I came directly to Bristol and took the train to Exeter. It was a rum go! I have thought since that yon chap was after running off to America to get rid of his wife and babby. It was a quare start! His wife was very much astonished to see him. And it was a very unlikely place for them to be there under the bank. They must have walked down there from the foot of the zig-zag. Do you happen to know the chap's name, sir?"

"I think he is called Butler," replied Barston.

"That's it! I had forgotten; but I heard the cappen say 'Good evenin', Mrs. Butler,' when she went aboard. By the bye, the *Pallas* sailed twelve hours before her time. Mebbe yon chap intended to take his wife, after all."

Mr. Barston had arrived at a conclusion. It was all plain to him. Butler had taken Kitty and Nellie to America. He knew the bracelet, which he had given the child at Stirling; and Butler's hatred of all the Harwoods, and his malignant character, would account for his abduction of Nellie. Only one thing was to be done—to follow.

"Captain, how can I get to America most rapidly?" he said, after an hour's silence, in which his thoughts had been busy.

"Take the *Princess* this mornin', sir," answered the sailor promptly. "Tide will be three quarters flood at daylight. She will sail at or near seven o'clock. She goes to Cork, and you will be certain to overhaul to-day's Cunarder in Cork harbour. By tomorrow night you will be off Cape Clear."

"It is settled, then," said Barston, decidedly. "My dear

Mobby, I have given you many lectures upon Providence. Hear one more. I have a first class ticket in my pocket, but I could not get a smoking carriage, and the guard put me in here; and so I have had your agreeable company and obtained valuable information from you, which would not have happened if I had not obstinately resolved to have my cigar, though I had to relinquish cushioned seats and probably a comfortable nap. Now I would have given twenty thousand pounds for your touching little history of that encounter on the banks of the Avon if I could not have obtained it cheaper. And you have awakened so keen an interest in my heart in that little girl that I am going to America to-day, simply to find her; and I may add," he continued, through his teeth, " I shall never return until I do find her. And if you will excuse me I will try to get a small nap in this corner. Take another cigar, captain."

In two minutes Swiss was asleep.

" I've told Cappen Spencer a hundred times," said Mr. Mobby to himself, " that Mr. Barston was a reg'lar loonatick! He is a jolly good gentleman, and his cigars are prime A 1. But if he ain't a loonatick I want to see one! Twenty thousand pounds to hear me talk! And when he said his heart was in love with that precious babby he was a gritten his teeth. He's a reg'lar loonatick or I'm blowed !" In giving the sleeper this title he always accented the penultimate.

Then the captain put his unlighted cigar carefully away in his pouch and fell asleep in his corner.

———

CHAPTER XLV.

ADIEU!

THERE was very little sleeping done at Vincent Lodge that night. Messengers came at all hours, with the same dismal report, "no tidings," and Lady Lacy spent the weary hours in constructing hypotheses to account for the absence of Kitty and the child. If Barston had thought of it, he might have enlarged upon the kind Providence that led Mobby to the spot where the bracelet was found, instead of allowing some one of the searchers to find it. As no one had seen the embarkation of the child and her nurse excepting the people on the ship, now steaming down the channel, or those on the tug, now ploughing her way back from the mouth of the Avon, the conclusion would have been irresistible that both Kitty and Nellie were drowned.

Lady Lacy consulted time tables, and had fixed in her mind the hours at which Mr. Barston might possibly arrive. If he received the despatch without delay, the earliest possibility was the approaching dawn. The more she thought of him the more she expected him to restore Nellie. She recalled stories she had heard of his prowess, and there were not a few of them; and in spite of the harrowing anxiety that tortured her, she found her hopes reviving as the gray light began to appear in the eastern horizon.

It was only a possibility that all had gone smoothly, and that he would come with the sun, but she put a waterproof cloak on, drew the hood over her head, and walked down the drive and out upon the Clifton road. As she passed through the hall she saw the rector sitting at the table, his head resting on his arm, asleep. He had been watching there all night, and the fatigue had overcome him at last.

Down the Clifton road all was blank. There were stripes of orange and pink in the sky over the little hillock that bounded her view. Then the orange faded and the pink grew into crimson. Then

"Up leaped of a sudden the sun,"

and something appeared against his lurid disc. It was a vehicle approaching at a rapid rate.

Lady Lacy drew aside as it came near. It was a Hansom cab, empty!

While she was choking down her disappointment with a sob, the driver pulled up his panting horse at the gate and touched his hat to her.

"Vincent Lodge, mum?" he said.

"Yes, where are you from? What have you to tell?"

"Nothin', mum! I on'y want to speak to Lady Lacy."

"I am she," said Ret, throwing back her hood, "speak quickly, man, if you do not wish to drive me mad!"

"Beg pardin, my lady," returned cabby, "but the gent said I was to go to the 'ouse and give the letter to Lady Lacy herself——."

"Mr. Barston?" said she, with a flush of joy spreading over her face.

"Yes, my lady. It is all right if you know who sent it. Here is the letter. He told me to wait."

She made an assenting motion with her hand, took the letter, and re-entering the grounds, sat down on a garden seat near the gate and tore the envelope open. Something dropped out and fell at her feet. With a low cry she snatched it up and covered it with kisses. It was Nellie's bracelet. And while the fast flowing tears which fell like heavenly dew from her aching eyes dimmed her sight, she read the letter. You have peeped over her shoulder before, reader. Do it again.

> "BRISTOL—ON BOARD THE 'PRINCESS,'
> "6 O'CLOCK, A. M.

"MY LADY—I have traces of Nellie; nay, I know where she is, and that she is safe! I enclose her bracelet by way of proof. She is safe and well. Be comforted, oh mourner! Do not repine at delay that cannot be avoided. Let the one thought possess you. She is safe and well, and I am about to cross the ocean to regain her and restore her to you.

"Butler married Kitty at Stirling. Did you know it? He met her and Nellie at the foot of the cliff yesterday—I suppose at the upper end of Clifton. He was on board the ship *Pallas*, bound for New York, and while the vessel was accidentally detained, being aground, he took Kitty and the child aboard, and they are two days ahead of me. I shall catch to-day's Cunarder, from Liverpool, at Queenstown, where I shall be to-night, and if the same overruling Providence that revealed this much to me by a half miracle will still befriend us, I shall arrive in New York almost if not quite as soon as the *Pallas*. Is it necessary to say that I will never return without Nellie—that I will hunt every possible locality—that I will leave no means untried, no agency unemployed, that has the feeblest prospect of success?"

"Trust the Providence! Two years ago I was driven to America by dire calamity and distress, and while there I learned some of Butler's haunts. I have the most sanguine expectation of finding him and Nellie quickly. Do not doubt it.

"I am writing very hurriedly, as the ship sails immediately. May I say one word? You will be praying sometimes that Nellie may be restored to you; will you please add a little petition in behalf of her searcher?

> "LACY BARSTON."

"P. S.—I told cabby that you would perhaps drive to the Downs, and let me see you as the ship passes—say at the foot of the observatory. It has been two years since I saw you, and it would comfort me no little if my last look might rest upon you. I ventured to order him to wait until you read this missive."

"Oh, my darling!" said Lady Lacy, kissing the bracelet once more. "I shall see you again! My love, my love!" and in her confusion she got the bracelet and the letter mixed, and kissed them both. Then she hurried out to the road and entered the cab.

"Drive to the Downs," she said; "no time to lose!"

Seated on the bench below the observatory she could see a long stretch of the river, up and down. Far down towards the channel there was a tug coming up rapidly with the flood tide. The high bank hid the upper part of the river, trending northward, and she kept her gaze riveted upon the point where the Cork steamer must appear. Presently the prow was projected beyond the bank, then the foremast, then the slowly revolving paddles, and finally the whole vessel appeared less than a mile from her elevated perch. She started up, throwing off her hood, and the rays of the morning sun were glinted back from her beautiful hair, as she stood like a lovely statue upon the bald rock at the base of the observatory. Upon the paddle-box of the steamer now gliding by stood Lacy Barston, his arms stretched upwards towards her. She kissed her hand to him again and again, trying to think of some gesture that would show him her gratitude and admiration, and wondering at her own stupidity, while her lover stood watching her, his arms uplifted, until the ship passed out of sight. And in their after lives both of them often recalled that mute adieu and thanked heaven for the comfort they found in it.

When the cab reached the entrance to Vincent Lodge, Lady Lacy produced her purse.

"I'm paid, mum! beg parding, your ladyship! Muster Barston paid me for the whole job."

"How much?" said she.

"A sov'run, mum, your ladyship."

"Here is another. And if you ever need assistance come to me and get it," and she entered the grounds, robbing cabby of the most perfect vision of loveliness that his eyes had ever seen.

The rector was at the door, looking with amazement at her

cheerful countenance as she approached. She put Barston's note in his hand, and waited while he read it.

"Hurrah!" shouted Parson Johnny, throwing up his hat. "Swiss after her!' Ret, my darling sister, kiss me! I tell you, Ret, there is no man on this planet to compare with Swiss! He is as certain to find Nellie as if she were hidden in this hall. He is relentless as death, and will hunt America over on his hands and knees before he relinquishes his search. Trust Providence, and trust Swiss! Come, are you going to the Downs, as he requests?"

"No," she answered, composedly, taking her letter back.

"No! Why, Ret?"

"It is too late, Johnny. The ship sailed at daylight; it is now seven o'clock. I must run to Clare with the news."

"Well," said the discontented parson, as she flitted out of the hall, "women are 'kittle cattle,' as the Scotch say. Now, a man with one spark of gratitude in his body, would get a horse and ride down to the mouth of the river to say good-bye to a fellow under these circumstances. Poor old Swiss!"

While the trio were at breakfast, a messenger arrived with a note for Lady Lacy. It was as follows:

"*From the ex-gamekeeper to her high and mighty ladyship of the Harwood blood. Greeting:*

"I have taken my wife from under the protection of your ladyship. She had your child in charge, and could not leave her on the river bank. It was no part of my purpose to take the child, and she shall suffer no harm. You may know this, as she will be under Kitty's care until we can get her back to you. As she is only half Harwood, I can forgive her that misfortune for the sake of the better blood in her veins. I write this, not to relieve your anxiety, but because I promised my wife, and am not in the habit of lying."

"How did this come?" said the rector, starting up.

"A lad brought it, sir," answered the servant. "He says it was given him by the captain of a tug-boat, at the foot of the zigzag."

The rector found the boy at the door, who told the same story. A man on board the tug had thrown the note, tied to a lump of coal, ashore, and told the boy he would get half-a-crown for taking it to Vincent Lodge.

"An' I vants the arf-crown, please sir!" said the urchin.

And the Parson paid it.

CHAPTER XLVI.

ON THE TRACK.

BARSTON'S first question when he landed on the Cunard wharf at Jersey City related to the *Pallas*. A custom house official informed him that she had arrived on the previous day. The wharf was crowded with passengers, porters, sailors and custom house officers, and was a first class Babel. After some slight delay, Mr. Barston, committing his scanty luggage to a hotel porter, escaped from the wharf, and crossing the ferry, was swallowed up in the crowds of the American metropolis. He had learned the locality of the *Pallas*, and with the prompt decision peculiar to the man, he went directly to the pier where she was discharging cargo.

When he boarded the steamer at Queenstown he was not Lacy Barston, but John Smith. It had occurred to him that the New York newspapers published a list of passengers, and Mr. Butler might consult them and find his name, and make his search more difficult. This habit of considering all minor details was another peculiarity. He incurred the risk of encountering some acquaintance on the steamer, but it happened that all were strangers to him.

He found the purser on board the *Pallas*, and obtained his stock of information in a few minutes.

Mr. Butler had started with them from Bristol. The ship had grounded in the Avon, and Mrs. Butler and the child happened to be on the bank. "It was a touch and go business," the purser said. They had had a good passage, and the little girl was the idol of the ship. Her parents had kept her jealously with them, and were disinclined to allow any conversation with the bright little angel. He could not say positively where they had gone, but he thought to Chicago. Mr. Butler had asked a great number of questions about the West, and the purser knew that they had started from the *Pallas* for one of the railways. He thought it was the Erie.

This was all. Hunting for a needle in a haystack was a promising occupation in comparison with an expedition to Chicago with the very insufficient clue the purser furnished. Nevertheless, it

was the only thing to be done. Mr. Butler was twenty-four hours
ahead. This might be made up by express travelling night and
day. There was no train until six o'clock, so Mr. Smith went to
his hotel and dined. He had provided himself with all needful
funds in Cork, and now exchanged a hundred pounds for American currency, and he saw the sun set from the car window twenty
miles west of New York.

In the station at Chicago on the second day Mr. Smith began
his explorations with patient philosophy. He was looking for a
lady and gentleman and little girl. They had arrived six, twelve
or eighteen hours previously. The various officials he questioned
had each seen the very party he described, and upon cross-exam-
ination each gave a description totally at variance with all the
rest and entirely different from the reality that Mr. Smith sought.
One gave the gentleman red hair and beard, another made him
quite gray, and a third deprived him of all hirsute adornments by
describing his head as "smooth as a pumpkin." It was very remarkable that there should have been so many arrivals of trios in
less than one day and that they should have been so dissimilar,
each from the rest. He went to a hotel and wrote a cheerful
letter to Parson Johnny, reporting his arrival and promising a
weekly letter thereafter unless he should get out of the reach of
mails. He recounted such portions of the purser's story as referred
to the good health and happiness of Nellie with great care for the
comfort of her mother.

He spent a week at Chicago. Particular inquiry at every hotel
in the city revealed the fact that Butler had not been in any of
them. He must go elsewhere. There was a new town in Kansas
where people where flocking, "especially Britishers," and he would
go there next. Before his departure he wrote his second letter,
making light of the difficulties and warning the rector that "there
were so many places in America, and the distances were so great
between them, that he might not be able to give *positive* information until the coming spring." He thought, however, that he was
on the track, and he would certainly continue the search until he
found Nellie. She was traced positively to New York, and the
rest was only a matter of time. "If I only knew," he concluded,
"that your sister was patient and hopeful, and that she trusted
my sagacity and perseverance, I could enjoy every part of my
search, even its frequent disappointments, for I know I shall find
my darling at last, and I am willing to wait the developments of
Providence—Ebenezer!"

Arrived at New Washington, the Kansas metropolis that was to be, Mr. Smith renewed his inquiries, and here he fell into "a famous streak of luck," according to his landlord's opinion.

There was a party, father, mother and daughter, and the latter was named Nelly, that had arrived and departed two days ago. They were in haste to reach their destination, which was a farm out on the "peraira," and the landlord had only had a glimpse of them, as they stopped less than an hour. The child was a "mighty spry little gal;" but his interlocutor could give Mr. Smith nothing approaching an accurate description. They had come from New York, as he knew by the labels on their baggage, and he had over-heard the mother call the child "Nelly." They certainly went to Carthagenia, a station twenty miles distant, and their farm was in the vicinity of that renowned city. Mr. Smith went immediately to Carthagenia.

It was dark night when he arrived, and he was escorted to the hotel by a man carrying a lantern. This edifice was of one story, and the proprietor had not had time to adorn it as much as he could desire. It was builded of logs and contained four apartments; one was a kitchen, which was also the bar room and the dining hall; another was the sleeping apartment of the host and his partner in distress; a third was occupied by the progeny of this pair, numbering "seven head," as the landlady apprised him with com-mendable pride, and the fourth was the guest chamber, and already occupied by a returned soldier who had "got hurted in the war." Mr. Smith was assured that this warrior would share his couch with him, but as the last comer thought from his appearance that he would probably share some other things, he rapidly made up his mind to decline the favour. He cautiously inquired of one of the seven pledges whether there were "many hotels" in Carthagenia, and the pledge, with untutored hilarity at his heathenish ig-norance, informed him that the hotel he now sat in and the rail-way station were the only buildings of which Carthagenia at present boasted, excepting the stable attached to the hotel.

Mr. Smith had encountered some rude experiences in his journey through life, but this seemed to him a little more desolate than any former adventure. He was a smoker, and after a supper of fried bacon, Indian corn-bread, which his uneducated palate could not appreciate, and muddy coffee, he asked permission to walk out and smoke.

"You can smoke as well hyar, stranger," said the mistress of the mansion. "None of us objects to smoke in the least."

Thus encouraged Mr. Smith produced his cigar case, and politely offering one to the wounded veteran and one to his host, they were soon enveloped in a fragrant atmosphere, the more noticeable from the contrast it afforded to the prevalent odour of the hotel.

"Landlord," said the philosopher, after a whiff or two, "I have decided to sit up to-night, with your permission. I slept enormously last night."

"Don't see why you can't bunk with the soger," replied the landlord.

"My dear sir, I am engaged in an investigation that requires a great deal of patient thought——"

"You can think in bed, I guess."

"But I have not time for entomological studies, my dear sir," replied Mr. Smith, coolly. The other smokers stared at him through the smoke. The big word vanquished them.

"Air you a preacher?" said the host, after a pause.

"No."

"Air you a doctor?"

"No. I have dabbled a little in medical lore, but I do not belong to the profession."

"Air you looking for land hereaway?" persisted the host.

"No. I am looking for a lady and her husband, and a little girl named Nellie, who have recently arrived in this neighbourhood from New York—probably two days ago."

"Yaas!" responded the landlord, "that's Sponder! He bought yon farm on the peraira. It's a good farm, too. Sponder bought it a month ago. He went to Noo Yawk after his wife and darter jist two weeks ago. The little one is a spry gal. She is about the size of my Sally thar," and he pointed to a ten year old pledge. "Her name is Nellie. Her har is as black as the dickens, and so is her eyes! He got here night before last, and I hauled him and his plunder out to his farm."

Mr. Smith smoked quietly for several minutes and meditated. The description so rapidly given of the black-eyed Nellie did not at all correspond with his anticipations.

"Did you know Mr. Sponder before he came?" he asked.

"Oh yaas! We was pardners over in Illenoy in land speckillations. He has been here off and on a dozen times this summer." He rose as he spoke and lighted a lantern. "I hear the down train coming, and must go to the deep-o."

"I will go with you, landlord," said Mr. Smith. "I have decided to return to New Washington. Mr. Sponder is evidently not the gentleman I seek. Allow me to settle for my entertainment. I have the honour to bid you good night, madame."

It was raining as they left the hotel. The wounded warrior sat stolidly sucking at the stump of his cigar. Over the roar of the approaching train the hotel inhabitants heard the cheery tones of Mr. Smith's voice singing lustily,

> "A wet sheet and a flowing sea,
> And a wind that follows fast!"

" He sings prime!" said the warrior decidedly, "and his cigars are prime. But my belief is that he's a Johnny Reb, and he's after no good up hyar."

" Reb be hanged!" said the landlady, " what put that notion in your head ?"

" Well, ma'am," replied the soldier, " he talks jist as smooth as grease ; he slings his cigars about as if they was made of Connecticut tobaccer at a cent a piece ; he gave your little girl a dollar greenback—I seed him—and he is so bloody polite! I tell you, ma'am, he's a Johnny Reb. I hev bin among them cattle, and I know 'em. He's a Johnny Reb!"

CHAPTER XLVII.

ON THE RIGHT TRACK.

THE patience with which Mr. Smith encountered his various disappointments was very remarkable. In his weekly letters to his friend the rector, he recounted the salient points in his adventures, and always had a new theory to suggest upon which he would act in the coming week. He spent the entire winter in explorations of western towns, always in vain, as the reader knows.

He was at Omaha in the last week of March, and pursuing his steadfast plan of asking questions whenever he could find an interlocutor civil enough to answer him, he suddenly fell in with the only man in America who could have given him the information he sought. He was a " switch tender" in the railway station,

16

and Mr. Smith found him because he made it an invariable rule to interrogate every railway official he could induce to listen to and answer him. This one was a countryman, and had come over in the *Pallas!* As soon as Mr. Smith learned this fact he ascertained when the man would be at liberty, and invited him to meet him at his hotel and dine with him. The switchman was punctual, with a clean face and decent apparel—his Sunday suit, in fact.

They had dinner in a private room, and when his guest was as full of dinner as his capacity would allow, Mr. Smith pumped him dry.

He knew Butler on the ship, went with him and his wife and child to the railway station in New York, saw him buy his tickets and saw his luggage checked to a town in New Jersey within forty miles of New York. Mr. Smith pressed a twenty dollar note upon his countryman, paid his hotel bill, and started the same night for New York.

It was all plain sailing now. He wrote the shortest letter of the series to Mr. Harwood, full of joyful anticipations, and promising full details a week later; and when he arrived at the Jersey village he suddenly remembered that it was the post-office address given him by Hawder the year before. The first step was to find Hawder.

He had dressed himself in homespun garments, which he had procured in the West, and with a knapsack on his back he began his search in the village. The post-master informed him that Hawder lived a few miles off, and directed him to "Baird's Tavern," whence he could be directed to Hawder's residence by a straight road. It was afternoon, horribly inclement, a sharp storm of rain mingled with sleet was progressing, but Mr. Smith resolutely set out, in defiance of wind and weather.

The gentle reader is thus brought to the opening chapter of this truthful history. Before midnight Barston knew where the child was, and had decided accurately how to gain possession of her.

He went to Baird's tavern, where Nellie, totally unconscious of his presence, once or twice flitted momently in sight. The strong man could scarcely restrain himself when he saw her, but he did. Near midnight, having ascertained where she slept, he got a ladder from the stable and entered her room from the window. She was asleep in her crib, and kneeling by it Barston took her in his arms and held her close to his beating heart. He pressed his lips to hers as she opened her eyes, and whispered:

"Nellie, Nellie! my darling, don't speak. If you know me, kiss me!"

"Cousin Lacy!" said the child, clinging to his neck. "Oh, take me to mamma!"

"I will, my precious baby; but don't speak above a whisper."

He had a railway rug on his arm, and wrapping the child in it after he had enveloped her in his own coat, he gathered up her clothing, and taking her in his arms again descended the ladder and walked swiftly to Hawder's house. When he arrived there he remembered that he had been cautioned against possible contagion, and alarmed for the child he continued his walk, crossing the bridge at the mouth of a creek, and then taking the high road he walked a dozen miles before he reached a railway station. Here he found a little fury of a stove, red hot, and by its light he dressed the happy child in her proper garments. A freight train, with one passenger car attached, passed the station as the dawn appeared, and a little after sunrise he was in New York.

He had been a week within reach of Nellie before he could accomplish his purpose. Hawder was sick of enteric fever, and he had nursed him a night or two. Afterwards he was baffled once and again by Butler's watchfulness, and on the night of his bold attempt he had seen this worthy drinking himself into a state of utter helplessness.

It was Sunday when he reached New York. He took Nellie to his hotel and locked himself in his chamber with her; and then his manhood deserted him, or he attained a new advance in manhood, whichever the reader pleases. He threw himself on the bed and burst into tears.

Nothing could be more touching or more charming than the tender ministrations of the little fairy he had rescued. She fluttered round him, cried with him, kissed him, patted his cheek with her hand, wiped his eyes with her pinafore, promised him unlimited good things when they got home, and finally got him to sit up and take her on his knee.

"My darling," he said, "we cannot get a ship for three days, then we will go home. But you cannot be out of my sight one solitary minute until we see your mamma. I must take you wherever I go. And now I want you to go to sleep while I wash my face and order breakfast. Don't tell anybody that you saw me crying."

"No, only mamma."

Lacy blushed like a girl. "My dear," he said, "I fear you have made the worst possible exception."

"I *must* tell mamma. She likes me to tell her everything about you."

"Does she?" said Swiss. "Well, you are a wise little woman, and I will think about it. Will you go to sleep now?"

"Yes. Kiss me good night. Won't we have a good ride on Roland when we get home!" and she coiled herself up in the bed and was asleep in five minutes.

Mr. Barston took advantage of the opportunity to resume his ordinary habiliments. He could not buy any garments for Nellie, as it was Sunday, so he spent the day in his room with her. She was amiable, and allowed him to smoke *ad libitum*.

The next day he procured all the attire that Nellie needed, and a good lot that she did not need, then went with her to the office of the steamship company and secured passage for Wednesday.

On the next day he took Nellie to see the ship and arrange their luggage. He had bought a lot of toys, which filled one trunk, and at last got their stateroom arranged to his satisfaction. Before he left the ship he learned that "Mr. and Mrs. Barston" were going in the same vessel, and that they had the opposite stateroom. Thinking the name rather peculiar, he drove back to the agent's office, as he could get no information on the ship, and there he learned that Mr. Barston was a very nice gentleman, with a red scar on his forehead. Then Mr. Smith asked and obtained permission to transfer his ticket to Mr. Jones and son, as Mr. Smith and daughter were obliged to change their plans.

The rest of the day was employed in procuring a new set of habiliments for Nellie, and explaining to her why the disguise was necessary. He did not dare trust Butler, though he felt certain that he would not interfere with the return of the child. He would not wait for another ship, and the only course left was to disguise himself and Nellie both. They were transformed into Mr. Jones and son before dark, and as the ship was to sail early in the day, they went aboard on Tuesday night.

Captain Strong has already related the main incidents of the passage. Mr. Jones and son landed at Queenstown, and proceeding to Dublin, crossed by the fast mail to Holyhead, and reached London the next morning. Pausing only long enough to ascertain that Lady Lacy was at the Red Hall, he went directly to Lavington. As he and Nellie had a compartment to themselves, he changed her dress once more, though he had no opportunity to resume his own identity. He was too eager to wait, and on the arrival of the train he took a cab and drove to the Red Hall with all possible speed.

His last letter had announced Nellie found, and Lady Lacy, expecting fuller intelligence by the mail just due, was driving into Lavington, hoping to find letters at the rectory. Swiss saw the carriage half a mile distant. A sudden fit of shyness seized him, and stopping his vehicle, he kissed Nellie, wild with delight and excitement, set her out on the roadside, and bade his jehu retrace his steps. He looked out of the back window and saw the carriage stop, Nellie fly to the side, and clambering up the steps, get torn into bits between Miss Tamworth and her mother, as they fought over the child like a pair of raging tigresses. Then the carriage turned backward also, and as it disappeared Mr. Barston lighted a cigar and soliloquized:

"It would have been very absurd of me to have shown myself to those lovely women in this sort of a costume. I don't think they would ever get over the shock! How they did claw my poor little baby! How their precious tongues will wag the rest of this day! What yarns Nellie will spin! Hum! My lady likes her to talk about me, does she? Well, let the child talk! Ah, Ret!" and he shook his fist at the retreating carriage—"the next time we meet, you will be mine—or, by the three kings, I will steal Nellie again!" and he laughed gleefully.

The cabby plodded on at a jog trot. He had earned his fare by the fast driving towards the Red Hall. The "old gent" did not care to get back so rapidly, so he would take his time. He had no special directions, but concluded the old gent wished to go to the inn, where he had sent his luggage. He peeped once or twice through the trap in the roof, but could only see the outlines of the old gent, as a fine cloud of smoke enveloped him. He seemed to be more than half asleep. But the inn was reached at last, and when the old gent blundered out, and into the sanded common room, he very nearly upset another "gent," who was not so old, and was quite surprised to recognize his compagnon de voyage, the *soi disant* Mr. Barston.

CHAPTER XLVIII.

The Cain Mark.

IF the gentle reader will go back to the twentieth chapter of this history, the very abrupt manner in which Sir John Lacy was dismissed from the narrative will be apparent. The time has now arrived when it will be in order to take up the thread there dropped, and the author recurs to that time with the greater reluctance, because it adds another to the already multiplied indications that the story is drawing to a close.

After Barston had parted from him, the baronet rode slowly along, thinking of the exciting colloquy just over, and the change wrought in his purposes and sentiments.

"I must tell Ret all about it," he thought. "Poor girl! she has been annoyed, no doubt, though she has said nothing. I must also manage to get her diamonds back;" and he took the box from his pocket and looked at the gems, flashing in the moonlight. The satellite was just appearing, full, above the horizon. "I wonder how much the trinkets are worth? Here is the Dark Wood. It will save a mile to cross here. The hedge is low. So! Saladin! Over we go!"

As the horse leaped and alighted at the edge of the wood, a man started up from the ground and confronted the rider.

"Hillo!" said Sir John, thrusting the jewel case into his bosom, "who are you?"

"I was about to put the same question to you," said the stranger, coming a little more into the moonlight, "but I believe your name is Lacy?"

"Having discovered this fact," replied Sir John, "you will perhaps acknowledge that I am on my own land and have the right to ask your business."

"I am not so sure of that," said the other, laughing disagreeably, "your title to the land may be questioned, perhaps. You are married, I hear?"

"What the devil do you mean by this insolence?" said Sir John. "Get out of my path and get off my property. You are a tresspasser."

"Softly," replied the stranger, "you are making too many assertions in one. You cannot pass until I have some speech with you. I thought of calling upon you at the Red Hall, but this is better."

" If you are drunk I can overlook this offence. If you are sober, I caution you to take yourself out of reach. I am a magistrate, and am bound to have you up for trespassing on a gentleman's grounds, unless," he added, shaking his rein and touching his horse with the spur, " unless you choose to apologize and decamp."

" How easily I can change all that lordly air," said the trespasser, laughing again, " with a word or two. You cannot pass, I tell you, until I have had my say !"

Sir John snatched his sabre from the scabbard and shook it wrathfully over his head.

" If you do not clear the path on the instant," he said, sternly, " I swear I will cut you down, you scoundrel !"

" Pooh !" said Butler, composedly, " the greater part of my life has been spent among real swords, where they were thicker than the twigs above your head ! Put up your holiday weapon, and keep it to frighten boys withal. You dare not use it upon me !"

Something in the man's manner impressed Sir John, and he lowered his weapon.

" Say what you have to say, then," he answered, " and oblige me by being brief as possible. I yield to your madness, for you must be mad, as you are clearly not drunk. What is your business ?"

" I have not decided fully," said Butler. " Perhaps I may let you off easily, as you have lowered your tone. I want to know more about your wife before I can tell you what I require."

" Hark you, Mr. Mountebank," said Sir John, struggling with his rising temper, " speak respectfully of Lady Lacy, or——"

" Pshaw !" said Butler, rudely, again laying his hand on the bridle, " you had better be sure that she *is* Lady Lacy before you lose your temper. What are you doing ?"

" Out of my path on your peril !" said the baronet, rising in his stirrups as his sabre circled round his head. " By Heaven, your life hangs upon a thread ! I will cleave your head in three seconds if you are within reach of my sword. One, two, three !" and the bright blade, flashing in the moonlight, descended like a bolt from the heavens.

" Madman !" said Butler, throwing up a thick stick he had plucked from the hedge, " would you kill your brother ?"

The keen blade cut through the tough cudgel, and though the force of the blow was broken by the parry, it bit deeply into the upturned forehead of the trespasser, blinding him with the quick flowing blood. Pressing heavily upon the bridle, the horse reared, struck out with his forelegs, and fell over upon his rider. Elbert Lacy passed his hand over his eyes as the horse, struggling to his feet, galloped away towards the Hall, snorting with fright.

He drew the motionless body of his brother into the moonlight and looked anxiously upon his pale face. The frown was rapidly fading from his countenance, giving place to an appalling calm which Elbert knew from many experiences betokened death! He put his hand—first cleansing it from blood stains, on the dewy grass—upon his brother's heart. It had ceased to beat! As he withdrew it from his vest a small jewel case fell upon the ground. He raised it, read the inscription "Lacy," and placed it in his own pocket. The sabre had fallen from the dead man's hand. Elbert raised it, wiped the stain upon his coat sleeve, and returned it to its sheath.

All this time the sound of the hoofstrokes of the flying horse came floating back upon the breeze.

"Dead!" said Elbert, "and by my hand! And he has left the Cain brand on my forehead to abide while my life lasts! Of all the horrors that have darkened that life this is the culmination. Guiltless in the sight of heaven, I swear!" and he lifted his hand solemnly to the solemn sky, "yet no stream can be found to wash away this stain! Oh, Jack, how joyfully would I change places with you, poor boy!"

He sat down upon the ground, took out the jewel case and opened it. The diamonds seemed to gather up all the rays of the moonlight and flash them back into the eyes of Elbert Lacy, mocking him with their weird and devilish glitter.

"Ay, ay!" he said, "I have heard of you many a time, and I would recognize you anywhere on the earth! No Lacy can die by Lacy's hand unless you are near!"

He thrust the box back into his pocket and rose from the ground, picking up the two pieces of the cudgel and looking curiously at the cut in the tough wood. It was a clean transverse cut, looking as if it had been made by the blow of an axe.

"The boy was a good sworder. If I had not chanced to pull this from the hedge it would have been Elbert Lacy lying there so still and calm. As it was, he has cut me to the bone! He died aflame with rage, and I have killed him, without design and without anger. It will take a portion of my life-long remorse away to remember that! It was the cursed curb that caused it all! The brute reared up and tore the rein from my hand at the very instant that Jack cut at me!"

He knelt down by the body and looked earnestly at the up-turned face, calm and beautiful. There was a strange composure in all that this outcast did, and his passions and feelings, tumultuous as they were, undoubtedly, were still held in perfect check. Under happier tutelage his marred life would perhaps have been brilliant and beneficent, for he had the attributes of noble manhood, albeit all warped from their normal tendencies.

"How handsome he is!" he said, sadly, and he leaned over him and kissed his cold forehead. "I would have died for you, brother," he continued as he rose, "but it was not to be. The curse that clings to the Lacy line has found you, Jack. My turn next, and I care not how soon it comes!"

With the fragments of his cudgel in his hand he crossed the hedge, swinging clear of it by an overhanging bough, and entering the wood on the opposite side of the road which divided the Lacy lands from the estate of Lord Morton, he suddenly found the death he courted waiting for him.

In an open glade, so near that he could hear the trampling of their feet, three men were pressing hardly upon a fourth. He could see the flash of a knife in the hands of one of the assailants, and without a moment's pause he dashed into the fray.

"Three upon one!" he shouted, as he felled the nearest with his short cudgel. "Shame upon you, cowards!"

The others turned upon him with curses, leaving their intended victim, who sunk bleeding to the ground. He had been cut in the arm by the knife, which the younger still held in his hand, as he rushed upon Elbert Lacy. The latter, avoiding his assault by springing aside, snatching a gun from the ground, discharged it at the baffled robber before he could stop in his career. He fell with a groan, and Lacy grappled immediately with the other, receiving an ugly blow upon the head, but holding his grip upon the throat of his brawny assailant with iron muscles. The wounded gamekeeper crawled to his assistance, and between them the poacher was borne to the earth and his arms pinioned. The others were already *hors de combat.*

The struggle occurred near the road-side, and the sound of the gun shot attracted a passing laborer, who came rapidly to the spot, directed by the shouts of the gamekeeper. And as Elbert Lacy saw the newcomer approach, his grasp upon the prostrate poacher relaxed, and he rolled over in a swoon by his side.

CHAPTER XLIX.

The Kinsmen.

"WELL met!" said Mr. Butler, as Swiss recoiled, "I was thinking of you this moment!"

"Mr.——Barston?" said Swiss.

"Well, no!" replied the other, "that was only a temporary title, which I assumed for a purpose. Come into my room and I will tell you about it."

He threw open a door as he spoke, and old Mr. Jones obeyed his courteous gesture and entered the room. The other followed him, and closing the door turned the key!

"It would be inconvenient to be interrupted," he said, apologetically, "take a seat, pray. But if I may venture to say so, you look so confoundedly ugly in that old tow wig that you would do well to take it off! So!" he continued, as Mr. Jones disappeared, wig and gray beard and stooping shoulders and all, while handsome Lacy Barston emerged from the ruins; "that is better! and now, Lacy Barston, I may say to you that I knew you on the ship as soon as you spoke!"

"Indeed!" said Barston, coolly.

"Yes! I recognized the Lacy burr. There is no mistaking it."

"True," said Swiss. "I think I knew you, Elbert, or at least that peculiarity of speech helped enlighten me. My dear cousin, I offer you my hand with true affection."

"Stop a moment!" said the other, a little startled, "you don't know yet what stains are on my hand——"

"Neither do I care, Elbert. If your hand would 'incarnadine multitudinous seas,' it is still the hand of my only living kinsman. Give me your hand, Elbert!"

The other stood gazing irresolutely at him a moment, and then sat down near him, his hands thrust into his pockets.

"Lacy," he said, speaking slowly and without any sign of emotion, "I told you a large part of my miserable story on the ship yonder. I was half mad with drink, but I deliberately told you every word because I would not sail under false colours with you. But there are some things that I did not tell you, and you must hear them now. Where is Nellie ?"

" In her mother's arms. Where is your wife ? I desire to be the first to address her as Lady Lacy !"

" Never !" said his cousin. " She can never have the title. It is a hateful name to me, since one of those cursed Harwoods has borne it !"

" For shame, Elbert !" said Barston, reproachfully, " you come of a gentle strain ; do not contradict your better instincts, and do not insult me by rude speeches against the lady I love ! Ret Harwood will be my wife if I ever have a wife.'

" Is it so ? Well, I will say no more, and will try to forget her haughty insolence. There ! there ! I have done. Kitty is abed, slowly recovering from the effects of the voyage. You shall see her anon, and if you wish to call her by the title you name, after you hear my story to the end, I shall not hinder you. Will you listen ?"

" Assuredly."

" You know all about me up to our parting at Liverpool, when we came from Australia, except that I had been fortunate at the gold diggings and brought some money home."

" I knew that, too, Elbert," said Barston ; " the captain told me of the bag of gold dust you gave into his charge."

" Ay, ay !" replied Elbert, " I gave him that before several witnesses. My object was to make all who knew it suppose that was all my wealth. It was not the tithe of it ! I had ten times the sum belted round my waist, in Bank of England notes ; and I have it still, or Kitty has, which is better."

" It makes little difference, Elbert," answered Swiss. " I have more than I can spend, and my purse is yours whenever you need it."

" You are kind, but there is no need. Well, after you saw me and Kitty over yonder at her house, I wandered away into the country around Lavington, trying to humanize myself by recalling events of my boyhood. Alas ! every spot I saw and recognized amid the changes wrought by the lapse of a dozen years and more, only brought back the memory of the wrongs that drove me from these scenes ! I spent the day brooding over these wrongs, and at nightfall I was alone in the Dark Wood, when

Jack came suddenly upon me, leaping his horse over the hedge. Ah! I see you anticipate what is to follow. He did not know me, and I, moody and irritable, chafed him with rude words. Before I knew it he had torn his sword from the scabbard, and——gave me this—this—accursed Cain brand!

"It is a Cain brand, for I killed him! I had my hand on his bridle, and when his blow came, like a thunderbolt, I called my name to him, and pressing on his rein, his horse reared and fell on him, crushing out his bright young life, and taking the last vestige of human emotion out of mine. I killed him—innocently, I need not tell you—but I killed him—my brother!

"Will you take my hand now, Mr. Barston?"

"Yes," said Barston, clasping his extended hand while he passed his other arm around the other's neck. "Poor old Elbert! I am so sorry for all you have suffered! But your sufferings are over, I hope. In the first place, your story does not happen to be true. You did not kill Jack!"

"What say you?" said Lacy, starting to his feet. "You mean I am guiltless of intention but guilty in fact——"

"I don't mean any such rubbish. Jack did not die of any hurt inflicted by you, accidentally or otherwise. He died a natural death!"

Elbert sat watching him with wonder in his eyes.

"It is true, Elbert. You know I would not lie to you! Poor Jack's life hung upon a thread. He had organic disease of the heart. I knew it years before, for I have studied the science of medicine. Dr. Holly knew it, and pronounced it the cause of his sudden death; and finally Dr. Cardon, who is the ultimate authority on heart diseases in England, pronounced this case a perfect specimen when I told him Jack's symptoms. Cheer up, Elbert, and spend the rest of your days in thanking Heaven that this burden is lifted from your heart."

"Can this be true?" said Lacy, as if stunned. "Have I been withering under this blighting curse all these years! Why, if your story is true, Barston, this beauty spot of mine may be obliterated also!"

"Perhaps. Let me look at it. Of all the sworders I have ever known Jack was the best, excepting only his teacher. I marvel that you lived to tell the story of that encounter."

"I had a tough ashen staff in my hand, with which I parried the blow. He cut through it as if it had been a pipe stem. I had been sped, no doubt, if his maddened horse had not reared at the same moment. Can the scar be cured?"

"It can be made much lighter, at least. Will you submit to some pain and annoyance for a few weeks?"

"To get this accursed mark off my face I would submit to a year's torture upon the rack. When will you begin?"

"Nay, you shall have no bungler," said his cousin. "I will get Cardon. Let us go to London and consult him. I will go with you."

"When?"

"To-night, if you will."

"Agreed. My dear Barston, there is no man like you on the earth! If I could make you know how this hideous scar bites into my brain you would not wonder at my eagerness. And now hear a word or two more. I never intended to take little Nellie away. You discovered that I married Kitty at Stirling. I persuaded her to call herself Miss Tamworth because your parson friend was spooney upon her, and I was sure he would hear of the marriage. It was pure spite against him that prompted me. When I met Kitty at Clifton it was accidental. She had Nellie with her, and we were compelled to take her. I confess that I enjoyed the thought that her mother would be distracted, but I sent her a note by the tug to relieve her anxiety. When we reached America I could not bear to take the child far out into the West; and indeed my wife would not consent. She is Jack's child, and I was a prey to remorse on his account, and I drank myself drunk nearly every day to escape from memory. Kitty told me the day after you took the child that you had done it, and she pleaded so earnestly to come back to England that I had to yield. One day at sea, and your disguise and Nellie's were wasted on me. The odour of salt water brought back all my faculties. It was pleasant to watch you and Hawder and let you think you were unknown; but I have had no unkind thought in my heart at any time against you, and more than once I have been on the very verge of a full confession to you when your woman's voice was singing in my ears! Ah, Barston! no woman can withstand you. If she listens she is vanquished!"

Swiss blushed and laughed.

"Now I will go tell Kitty. You will be ready at train time? And if your London doctor undertakes this cure you will stay by me until it is done?"

"I will. We have an hour or more. I will meet you at the station. Greet Lady Lacy in my name and tell her that her husband's cousin is her cousin also, and claims kindred."

"Stop, Barston," said the other, as he unlocked the door, "until this blot is removed, no Lady Lacys, if you please; no Sir Elberts, but—my old name—inherited from the pirate captain, the greatest thief and scoundrel that ever cursed the earth with his presence—Mr. Butler!"

CHAPTER L.

LOVE TOKENS.

WITH patient self-denial Lacy Barston staid by his cousin's side while Dr. Cardon wrought with the stubborn scar. He talked, read the papers, explained multitudes of conventionalisms of which Sir Elbert was totally ignorant, but which must be known by all who move in refined society. He drove out with him through the brilliant streets at night, when the bandaged head of his cousin could not be seen, in their Hansom. And when the baronet retired for the night Swiss would steal an hour or so from his own slumbers to write to Parson Johnny.

He could only tell him that he was kept there in attendance upon a friend, undergoing a prolonged surgical operation, and that he would fly to Lavington as soon as this duty was accomplished. Elbert steadfastly insisted upon maintaining his incognito, until he could face the world without a blemish upon his countenance.

One day Barston was walking down Regent street, and he suddenly ran against the rector. With a shout of delight he clutched his arm, and hurrying him into the Haymarket, entered the Western Club. Seated in the smoking room Swiss bade him "talk and tell him everything he knew."

"The best news I have, dear old Swiss, is that Clare and Ret have just gone to Paris——"

"Well, that is a promising beginning!" ejaculated Swiss, with an elongated countenance. "How long will they stay?"

"I cannot tell," replied Mr. Harwood, with a little blush; they are on a shopping expedition. Miss Tamworth is to be married a month hence, and said she must go to Paris to get some 'things.' I don't know what they are."

" Where is Nellie ?"

" At Harwood House."

" Why did you not accompany the ladies ?"

" They would not allow me. I am permitted to go after them when notified. My dear Swiss, in one month from this day I shall be invested with authority to regulate the movements of one of them, at least. In the meantime submission to all sorts of absurd whims is my daily lesson."

" Learn it well, Parson. You will find the knowledge useful hereafter. Please give me the ladies' address."

" Hotel de Lisle et Albion," answered the rector. " Lord and Lady Morton are there. Come with me to Harwood House, Swiss."

" I cannot, Johnny. I am sorry, but I must attend upon my friend here for a week or two more. He is undergoing a painful and tedious operation, and I promised to stay by him."

" Who is it, Swiss ?"

" Ah ! that is a secret. I will tell you later. This is the fifteenth. Do you mean to tell me that you will be married on the fifteenth of August ?"

" That is the happy day, Swiss. Oh ! how I wish you also——"

" Thank you, Johnny. I think I shall ! Don't ever tell that I said so, I pray you. But I shall set my wits to work to bring it to pass ! It would be jolly to be married on the same day with you ! Where do you go for the honeymoon ?"

" Through Scotland, the Lochs, the Trossachs, everywhere, anywhere. You know I missed that trip last summer."

" So did I. The route is faultless. Would you object to have Ret and me in the party ?"

" Object ! Oh, Swiss ! Poor Swiss ! Have you spoken to Ret on the subject ?"

" I have not spoken to her for three years ! When I speak to her again I will speak to purpose ! My dear Johnny, my whole soul is full of her ! Without one word of encouragement I am still so happy, whenever I think of her, and that is always, night and day, asleep and awake, that I know I shall win her ! If she did not love me in requital for all the volume of love I feel for her— why, Parson, it would be like a vacuum in nature. I am *sure* of her ! The horror, the dismay, the madness of failure—Pooh ! It is one of those things that are simply inconceivable !"

" Poor Swiss !"

"Get out, you sleek old rascal!" said Barston, "do you suppose that you are the only man that knows how to court?"

"Ah, Swiss! if it were anybody but Ret! I have tried to get her to talk of you a dozen times since you brought Nellie back. She listens to all I say, but she never mentions your name!"

"Don't she?" said Swiss, with a grin.

"No," answered the rector, a little nettled—"and Clare tells me that she has attempted once or twice to joke her about you, and that she receives all these attempts with imperturbable gravity."

"Does she?" said Swiss, the grin broadening.

"Upon my word, Swiss, your conceit is intolerable!" said the rector, in a rage. "It is bad enough for me to see how hopeless your case is, without having to endure that complacent smirk too!"

"Why, you poor old dunderhead!" said Barston, "all the symptoms you have described are highly favourable! I am more than ever convinced that she has a liking for me."

"Please enlighten me, then," said the bewildered Parson, "for I vow I am entirely in the dark as to your method of extracting comfort from the signs I have given you."

"Promise to keep the secret, then."

"I promise."

"*Eh bien!*" said Mr. Barston, leaning back in his chair, "to begin——"

"Stop, Swiss!" said the rector, suddenly. "I have one more shot before you begin. Do you remember sending a note to Ret when you sailed from Bristol? Well, she handed it to me. I read it. You requested, poor boy, that she would show herself to you from the Downs! Ah! you remember, I see. I caught up my hat, and bade her come to the Downs before your ship passed, and she——"

"Go on, Parson! what the mischief are you stopping for?"

"I don't like to tell you, Swiss! She took back your note, folded it coolly, and said, 'Too late, Johnny! the ship must have sailed at daylight,' and *she* sailed out of the room with the most perfect indifference—— What ails you? You will have a fit if you cough and splutter in that fashion! Laugh out, you goose, if you see anything amusing and encouraging in my story!"

"Excuse me, Parson!" said Barston, recovering his gravity. "I will explain my hilarity anon. To begin: Women were intended by Nature to govern the world. All of these modern 'womens' rights' leagues are miserable caricatures of a grand truth. Also, all of this awful rubbish about ' natural selection ' has a golden thread of truth mingled with enormous masses of lies and bosh ! and that truth is the essential domination of woman. Do not misunderstand me. Her husband is her lord, and the true woman delights to acknowledge his authority. But she does verily reign in and through him with despotic sway. You spoke of your 'authority' a little while ago. Why, you. simple-minded Parson, do you not know that one tear would melt your authority at once ! And what do you think would be the power of a pint of tears all poured out at once ? They keep them, man, subject to call ; an army of rain drops ; swift, prompt, irresistible. No man who is not a brute can withstand a true woman's tears !"

" That sounds quite rational !" quoth the Parson.

" Rational ! Of course ! Now, secondly, they have another troop of invincible forces—warriors, called smiles. Don't you know, Johnny, that you would jump in the river to gain a smile when it is withheld ?"

" Yes, perhaps !"

" Then, Parson," continued the orator, " women are secretive in all matters pertaining to their affections. I cannot say they deceive you, but they allow you to deceive yourself, and if there is any one thing which a spooney man is sure to do, it is to make a goose of himself whenever occasion offers. Ret never said she disliked me, did she ?"

" No ; I tell you she says nothing whatever about you !"

" And, therefore, you stretch your long neck up and think you have read her heart ! 'If she did not dislike Lacy Barston she would be certain to speak of him.' Now, try the other proposition ! If she did not *like* Lacy Barston she would be *certain* to speak of him !"

" Very well, Mr. Swiss," said the rector, " have it your own way. You forget that I have known a long time that you loved Ret, and that I have watched very anxiously for some symptom that was favourable. In vain, Swiss, in vain !"

" Keep on watching, Parson," said Barston, " but keep your mouth shut."

" No use to watch, Swiss ! That morning at Clifton satisfied me ! Why, if you had written that note to me I should have crawled to the river on my knees if I could have got there no otherwise. Just think of it ! here you were about to start on a long journey, three or four thousand miles, to look for her own child, and all you asked was just to look at her as your vessel passed the place! Why, if she had hated the sight of you she might have done it out of mere gratitude! It was all humbug about the ship starting too soon. I remember now that the cab was there! Ah, Swiss, it was heartless! heartless!"

Barston rolled about in his cushioned chair in strong convulsions. Mr. Harwood took his hat and stalked with dignity to the door.

"I must bid you good morning, Mr. Barston," he said, "and I beg you will not restrain your merriment on my account. I have read of laughing hyenas somewhere, and," he concluded sardonically, "I have also heard of people who laughed on the wrong side of their mouths!"

CHAPTER LI.

SIR ELBERT LACY.

IT was the first day of August, and all Nature was baking. The various personages, in whose fate the charming reader is specially interested, were all in fair Devon. Morton Priory was inhabited. Clare, with numberless trunks, had taken up her abode there; Lord and Lady Morton claimed her, and Ret relinquished her at their urgent solicitation. Distracting parcels came from Paris day by day, and Miss Tamworth spent many hours in fluttering from one trunk to another, gloating over the flimsy wealth wrought by the nimble fingers of French *modistes*.

Sir Elbert Lacy and Mr. Barston had returned from London on the previous day. The scar upon the brow of the baronet was nearly obliterated; a faint line remained, visible only when some strong excitement sent the Lacy blood to his forehead.

Lady Lacy was at the Red Hall. She was in the Lollard's room, near the library, when a carriage came through the arch, and grated on the gravel. While she wondered who her early visitors might be, a servant brought the cards:

"*Sir Elbert Lacy.*"
"*Lady Lacy.*"

With increased astonishment Ret directed the servant to show the new comers into the library, and recognized Mr. Butler and

Kitty, both in faultless apparel, as they entered the apartment. Ret arose and stood by the library table, while the visitors quietly took the seats the servant placed.

"I owe you an apology, madame," began Sir Elbert——

"Pardon me!" said Ret—"William, ask Mrs. Froome to come to the library." She still stood, gazing intently at the composed faces before her, until the rustling of Mrs. Froome's dress announced her presence.

"Proceed, sir," said Ret.

"Ah, Mrs. Froome!" said the baronet; "I might safely rely upon you to recognize me. We have met once or twice within the past few years; but you must now go back a score of years to recall the features of Elbert Lacy!"

The old woman went up to him, peered anxiously in his face, then took his hand and kissed it.

"It is Sir Elbert Lacy, my lady!" she said, turning to Ret. "It is Master John's elder brother!" Ret looked at her with silent incredulity. "Nay, my lady," continued Mrs. Froome, "if you have any doubt, look here!" She went to the opposite wall and tore aside the crimson curtain from the portrait of the Red Lacy. Sir Elbert laughed, while a disagreeable sneer passed over his face, and the red line on his forehead came into view. The resemblance betwixt him and the picture was certainly very striking, and Ret began to have some glimmering of the truth.

"Mrs. Froome," said Sir Elbert, "I remember a certain bin in the wine cellar where my father had some South Side Madeira. Do you think you could find a bottle?"

Mrs. Froome rattled her keys, and looked doubtfully at Ret, who was passing through certain mental exercises with lightning rapidity.

"My lady!" said she.

"Really, Mrs. Froome," said Sir Elbert, rudely, "there is no necessity for this appeal. And the title is inaccurate also, unless madame may inherit it from the gentle Harwoods! There is no Lady Lacy here excepting this lady by my side."

"Why have you not asserted your claim earlier?" said Ret, the haughty Harwood blood mantling on cheek and forehead.

"Certain obstacles prevented, madame," returned the other; "besides, I thought I would wait for my birthday. I believe I was born on the first of August, Mrs. Froome?"

"Yes, Sir Elbert; at sunset."

"Well, the Ides have come, if not gone. May I trouble you to get the wine, I am athirst?"

Ret signed to Mrs. Froome, who rustled out of the room.

"Be seated, madame, I beg," said the baronet. "The owner-ship of the old Madeira will hardly be questioned, I presume. I shall have the pleasure of drinking your health presently. My dear, remove your bonnet, and bid Mrs. Lacy welcome!"

Ret glanced from the window at the western sky. A dark cloud was overspreading the heavens. She quietly put on a dainty little chip hat that was lying on the table, and threw a waterproof cloak over her shoulders. Mrs. Froome re-entered the library, followed by William, with a tray containing wine glasses and biscuits. Mrs. Froome placed a cobwebbed bottle on the table, and William drew the cork with exemplary caution. The odour of the wine filled the apartment. Ret was moving to the door, when Kitty started up and caught her cloak.

"Oh, my lady!" she began——

"Perdition!" said her husband. "I cautioned you against this folly, Kitty, before we came. Please remember that you outrank this lady, who comes of a mushroom stock in comparison with the Lacy strain. She is the widow of a cadet of the Lacy blood, and that is all."

"You are mistaken, sir," said Ret, coldly. "The Harwoods were nobles of England some centuries before the Lacys were ever heard of. Allow me to pass, Kitty, I am going out."

"My carriage is at your service, madame," said Sir Elbert, "but as a storm is approaching, I think you will be wiser to remain. I hope you do not take offence at my remark; it was rather intended for Lady Lacy's ears than for yours. Moreover, I remember that you rushed out, a few years ago, with haughtier greeting to Lord Morton's discharged gamekeeper. I think it was just below this window!"

"I leave you here," said Ret, with no mark of emotion upon her features, except a slight expansion of her nostrils, "not knowing whether you have rights here or no. If you have not you are not welcome. If you have I should stifle in the atmosphere of your house if I remained. I decline your carriage, with thanks——"
The door opened as she spoke and admitted Swiss—"Oh, Lacy Barston!" she said, while strangely mingled tears of rage and joy rained from her eyes—"take me away! take me away!"

Barston caught her hands, drew them passionately to his breast, with an inarticulate cry, and then taking her hand upon his arm, faced Sir Elbert with stern displeasure.

" You have not done well, Elbert Lacy !" he said, while the other coolly sipped the wine.

" Take a seat, Barston !" returned the baronet ; "you are most welcome to the Red Hall. The last time you were here you left somewhat suddenly, I remember. Ha! ha! You did not know that I witnessed your abrupt flight, and your doleful countenance ! Forgive me, kinsman, I did not know you so well then, and I was playing a game against heavy odds. There were madame, yonder, Lord Morton, the dainty little Parson Harwood and yourself, all sworn to thwart me. Yet I befooled you all ! Ha! ha! allow me to offer you a glass of wine! It is the old Seventeen Madeira."

" You knew of this, and did not warn me !" said Ret, reproachfully.

"I only arrived last night, Ret, and I have been seeking you all day. Johnny told me you were at the Priory. I have been there. Nellie is there and I had to take her for a little gallop. And then I came directly here, across fields, in a straight line. And when I left Elbert, last night, it was agreed that we should come here together this morning. And my errand now was to notify you. Do not look so reproachfully at me !"

" Sit down, Barston," said Sir Elbert, "you must positively taste this wine. Kitty, take a glass. What ! no ? Mrs. Froome, pray take my lady somewhere to lie down. Do not disturb Mrs. Lacy, I beg !"

" Come .away !" said Ret, stamping her foot impatiently, and drawing Barston to the door—" come away !"

" Stop, Barston," continued his cousin, with courtly ease, "stop, I desire to recall that ride of yours. How it rained ! Surely you do not intend to encounter a similar storm. It will be here in five minutes. Sit down, man, and persuade that irritable lady to control her Harwood impatience, at least until the storm passes."

"Come away, I tell you!" exclaimed Ret, vehemently. "Will you subject me to this insolent treatment another minute ? Away !"

Swiss looked out at the scowling face of the heavens with deliberation. Peace was in his soul, because she clung to him and would not leave him, though he still lingered. He quieted her with a gesture and turned to his kinsman.

" Elbert," he said with grave dignity, "you wound me deeply.

If any other man would dare do what you have done, he would have to render account to me. I cannot quarrel with you, because you are my mother's kinsman. I must stifle my just resentment for her sake, and forgive you. If this rude entrance upon your rightful inheritance is excusable at all, it is only because you have fallen back into your intemperate habits, and are not yourself. For your own sake, cousin, I pray you apologize to this lady. She is the widow of John Lacy."

"I apologize to the widow of John Lacy," replied Elbert, rising, while the purple line in his forehead appeared again. "His memory is dear to me, and no one deplores his death as I do! I do not like this lady for her own sake, and I have just cause for resentment, I think, against all of her race. But let that pass. I did not intend this rude entrance. I came to say to her that my rights should remain in abeyance while she chose to occupy the Red Hall, but she received me with all the infernal haughtiness of those Harwoods, and exasperated me. Do you think I am dog enough to eject a lady from my house? Shame on *you*, Lacy Barston, for taking the part of any one against your only living kinsman!"

"This is a lame apology, Elbert——"

"Madame," said the baronet, approaching Ret, who recoiled and clung more closely to Barston. "Madame, I pray you pardon my rudeness. I foresee that you will not accept my hospitality, but you will take sore revenge for all my rudeness if you leave the Red Hall in the face of this storm. If I am wanting in decorous manner or in proper forms of speech, I pray you attribute it rather to my rough training than to any desire to offend you. I cannot profess a friendship that I do not feel, but I sincerely offer you the shelter of this roof so long as you will accept it."

"Come away!" said Ret. "I thank you, sir, but other duties call me away. Come away, I tell you, or I shall go mad!"

CHAPTER LII.

THE DROWNED RATS.

A S they issued from the door of the Red Hall, Barston glanced
anxiously at the gloomy heavens. Far down in the east
there was a strip of blue sky, but all the rest of the vault was the
blackness of darkness. A long, ragged tongue of cloud stretched
down from the zenith, seeming to touch the tall tower of Lacy
Keep. The leaves were motionless upon the trees, and a horrible
calm, full of dismal portents, overspread the face of nature. The
swallows, which had their nests builded under the coping of the
tower, were sweeping on swift wings to the shelter of the spruce
plantation, beyond the ruined arch. It was not much past mid-
day, yet the gray light was more like the gloaming in high latitudes, with the added obscurity of approaching storm.

"'Ret," said Barston, "look around you and pause; there is no
mistaking these signs. Come with me to Mrs. Froome's room, and
wait until the tempest passes."

"Away!" she answered; "take me away! No tempest can be
worse than the shelter of that roof!"

"Will you wait until I order the carriage——"

"No carriage! It is his!" she replied, with haughty vehemence.
"I can walk! Take me away!"

Barston led Roland from the arch and leaped lightly into the
saddle.

"Stand, Roland!" said he, throwing the bridle upon the neck
of his horse. "Give me your hands Ret—both of them—so. Place
your foot on my boot. Up!" and he swung her before him on the
saddle bow. "Ten stone, by the three kings!" he muttered, as
he gathered up the rein. "Roland, my bonny bay, you carry
more than Cæsar and his fortunes! Away, brave Roland!"

Roland reared his magnificent body, throwing out his fore legs
as if he were bearing a handful of thistledown. Then bounding
lightly away he passed through the arch and down the drive, as
if he had been projected from some enormous catapult. At the
same instant a sheet of flame leaped from the bosom of the ragged
cloud, accompanied by a crash that seemed to rend the earth
under Roland's flying feet. As they turned into the high road
Barston looked over his shoulder. They were on a bit of rising
ground, and the Red Hall was in full view.

Torn by a hundred conflicting emotions, Lady Lacy was for the nonce oblivious of conventional proprieties. Overbearing all other considerations was the sharp sting of humiliation, as she remembered her haughty treatment of Sir Elbert Lacy a year or two before, and the undeniable fact that she had been living, ever since her marriage, in his house and upon his land. When Barston acknowledged Elbert's identity, all doubt concerning his legal rights vanished, and she could find no answer to the mocking words of the new claimant. The one impetuous purpose upon her mind was to get away from Lacy Keep; and while burning with resentment against the intruder, her keen sense of right recognized the validity of his title and her consequent trespass. A dozen schemes, looking to the payment of a full rental for all the years she had lived at the Hall, flitted through her mind, as the thought of living under obligations to Elbert Lacy, late Butler, was monstrous. Then, mingled with these reflections, was the blissful thought that he, her hero, Lacy Barston, had at last come to claim her. Since the day when he held up his arms to her, from the deck of the steamer, she had watched and waited for him, and now, when those strong arms were around her, and those dauntless eyes looking so longingly into hers, what marvel that she yielded so promptly to his invitation. One swift glance at his face was enough to tell her where her true resting place should be henceforth; and perhaps also, for that recognition of lordship, of which every true woman, truly mated, is conscious. Hence her prompt obedience when Barston bade her mount Roland.

"Ret," he said, "I see Mrs. Froome at the door, beckoning with frantic eagerness. Shall we return?"

"Never! Put me on the ground, if you wish to go. Never more will I set foot on Lacy land!"

"Put you down!" said Swiss; "go one way, and leave you to go another? Hark! Do you hear the roar of the storm? Are you frightened?"

She drew the hood of her cloak over her face and leaned it upon his sturdy shoulder.

"It seems that I am fated to ride away from the Red Hall in the rain," said Barston. "Here it comes! What a crash was that! Ret, we must get away from the trees."

"Anywhere, any way, only not back. I am not frightened."

"Here we are, at the edge of the Dark Wood. Ret, I parted with Jack just here."

" Did he give you the diamonds ?"

" What do you say ?" said Barston, with a start.

" The diamonds ! the Lacy Diamonds !"

" I never had the diamonds, Ret. He gave me nothing."

" Oh, dear !" said Ret, plaintively. " What wretches there are in the world! Mr. Bottomry and Mr. DeVere both told me that *you* held Sir John's securities. I have waited seven years for you to bring them back to me."

" I never had securities, Ret. How could you think so meanly of me ?"

" It has almost killed me," she answered, passionately. " I knew the necklace was worth thirty or forty thousand pounds. I saw him take it that morning, and when he was found it was gone. He had seen nobody but you."

" Yes, he had seen one other. I will tell you hereafter, it may be. You drove me away, saying you hated me."

She murmured something about fear of falling, and slipped her shapely arm around his neck.

" It was a big story," she whispered.

" Sometimes, when I have been on the tossing sea, Ret, or in the quiet woods, I have recalled your words and looks, and it has seemed to me that you meant to say ' I almost love you, Lacy Barston !' "

She clung closer to him, but said nothing.

" Because," he continued, " with my profound sense of unworthi-ness, there was always mingled the conviction that you were the only woman in the wide universe that I ever loved, or could love, and I thought the very force of my devotion, which you know is old as my life, must conquer your repugnance at last. Do I annoy you ?"

" No," she whispered, softly.

" And I hoped that some mistake—some slander, perhaps, had damaged me in your eyes, which time would reveal and remove. Tell me why you thought I had your diamonds ?"

" I saw him take them that last day. I knew he was sorely pressed for money, that he owed Mr. Bottomry and Mr. DeVere. When he was found the diamonds were gone. After a year I ap-plied to them both, and they both said you must have them, because you had paid them all Sir John's debts. All that I could hear of were about fifteen thousand pounds, and the diamonds had been valued at Amsterdam at a much larger sum. I have never told any one before that they were gone, and I hoped, year after year, that you would bring them back to me. My father, who tells me everything, told me two years ago that I would in-herit from him fifty thousand pounds, and that I could have it whenever I pleased to take it. Then I thought I would get back the diamonds."

"There was something else, Ret."

"Yes, I thought I heard you making love to Kitty. It was in the conservatory at Morton Priory. You said she must go live at Oakland."

"Oh, Ret! how could you so woefully mistake me?"

"I found out my error after you left me! How could you get your own consent to ride away in such a towering rage? And the rain! I thought you would be drowned!"

All this time the rain was lashing the earth with a roar, but these simple creatures heeded it not, or knew it not. With his left arm around her, holding her close to his heart, Swiss was un-conscious of all the phenomena of convulsed nature. He would not have noticed an earthquake. Ret, nestled so securely there, only knew that she had found peace at last. If Roland had been equal to it, Ret would have enjoyed the little excursion, if it had lasted the day.

Roland said nothing, but pounding the road with his heavy hoofs, galloped on elastically. Ten stone additional was nothing to him.

"What did you mean by 'ten stone,' Mr. Barston?" she said.

"Er—hem. What did you say, Ret?" replied Swiss, with mani-fest confusion.

"What did you mean by 'ten stone,' sir? That is what you said, when you lifted me up!"

"Ten stone means one hundred and forty pounds avoirdupois," replied Mr. Barston. "I was probably thinking——"

"You were probably swearing at so much additional weight on your poor horse! It is a story, though! I don't weigh nearly so much. Let me down, sir, I can walk!"

"Swearing!" said Swiss, holding her more tightly. It is the author's deliberate opinion that this is precisely what she expect-ed. "Swearing! Let you down! I will never let you down, Ret, while Roland can keep on his legs, until you tell me you love me."

"Do you want me to tell stories?"

"No."

"That night you were singing on the terrace—'*Ah ! che la morté,*' 'you almost broke my heart! And the letters you wrote to Johnny —here they are, all of them. They all tell the same story. They all say you love me, and they have never been out of my reach since they came. I have read them every day, and wept over them, and wondered if you would never, never, *never* come for me! My hero! my darling!" and she threw back the hood, drawing his head down to her, and kissed him.

"Love you?" she continued—"Ah, how little do you know how I love you! I love you so much that I am jealous of Johnny, of Nellie, my baby!"

"You need not be jealous, Ret. Your place in my heart is not accessible to any other. I have never lived a conscious hour since we were children, when you were not uppermost in my thoughts and love. My own Ret! All that I have suffered in waiting for this hour shrivels up into nothingness. I have not lived hitherto. I have dreamed away the quarter of a century to no purpose. Ah! what possibilities are in my future, with you by my side!"

"Why did you not tell me that you loved me, long ago?"

"Oh, Ret, I was so poor——"

"Shame on you! If you had but whispered to me that you loved me, do you think I would have asked about your money? And now that you have money, I won't have you! I am poor now!"

"You just told me you had fifty thousand pounds."

"Yes, but you ought to have more than that——"

"I hope for more. I want one hundred and forty pounds more. Oh, you dear little gossamer butterfly! how I love you!"

"Let me go, sir! Here is the Priory! Put me down this minute! Oh, you poor drowned rat! how wet you are!"

Ret walked demurely up the drive, and Swiss followed, leading Roland by the bridle. Roland had made no complaints, but he was laughing in his sleeve at his master and mistress, as they lingered in the downpour, to murmur delicious nothings to each other. But the terrace was reached at last.

"Here are two drowned rats!" said Lord Morton. "Why, Ret! How did you get caught in this storm? Come in, child. Parson! here is Mr. Barston, carrying a hundred weight of rain in his habiliments. Take him to his room, Parson, and rub him down! Luncheon is just ready. But we will wait for the rats! Away with you!"

"My lord, Johnny, my lady!" said Swiss, as Ret slipped through the hall, and up the staircase, "let me take all your hands at once! That dear, precious, darling Ret, sneaking away yonder, has' promised to be my wife! Wish me joy!"

Lady Morton kissed him.

The rector hugged him, and got his coat sleeves wet in the operation; also his shirt front.

Lord Morton shook his hand warmly.

"Go to your room, Swiss, my dear boy—my dear son—and get dry clothing. Your traps are there. I sent for them while you were away. Take him away, Parson, and hug him after he is dry! I give you twenty minutes. Go after the other rat, my dear!"

An hour later the joyful household, at the luncheon table, were admiring the glorious sunlight that had succeeded the storm. And while the laugh and jest were passing round, a messenger arrived with terrible tidings.

The Lacy Keep had been stricken by lightning, and Sir Elbert killed at the moment that Swiss and Ret had ridden away. The Keep was in ruins, having taken fire, and the old wainscot and flooring burning like tinder, were all consumed, leaving only the naked and riven walls of the old tower, a landmark that still adorns that beautiful landscape.

CHAPTER LIII.

A CONFESSION.

THE storm through which the happy couple passed, courting under difficulties, was an exceptional storm in that peaceful latitude. Swiss, in reading a description of it in the Lavington paper, pronounced it a first class West Indian hurricane. His mind was so entirely occupied with the ten stone treasure he carried, that he did not remember any meteorological phenomena, excepting the primal flash and its accompanying roar. It was this bolt that shattered the Keep, and struck down its new lord, and the last of the Lacy line. Mrs. Froome and Kitty, with William's assistance, carried the body of Sir Elbert to the newer portion of the Red Hall, which escaped the conflagration that destroyed the old Tower. He was buried in the ancient cemetery, and his funeral was attended by all the gentry of the neighbourhood. Mr. Parchment came from London, and Mr. Macdower from Stirling, all under Barston's management, to identify the baronet and his widow, and to comply with the legal requirements to fix the succession. It is worthy of note that Mr. Macdower was somewhat doubtful as to Kitty's identity, in her black attire, until Swiss borrowed the diamond brooch, which she fastened on her breast. Then the Scot swore to her, point blank. This shows the value of circumstantial evidence.

The lands passed to Barston now in spite of his opposition. His first act was to convey them to Ellen Lacy, infant, to her and her heirs forever. As he had some new schemes in view, he burnt the will he had made at her birth, in which he had made her his sole heiress. Ret's zeal to pay him the fifteen thousand pounds, over which they had formerly quarrelled, had gotten drowned out between the Red Hall and the Priory, on the first day of August.

·On the sixth day of the same month these two happened to meet in the conservatory at Morton Priory. The sashes were all opened and the beautiful lawn seemed to have pushed its way up to the house, coming in under the glazed roof of the conservatory, and mingling the odours of the out-door flowers with those of the tenderer plants within. Ret and Mr. Barston were seated in a secluded corner of the conservatory, where nobody would be likely to disturb them. There is generally an exception to all established rules, and Nellie was the exception this time.

"I want to go ride with you on Roland!" she began, as she crawled upon Mr. Barston's knee.

"Roland has lost a shoe, baby. I have sent him to Lavington to get a new one."

"Mamma says," said Nellie, while a tear rolled out of each round eye, "that I mustn't call you 'papa' any more!"

"Does she? Well, wait nine more days, and then mamma will teach you to call me papa again! Will you wait, Nellie?"

"Yes!" said Nellie, clapping her hands. She slid down from his knee, and seeing a butterfly on the lawn, bolted out in full chase. Ret looked at his placid face with blank astonishment.

"What do you mean by telling the child such absurd stories? It would be horridly indecorous. I shall not allow her to do anything of the kind!"

"When I call you wife, Ret," said Swiss, "you can surely allow Nellie to call me papa!"

"Yes," she answered, blushing, "but not before."

"Certainly not!" said Mr. Barston, taking her hand and kissing it. "I meant Nellie to understand that the happy time would come nine days hence, when Johnny and Clare——"

"Are you stark, raving, distracted, crazy?"

"Very nearly, Ret! The thought of waiting nine more days almost drives me mad! Oh, how long have I waited! And now I must pass nine more miserable days, forsooth, just because Johnny was such a booby as to appoint the fifteenth of August!" and he got her hand again, which she had snatched away, and kissed it once more.

"I am sure I don't know what you mean, Mr. Barston," said Ret, with great dignity, "you cannot have lost every grain of sense; yet the idea of proposing to a lady on the first of the month, and expecting her to marry you two weeks after, hardly admits of discussion."

"Two weeks! Is it thus you measure time, Ret? I asked you formerly, two—nay, three years ago! When do you think it will be proper to marry?"

"I don't know! in two or three years. Let go my hand, sir!"

"Don't you love me enough yet? Alas! I had set my heart on this, and I thought you would remember how long I have waited for you! Ah, Ret!" he continued, plaintively, "I cannot press this suit, because I feel unworthy of you——"

"I do wish you would try to talk reasonably!" said Ret. "Don't you understand that nobody in the world knows that you—you said all that to me, three years ago! I never told Mother or Father!"

"No, my darling," said Swiss, innocently. "I thought you had not, so I told them last night; also, Johnny and Clare."

"Really!" said she, biting her lips, "may I inquire what they said?"

"Ah, Ret!" said the hypocrite—"it will avail nothing to tell you. If you have only thought of me as your possible husband for six days, I could not ask you to marry me on the fifteenth, no matter what they think. By the three kings of Cologne! I'd die a thousand deaths before I would ask so monstrous——"

"If you will please stop swearing, sir," said the lady, with crisp politeness, "and tell me what Mother said—I don't care about the others! Johnny and Clare are half demented, and poor Father is just led about by the nose by these two. What did Mother say?"

"Oh, Ret," said the sly rascal, with a rueful face, "please don't ask me—and please don't say anything to any of them about it.

I am mortified enough as it is ! You will marry me in five or six years. Don't humiliate your future husband unnecessarily."

Ret felt a little like crying. But she thought she would rather scratch Swiss, just over his big eyes, looking so sadly into hers.

" If you can't tell me what Mother said, I can't tell what to say. You seem determined to distress me !"

" My beloved ! I will tell you. They *all* said, with one voice, that there should be a double wedding on the fifteenth. Your darling Mother—oh, how I love her, Ret !—was the first to say so."

" Why, you lunatic !" said Ret, starting to her feet. " It is wholly impossible. I—I—have no things—there ! and all the milliners and mantuamakers in Devon could not get me ready in this indecent haste !"

" Please sit down again !" said Swiss, plaintively ; " I have a confession to make ! I know it will ruin me forever in your eyes— but I cannot bear to deceive you any longer. Sit down, Ret ! I will make a clean breast of it—and then—I think I will go to sea again !"

Ret sat down, with amazement in her face. Swiss knelt on a flower stand by her side, and propping his head with his hand, half concealing his eyes, began his story. There was a melancholy intonation in his voice, that awakened her sympathy.

" Ret," he began, with sorrowful accents, " you know that I am entirely ignorant of all proprieties in this business ! You are the only woman that I ever spoke to of love. I have never thought of any other. And when I thought you might learn to love me, I did not dream of any difficulties in the way. I will ask her again, I said to myself, and if she says yes, I will be married with Johnny ! So, not having an opportunity to consult you—I—wrote to Clare at the Hotel de Lisle—and besought her to buy all the things for you that she was buying for herself ! I begged her to conceal her movements from you—as I had not yet had that blessed ride in the rain ! my *second* ride in the rain, Ret ! Oh, how hard hearted you are ! Well ! I sent Clare a cheque for a thousand pounds, as I did not know how much things cost. She has given me no change. She has about forty trunks and boxes up stairs, belonging to you. Stop one moment, Ret ! Hear me out, I pray ! She has been dying to get a peep at the things ever since they came, but has loyally refrained. She said you had milliners and all that sort of thing in Paris, and she knew your peculiar tastes—and so she made the purchases—and the things are in this house.

" And now, Ret, please say you forgive me! You can tell Lady
Morton that certain insurmountable obstacles are in the way at
present—and I—I have never been to Greenland. I will go to
Greenland, and wait there, until *your* time arrives to make me
happy!

" As for living on this island, within reach of you, within sound
of your voice, and yet know that I cannot call you my wife—and
call that darling baby my daughter—by the three kings! I'll
never stand it! Never! Never!"

As he turned away from her she rose from her seat and marched to the door.

" Please to sit down and wait for me a few minutes, sir. I will
return immediately."

When she whisked her dress through the glass door, Mr. Swiss
composedly took out his cigar case and struck a Vesuvius.

"Puff! puff!" he said. " Clare is about to catch it! I am
thankful that I am through my part, and still live. I wonder why
that rascally tailor has not sent *my* things down!"

CHAPTER LIV.

Ornithological.

THE author of this volume once had the pleasure of going into
a railway station behind a locomotive. It had " jumped
the track," as he was informed afterwards, and did not go into
the station very quietly. It is probable that Ret's entrance into
Clare's chamber was in very similar fashion. The gentlemen who
manage experiments in gunnery, at Shoeburyness, can calculate
to a nicety how hard a knock can be given by a hundred pounder,
projected by a given weight of powder. If these scientists were
within reach they might estimate the force with which a hundred
and forty pounds of sweetness, tortured by a villain like Swiss
into a state of " demnition sweetness," would go through that
chamber door.

Miss Tamworth was expecting her. She rose at her entrance
and ran to meet her, kissing her tenderly. Ret feebly repulsed
her.

" Clare !" she said, viciously, " this is a nice business ! Could
I believe that you—you—would have treated me so shamefully ?"

" What *do* you mean, Ret ?"

" Oh, you are very innocent ! That crazy man down stairs has
told me all about it ! I declare I feel so hurt ! Oh, Clare, it was
base !"

Clare began to whimper.

" There ! there !" said Ret, kissing her; " please don't cry. I
suppose it was not all your fault ! Ah !" she said, with pro-
phetic wrath, as she clenched her little hand, " won't I dress him
for this ! Just wait, my gentleman ! Where are the things,
Clare ?"

" I don't k-n-o-w what you m-m-mean !" whimpered Clare.

" Don't you, dear ? The lunatic said you had forty boxes and
trunks belonging to me—bought in Paris—under my own nose !"

" Oh ! yes, they are all locked up in the Blue Room. Here is
the key. May I go with you ?" she said, timidly.

" Of course. I shall want you to tell me what purposes the
things are to serve. Come along, pray."

" My love," said Clare, as she unlocked the boxes, " almost all
of these are duplicates of my own purchases. Some of the dresses
I made you select—you know, my darling, that I could not help
it. If you don't want them, they will all fit me, with very little
alteration. But I really thought, until last night, that there was
an understanding between you and the lunatic. I thought there
had been a little quarrel and that you had made it up. Oh, Ret !
that *poult de soie* is lovely, lovely, lovely ! Did you ever see more
exquisite taste ? Madame Lacroix is faultless. Please slip this
skirt on. Oh, Ret, I hope you won't like it ! Heigho ! I am so
sorry that I was misled—I did not know the man was crazy. My
darling child ! you shall never marry a crazy man ! This is the
poplin, Ret. That shade is *entirely* new, and it is lovely !

" Oh, Ret, I found out something ! Do you remember that story
of Mr. Barston and the French officer at Sebastopol ? Well, his
widow is Madame Dutilh, the milliner in the Passage de l'Orme !
She knows Mr. Barston ! He bought Nellie's hat there ! And he
ordered a bonnet and left her three hundred francs to pay for it !
And it is here ! Ret, my maid carried that dreadful box in her
hand all the way from Paris. She kept hold of it when crossing
that horrid channel, even when she thought she was dying ! I
have never seen it ! See ! it is sealed up, where the cords cross.

18

Shall we open it? Oh, that's a dear—where are my scissors? here—snip, snip. It is all wrapped in tissue paper. Ah, Ret!"

The two lovely ladies fell on their knees, one on each side of the bonnet box. It was a great deal worse than the golden calf business, as this idol was a flimsy thing, made up of a minute fragment of straw, and other fragments of lace and ribbons. They gazed, enraptured. At length, Clare took it up gingerly, and placed it on Ret's head, with a little shriek of joy. Ret allowed herself to be led to the mirror, where she half dislocated her superb neck, trying to look at the back of her head. They stood near the window, and Mr. Barston, lolling on the bench in the conservatory, overheard their comments.

"Did you ever see such a bonnet, Ret?"

"Never! never! Oh, Clare, it is a duck."

They were interrupted by the entrance of Lady Morton.

"Mother!" said Ret, "he wants me to marry him on the fifteenth!"

"He?"

"Yes, ma'am!" said Clare; "she means that wretched inebriate——"

"Whom do you mean, Miss Tamworth?" said Ret.

"I mean your lunatic, of course. My lady, *he* ordered this bonnet; just please look at it!"

"What superb lace, Ret!" said her Mother; "it is beautiful, indeed. Well, my dear, what did you tell him?"

"I did not tell him anything. If you say I must——"

"I think you must, Ret. I have loved the poor motherless boy ever since I first saw him. You are a happy woman, daughter."

"Where is Father?" said Ret, placing the dainty bonnet in its box.

"In the library;" and with one lingering look at the duck, Ret departed.

Lord Morton was poring over a parliamentary report. Ret took her seat on his knee, and put her arms round his neck and hid her face on his shoulder.

"He wants me to be married on the fifteenth, sir," she whispered.

"Of course, Ret. Why not?"

"It seems so dreadfully sudden, sir."

"Sudden! Pooh! The poor fellow has been courting you for three years! Do you love him, Ret?"

" Yes, sir, a little."

" Well, I love him very much as I do my other boys. When you know him better you will love him more, Ret."

" Have you any money, sir ?" said Ret, tossing her head.

" Money ! Certainly ! How much do you want ?"

" A thousand pounds, sir, please."

" Hum, that is a moderate demand, certainly. I do not usually carry such sums in my pocket. I shall have to write a cheque."

" That will do, sir. Thank you, sir."

Mr. Swiss came forward as she reappeared. He had resumed his melancholy air of resignation, and something in his attitude recalled Lady Morton's expression, " the poor motherless boy." He was a tolerably well grown orphan, too.

" Since you left me, Ret," he began, " I have been thinking what a wretch I was to order those things. It all comes of a habit of mine. When I have a purpose in view I always try to provide the minutest details. I reasoned in this wise: if she consents to marry me, she will require the same sort of preparation—things, in fact, that Clare is purchasing. I cannot ask *her* about the things until I ask her to take me. I cannot ask her to take me until I see her. If I don't get the things now, it will be too late when they come from Paris——"

" There ! there !" said Ret, " you need not make any more explanations. How did you become acquainted with Madame Dutilh ?"

" What ! you mean the milliner ?"

" Yes, sir, I mean the milliner."

" I found her in the Passage de l'Orme, soon after her husband, the captain, died. He was wounded in the Crimea."

" Yes, sir, I understand," said Ret.

" And I felt a great interest in her. He was a gallant fellow, Ret, for a Frenchman."

" And you naturally tried to comfort his widow ?"

" What do you mean, Ret ? She is a yellow, shrivelled little Frenchwoman, and takes snuff !"

" Indeed !"

" If you had not been so deeply offended, Ret, I meant to talk to you about the trip to the Highlands. I have been picturing to myself the most delightful honeymoon in the midst of that grand scenery. I thought you would climb Ben Nevis with me, and——"

"I thought you had concluded to try Greenland," said Ret, slyly.

"Not unless you drive me there. Ah, Ret! why are you so obdurate? If you will let me have my way this time, you will thenceforward own the most abject slave——"

"I don't want any abject slaves, sir!"

"Well, the most loyal subject, then, for you are my queen, Ret. You don't look quite so angry now. If you will only tell me that you forgive me about the things, I will not transgress again."

"I suppose not," answered Ret; "it is rather expensive. Here, sir! allow me to return the thousand pounds, with my thanks. You need not promise not to repeat the offence. It is not at all probable that you will offer your *wife* such a sum to spend in Paris!"

"Shall I go to Greenland, Ret?" said Swiss, as he put the cheque in his pocket-book. "This will pay all expenses at least. I may as well tell you that Lord Morton gave me a similar cheque last night, in settlement of my outlays——"

"Give me back that money!" said Ret. "There! let me go, sir, or I'll scream. Greenland! Ah, would you dare leave me again?" and she secreted and dropped a dozen tears in three seconds, which Swiss kissed away in the same space of time.

"May I ask you one question, my precious Ret?"

"Yes."

"Was the bonnet a regular duck, my love?"

She extricated herself from his arms, and walked with stately dignity to the glass door. Pausing at the threshold, she turned upon him a withering look, while he choked and coughed, trying to restrain his mirth.

"Yes, sir!" she said, severely. "It is a duck. And you will permit me to add, that you are a goose!"

CHAPTER LV.

¡ THE LORDS OF CREATION.

IT was late in October, and summer departed with great reluctance. All the country around Morton Priory was sleeping in beauty. Lord and Lady Morton, with their two sons, had gone to Essex, and were expected to return that afternoon to lovely Devon.

In the famous conservatory two American rocking chairs, made of split hickory, and exceedingly comfortable, were occupied by two happy bridegrooms, who had left their partners at the luncheon table. Were they smoking? Of course.

"These are the Colorados, Swiss," said the rector. "If any of your keys will fit Father's cigar case, there are some Oscuros there, I know!"

"Do you suppose I would commit petty larceny, you old burglar?" replied Mr. Barston.

"No indeed; we could put some of these light ones back; Father prefers them. It would not be robbery—only an exchange."

"Where did you get them, Parson?"

"In Father's dressing room."

"If mine wasn't lighted I would reject it with indignation, Johnny! Stealing is a mean vice at any time. But stealing from that great and good man, Lord Morton, is positively infamous!"

"Pooh! He left them there for us, of course. Isn't this jolly, Swiss?"

"Paradisaical, Johnny. How one's views of life are enlarged by matrimony! Do you know, Parson, that you and I have wasted all our former lives? We are now beginning our careers. You will preach a thousand times better——"

"Haven't written a sermon for nearly three months!" said the rector, dolefully. "I don't know where to begin. I haven't read a word in a book, and hardly looked at a newspaper."

"Books! you don't need books. You have the sweetest wife in the world, excepting one, and you can learn more in one hour's conversation with her than you could learn from forty books. And if she don't know enough, Ret can instruct her. *She* knows everything!"

"That is comical!" quoth the rector; "what little poor Ret knows she has learned from Clare! Swiss, she is the most superior woman in England!"

"It will avail nothing, Johnny, to discuss their relative merits. Since I have been married, I have begun to understand what is meant by the lordship of man over the intelligent creation. His dominion over the brutes is a small matter. But when he has a wife who spends her lifetime in studying his merest whims—who anticipates his wishes almost before they are shaped in his own mind, by her keen perception, and who yields her preferences with such charming grace and sweetness—it is then, and then only, that man appreciates his lordship!"

"Exactly!" replied the rector—"only sometimes one does not know precisely what one wants. Then the dear angel enlightens him, and he has his own way, without knowing it."

"Pish! You have not risen to the grandeur of my thought. Women have a faculty by which they perceive our hidden purposes, while our slower logic is plodding to a conclusion."

"Yes," responded Mr. Harwood; "Do you remember our ascent of Ben Lomond?"

"No," spluttered Swiss—"we did not ascend that inaccessible height. It was a foolish project——"

"Yes. That was what Ret said," replied the Parson dryly. "I suppose her quick perception had enabled her to discover that it would wear out her boots! Clare and I went to the top of that Ben!"

"And came back again as cross as two amiable grimalkins! Ret and I staid below in the heather, discoursing like sensible people."

"You made sad havoc with the dinner, though; I only got a small taste of the grouse pie."

"What a regular glutton you must be, Parson," said Swiss—"you have fallen into bad habits. Eating and smoking are not the chief end of your existence! Who is there?"

"I want you, please!" answered a sweet voice from the lawn.

"Do you want me, madame?" said Swiss, rising.

"No, I don't want 'me, madame;' I want the Reverend Mr. Harwood," replied Clare. "I can't come in there among all that horrid smoke! It would ruin my shawl! The odour would never come out. Never!"

"My dear Parson," whispered Swiss, "now is your opportunity. It is highly unreasonable to call you away from your smoke. Your digestive organs require——"

"What are you whispering about?" inquired Mrs. Harwood. "Are you coming?"

"In a moment, my dear!" replied the rector. "I cannot come with my cigar, you know. Will you wait for me?"

"Not a second!"

The rector glanced irresolutely at Swiss.

"Go!" said that worthy; "go! you hen-pecked old wretch! You deserve your bondage, because you have not had pluck enough to assert your lordship from the first. Go along with you!"

"It is only a Colorado!" quoth the rector, throwing his weed away and stalking majestically out.

Mr. Barston leaned back in his chair, and laughed until the tears ran down upon his beard.

"That dear Clare is a stunner!" he said, watching the couple as they walked away. "But she suits Johnny admirably. Evidently he does not appreciate the kingship, which he relinquishes so lightly. That was a famous dodge of his, to express his contempt for 'Colorados.' To such base subterfuges must the man come who does not reign in his own household. Poor old Johnny! His cigar was rather more than half smoked though. It will be jolly to tell him that I had two. I think I will light another."

"I don't think you will," said another melodious voice, as a plump arm was passed around his neck, and his cigar removed by dainty taper fingers. "This makes four to-day," continued Ret, "and you will soon require a dozen to satisfy you. Your system is full of nicotine, and you will have softening of the brain presently. The specific effect of that poison is to retard the circulation. Congestion—then paralysis——"

"Where in the world did you pick up all that lore, my darling?" said Mr. Barston, submissively.

"No matter where," replied madame; "it is sound doctrine, however. Faugh! the conservatory smells like a German beer garden! Come out!"

Swiss followed, with a hang-dog expression of countenance totally at variance with his discourse on lordship.

"My dear," said Ret, taking his arm, and following the grinning rector and his wife; "don't you think a man of your excellent sense should put some restraint upon so harmful a habit? *I* would never dream of interference, except for your own sake, my love. But when I think of you falling over in a fit of apoplexy, I am ready to scream——"

"Don't scream, you precious angel!" said Swiss. "I am sure that would throw me into a fit, without the aid of nicotine. I have such unlimited confidence in your judgment, my love, that I will promise to confine my fumigations within whatever limits you direct."

Ret squeezed his arm.

"Do you think I would put limits upon you? Do you think I would measure my feeble intellect with your clear, sound judgment? Never! never! All that I ask of you is to consider the matter, and I will freely promise to speak of it no more. Only remember how desolate your poor wife would be if you were to kill yourself with that dreadful nicotine!"

"Well, Ret," quoth Mr. Barston, with an air of superb royalty, "I will investigate the whole subject thoroughly. And, in the meantime, I will only smoke one more to-day; just one, after dinner."

They speedily overtook the rector and Clare.

"Where is your cigar, Swiss?" said Mr. Harwood.

"Smoked out, Parson."

"Won't you have another?"

"Not now, thank you. The truth is, Johnny, I am reluctant to smoke stolen cigars at second hand. I don't mind stealing yours, when I know you got them honestly."

"Very lame, Swiss!" said the rector. "Now listen, you old humbug! These charming ladies were hidden behind the lemon trees while you were discoursing so eloquently about lordship. They silently retired and concocted their little plot. My demure little wife called me out, and I obeyed. Your angelic wife collared you and brought you out. The next time you wish to enlarge upon the domination of the husband, you had better get in the open fields, or like that other old humbug, Demosthenes, upon the margin of the sea! Laugh at him, girls!"

"My dear Parson," said Swiss, his voice falling into the sweet tones that indicated earnest sincerity, "my experience has been large enough to teach me this much: It is so delicious to discrown one's self, and to lay one's diadem at the feet of one's wife, that domination culminates in the very act of yielding the sceptre. None but a king can relinquish dominion. They who resist that gentle sway, and tear away those silken chains, are not husbands—they are bluebeards; and the clearest records of the world's long history teaches the same lesson. No race has ever been dominant where women did not reign. The Roman, lord of the earth, growing corrupt in success, reversed this beneficent law of the race, and was exterminated by the rude Gothic tribes, whose distinguishing characteristic was deference to the gentle sex. And now that the domination has passed into Anglo-Saxon humanity, let us be grateful that deference to the woman, the queen of love and beauty, still distinguishes that race from all others on the surface of the planet. The reign of the distaff is the hope of the world!"

CHAPTER LVI.

L'ENVOI.

CERTAIN threads dropped here and there in the foregoing history remain to be gathered up. The author intended the concluding words of the previous chapter to be the concluding words of the story, but some critics who have patiently read thus far, profess great interest in the minor characters and demand a more minute account of their sayings and doings. They also complain of vagueness in portions of the story, where it was supposed the imagination of the reader would supply deficiencies, and fill up all lapses. Those of the aforesaid critics that object to weird and inexplicable touches here and there, now demand a matter of fact solution of those portions of the Red Hall legend that refer to the unexpected appearance of the Countess DeLys, at the crisis of Sir Ranald's history; and also an explanation of a prophecy spoken by a lady who was supposed to be comfortably defunct at the date of its utterance.

The ruins of Lacy Keep still stand, the walls now overgrown with ivy. On that part of the inner wall, where Sir Ranald's room was supposed to be, there is a fragment of a stone stairway, built in the thickness of the wall, connecting this room with the chamber above. No doubt this communication was hidden by wainscoting, which had been destroyed by the lightning-kindled conflagration, when Sir Elbert died. And sight-seers who visit the locality, and listen to Mrs. Froome's miraculous stories, point to this crumbling ruin, and assert, with great complacency, that the Countess had traversed this hidden passage, and after filling her auditors with terror at her dismal rhyme, had returned to her chamber, and died outright. The old dame rejects the hypothesis with high scorn, and holds to her original theory, as hinted in the body of this narrative. The modern portion of the Red Hall is uninjured, and occupied by Kitty—Lady Lacy—whose life is spent in the practice of unobtrusive charities, that perpetually contradict her cold, impassive exterior. The rare occasions when this coldness gives place to tokens of pleasure, are those in which Mr. Barston and Nellie pay brief visits to the Red Hall. Mrs. Barston has never revisited the place, since the day when the stately Keep was transformed into a ruin.

John Hawder is steward of Mr. Barston's estate. Sometimes he finds willing listeners, to whom he recounts certain portions of his American adventures, in which Mr. Barston figures once and again.

Tommy Dawson cultivates the soil at Ripple Farm. All his wounds are healed, except the portentous gash in his face, which his wife daily fills with dumplings. He still talks of his version of the descent of man, comprised in a short chapter that only tells of his rapid journey from the cliff to the beach below. The favourite item in this account is the "sawing of a 'ole in his 'ead" by Dr. Cardon; and Tommy describes his emotions under the "hoperation" with grisly minuteness, which is the more remarkable as he was in a comatose state when the sawing was done. Mrs. Dawson, the dowager, is the ultimate authority at Ripple, and Jenny is the most dutiful of daughters, and a prime favourite with the old dame, whose chief solace (after curd-making) is to coddle the later generation of Dawsons, with flaxen heads, and mouths constructed with due reference to dumplings. Mr. and Mrs. Barston take frequent equestrian trips to Ripple, accompanied by Nellie, who is the sole owner of a Mexican pony, that is a natural pacer and docile as little Laura's lamb.

The Diamonds. No one knows the fate of the Lacy Diamonds but Swiss and his wife. Both shrunk from telling the story, and if it were not that no secrets are withheld from each other, both would have refrained from the subject, even between themselves. On the day of their marriage, Mr. Barston presented his bride with the box he had picked up on the deck of the steamer. She opened it, and discovered a necklace of sparkling gems.

"My diamonds!" she exclaimed.

Swiss said nothing.

She took out the jewels, held them up to the light, kissed them, and dropped a joyful tear or two, and clasped them round her neck. Then she took them off and examined them narrowly.

"Where did you get them?" she said.

"Do you recognize them, Ret?"

"Yes. They are not the same diamonds that I lost."

"Will any one else detect the difference?" said Swiss.

"I think not. The necklace is a little tighter on my neck and the gold is brighter. They are almost exactly like the others. Tell me about them."

"I persuaded Clare to steal your brooch, and your Mother described the original necklace to me. A London jeweler did the rest."

" And you have spent——"

" Nothing. When you drove me away, three years ago, I went to Charleston. Before I left I bought a blockade runner and her cargo of cotton. She escaped, and reached Liverpool in safety. A week before Nellie was stolen away from you, I sold vessel and cargo. The necklace represents the difference between my outlay and the proceeds. The former owner was a young Englishman, who had invested all his fortune in this venture. The blockade was rigid, and the escape of the ship seemed impossible. He applied to me for advice, bringing his young wife with him. Oh, Ret, she reminded me of you ! So sweet, so gentle, so good ! They were British subjects, and could get through the lines, if they had the money that was locked up in the " Nellie " and her cargo. My advice was to sell the ship to me, to take what money I had to spare, and a cheque on my bankers in London for the rest. While I was irresolutely considering the matter, he happened to mention the name of his vessel, the " Nellie," and I was then *compelled* to buy her. On the next night there was an easterly storm, and I sent the ship out in the teeth of the gale. The blockading squadron was obliged to stand out to sea, and the " Nellie," cross-ing the bar, ran down the coast and escaped. It was my first and last commercial exploit, and I dedicated the proceeds to you.

" My darling ! if you and I can thus bury the story of the real Diamonds, as deeply as they were buried, 'full forty fathoms down' under the sea, I know of nothing except the joy of calling you my wife that could so much comfort me. Shall it be so ?"

The answer was audible, but inarticulate.

" Do you know, Ret," said Swiss, blushing like a girl, " that I cannot help rejoicing at the loss of those horrible diamonds ! My Mother has told me the story of the Red Lacy a hundred times, and I have always thought of the jewels as the messengers of Satan ! I had never seen them, until that night, when Elbert cast them into the sea, and I knew instinctively that they were the same accursed baubles that had been bloodstained a dozen times. My Mother said the necklace alone belonged to the Lacys. The earrings and brooch were added by Mrs. Lacy Harwood two or three generations ago. And now, my beloved, you have the full set, without the curse—for the curse is under the ocean. There were some lines that my Mother used to repeat, but they have escaped me——"

He was interrupted by Ret, who took the jewel case, and

removed the false bottom. A small piece of parchment fell out. It was yellow with age, and when Barston unfolded it, the antique characters traced on it were almost invisible. With some difficulty he read as follows :

> "The Lacy that holdeth the Red Hall and fee
> A score and a half score he never shall see,
> Till the jewel from kin-blood be washed in the sea,
> And tempest and flame
> Smite the last of the name
> With the hall of his fathers, this weird shall they dree!"

They sat in silence a few minutes.

" Ret !" said Bârston, with a puzzled air, " what do you think of these lines ?"

" I don't think much of them," she answered indifferently.

" But Ret ! these lines were written hundreds of years ago."

" I don't believe it."

" They were certainly written three or four years ago !"

" Yes."

" Well ! their accurate fulfilment is overwhelming to me !"

" The coincidences *are* a little remarkable," she answered. " Mrs. Froome told me the old story before I was married. It made a deep impression upon me, probably because of Mrs. Froome's dramatic manner. I forgot the lines she repeated, but retained the idea, and candour compels me to confess that *I* wrote the doggerel you have just read."

" But the old parchment ! the faded ink !"

" Oh, that was nothing in comparison with a hundred tricks of yours, you old deceiver ! I got some parchment from Father, smoked it, diluted some ink, and made the rhyme. I spent half a day over it !"

" The next generation," said Swiss, " will swear that those lines were written *after* the events. It is in this way that fellows who don't believe in ghosts or legends get rid of testimony ! But, my dear," he continued, with tremulous anxiety, " do you intend to grind out any more poetry ? I know a poetess in London who puts things in the magazines. She has a bald place on the top of her head, and wears green spectacles, and looks like the demented old idiot she is !"

" No more poetry, Mr. Barston. My first and last effort is this short requiem over

"THE LACY DIAMONDS."